THE
FAR TIME
INCIDENT

THE FAR TIME INCIDENT

A NOVEL BY
NEVE MASLAKOVIC

47N♦RTH

The characters and events portrayed in this book are fictitious. Any similarity to real persons, living or dead, is coincidental and not intended by the author.

Text copyright © 2013 by Neve Maslakovic

Grateful acknowledgment is made for permission to reprint excerpts from *The Complete Pompeii* by Joanne Berry. © 2007 Thames & Hudson Ltd., London. Reprinted by kind permission of Thames & Hudson.

All rights reserved.
Printed in the United States of America.

No part of this book may be reproduced, or stored in a retrieval system, or transmitted in any form or by any means, electronic, mechanical, photocopying, recording, or otherwise, without express written permission of the publisher.

Published by 47North
P.O. Box 400818
Las Vegas, NV 89140

ISBN-13: 9781611099096
ISBN-10: 1611099099
Library of Congress Control Number: 2012951474

To John and Dennis

PART ONE:
GONE

1

The door to my office flew open with a bang.

"Julia—the professor—he's been scattered across time!"

A parka-clad student had brought the news. Kamal Ahmad stood in my doorway trying to catch his breath, his sneakers heavy with wet snow.

I pointed him to a chair and went back to giving directions into the phone. Hoping the person at the other end hadn't heard what I strongly suspected was a student prank in progress and not an actual emergency, I said, "Sorry, where was I? Right. From Highway 94, turn onto Eagle Creek Road and stay on it for nine miles, then take the left fork at the old red barn. Follow it to the campus visitor parking lot—not bar, *barn*." I paused to let what sounded like a truck, an especially loud one, rumble by. It had been snowing steadily since midnight and the blogger who was driving up from Minneapolis to tour STEWie's lab this morning was caught in slow traffic. If I was wrong and this turned out not to be a prank—well, the lab tour could be canceled once she got here. I went on, "My office is next to Dean Sunder's, in the Hypatia of Alexandria House—no, *Hy-pay-sha*. You'll know you're in the right place by the photo out front. Long black hair, strong cheekbones—"

Before ending the call, I warned the blogger about the current hazard on campus, finals week. Bundled-up students with dark circles under their eyes bicycled the slippery St. Sunniva University walkways on their way to and from tests without much regard for pedestrians. You had to keep an eye out if you didn't want to get run over.

I hung up the phone, pushed my glasses farther up my nose, and gave my full attention to Kamal, who was slumped in the chair across the desk, still drawing air into his lungs in large gulps. Finals week was peak practical joke time. From previous experience I knew that students usually waited until after the last of the exams on Friday afternoon to hide research notebooks, glue lab doors shut, and so on. It was only Tuesday. Still—

"Kamal, did I hear you right? The professor—which one?"

"Dr. Mooney."

"Has been—"

"—scattered across time, Julia, *yes*."

That seemed pretty unlikely. Dr. Mooney was one of our senior professors. If I had to put together a list about him, it would go something like this: (a) popular with students; (b) knew his stuff; (c) took it in stride when budgetary decisions didn't go his way; and (d) had wowed everyone with his didgeridoo playing at the Science Quad Thanksgiving party—*and* had brought along a homemade pumpkin pie.

Kamal Ahmad, on the other hand, was a graduate student. More specifically, he was Dr. Mooney's senior graduate student and the teaching assistant for some of the professor's classes. Grad students have their own list. From (a) to (d), they are an underpaid, underfed, underslept lot, and often the source of a lot of trouble for the science dean's office. I took stock of Kamal's unzipped parka and his inside-out woolen hat, whose π *is a mathematician's dessert* logo was still readable backward. Had he run over from the Time Travel Engineering building in the snow, which was still coming down fast? Maybe this wasn't a prank after all. I said the first thing that came into my mind.

"What year?"

"Year? I don't know—all of them, I suppose. What should we do, Julia? He's gone. *Gone.*"

I reached for the phone again. Dean Sunder relied on his assistant—that'd be me, Julia Olsen. A descendant of Norwegian immigrants to a coal-powered nineteenth-century Minnesota, I had nevertheless ended up with solidly brown eyes and hair—which was a bit of a mystery, as I looked nothing like my parents, and the family photos of my grandparents all showed light-haired, prim-mouthed Scandinavian types. Where was I? Right. I was about to say that Dean Sunder liked to leave routine problems in my hands.

A physics professor scattered across the vastness of time was definitely not a routine problem.

2

By phone, I reached Dean Sunder at the *History Alive* exhibition just as he was pitching the need for a new STEWie generator to his guest, the actor Ewan Coffey, the university's most famous former attendee. (Everyone knew the story: As a junior, Ewan had packed a duffel bag and taken the train west to Portland, then a bus down the coast to Hollywood. The rest was movie history.) The dean was not pleased to be interrupted. After hearing what I had to say, however, he excused himself and stepped into the curator's office so that we could speak privately. The dean's voice carried strong over the line. "Julia, this is the last thing we need. Is Dr. Mooney's student sure about this? Let's get all the facts before we sound the alarm."

He instructed me to keep him updated and went back to wooing Ewan Coffey with the bagels, cream cheese, lox, and champagne I'd ordered for the occasion. I hung up the phone. Kamal had taken off the woolen hat and was twisting it in his hands, compacting the logo to read π *is dessert*. His breathing had calmed but he still had a glassy-eyed look. I got up and went over to the cabinet nestled under the winter-frosted window of my office to fetch the cookie jar I kept there. My approach to any crisis, large or small, was this: (a) offer food, and (b) make a list of things that needed to be done. I handed Kamal a napkin with a couple of butter cookies, then sat back down across from him, leaving the cookie jar open on the desk. Kamal wrapped his gloveless and icy-looking fingers around one of the cookies and wordlessly took a bite.

"I suppose you'll have to find another graduate advisor," I said. "I hear Dr. Little is taking on new students—"

I stopped to allow his coughing to subside.

"Julia," he said reproachfully, sounding more like his normal self, "how can you be so efficient at a time like this?" He hiccupped, then finished off the cookie as I pulled out my yellow legal pad to start a list.

"Tell me what happened. You went on a STEWie run with Dr. Mooney. What went wrong?" Something occurred to me. "And who else was with you?"

He quickly polished off a second cookie. "No one."

"It was just Dr. Mooney and you?"

"No, Julia. Dr. Mooney was alone, according to the log. Just him."

I looked up from the notepad, not about to write that down. No one went alone. STEWie teams consisted of a professor and a couple of grad students, with perhaps a postdoc or a visiting researcher tagging along for good measure. Three to four was the standard.

"It's my fault—though I don't know why Dr. Mooney went on a run—"

I pushed the open cookie jar toward him. "You'd better start at the beginning."

He reached into the jar. "It was my shift in the lab last night. I tried to switch with Abigail so I could get some last-minute studying done for Spacetime Warping: Theory and Practice—the exam is at noon today—there's going to be a written section and a practical one—it's Dr. Little's class and his tests are always hard—I still have a couple of hours left to study—that's not important, is it? The point is, I tried to switch with Abigail, but she has two finals today. Jacob was swamped with projects, and I couldn't reach Sergei, so Dr. Mooney offered to take over for me—he does that for his students sometimes—I had no idea, Julia, that he would—" Kamal stopped, as if he wasn't sure he should voice his thoughts, and bit into another cookie.

My pencil hovered above the blank page. "Kamal, are you saying that Dr. Mooney went on an unscheduled run last night and something went wrong?"

Kamal leaned forward, planted his elbows on the desk, and waved the cookie in my direction. "Dr. Mooney logged in around midnight. He never logged out. The basket came back empty. You know what that means."

It was only when I looked at my hand that I realized I'd reached for a cookie myself.

Kamal added, "I sat there for a while, trying to figure out what to do—your phone was busy—then Abigail came in, so I left her to guard the lab and ran over here." He sat back up in the chair. "Julia, we have to take STEWie off-line until we figure out what went wrong."

I wiped the cookie crumbs off my hands. "I'll call campus security and send out a memo that Dean Sunder is canceling all runs until further notice." I wrote that down under "(a)" and "(b)," then flicked my computer to life and opened STEWie's roster. "A blogger is scheduled to observe this morning's run—I was about to look up whose—"

"Abigail and Sergei with Dr. B."

I got to my feet and reached for my goose-down jacket. "Dr. Baumgartner? Why didn't you say so? We'd better hurry over to the lab. I can call campus security on the way."

∞

Petite, blue-eyed Abigail Tanner, whose short hair was spiky and neon orange today, stood with her arms crossed and her back against the opaque glass doors of the Time Travel Engineering (TTE) lab, blocking her graduate advisor's way. More than six feet tall, Erika Baumgartner towered over her student. I saw her jab a finger at the lab as Kamal and I rounded the bend in the hallway.

"It's my time slot and I'm going in—"

"There's no point, Dr. B. The calibration for our run—"

"—you have five minutes to get ready, Abigail, so you better hurry into the travel apparel closet. And get a cap to cover that orange hair." Anger had tinted the professor's cheeks red below the tight-fitting bonnet that hid her own blonde hair, and a tiny bit of spit on one corner of her mouth threatened to fall onto the white chemise that stretched across broad shoulders under a mushroom-colored bodice. A drab green skirt, a checkered apron, and a pair of wooden clogs completed Dr. B's peasant ensemble. Two cabbage heads and half a dozen eggs lay cradled on a bed of straw in the wicker basket on her arm.

Sergei, another of Erika Baumgartner's grad students, stood off to the side, also dressed in period clothes—a brownish tunic and breeches. Next to him was a mousy-looking, ginger-haired student, a recent addition to the TTE lab, who looked very interested in the proceedings. As Dr. Baumgartner turned to the security keypad to the right of the lab doors and started punching in numbers, the student said politely to me, "Good morning, Ms. Olsen." I saw his fingers inch toward the cell phone sticking out of his T-shirt pocket.

I wiped wet snow spots off my glasses with my sleeve and then slid them back on. "Call me Julia. And you are—?"

"Jacob Jacobson. Dr. Rojas's new graduate student."

"Jacob, that's right. Welcome to the lab. How are you settling in?"

"Fine, fine," he assured me, still very polite. Besides the ginger hair, he had an oval face and delicate, tan eyebrows. Like Abigail, he sported the normal student uniform, one that didn't change much with the seasons—jeans, T-shirt, and sneakers.

The security keypad had beeped green, but the lab doors did not yield to Dr. Baumgartner's insistent push. I saw why. Abigail had coiled a bike lock around the door handles and secured it. Good thinking on her part. (As a rule, young grad students were like scared sheep when it came to their advising professors, and understandably so—an advising professor had all but total control of a student's funding, access to lab time, graduation date, and future prospects. Abigail, however, was made of stronger stuff.)

"This is ridiculous," Erika Baumgartner, who clearly didn't agree with that assessment, bellowed in her deepest professorial voice. She shook the door handles again. "It's impossible for anyone to get scattered across time. STEWie has redundant safety systems built in. Xavier must have forgotten to sign out, that's all. It's happened before."

"The computer log says the basket came back empty, right?" Abigail said. "Besides, the calibration for our run was never done, Dr. B."

A look of terror crossed Kamal's face as the professor whipped around to face him. "Why was the calibration never done?" Before Kamal had a chance to answer, the professor turned to me, barely pausing for breath, the lace on her bodice threatening to come undone. "Julia, a blogger's coming to observe my run. She should be here any minute. We're going to bring back footage of Antoine Lavoisier conducting one of his combustion experiments. Also a few photos of, uh—other things. Penny Lind blogs about celebrity fashions…" The professor trailed off, a note of embarrassment in her voice.

"Penny couldn't reach you, so she called the dean's office to say that she's running late because of the snow," I said. Erika was one of our junior professors and needed the name-recognition boost that a popular blog could provide. STEWie runs were expensive, and Dr. B's research into the life of an eighteenth-century scientist, even if he was the father of modern chemistry, paled in comparison to more marketable time travel projects. One that had recently gotten a lot of media attention belonged to Dr. Presnik of the English Department; she had gone on a few well-planned runs to confirm that Shakespeare *had* written all of his plays.

I had assumed that Penny was coming in for the usual lab tour and to take a look at our steadily growing stock of snapshots from the past. She hadn't mentioned that she'd made a deal for exclusive photos of revolutionary France haute couture in exchange for publicity for Dr. B's pet research project. Nothing wrong with that. It was just that the dean's office liked to know about these things.

Jacob was typing something into his cell phone. Over his shoulder I read *Something wrong with STEWie—Dr. Mooney gone, Dr. B furious, her run cancel—*

"Don't tweet that," I said, which turned out to be unnecessary. Hitching the wicker basket farther up her arm, Dr. Baumgartner snatched the phone from Jacob. She deleted the tweet and let out an angry explosion that shook the basket, cracking two of the eggs against each other. (I knew that underneath the eggs and the cabbages was a hidden stash that included a pen, a notebook, and a miniature camera, along with hand and nasal sanitizer—standard time travel gear.) "It's almost ten! I tell you, there must have been a glitch in the log—"

"Then where," said Abigail, who seemed to be doing just fine even without my help, "is the professor?"

"Let's check the bathroom, the cafeteria, the lake—maybe he went ice fishing. Or he's coming in late this morning because of the snow—"

"Dr. Mooney's not answering his cell," Kamal spoke up from his position of safety behind me. "And his bike is right outside, in the bike bay." He jerked his thumb in the direction of the front steps of the Time Travel Engineering building. We had spotted the professor's bike in the glass-encased TTE bike bay on the way in. It was one of a kind and hard to miss: the body was a very-visible-in-all-seasons bright red, the handlebars stuck out at an odd angle that the professor claimed worked wonders for his back, and the bike's nickname, Scarlett, was etched on the seat.

Across the hallway, the door to Dr. Mooney's office stood wide open, and I could see the professor's desk, which was overflowing with books and papers. The chair behind it was empty. A bookcase along one wall held his collection of antique musical instruments, most of them acquired on STEWie runs.

"Dr. Baumgartner, I'm afraid we've got to assume the worst. Campus security," I added, raising my voice a notch but keeping my anger in check (I was aware of the pressure Erika Baumgartner and other untenured professors were under to produce publishable research), "will be here any minute, as soon as they deal with a snow emergency. They'll take statements and help clarify what happened. Until then, I suggest we all go back to our offices. Thank you, Abigail, I'll take over from here."

Abigail scurried off into the graduate students' office down the hall before I could remind her to take off the bike lock. Kamal followed, looking relieved to be out of the line of fire. Having retrieved his phone from the professor, Jacob resumed typing and just managed to avoid a collision with the doorframe of the student office on his way in.

"No tweeting, Jacob," I called after him, but I wasn't sure if he heard, as I was distracted by the withering stare Dr. Baumgartner shot in my direction. Clogs echoing on the tile floor, she stormed into the travel apparel closet. Sergei looked down at his tunic and breeches, shrugged, and headed for the vending machine farther down the hallway.

I was leaning in, trying (unsuccessfully) to catch a glimpse of the interior of the lab through the crack between the double doors, when the sound of approaching conversation made me turn. It was Dr. Little, the younger and shorter of our two junior TTE professors, in a buttoned argyle wool vest. "Using STEWie to confirm the Snowball Earth hypothesis has academic merit, Ty, but how would you do it?" he was saying to the grad student accompanying him.

"Uh—I've got it, Dr. Little—send a balloon with a camera back in time. Then, when it reaches altitude, have it snap pictures of Earth iced over."

Dr. Little, who seemed oblivious to my presence and the fact that something out of the ordinary was going on, pounced on the student's statement as they passed by. "Yes, that's all very well, but how would you solve the problem of getting the balloon *back* into STEWie's basket?"

They walked out of earshot and I called out Abigail's name in an undertone. She and Kamal were standing just inside the open door of the grad student office, talking in hushed voices. Jacob Jacobson's head bobbed out occasionally as he kept an eye on the developments and, I suspected, sent out tweets to fellow students and the rest of the world against my explicit instructions.

Abigail hurried back and I said, "The bike lock combination?" As she entered the numbers (18-6-7, I noticed, the birth year of one Maria Sklodowska, a.k.a Marie Curie), I asked, "Where is Dr. Rojas?"

Dr. Rojas was a senior TTE professor, along with Dr. Mooney.

"In the Coffey Library giving his Physics for Poets students an oral exam. Kamal and I weren't sure whether we should call and interrupt him."

"I'll take care of it. You didn't inform Dr. Little?"

"It never occurred to us."

I decided I might as well wait for campus security inside the lab and typed in the access code. Abigail followed me in, having left the bike lock hanging from one of the door handles in a droopy coil. The doors creaked shut behind us, reminding me that I'd been meaning to put in a call to Maintenance to have them check and oil the hinges.

"I'll try Dr. Mooney again," said Abigail, dialing the phone in her hand. "I keep getting his voice mail. I've also sent him an e-mail, posted an inquiry to his CampusProfs page, and sent several text messages to his cell."

"He's okay with students sending him text messages?"

"He's the only professor in the department that allows it."

"I'm not surprised. Not that Dr. Mooney lets his students send texts, I mean—well, that doesn't surprise me either—but also that other professors don't. It's hard to explain to students that there is a fine line between—wait, where is that coming from?"

"I hear it, too."

We looked around the cavernous lab, with its labyrinth of lasers and mirrors under a balloon roof. A faint ringing emanated from somewhere, breaking the monotony of the quietly humming equipment. The ringing stopped abruptly, and through the phone in Abigail's hand I heard Dr. Mooney's voice offering the caller the option of leaving a message, followed by a very long beep.

"I'll redial," Abigail said.

The *ting-ting* of a phone started up again.

"There." I pointed.

We moved toward the corner of the lab where there was a short row of head-height lockers for storing personal effects during STEWie runs. Three of them gaped empty, their metal doors ajar. The door to the fourth was shut, but the lock, like the bicycle one that Abigail had left on the lab doors, hung loose. Abigail and I exchanged a look, the eeriness of the deserted lab starting to get to us. My heart in my throat, I reached out—I could almost feel the gray metal vibrating with the faint ringing coming from within—and swung open the narrow door.

3

What was the matter with me? I don't know what I expected to see. Besides the cell phone, the only things in the locker were a black wallet, a winter hat with a bicycle headlamp still attached, and a man's leather belt.

I sent Abigail to the grad student office to make sure Jacob and the other students weren't tweeting about Dr. Mooney's disappearance, and turned away from the locker, moving toward the heart of the lab to wait for campus security. My wet boots squeaked on the tile floor and I subdued an impulse to shout into the cavernous space to see if my voice would echo. To me, STEWie had always looked like a dishwasher—a giant's dishwasher, if such a thing existed. Like gleaming tableware, mirrors fanned out from the array center, the smallest the size of a file folder and the biggest almost reaching the balloon ceiling, all gently curved into a dish shape. The dim floor lighting threw soft shadows on the ring lasers that circulated around the mirrors.

STEWie. The *SpaceTimE Warper*, a.k.a, the Time Travel Machine. Sort of. It wouldn't always take you where you wanted to go, only where History allowed. All summer, a team from the Linguistics Department eager to decipher Rongorongo had tried to interact with the fifteenth-century inhabitants of Easter Island. They hadn't been able to take more than a step away from STEWie's basket, as their attempts at getting their clothing and mannerisms right had fallen far short of what was needed for them not to disturb history. Similarly, a recent attempt to get footage of Galileo spotting Jupiter's moons had failed, even though the History of Science team had arrived at night—they could not move stealthily enough to get near the telescope and its builder and were forced to turn back.

The square of thick glass mounted on a knee-high base in the center of the array felt cold to the touch, as usual. A steel frame sat rather incongruously on top of it, like a waiting elevator. But this elevator had no walls, no ropes attached to it, and didn't go up or down. The frame and platform delineated STEWie's basket, which was visible only to instruments.

The basket was, as Kamal had said, quite obviously empty.

I shivered. The lab was always chilly—the result of the cryogenic equipment under the floor, needed to keep STEWie from overheating during time travel send-offs.

The project badly needed funding for a new generator—after the first whirlwind year, the excitement had worn off somewhat and the prospect of yet more panoramic photos of battlefields and unflattering close-ups of secondary historical figures, yellow teeth and all, had been greeted with a large yawn from the public and with mumbling about more practical ways of spending money. Not to mention that MIT and other schools were starting work on their own time travel labs with bigger and better STEWies. Maybe they would have more luck getting close to the men and women who anchored history, I thought, moving away from STEWie's basket.

My cell beeped, interrupting my chain of thought. Oscar, the building doorman, with a two-word text message: *Security here.*

I looked up from the phone to see two shadowy outlines appear outside the opaque lab doors: a solid, square one and next to it, a harder-to-make-out tall one. Campus Security Chief Kirkland stuck his head through the door. "Ah, Ms. Olsen."

His squat companion was a uniformed campus officer I hadn't met before. They were an odd pair: while the officer's uniform looked a size too small—the fabric stretched tight across his wide thighs—Chief Kirkland's looked like it had been custom-made. It might have been, given his lanky height. The chief's parka was unzipped, as if we were in the middle of the March melt-off and not in the grips of December, and he had his hands in his pants pockets, not in a slouchy way, but in a comfortable-in-his-own-skin kind of way. He had once told me—in a rare personal slip—that his grandparents hailed from here and from north, east, and west of us: the Dakota peoples, Quebec, Scotland, and Sri Lanka, which explained his dark complexion and hard-to-place features.

"Van Underberg," the security chief introduced his new officer after the two of them had filed into the room. "This here is Ms. Olsen."

"Ma'am," Officer Van Underberg said politely. As the lab doors closed behind him with their usual uncomfortable creak, the officer removed his fleece hat and took a somewhat nervous look around. His superior surveyed the room, too—calmly, with interest. No one could fail to be impressed by their first look at STEWie.

In the seven months since our previous chief had retired, Chief Nate Kirkland and I had crossed paths a few times. He mostly kept to himself and had a square jaw that he used sparingly for conversation, as if he was the one with the Norwegian ancestry, not I. He had come to us from the state park system, and at first he'd struck me as being somewhat out of place at St. Sunniva, where there was not much for the security office to do except (a) issue parking permits, speeding tickets, and fishing licenses; (b) provide directions to visitors who were confused by the circular campus layout; and (c) intervene in the occasional fender bender or student party gone out of control. This, however, seemed to suit Chief Kirkland just fine. The most recent problem we'd called him in for had involved petty theft of food from a shared fridge in the Rosalind Franklin Biology and Genetics Complex. A well-hidden camera had revealed the culprit to be a visiting research fellow with a somewhat loose definition of public property. But he had also been quite brilliant in his subject, experimental genetics, so we'd put up with the nuisance until his three-month term ran out. He was now somebody else's problem.

Once, right after he'd taken up the post, I had asked the security chief to call me Julia—everyone did—but his answer had been that he preferred to keep things formal on all official business. I hadn't repeated the offer since.

Chief Kirkland tore his gaze away from the largest of the mirrors and turned to me. "What happened here, Ms. Olsen?" Officer Van Underberg readied a pencil and a little spiral notepad from his parka pocket.

I opened my mouth to speak, then closed it, realizing that blurting out that a respected physics professor had been scattered across time was probably not the best place to begin. Chief Kirkland waited, not exactly patiently, while I composed my thoughts. I took my hands out of my jacket sleeves, where I had slid them in an effort to keep my fingers warm, and plunged into the story, pointing to STEWie's basket and the lab lockers at the appropriate points in the narrative. After I finished there was silence. Officer Van Underberg, who had stopped taking notes about halfway through, stared at me wide-eyed, rather like Kamal had when he'd brought the news to my office. The tip of his pencil had broken off. Even Chief Kirkland, who always seemed perfectly composed, looked a bit disconcerted.

"Let me begin again," I said. "Surely you've heard of STEWie?"

Chief Kirkland beckoned me to go on, but Officer Van Underberg looked at his pencil sadly and said, "Pardon me, ma'am, is this—is STEWie the Time Travel Machine?"

The Time Travel Machine was what everyone outside the academic world called STEWie.

"It's not quite as exciting as it sounds," I explained quickly. Officer Van Underberg had a chubby, caramel-colored mustache that he kept stroking nervously with the back of one hand. His freshly trimmed hair—regulation for new officers?—contrasted with the chief's black strands, which hung below his ears to his shoulders. "STEWie ferries researchers to past places and times, where they can take notes and photos, even footage on occasion. But they *cannot change anything of significance, however small.*" I always tried to emphasize this; it was everyone's first question. "That is, they can't go wherever they want, or near anyone they want. The photos and eyewitness accounts go into the *History Alive* exhibit at the university museum. Our researchers also write articles and books, deliver presentations and workshops, and teach classes. Most of the travel slots go to the History Department, including History of Science, where the dean's offices are, but we also get archaeologists, linguists, anthropologists, paleontologists, evolutionary biologists, the occasional geologist—"

"In a nutshell, then," Chief Kirkland summarized, "STEWie is like a tourist bus. Travelers carry cameras, go where the bus takes them, and come back with photos. And this Dr. Mooney?"

"You've probably heard his name before. One of the original minds behind the project. A physicist who applied his talents to time-travel engineering."

"And he is missing."

I shivered again and wrapped my arms around my body. It was a toss-up between whether it was colder inside or outside. "I'll take you to see Kamal Ahmad and Abigail Tanner in a minute. They were first on the scene. The joint grad student office is just down the hall. You'll probably also want to talk to Oscar. And Dr. Rojas. He and Dr. Mooney are—were—the two senior professors in the TTE Department."

"Oscar?" inquired Officer Van Underberg, his stubby pencil hovering above the notepad.

"The doorman who walked you in. Aged, wiry-looking fellow with alert eyes who looks like it would be a bad idea to cross him? Ex-Marine. Raises miniature roses in his greenhouse and rarely sleeps. That big pile of toys in his station is for Toys for Tots."

"We'll also need Dr. Mooney's home address," the chief said.

"It's on file in my office. I can text you the information, if you have a cell number where you can be reached—"

Chief Kirkland nodded to his officer. "Van Underberg."

I watched as Officer Van Underberg scratched down the number for the phone sticking out of his parka pocket. He carefully tore the page from his notepad and handed it to me.

"We'll need to see Dr. Mooney's office," Chief Kirkland added. "Is it in this building?"

"On the other side of that wall. The door is open. Anything else?"

"We'll probably have more questions for you as the accident investigation progresses, Ms. Olsen."

"You know where to find me, Chief Kirkland."

"I need to fetch my pencil sharpener from the car," said Officer Van Underberg, and he left to do so before I could point out that there was bound to be one somewhere in the lab.

I led Chief Kirkland to the locker that contained Dr. Mooney's personal things and pointed out a nearby office chair where a sweater, a jacket, and a pair of bicycling pants with reflective stripes along their length lay neatly folded. On top of the pile of clothing sat one of the lab cameras. "Dr. Mooney must have changed into period-appropriate clothes, but apparently he decided he didn't need a camera."

"Period-appropriate clothes?" the chief asked as he examined the professor's wallet.

"We don't yet know what era he was visiting, so I'm not sure what he might have been wearing. The TTE Department keeps a wide selection of outfits in the travel apparel closet across the hall. Tunics, sandals, robes, wigs, and so forth, whatever the professor might have needed. I'll ask around to see if anything is missing... There was quite a bit of discussion," I added, straying from the strictly relevant, "about whether the clothes should be kept unwashed and unmended and the shoes muddy and uncleaned to allow our travelers to blend in more easily in earlier time periods. The obsession with laundering is a relatively recent one. Some professors drew the line at personal—uh, odors. Others felt it was a necessity they were willing to put up with for the sake of knowledge and discovery. Xavier Mooney is—was—one of them. We settled on laundering everything and spraying the clothes with a synthetic compound that mimics human sweat and dirt as needed. And no one," I added as we turned away from the lockers, "not even the researchers who prefer to appear authentic, minds the periodic bed bug treatments."

"How's Quinn?" Chief Kirkland asked as he held the lab door open for me. "We haven't seen him at the Walleyes lately."

While the security chief had never deigned to call me Julia, he was on a first-name basis with my ex. Both of them had belonged to the Walleyes, the town's fishing club. I had already decided I wasn't going to sugarcoat things when people asked me about Quinn. The reactions I had gotten to the disintegration of my marriage had ranged from expressions of condolences to comments of the I-never-liked-him variety.

"Quinn took a job in Phoenix," I said. "Real estate. He left town with Officer Jones. You didn't know?"

"So *that's* why she quit so suddenly," he said without a change of expression. "I wondered. I thought it was because she didn't like me for some reason."

I snickered at this unexpected bit of humor from him and the awkwardness of the moment dissipated.

"It was the cooking, mostly," I explained half-seriously as we stopped outside the open door of the grad student office. No work or studying was being done inside. Kamal, Sergei, Jacob, Abigail, and two other students stood huddled around Abigail's desk talking about what had happened to Dr. Mooney.

"Quinn didn't like your cooking?" He sounded a little baffled.

"He expected me to cook. There are many things I can do, but that's one list that cooking is not on. Scrambled eggs mystify me. They always stick to the bottom of the pan. And my chicken invariably turns out dry and my pasta squelchy."

Chief Kirkland gave me a look I couldn't interpret before nodding at me and heading into the student office. Taking that as my cue to leave, I hurried back to the Hypatia of Alexandria House. Penny Lind had already arrived and was tapping an impatient leopard-print, two-inch-heeled boot in front of my closed office door. Her face, framed by fluffy earmuffs, was pink from the cold above her cream-colored coat.

"Penny Lind. Of the *Les Styles* blog, fashions past and current. Am I late? Professor Baumgartner hasn't left, has she? The snow—"

"No, you're not late. She's still in the present." I opened the door and hung my jacket and scarf on the coatrack just inside of it. I offered Penny the chair that Kamal had sat in an hour ago. Her own coat, which she left on, had large splash marks down the back. I decided not to point them out.

She draped her purse on the back of the chair before lowering herself into it, taking care not to sit on the coat. The purse was the kind that I would have trouble fitting a hand into, much less actual stuff. It matched the boots.

I held open the cookie jar. She shook her head. "I wish. Carbs are the enemy—even for those of us who only work behind the computer screen. You don't happen to have a fat-free latte on hand?"

"The vending machine has hot chocolate but no lattes, sorry," I said. A quick peek at the *Les Styles* blog while I was on the phone with her earlier had revealed that most of its glossy photos had little to do with Minneapolis and its dress styles and much more to do with what celebrities were wearing in two more-trendsetting cities, one on each coast. Also that my whole wardrobe was just not *it*.

Penny Lind stretched out her feet in the soggy boots to one side of the desk. She glanced with disdain (mixed with perhaps a touch of envy) at my treaded, puffy, waterproof boots. "I had no idea it was such a *long* walk from the parking lot."

"We encourage walking and biking at St. Sunniva," I explained, sitting down across from her.

"I've always thought of walking and biking as summer activities."

"In the winter we encourage bundled-up walking and biking."

"Of course you do. Who's Sunniva?"

"Patron saint of Norway's west coast. She was a tenth-century Irish princess. As the legend goes, she fled aboard a ship to escape marriage to a heathen king. She and her followers hid in a cave on the island of Selja, just off the coast of Norway. They died after a rockfall. We're working on confirming the story," I added as an aside, then went on. "St. Sunniva was founded in 1890 as an all-girls Lutheran school by an immigrant couple, Knut and Agnes Hegge. In 1968, we turned coed and nondenominational."

"And the dark-haired, strong-boned woman whose photo is by the front door?"

"Hypatia? A scientist and a philosopher in Roman Egypt. A story with an unhappy ending. She was murdered by a religious mob."

I saw her eye one of the black-and-white photos on my wall, this one taken the usual (not time travel) way, which showed the 1929 varsity football team. The cheerfully grinning women wore bulky and very non-revealing gym uniforms. They wouldn't have made it onto *Les Styles* even if blogs had existed back then. Below the photo was a large world map riddled with pushpins. I stuck one in after every successful STEWie run. Without saying anything, she got to her feet. "Right. Shall we get to it? The Time Travel Machine isn't far, is it?"

I hated to break the news that the only place she'd be going was back to her car. A quick glance through the window showed me that the campus path had yet to be cleared; a bundled-up student was pushing a bicycle in the direction of the glass-encased Emmy Noether House for Mathematics.

"Ms. Lind, I'm afraid—"

"Penny." She slipped on thin leather gloves and swung her purse across one shoulder.

"Penny, I'm afraid we'll have to postpone the tour of the TTE lab. Sorry. Unforeseen circumstances. We've had to temporarily halt all STEWie runs."

Her eyes narrowed under her pencil-thin eyebrows, and her perfect nose wrinkled ever so slightly, like a well-groomed dog picking up a scent. "I thought I heard something over the phone. Unforeseen circumstances, you say…I think I might have that hot chocolate after all."

I got up and returned a couple of minutes later with two hot chocolates in Styrofoam cups. Penny Lind had her cell phone out. She flashed the screen at me, her voice taking on a salesman's tone. "My readers have left a lot of comments. They've been looking forward to the photos Dr. Baumgartner promised me—pouf hairstyles, gowns, men in wigs and stockings—"

I set the hot chocolates down on the desk, leaving one in front of Penny. I wondered what she would have made of Dr. B's clogs, peasant dress, and egg basket. Erika Baumgartner's research subject, the chemist Antoine Lavoisier, had, like Hypatia, met with an unhappy end, his involving a guillotine in revolutionary-era France. His wife, Marie-Anne, was Abigail's thesis topic. The professor's choice of peasant-wear had been a strategic one. The rule of thumb was that foot soldiers—maids, milkmen, washerwomen, chimney sweeps, and so on—usually went about their jobs unnoticed. Donning the mantle of an average Jane or Joe made it much easier to move about in the past.

Looking about as far from a peasant as humanly possible, Penny Lind took a delicate sip of the hot chocolate, which left a mustache above her upper lip, and asked, "Is it true that Erika Baumgartner would have been back in less than an hour with the photos?"

"Yes—a day in the field takes about fifty minutes of lab time." I waved that aside. "I can give you a tour of our other science buildings if you'd like—"

"Will there be any time travel in them?"

"I'm afraid not."

It was not a good idea to send her into the office of the probably still-fuming Dr. Baumgartner, that was certain. For a wild moment I considered walking Penny over to the museum so she could snap a few photos of Ewan Coffey for her blog, but decided the actor might not appreciate that. And we did need his checkbook, as crass as that sounded. Probably now more than ever, the unpleasant thought shot through me, given what had happened to Dr. Mooney.

Penny tapped an impatient leopard-print boot.

"How about this? I'll arrange for you to observe a second project after we resume STEWie runs." I flicked on my computer and opened STEWie's roster. "Maybe with someone from the History Department—let's see—yes, here we go—there's a team scheduled to travel to 41 BC to gather data on Cleopatra, the last of the Egyptian pharaohs."

Whatever had gone wrong last night with STEWie, I hoped it would be dealt with soon; otherwise there were going to be a lot of unhappy researchers roaming the halls and snapping at the students who remained on campus during the winter break.

I went on, "The Cleopatra team will try to find out if the source of her power was her beauty, as has been rather fancifully reported down the ages, or if it was the more practical combination of intelligence, charisma, and political smarts. Should they return with photos, the question will be answered once and for all."

"The question?"

I leaned forward. *"Did she have a large nose?"*

∞

The day's exams proceeded as scheduled; school life, like the proverbial show in Ewan Coffey's line of work, had to go on. After resolving a problem that had arisen during the freshman Human Biology test (there was a reason cell phones, with their

25

memory and messaging capabilities, had been banned from exam rooms), I printed out the press statement I'd prepared for the dean's review. I usually e-mailed inter office documents to him, but something stopped me from doing that this time.

To seek company is the instinctive human response to death.

Though I was keeping my fingers crossed that the professor would be found at home or in the special collections section of the Coffey Library attending to the formerly lost volumes whose copies he had obtained on STEWie runs, I did not hold out much hope. Officer Van Underberg had kept me updated on the progress of the investigation via a series of texts. Chief Kirkland and the officer were checking all the obvious places for any sign of the professor, starting with Dr. Mooney's house on the edge of campus, on the off-chance that he had changed his mind about biking home once he saw the snow and had made it there by walking or hitching a ride, and then overslept after a long night in the lab, missing our many calls to his home phone number. They were not back yet.

Dean Sunder stood at the wide windows of his office, lost in thought. At first I assumed he was looking out at the still-falling snow, but then saw that he had a PhD thesis in his hands. It was bound with the red cover the school had used before switching to blue in 1980, fifteen years before I enrolled in the Business Administration program at St. Sunniva. Xavier's old PhD thesis, I suspected, from the dean's personal collection. I cleared my throat and Lewis turned toward me. He shut the volume, put it aside, then held out his hand. "Julia. Is that it?"

He took a minute or two to read over the press statement. I had taken care in crafting it. It wasn't very long, just a paragraph or two explaining that the school was looking into the incident, with some inspirational words at the end. *Well-respected scientist at the tail end of his career may have sacrificed all for the benefit of mankind and the advancement of knowledge,* that kind of thing. Whatever the reasons for Dr. Mooney's unscheduled run, I was sure that my words weren't far from the truth.

"Yes...well done, Julia." The dean reread the statement, slipped it into his briefcase, and opened one side of the mahogany cabinet that took up a wall of his office. Extra shirts, assorted ties, and a bottle or two of hair spray waited inside. He loosened the lively red tie he'd worn to the museum breakfast meeting with Ewan Coffey—which had turned out to be very productive, he said—and hung it on the tie rack. Like me, the dean seemed to have a need to talk. "What a terrible thing—for Xavier—and the department. I know Chief Kirkland is still checking, but at this point it's a formality. The basket came back empty and there's only one thing that can mean... Nothing like this has ever happened on my watch. This has been my office for a long time, coming up on, what, nineteen years?" he said, rummaging among the ties without seeming to really notice them.

I couldn't help but throw a glance at the diplomas, awards, and photos with St. Sunniva's chancellor, Jane Evans, and other dignitaries that graced the wall behind his desk. I corrected him gently. "Twenty this January, Lewis." I'd already ordered a silver wall clock for his office with an appropriate inscription. *To Lewis Sunder. From his grateful students, professors, and staff.*

"Twenty, Julia, really? You've been my assistant for, what—"

"Seven years. How about this one? Dark gray is always appropriate."

He took down the somber dark-gray tie and faced the mirror inside one of the cabinet doors. "Did you know that Chris, my assistant before you, retired early to grow palm trees in Florida? It wasn't the winters that drove him away, he said. He'd had enough of students and their problems and wanted to work with something that wouldn't complain all the time." He chuckled, then grew serious again as he wound the tie into a perfect knot. "Xavier and I go way back, have I ever mentioned that? He and Gabriel Rojas and I worked on early attempts at spacetime warping technology as graduate students, back when time travel was just an idea on the back of a napkin. We were young and full of ideas—practical, ambitious, doable, impossible. It was difficult to get funding, a constant struggle. We were barely able to keep things going from one semester to the next. I moved on to other things. After tenure, I had the honor of being offered this post and I jumped at the chance. From that point on, I made it my mission to expand the science departments, bring in new talent, and do all I could to help my researchers."

He had certainly done that. St. Sunniva's eight science departments, from the Mary Anning Hall of Earth Sciences to the Maria Mitchell Astronomical Observatory, owed a lot to him. He had fought for support for many a student and project, and had helped Dr. Mooney and Dr. Rojas scrape for funding at the bottom of the budget barrel until their joint project and the budding Time Travel Engineering Department had taken off. There had been criticism, too. There had been those who felt that St. Sunniva's past as an all-girls school would be best honored by giving admission preference to female students. Lewis Sunder had been adamantly against that and had voted for blind (or as near as could be) admission decisions. But he had also done his best to bring women faculty members into the science departments and had been the one to suggest that naming buildings after Marie Curie and other women scientists would be a tangible way of honoring St. Sunniva's past.

"This will shake up the TTE lab—we'll have to regroup, start fresh. And I have no idea how it will affect our chances in Stockholm. Don't go spreading this around, but I've heard that Xavier and Gabriel were high on the list." Lewis sighed and brushed a bit of lint off his suit. It wasn't just vanity; he represented the science departments through good times and bad. They were expecting him at the campus TV station for the taping of a special announcement. "By the way, I've had to promise Erika the first spot when STEWie runs resume," he added before picking up his briefcase and coat. I followed him out and then headed down to the building kitchenette. I grabbed cheese and grapes from the fridge, stacked several boxes of crackers on top, and hurried over to the TTE building. A meeting to discuss Dr. Mooney's accident had been called; since Lewis was needed for the TV taping, I would be representing the dean's office.

Chief Kirkland was in the conference room. He'd taken a chair not at the rectangular table, but by the narrow windows at the far end of the room, where the blinds were drawn against the falling snow, giving a cozy feeling to the otherwise rather utilitarian space. He sat there with one of his long arms draped over the side of the chair, watching Dr. Mooney's colleagues shuffle in—and his students, too. The professor had made many friends and connections in his years at St. Sunniva. Everyone wore that slightly stunned look people get when something bad happens unexpectedly. I hoped there would be enough refreshments to go around. (Providing a food spread wasn't technically part of my job description, but I found that it made meetings run more smoothly, and thought that it might be especially needed today.)

As I walked in carrying the food, Chief Kirkland shook his head at me, seeming a little less standoffish than usual. "He wasn't at his house. Neighbors had no idea where Dr. Mooney could be or where he might have been planning to go. Things were in a bit of a disarray inside the house," he added. "Old books were strewn all over, with notes penciled in margins. Also a lot of chocolate bar wrappers and empty pie containers."

"Dr. Mooney had a bit of a sweet tooth. And the books wouldn't be unusual for any of our professors," I said, trying to wrestle open a goat cheese log by puncturing its wrap with a plastic knife. As Kamal came in and took a seat near the door, I finally succeeded in getting the package open and plopped the goat cheese down, rattling the platter of food. Abigail hurried in a few minutes later. While we waited for Gabriel Rojas—the mild-mannered professor often forgot about meetings, though I was sure he would make this one—I offered cheese to Officer Van Underberg.

He shook his head politely. "No thank you, ma'am."

"There's Brie, a goat cheese log—or what used to be a log—grapes, Gouda—"

"Appreciate it, ma'am, but I'm on duty." He took out his pencil, which appeared to have gone dull yet again, and sharpened it before tucking both the pencil and the sharpener—a square one that collected its own shavings—back into his uniform's front pocket.

"I find that a pen is more reliable than a pencil for taking notes, Officer Van Underberg," I pointed out helpfully.

"Yes, ma'am. It's just that I'm worried about getting ink stains on my new uniform, ma'am."

I set the cheese tray back on the conference table and asked Chief Kirkland, who shook his head at the food, "Why does your officer keep calling me ma'am?"

"Van Underberg's new at this."

The security chief's gaze barely brushed me before settling on Dr. Rojas, who had hurried in at last and taken a seat. I was a bit surprised by the chief's demeanor, but supposed that even accidents merited a thorough investigation.

From the head of the table, Dr. Baumgartner, her blonde hair falling freely around her shoulders now that she'd exchanged the peasant-wear for casual slacks and a sweater, nodded to thank me for the refreshments for the meeting she was about to chair. She seemed to have accepted that something had gone badly wrong in the TTE lab, and her anger had been replaced by a certain grimness. She cleared her throat and opened the meeting. "I am sorry this sad occurrence has brought us here. But," she added, wasting no time in dispensing with the formalities, "let's face it, we've always known that something like this could happen. It was only a matter of—uh, time."

Dr. Steven Little, the second of our two junior TTE professors, was seated on her right, across the table from Kamal, Abigail, and me. He grunted in agreement without looking up from his laptop. The clean-shaven professor was striking keys with astonishing speed, his fingers moving almost independently of the rest of him, his thickset shoulders hunched forward under the argyle vest. The newest of the four TTE professors—the others being Dr. Mooney, Dr. Rojas, and Dr. Baumgartner—Dr. Little had recently been wooed over from a postdoc position at Berkeley with promises of funding, plentiful STEWie roster slots, and tenure down the road. His first months at St. Sunniva had already shown me that he'd have to be goaded into doing his share of chairing meetings—he clearly felt that stuff was for minds less brilliant than his own.

"I've canceled all runs indefinitely," Dr. Rojas said from the other end of the table. Framed between an unruly mop of gray hair and equally gray and unruly eyebrows, his brow was deeply furrowed. He ran a hand through his hair, disheveling it further. "For as long as it takes to figure out what went wrong."

"Indefinitely? Let's not be hasty," Dr. Baumgartner said, her face falling. "This could still turn out to be a glitch in the computer log. I mean—are we absolutely sure that Xavier is gone?"

In a few clipped sentences, Chief Kirkland summarized for the room what we knew so far. Oscar, the doorman, had seen Dr. Mooney arrive on his bicycle, wheel it into the bike bay, and enter the TTE building at about an hour before midnight. He had not seen the professor leave. Anyone else might have been suspected of dozing off on the job, but not Oscar, who was a well-known insomniac. According to him, the chief said, after Kamal had left for the evening, no one else had gone in or out till morning, when the usual crowd of professors, postdocs, and students had started trickling in, everyone a bit late due to the snow.

The subject of Kamal having been the one signed up to oversee last night's calibration came up.

As Kamal opened his mouth to explain, Dr. Baumgartner clarified the process for Chief Kirkland's benefit. "The equipment must be calibrated for the next day's run. It's a sensitive undertaking, so the graduate students take turns babysitting STEWie overnight." I saw Officer Van Underberg, who was leaning against the wall next to me, pencil this down.

All eyes in the room turned to Kamal. He squared his shoulders and sat up, his earnest young face pulling at my heartstrings for some reason. He gave his explanation unapologetically and with honesty, or at least he began to. "Dr. Mooney was kind enough to offer to take over my shift so that I could get in some last-minute studying for my Spacetime Warping: Theory and Practice exam. I mean, your Spacetime Warping exam, Dr. Little—I've just come back from it—"

"Ah, my teaching assistant brought the exam papers to my office. I haven't had a chance to read them yet." Dr. Little looked up from the laptop and reached around it to spread a lavish layer of goat cheese onto a cracker. "And how did you find the test? Too easy? Not long enough?" He popped the cracker into his mouth.

"Uh—well, I wouldn't say it was too easy, no," Kamal said. "As to last night's calibration, it was kind of Dr. Mooney to offer to take over. I had no idea what would happen... If I had known..."

"No one is blaming you, Kamal," I said firmly.

Dr. Baumgartner was eying Kamal as if she still thought the whole thing might turn out to be an end-of-the-semester student prank gone wrong. Dr. Rojas came to his rescue. "I'll start running tests this afternoon to see what I can find out. Until then, let's keep all this guessing to a minimum."

"Surely you're not planning on going on any STEWie runs, Dr. Rojas," I said. "I don't think Dean Sunder is ready to approve anything of that sort yet—"

"And he would be quite right, Julia. No, the Genetics Department is lending us a fish so we can run tests and pinpoint the malfunction that caused the mirror-laser array to lose focus—"

"—and send Mooney into a ghost zone," Dr. Little finished the sentence for him. "The dangers of cutting-edge research," he added matter-of-factly, offering the well-known platitude (one that, I had to admit, I'd used myself in composing the dean's press statement). "Instead of arriving at whatever year and location Mooney wanted, he found himself trapped in a ghost zone with no way out." As if to add emphasis to his words, the young professor broke the cracker in his hands in two with a snap. I winced and noticed that Abigail, next to me, had scrunched up her eyes, like she was either getting ready to cry, or getting very angry. I rather fancied it was the second. Her spiky, neon-orange hair made her look like a petite warrior. Kamal, next to her, wasn't looking too happy, either.

"And a ghost zone is...?" Chief Kirkland asked Dr. Little, who was deftly toothpicking one of the Gouda cubes. Our newest professor looked like he was well on the road to gaining the tenure-track twenty and contradicting his name in the horizontal dimension, I noted somewhat uncharitably as I got up to empty a fresh package of crackers onto the platter.

Dr. Little disposed of the Gouda cube and said, "A ghost zone is the easiest way for History to protect itself." Like everyone connected to the TTE program, he spoke the word with reverence, a capital *H*, as if History was a force to be reckoned with. "Nothing cleaner than sending a time traveler to the bottom of the ocean, or into outer space, or onto the Bikini Atoll on the morning of March 1, 1954. The traveler would be able to move quite freely on the atoll. Not for long, though. That's what a ghost zone is—you perish seconds after you step foot out of STEWie's basket, your body decomposes as time passes, nature spreads your molecules all around...so you do come back to the present, just not in one piece. We call it being scattered across time."

He reached for another cracker and Dr. Rojas took the opportunity to clarify things for the chief and an agog Officer Van Underberg. "That's why we perform a calibration before each run, to sidestep any possible ghost zones. Our early tests with fish and robotic vehicles resulted in quite a few losses."

I brought up a thought I had been holding on to. "What if Dr. Mooney arrived safely but was for some reason unable to get back to STEWie's basket? Would the professor be able to contact us?"

"You mean, could he carve a message into stone and leave it somewhere for us to find?" Dr. Little liked to pounce when a scientific point came up, especially if someone had inadvertently spoken with imprecision. "First, the basket would never have returned empty. That only happens if the traveler is—"

"Dead," Kamal croaked out the word.

"And second, even if Mooney did somehow manage to write a message for us, it wouldn't matter."

"Why not?" I hoped Dr. Little wouldn't ridicule me for what I was about to ask. "Couldn't we send a rescue basket after him if we found a message telling us what went wrong?"

Dr. Little opened his mouth to answer but Dr. Rojas got there first. He briefly shook his head. "It's all in the past, Julia. He would have already lived out his life."

"Right, of course," I said.

"Any message he might have left for us could only have served one purpose—by letting us know what happened, it would help us avoid future incidents." Dr. Rojas continued in the same pensive tone. "I wonder why Xavier decided to do a run alone, though it's not unlike him to go off protocol—"

"Exactly," said Dr. Baumgartner bluntly, looking up from the journal article she had discreetly started editing. She had a while to go before acquiring tenure (the holy grail of academia, a professorial position that could not be terminated). "Xavier was always full of ideas and eager to tinker with things." She said it with admiration, not criticism. Dr. B had been a postdoc in the school (the shortened version of her name had been coined by fellow postdocs) before being offered a joint tenure-track position in TTE and History of Science. She herself seemed to prefer action to theory. "Most likely, Xavier probably saw that something needed tweaking when he was overseeing last night's calibration, so he jumped in STEWie's basket to test a Band-Aid solution he'd come up with—and it failed badly. Isn't that what everybody's thinking but no one wants to say it?"

Again, it wasn't said as a criticism, but a sudden awkward silence did descend on the room.

"Dean Sunder," I said into it, "has canceled this year's December holiday party. We'll be holding a memorial service on

Friday, after the last of the exams. Anybody who wants to say a few words about Professor Mooney or share any memories from his almost four decades at St. Sunniva, please let me know."

"Let's try and get to the bottom of this unfortunate matter as soon as possible," Dr. Little said, resuming his typing. "Everyone has work to do. Who'll take over Mooney's courses, Julia?"

"Dean Sunder will try to figure something out before the start of the next semester. As for his current classes, Introduction to Time Travel Physics had a final project and no exam. Dr. Mooney had already graded the projects before his accident. There was a list of final grades on his desk. Ghost Zones in Time: How to Find Them and Avoid Them has a final project as well, doesn't it, Kamal?"

Kamal, who was the teaching assistant for that class, nodded. "He sent me the final grades yesterday."

"I took Ghost Zones in Time last year," Abigail spoke up for the first time. "In that classroom, just around the bend of the hallway. For the final project we had to propose a historical event or geographic location that constitutes a ghost zone, suggest an itinerary that circumvents it, and compute coordinates. I chose the Tunguska Event of 1908."

Erika Baumgartner looked up from her journal article again. "It would be quite interesting, wouldn't it, to travel to Siberia of that year and settle the question of whether an asteroid or a comet impacted in the area? It wouldn't be relevant to your thesis topic, Abigail, but perhaps we could get a paper out of it," she said, then stopped abruptly, as if remembering why we were all gathered here.

I didn't begrudge her the editing of the journal paper (*publish or perish* was the imperative phrase in academia), nor her momentary lapse of memory. This was merely a department meeting to figure out how to deal with the aftermath of Dr. Mooney's accident; the memorial service would come later. It was also true that sometimes people dealt best with bad news by focusing on other matters.

As everyone started to shuffle out of the room, Chief Kirkland raised a hand. "I have a question," he said in a quiet tone that nevertheless made everyone stop and turn in his direction. (The chief seemed to have a talent for bringing other people's conversations to a halt. Maybe it was the uniform. I usually had to pull on sleeves and tap shoulders.)

Dr. Rojas shifted in his chair to face the chief. The grayhaired professor had not eaten anything, I noticed, and looked too distracted to bother with class arrangements or asteroid-event discussions. "Sorry, Chief Kirkland, I should have made sure that we'd clarified everything. What is your question?"

"The Time Machine—STEWie—even if we don't know what went wrong, wouldn't the machine settings show where Dr. Mooney had been aiming to go? We know he left his clothes behind. What kind of costume did he put on?"

"We've all taken a look at the travel apparel closet," Dr. Rojas said. "Impossible to say for sure what's missing. As for STEWie's settings revealing Xavier's intended destination—" The bags under Dr. Rojas's eyes seemed to deepen. "That's the really odd thing. They don't."

4

Nightfall, hushed and starless, came early. (We were only ten days from winter solstice, the shortest day of the year and the traditional date of St. Sunniva's Science Quad holiday party. This year we would have a much less jovial event, one which I had already started organizing.) Outside my office window, snow still fell thick and quiet. The phone had been ringing all afternoon. Mostly with expressions of condolences from various parties and questions from news reporters, but I had also fielded quite a few calls from worried parents. One had demanded that her son, a junior who was on the far side of campus in a Method Acting workshop for his School of Drama degree and had probably never set foot in the Science Quad, be kept at what she termed a *safe distance* from the TTE building.

"We're not sure yet who will be teaching the course, but there will be no disruption to the schedule," I'd reassured a parent who was curious about who would teach his daughter's Introduction to Time Travel Physics: Part II spring semester class now that Dr. Mooney had been lost to time. "I'm sure one of Dr. Mooney's colleagues will be happy to take over the course—"

I had dealt with all the condolences, questions, and outright demands as patiently as I could, but I was approaching some kind of wall and was glad that the ringing of the phone and onslaught of e-mails had tapered off. I turned away from the window. In a few minutes Dean Sunder would go home to his family. With the Science Quad empty save for a handful of grad students and research staff monitoring lab experiments, I'd finally be able to get around to finishing the day's paperwork, a task that had gotten pushed aside given the odd events of the day.

"Still working, Julia?" said a strong voice that carried into every nook of my office, trained as it was by the years of public speaking that were at the core of a professor's job. A familiar head of long, silver hair poked in through the open door.

I waved in Dr. Helen Presnik, historical linguist and a well-known face in the TTE lab for more than one reason. She sank into the visitor's chair, deposited a thick sheaf of final exam essays in a free spot on my desk, and loosened her scarf. She had been letting her silver hair grow so that she would fit in better during her runs to Renaissance England, and it now reached halfway down her back. She looked at me and got straight to the point.

"I was in the reference section of the library all day. I just heard about Xavier."

"I'm so sorry, Helen. Do you want a cookie?" I made a move toward the window cabinet.

She stopped me. "That's not necessary. It's certain, then?"

"Oscar saw him enter the TTE building but not come out. His bike's still outside the building, and no one's seen him or heard from him."

She didn't bother asking if Oscar could be trusted to report accurately on happenings in the TTE building. Everyone on campus knew Oscar. With his strange bodily rhythms, he was a favorite subject at the Sleep Lab in the School of Medicine across the lake.

I recapped what we knew so far, then added, "Chief Kirkland will keep an eye on Dr. Mooney's house in case he went somewhere without telling anyone and forgot to take his phone and his wallet—"

I stopped, aware how utterly ridiculous the scenario sounded.

Helen seemed to share my opinion. Her voice softening just a shade, but still brisk, she said, "I see."

"Helen—did Xavier ever express any wishes about—well, what to do in a situation like this?" I paused to frame my words carefully. "Seeing as a funeral is not technically possible, Dean Sunder suggested a memorial service in the Great Hall of the Coffey Library on Friday evening, after the last of the exams, but if you have other thoughts on the matter—"

All softness forgotten, she snorted. "Colleagues and adoring students giving speeches about what a great educator and researcher he was? Xavier would have loved that. All the world's a stage and Xavier liked his place on it. Is it true that it was an unauthorized run?"

I decided that the unadorned truth was the best way to go. I flicked on my computer and scrolled down STEWie's roster. "I looked it up for Chief Kirkland. Xavier wasn't on the roster until next month. Here—late January. He'd asked for a ten-day run to track down a long-lost Arabic manuscript. Al-Khwarizmi's *The Book of Sundials*."

"The Persian mathematician whose name was Latinized into *algorithm*? Another wild-goose chase. Perhaps Xavier was trying to get a head start on locating it," she added, somewhat contradicting herself.

"You mean he might have been testing the viability of the landing site coordinates or something of the sort? Could be. It might explain why he changed out of his everyday clothes and into—well, we're not quite sure what. You know what the travel apparel closet is like. It's impossible to tell what's missing. For now, Dr. Rojas is operating under the assumption that the scheduled calibration stalled for some reason and that Xavier was checking the equipment when the mirror-laser array lost focus, causing him to slip into a ghost zone. Maybe there was some technical reason why modern clothes couldn't work for what he had in mind." I had a sudden thought. "Helen, would you like a glass of wine?" In the white cabinet under my office window, behind the backup boxes of cookies, paper plates, and napkins, I kept a couple of bottles of the stronger stuff. For those times when things went more wrong than they ordinarily did.

"Thank you, Julia, but I better not." She sighed, the news about Xavier clearly foremost in her mind, and ran a displeased eye over the stack of exams. "I need to grade these tonight. The first one I looked at seems to be half-full of Internet slang. A paper for my class, can you believe it?" Helen's specialties included classical Greek and Latin, along with Shakespeare's English. "I can't even understand the title. Look"—she tapped the paper—"four acronyms one after another: WRT F2F NBD IMO. Brevity is the soul of wit, but this is taking things too far. It's like trying to decipher a vanity license plate."

"Wait, I know that one. *With respect to face-to-face, no big deal in my opinion.* Can't say that makes much sense, however. What was the topic of the paper?"

"The difficulty of personal interaction with the local populace on time travels to Shakespeare's London."

"Ah, there you go."

"I wanted the students to roll up their sleeves and think about what a STEWie research run entails." She tapped the paper again. "I don't think there's a single comma anywhere. It will be returned with a *Redo* instruction."

"I suppose one could argue that it's a language in the making," I said, trying to appeal to the linguist in her and glad for the brief change of topic.

"Until it *is* a language of its own, it has no place in an academic setting. And by the time it does, I'll be long gone," she said, whether referring to future retirement as a professor emerita or the other outcome, I wasn't sure. "I wish we could ban the things from campus," she added.

"What things?"

"Cell phones and laptops and e-readers and tablets and such. I've tried telling the students I don't want their electronic devices in my classes, and they all nod like they understand, but I see fingers twitching and moving under desks as they text and tweet and blog and who knows what else. I never know if they hear a word I say anymore."

"I'd think we'd have a mutiny on our hands if we tried to ban cell phones and laptops in classrooms, Helen, though I do somewhat agree with you." I relayed the story of the cell phone and the biology exam.

"Is my complaining a sign that I'm getting old? Don't answer that." She added, "I suppose I have to give credit where it's due—technology made it possible for me to have the honor of watching the very first performance of *Hamlet* at the Globe"—she sighed again, but this time happily—"as an audience member. That was my first STEWie run and Xavier accompanied me. We had to put our differences aside. Speaking of which, how have you been doing, Julia?"

"You mean since Quinn left? Quite well, actually."

"I know you've been telling everybody that it was the cooking—"

"It was. Why did he have to rely on me for his meals? He's a grown man."

"—but I know it was more than that."

She was right, of course. I said, after a moment, "We just couldn't make it work. Our jobs kept getting in the way. I think he assumed that once we got married, I'd turn into someone who was happy to battle the home front problems while he went out and conquered the world. It's just that"—I had no problem admitting this to Helen, who would know what I meant—"I kind of wanted to conquer the world myself, in however small a way. The bottom line was that Quinn didn't like his job—any desk job, really—but I like mine. We had these never-ending arguments about my long work hours. His were nine to five, but school hours just aren't like that, are they?" I was usually in by seven thirty and not home until seven, and often worked weekends. As for Quinn, his new project, flipping upscale houses in Phoenix, hadn't come as a surprise. The last few months before he left, he'd spent much of his free time looking at online photos of Arizona bungalows and backyard pools as he searched for something grander than his then-job as an accountant for the town's electrical plant. One morning, he'd emptied our joint bank account, taken the more reliable of our two cars, and headed south on I-35 with Officer Jones. At least the house was in my name only.

Helen got to her feet, the ungraded essays in one hand. "Well, you're probably better off in the long run." She paused on the way out to make one final remark. "I've always known he'd come to a bad end."

The door closed behind her with an abrupt click.

I knew whom she meant, and it wasn't Quinn.

Drs. Xavier Mooney and Helen Presnik were ex-spouses.

∞

I had just gotten around to sorting a stack of office-supply request forms, which needed to be turned into orders by the end of the day, when Dean Sunder stuck his head in. "Julia, I'm going to take off now, unless anything else needs my attention."

His suit still looked pressed to perfection and his salt-and-pepper hair was arranged just *so*. My hair, on the other hand, had slowly started slipping out of its clip as I'd fielded phone calls, e-mails, and text messages, finding its way into my eyes and onto my neck. I sat up, pushed my glasses up my nose, and grabbed a firm hold of my brown locks, pinning them back into submission. No matter how unusual the circumstances, slouching and loose hair went against the aura of efficiency and competence that I aimed to project. "We've been getting a lot of phone calls from anxious parents and reporters wanting a quote, but nothing I can't handle."

"Well, coddle the first and dodge the second, as usual," he said from the doorway. "I was thinking—I'd like you to accompany campus security if they request additional interviews with our staff. We should extend them our full cooperation, of course, but I don't like them wandering around the buildings, asking unnecessary questions. I understand the difficulty, since there's no body and all…but this was just an unfortunate accident, after all. We're all very shaken by what happened." He added pensively, "It falls to me to think about what's best for the school."

I understood what he meant. Donations. We were in the middle of the end-of-the-calendar-year push. Alumni had a standing invitation to drop in on any departments and labs to look around and see what their old school was up to these days. We did not want anyone to be scared away by the sight of Campus Security Chief Kirkland and Officer Van Underberg roaming the halls. If I accompanied them, I'd be able to reassure everyone that the school had things under control.

To an outsider, Dean Sunder's concern about alumni contributions at a time like this might seem crass, but in fact it was the opposite—where fundraising was concerned, the dean had always tried to take as much as he could off the shoulders of the researchers in the science departments and onto his own. His efforts fell into two categories: tapping government grants, which usually favored safe, baby-steps research projects; and targeting alumni, private patrons, and foundations, who were more willing to take on risky research projects like STEWie. Ewan Coffey's donations to the school had been instrumental in getting STEWie up and running. The actor had been following the project's results with keen interest—and with the satisfaction, I thought, of a gambler who had backed the right horse. (After his morning meeting with the dean, Ewan had returned to his movie set; the actor was back in Minnesota for the shooting of what rumor had it was the thrilling tale of a cabin-vacationing lawyer battling an angry Bigfoot in a blizzard, all while trying to win the heart of his somewhat younger but equally attractive next-door neighbor. It would no doubt do as well as all his other flicks.)

Dean Sunder glanced behind him with that last sentence, as if there might be potential donors wandering around the 120-year-old halls of the Hypatia of Alexandria House at this late hour, or a few of Xavier Mooney's molecules floating down the dimly lit hallway that his corporeal form had graced many times over the years. The dean turned back with a small shudder. "We really need more indoor lighting in here. It gets dark so early in the winter. See if you can get Maintenance to install a few more ceiling lights, Julia."

"Lewis, you knew Xavier better than I did—did he have any family other than Helen Presnik?" I asked, immediately regretting my choice of words. I wasn't sure I looked upon Quinn as family anymore and I had no idea what Helen's opinions on the matter might be; ex-spouses were a gray area family-wise, their status to be determined on a case-by-case basis.

"I think there's a sister. Mary and I met her at Xavier and Helen's wedding."

"I'll see if Helen has her address. Helen didn't know of any particular wishes he might have had regarding a memorial service. I'll schedule the Great Hall in the Coffey Library for Friday evening, like we discussed. I called Ingrid, hoping she'd be able to put together a light buffet at short notice. She said it would be no problem."

Ingrid was one of the linchpin personalities in town, always ready to take up a cause when someone needed help or to drop by with a stack of Swedish pancakes with lingonberry jam from her restaurant when a family was in trouble.

"I suppose we should have flowers?" the dean said.

"Sven's Shop can provide them."

"And some kind of music, do you think?"

"The Music Department offered to send over students to play something lively on Dr. Mooney's collection of historical musical instruments. I also thought I might get an enlargement made of Dr. Mooney's CampusProfs page picture."

"You've thought of everything, Julia. I don't know what I'd do without you. I'll see you in the morning."

Mary, his wife of thirty years, and their two dogs awaited him at home.

"You have a press conference at eight," I reminded him as he left to dig his BMW out of the snow. "I expect it will be well attended."

I heard the sound of voices in the hall, and a moment later Chief Kirkland's lanky figure appeared in the doorway. I put down the stack of office forms I'd only just picked up again. "Chief Kirkland, any news?"

He shook his head in a curt and unambiguous negative.

"We've checked everywhere we could think of. I'm sorry."

"Oh." I felt my eyes begin to sting with tears. I took off my glasses and gave them a firm wipe with the lens cloth I kept on my desk. I had known Xavier for the seven years I'd been Lewis Sunder's assistant; still, we'd only had infrequent contact regarding school business and exchanged small talk at the occasional lab party. I seemed to be overreacting. It was due to one simple fact, I realized. The professor had been a positive force in a complicated world.

On the window cabinet, a folder bulging with conference travel receipts and reimbursement forms suddenly flew open as its rubber band gave out, spewing papers all over the floor. My administrator's instincts kicked in and I left my glasses on the desk and hurried over to pick up the forms.

"Looks like the snow isn't letting up anytime soon," Chief Kirkland said, bending down to help me. Outside, a compact snowplow chugged along under a streetlamp with the familiar grating noise of steel on asphalt; the path behind the snowplow had already acquired a layer of powder. "Are you heading out, Ms. Olsen, or—I'm sorry, is your name still Ms. Olsen now that Quinn has, uh, moved to Arizona?"

"It is. I mean, I never had to change it. Both he and I happened to be Olsens when we met. I thought it was a sign that we were fated to be together." I snorted at the recollection and went back to my desk for a fresh folder to transfer the papers into.

The lanky figure by the window chose not to remark on that. "If you're heading out, I'd be happy to escort you to your car to make sure it starts up in the cold—"

What, was he being gentlemanly or was that a dig against my admittedly aged Honda? Deciding to give him the benefit of the doubt, I reached for my glasses, slid them back on, and said, "Thanks, but I have to finish these forms on my desk tonight. In the spirit of redundancy, Central Accounting wants both hand-filled copies and online ones." I noticed that his usual shadow was not behind him. "Where's Officer Van Underberg?"

"At the station typing up his notes. I'll be heading over there later—I suspect we're in for a busy evening, with motorists stuck in snow and cars refusing to start. Wanda—my spaniel—will be wanting her dinner and a walk first. I was on my way home, but I noticed that your light was on." He hesitated, then went on. "Losing a colleague is not—easy."

From the way he said it, I sensed there was a story there, but did not want to pry. Instead I said, mulling over what he'd said like it was a matter of cold and indifferent semantics, "I don't know if *colleague* is the right word. Xavier was a teacher and a researcher—there have been rumors that he and Dr. Rojas were up for next year's Nobel Prize—and I spend most of my time making sure forms are filled out correctly."

"Don't sell yourself short, Ms. Olsen. Professors Mooney and Rojas would hardly have been able to accomplish Nobel-worthy research without the support of the dean's office. Though I have wondered why you're content to be a dean's assistant," he added in what was for him an unusual outburst of curiosity. "You could be dean yourself. You practically run the place anyway."

"You need a science degree to be a science dean. Besides, Lewis spends most of his time shaking hands, smiling, and making small talk at fundraisers. His position is a political one, and I…well, I do my best to find solutions to the daily problems that arise around this place. When a bigger issue comes up, like Dr. Little and Dr. Baumgartner disagreeing about whether pure and applied research should be funded equally, Dean Sunder gets stuck in the middle. Meanwhile I prepare the budget and, as you say, practically run the place. That's pretty satisfying to me, Chief Kirkland."

"Still. I used to be an officer in my young days. It's better to be chief."

"There's nothing wrong with being an assistant," I snapped, surprising myself. I decided not to point out that he, too, had a boss—as head of campus security he reported directly to Chancellor Jane Evans. "If I were in Dean Sunder's place, the first thing on my to-do list tomorrow would be to make another statement to the media. He won't have anything new to tell them because it will take Dr. Rojas some time to figure out what went wrong with STEWie. And after that, he has a tenure review meeting, then a fundraiser luncheon, then a committee meeting to determine whether the cutoff for the Dean's List this semester should be an A grade point average or an A-plus, a discussion that will probably drag well into the late afternoon. Need I say more?"

"Fair enough. So Dr. Mooney wasn't a colleague, then. A coworker and a friend?"

"One I'll miss."

5

By the end of the week, the final exams were behind us, Dean Sunder had given a heartfelt speech at Dr. Mooney's memorial in the packed hall of the Coffey Library, and the campus walkways and roads had all been cleared of snow. The first quiet Monday of winter break began with Abigail walking into my office and demanding, "Where is Dr. Mooney's didgeridoo?"

I hit the Send button on a mass fundraising e-mail directed at science degree alums and looked up. "Abigail, you're in early." Graduate students were usually late risers, particularly during school breaks.

"I wanted to stop by Dr. Mooney's office one last time—just to say good-bye—"

"Abigail, here, come in and take a seat." I got up and hurried to get the cookie jar. Her hair was a more somber dark purple today and framed her face instead of sticking up above it. She didn't talk about her childhood much, but I knew that it had been spent in and out of foster homes. Every textbook I'd ever seen her carry had a *USED* sticker on it. She seemed to have found a home here; other than the time she spent with her boyfriend, who was in the Athletics Department, she was always in the TTE lab. Dr. Mooney, in particular, had become a bit of a father figure in her life.

into the room, because everything smelled like Thanksgiving... Then I found myself by the musical instruments shelf—the Music Department students had put everything back in the wrong place, but that wasn't the problem. The Babylonian rattle, the Portuguese castanets, the Hawaiian nose flute, they were all there, but the didgeridoo from Dr. Mooney's Australia far-time trip wasn't. I took a good look around the office but the didgeridoo was definitely not there. It's not like you can miss it, it's pretty large, right? The movers said they hadn't seen it or packed it away."

"Maybe someone from the Music Department kept it a little longer. I'm sure they'll return it."

"I asked. They said they didn't take it."

Now that she mentioned it, I didn't remember the didgeridoo among the instruments showcased at Dr. Mooney's memorial.

She added, "I was hoping we could keep it as a memento in the grad student office—not to play, of course, just to have—though I don't know who I should ask about that."

"Dr. Mooney left everything to the school in his will," I said. "I'm sure something can be arranged."

Abigail grinned at me and got to her feet. "Thanks, Julia. Can I have one more of these?" she asked, hand hovering above the open cookie jar.

"Have several."

From the doorway, she added, "And you'll find out who might have the didgeridoo, right?"

"I'm taking the budgetary forms around the buildings today. I'll ask around."

∞

After resolving a travel visa issue for an exchange student who was arriving from China for the optimistically named spring

Abigail accepted a walnut cookie. "Thank you, Julia. You're very nice, you know that?"

"So you went into Dr. Mooney's office," I said, setting the open cookie jar between us in its usual spot on the desk and dropping back down into my chair. "How did you get in, by the way?"

"The door was unlocked. The movers are there."

Dr. Mooney's office was being packed up into storage until the department decided what to do with his belongings. I made a mental note to ask Oscar to keep an eye on things. We couldn't have students, even well-meaning ones, wondering in and out of the late professor's office without permission.

As if sensing my disapproval, Abigail pushed her thin, purple hair behind her ears and explained, "I just wanted to look around, that's all. Other than a few half-packed boxes, everything was the way the professor always kept it—"

"Cluttered, untidy, and teeming with interesting things," I summarized the usual state of Dr. Mooney's office for her.

She relaxed and a smile crossed her face. "I was going to say that it was in a state of controlled chaos. The movers had only just gotten around to packing some of Dr. Mooney's books. I took a moment to—to touch some of them—like the Hipparchus trigonometry tables that he brought back last year, you know the ones—" She paused to eat the cookie.

The photographic copies Xavier had made of the ancient Greek astronomer's work were one of his—and the ancient manuscript depository in the Coffey Library's—most prized possessions.

Abigail, having wolfed down the walnut cookie, reached for another. I had a sinking feeling that the cookies were destined to be her breakfast for the day. (Like early rising, grad students and nutritious meals were not a compatible combination.) "I rummaged a bit in the basket with all the snapshots he'd taken on STEWie runs... Someone must have plugged an air freshener semester (which started mid-January) and rearranging a pair of tenure review meetings that had come into conflict scheduling-wise, I was ready to tackle the next big item on my to-do list, the budget for the next school year, due the first day of the new year. While the details had mostly been hammered out in meetings, I had yet to receive the necessary paperwork from a handful of professors and research staff. This state of affairs wasn't unusual in the least, and would easily be resolved. Winter break meant that everyone would be holed up in their labs or offices. I donned my goose-down jacket, picked up a stack of blank Supply, Laboratory Space, and Office Space Request forms, and slid them into my bag along with several black-ink ballpoint pens, which were the best for filling out forms in triplicate. Prepared for my mission, I headed out.

 The building doors closed behind me as I paused to slide on my gloves and let my eyes adjust to the sunlight. Winter was the brightest of the four St. Sunniva seasons—the sun's rays were reflected to summer strength by the freshly fallen snow, and the lake was like a large, round mirror, its surface a solid block of ice. (The 270-acre lake sat firmly on the official list of Minnesota's ten thousand, though Dr. Braga of the Department of Earth Sciences had recently informed me that there were actually 11,842 lakes in the state.) On its shores, the stately birch and oak trees that shaded the brick Hypatia of Alexandria House in the summer held a reminder that spring was very much *not* just around the corner, their bare brown branches stark next to their evergreen cousins. The cold was character-building. At least it was a dry cold, I thought as I reached for my phone to turn it off so that any calls would go directly to voice mail. Then I took off a glove and had another go at it (the phone tended to ignore any activity made by gloved fingers). Before heading to work, I'd donned my "astronaut" boots—the warm, puffy, white ones with treaded soles that Penny Lind had both envied and hated—in anticipation of the walking I'd be doing around the science buildings. The only one that would require driving was Astronomy, which was located north of the lake, on the biggest hill on campus.

I let a bundled-up student on a bicycle pass me, then set a course for the Earth Sciences building, the one nearest to the boat dock. From the dock, counterclockwise, the path brought visitors first to the Science Quad, then the Humanities Quad; the path then touched the south parking lot and continued on to the School of Law and the School of Medicine, known as the Law-Med Quad; then came the fourth, unnamed quadrant which housed the Coffey Library, the History Museum, and student housing, after which the path came full circle, ending back at the boat dock. Today a group of students who'd stayed on campus during the break were playing ice hockey next to the dock.

A slow and steady plod took me from the stately Mary Anning Hall of Earth Sciences to the oversized Marie Curie Chemistry and Physics Annex to the elegant, glass-dominated Emmy Noether House for Mathematics, during which I (a) alternately removed and donned my jacket and gloves; (b) listened to the latest lab news while waiting for professors and researchers to fill out forms; (c) watched a chemistry demonstration in which a gallium spoon melted into hot water; (d) fielded a thinly veiled, inappropriate comment about my astro-boots from a senior researcher who clearly needed a refresher course in workplace sexual harassment; and (e) failed to find anyone who had seen the didgeridoo from Dr. Mooney's office. The sun had progressed well along its low arc in the sky when I decided it was time for a lunch break and a fresh supply of forms.

I returned to the Hypatia of Alexandria House nursing a cut on my finger—a black, glossy specimen that had caught my attention on a Geology Department lab bench had turned out to be unexpectedly sharp. I bought a hot chocolate and a ham sandwich from the kitchenette vending machine, and carried my lunch past the multicultural winter holiday display in the hall and into my office, where I spent a few minutes rummaging around in the window cabinet for a Band-Aid. After the Band-Aid was in place, I unwrapped the ham sandwich, took a warming sip of the hot chocolate, and hit the answering machine button on my desk phone.

The first message was from Dean Sunder. He was driving to St. Paul to meet with a potential donor who was hinting that she might offer up a significant sum for the school. I jotted down a note to ask him for details when he got back; the dean kept a running tally of donation promises in his head and sometimes forgot to relay them to me. It helped speed matters along if I sent a follow-up letter printed on the finest and thickest university stationary reminding the donor of his or her promised sum.

The next three messages were from researchers wondering when STEWie would be back online, followed by two from news reporters. I had seen the headlines. *Has Science Gone Too Far? Is a Life Worth a Journal Article? The Death Price for a Photo?* Perhaps, I thought, replaying the reporters' messages, Dean Sunder needed to compose a press statement about the adventurous journey that is science, a journey of curiosity and exploration that only occasionally leads to mishaps. I jotted that down on my yellow legal pad, then played the last message, a long, rambling one that filled the rest of the phone machine's memory. It had been left by an uninformed gentleman who was *certain* our scientific experiments would destroy the world's past; this even though the school had gone to great pains to explain to anyone who cared to inquire that changing the past was impossible because History always protected itself.

The real problem, I thought, hitting the Delete button, was that we now knew *more* about History, more about its warts and scars and soiled undershirts. Stuff that up until now had been glossed over by the passage of time and the vagaries of the pen, as deeds and accomplishments got exaggerated and the lucky and the successful became valiant and brave—and the unlucky, for whom the inevitable coin toss had landed on the wrong side, sank into oblivion. Much of what used to fill history textbook pages now had an asterisk next to it.

I shook the thought out of my head. A pensive mood had come over me after Dr. Mooney's accident. I sent off a bunch of e-mail replies, finished off the sandwich and the now-lukewarm hot chocolate, and headed to the Rosalind Franklin Biology and Genetics Complex, next on my list. Once I was done there, I moved on to the TTE building, briefly chatted with Oscar about roses (the ones in his garden were covered for the season, of course, but the ones in his greenhouse were flourishing, he reported), and then went inside.

I left my goose-down jacket hanging on the coatrack just inside the building's front door, having stuffed my hat and gloves inside a sleeve. Unlike the compact, brick Hypatia of Alexandria House, which was as old as the school itself, the one-floor, balloon-roofed cement building that housed Time Travel Engineering was a modern affair, built to house an ambitious chemistry experiment that had never gotten off the ground because of funding difficulties. The main hallway of the building followed the angular bends in the lab walls; from it sprouted the offices of the TTE professors, postdocs, and grad students like petals on one of Oscar's roses. Intermixed with the offices were two classrooms, the conference room, the printer and office supply room, and the travel apparel closet with its changing area.

Dr. Rojas was not in his office, the first on the right, but I had expected that. He had been holed up in the TTE lab for the past week, endeavoring to find out what had taken away his longtime colleague and friend, only making an appearance for the memorial service. I turned away from the closed door to his office and went past the first bend in the hallway, raising my hand to type in the lab entry code. Then I changed my mind and turned instead toward the open door of Dr. Mooney's office across the hall. I could hear the movers joking around as they packed up his things. It sounded like they were dropping them into boxes.

They were. Books.

"Please be careful with those," I called out from the doorway. "Some of them are very valuable."

Two young, muscular guys looked up. Their jackets lay on the floor in a heap and they both sported crew cuts, jeans, and white tank tops. "No problem, lady," the one at Dr. Mooney's desk said. "We're always careful with the fragile stuff—we double wrapped the desk lamp." He tossed one of Dr. Mooney's books across the room to the other mover, who dropped it into an open box.

"Never mind the lamps," I said. The lamps and the rest of the office furniture weren't supposed to have been packed at all. "The books are probably more valuable than anything else in this room."

He shrugged, as if used to dealing with overprotective home owners. "The insurance will cover any damage." He tossed another book across the room, a bound photographic copy of a Maya codex. Its pages fluttered as I stepped in and caught it. "Someone went to a lot of effort to obtain these."

They gave me a blank look.

"Never mind," I said, gently lowering the Maya codex into the open box. "Just—well, you are packing away someone's life's work, not office paraphernalia that can be easily replaced."

"Not to worry, lady." He made a deliberate show of walking across the room and gingerly handed a stack of lab notebooks to the other mover, who just as gingerly lowered them into the box.

"Well, that's all right then, I guess," I said. As Abigail had mentioned, the room smelled strangely like Thanksgiving—an herby, cinnamon aroma permeated the space around the stacked and open boxes. I decided against asking the movers if they had been the ones to spray air freshener in the room. It seemed unlikely.

"Did the purple-haired girl find her whatsits?" one of the movers asked as I turned to go. I shook my head and crossed the hallway back to the TTE lab, entered the code, and went in. The double doors closed behind me with their usual creak. Maintenance, after some prompting, had promised to oil the hinges by the end of the week.

I found Dr. Rojas—*hovering* is probably the right word—by the aquarium tank that was placed squarely in the middle of STEWie's basket. The tank looked like it had been put there for the purpose of displaying the single fish that was swimming irritably behind the encrusted glass, not as a vehicle for a time-traveling aquatic. The outside of the tank was wet and water was trickling onto the floor from it, forming small icy patches. The fish was about the length of my arm, elbow to fingertip, yellow, bug-eyed, with vertical blue-black stripes. Dr. Rojas seemed to be feeding it little pieces of broccoli.

He started when he saw me and said, "Julia." He added with some embarrassment, "The zebra tilapia was getting hungry, so I thought I'd better give it something to eat. It's an experimental fish," he clarified for some reason.

Not being the caretaker of any pets, I was wondering how one knew when fish needed to be fed, when the zebra tilapia sucked up a mouthful of gravel from the bottom of the tank, charged upward, and spit it out in our direction, managing only to shower the aquarium glass facing us. Dr. Rojas hurriedly dropped a handful of broccoli pieces through the small, uncapped opening in the tank lid, and the zebra tilapia snatched them up one by one. After a moment, the fish's stripes seemed to brighten to a light blue.

"Did it just change color?" I asked with interest.

"The color varies according to its mood. It hasn't been harmed by any of the runs we've sent it on, but I have to say, I wish the Genetics Department experimented with more pleasant fish. I'm not quite sure they even want it back. I've left repeated phone messages telling them that I'm done with their tilapia."

"I suppose a fish with personality makes for interesting research," I said. I pulled a tissue out of my sweater pocket and bent down to scoop up a trail of tiny gravel pieces that had lodged themselves against the base of the platform. Not gravel, but peppercorns. Perhaps Dr. Rojas had peppered the broccoli for the fish's enjoyment, I thought. I turned to ask him, but he had set the dish with the broccoli aside and was wiping his palms on his slacks as he headed for one of the computer terminals. His clothes were rumpled and his gray-streaked mop was more disheveled than usual, as if he had spent the night in the lab. Come to think of it, he probably had. I thought about suggesting that he find a change of clothes in the travel apparel closet and take a shower (the emergency eyewash and shower stations that had been built for the never-realized chemistry lab had been converted into a decontamination unit for returning time travelers), but only said, "You're finished with it then? The fish?"

"Yes. There's not a thing wrong with the equipment."

"Dr. Rojas, are you sure?" I said, following him over to the computer terminal.

Now perched on a barstool-like lab chair, he was giving his attention to long screenfuls of incomprehensible (to me, at least) number-symbol sequences. "Hmm? What's that, Julia?"

"You're sure there's nothing wrong with the equipment?"

"What? Yes, yes. Absolutely."

"The researchers who've been deluging me with messages asking if STEWie is back online will be glad to hear that. But, Dr. Rojas—"

"Hmm?"

"What went wrong, then? With Xavier Mooney's run?"

"The equipment does what we tell it to do, Julia," he answered a bit testily, as if my presence was distracting him from more pressing matters. "Now, where—"

It seemed to me that he was hinting that Dr. Mooney had goofed up in programming a run, like Dr. Baumgartner had suggested. I decided not to push him for now, figuring that he would let Dean Sunder and me know as soon as he found anything conclusive. "So we can restart the runs? As I said, a lot of people are eager to—but you already know that. I came by to ask if you've seen Dr. Mooney's didgeridoo—no? Also, I need you to fill out one of these." I set the blank Supply, Laboratory Space, and Office Space Request form on the table, next to the computer monitor. He glanced over at the form, said, "Oh yes, we need a couple of extra desks in the grad student office for incoming students," and returned his attention to the computer, muttering, "If I didn't know better, I'd say someone had—yes—but *where*—?"

"Dr. Rojas?"

"Hmm?"

"The form?"

He gave a vague wave without looking away from the screen. "Yes, yes. Just leave it anywhere. I'll get to it later. There are more pressing matters at the moment—I wasted a week—could it be that simple—?"

I picked up the form again, deciding that maybe I *did* need to push him if I wanted to finish my day's work. "Dr. Rojas, is something wrong? You seem a bit distracted. And where are your students?" I looked around the lab, noticing for the first time that it was studentless. Unlike undergrads, who stuck around during the holidays only if traveling home was too expensive or too hard to arrange, grad students usually stayed on campus to work on their research and dissertations. Abigail had no family to visit, Kamal had been home to Egypt over Thanksgiving, and Jacob's parents, I'd learned, lived in town. The three of them should have been around.

"The students went to get something to eat. I took the opportunity to test an idea—" He brought his eyes closer to the monitor and squinted in concentration. "Have I been looking at this all wrong? But that must mean—"

I moved closer, budget form in hand, until my arm was almost touching his shoulder. Whatever was on the screen meant nothing to me, but his demeanor did. I felt a shiver travel down my spine. I brought my voice down an octave.

"Gabriel, what is it?"

His fingers had frozen above the keyboard.

"Gabriel?"

"Julia—we need to call Chief Kirkland back."

"You've found the cause of the accident?"

"It wasn't one."

"Not an accident? Gabriel, are you saying—you can't possibly mean—"

He ran his fingers through his hair, like people sometimes do when they're fighting disbelief, then turned and locked eyes with me.

"I hesitate to say this, but no other explanation befitting the facts has presented itself. Julia, we're looking at foul play."

6

I reached Chief Kirkland in the middle of Sunniva Lake, where he and Officer Van Underberg were dealing with a pair of first-year grad students unaware of the no-snowmobiling-on-campus rule. (The lake was especially off-limits, whether the ice was firm or not.) Some fifteen minutes later, Oscar guided the chief and Officer Van Underberg into the TTE lab. They strode in through the propped-open doors and over to where I waited by Gabriel Rojas's workstation. I had sent the professor to freshen up and get something to eat. We needed him at his best for what was to come.

Sabotage.

I imagined the word spreading by word of mouth and the beep of electronic gadget through the hallways, lab to lab, building to building, all around Sunniva Lake. Only it wasn't. The chief had instructed me over the phone to keep Dr. Rojas's finding under wraps for now.

Chief Kirkland's eyes swept the lab. Last time, he had taken it in with the curiosity and interest of a first-time visitor to STEWie's home; this time, it was done slowly and with care, like he was a researcher rolling up his sleeves prior to commencing a particularly tricky experiment whose outcome was uncertain.

"It's cold in here. Was last time, too," he said when he finally turned back to me.

"It always is. There's cryogenic equipment under the floor, to prevent STEWie from overheating. Our Minnesota climate helps to keep the building cool—though our electrical bills are quite large in the summer."

"I had a feeling that there was more to this case than met the eye," he went on.

"I didn't," I said quite honestly, wondering if he was just saying that or if he'd really had a feeling all along that this was more than just an accident. Then I remembered how the chief had taken an unobtrusive seat in the back of the conference room the day the professor's molecules had been spread over time, and listened as the professor's colleagues talked about him. Well, perhaps he had had a feeling after all.

As if he could tell what I was thinking, the chief explained, "It's my job to expect the worst from people. While hoping for the best, of course," he added as Dr. Rojas hurried back into the lab. He looked like he had splashed water on his face but was still wearing the same set of rumpled and slightly smelly clothes. He had a granola bar in one hand.

Chief Kirkland, wasting no time, said to the professor, "STEWie and time travel. Tell me more about how it works."

Dr. Rojas, looking somewhat taken aback by the security chief's abruptness, sank onto a lab chair and said, "Where to begin?" He absentmindedly unwrapped the granola bar and took a large bite as if it was the first thing he'd eaten all day (which it probably was), then waved the security chief over to a second lab chair. Chief Kirkland shook his head and indicated to Officer Van Underberg that he should sit. The officer plopped himself down and readied his spiral notepad and pencil.

I noticed that Jacob Jacobson had followed the professor in. The ginger-haired youth had taken a seat at a desk by the lab lockers, propping a textbook open in front of him. Jacob's parents ran the town bookshop/antique store, I'd found out, so he biked home every night. I'd also heard that he was having trouble in some of his classes and had requested extensions to finish all of his projects. I could see his fingers moving behind the textbook, like he was typing something. I wondered how the chief intended to keep the happenings in the lab quiet. I thought I'd better inquire, "Chief Kirkland, do you want me to limit the audience?"

"What? I mean, I beg your pardon, Ms. Olsen?"

I indicated Jacob with a nod of my head.

The chief turned on his heel. "Didn't see him there in the corner. Yes, let's get the students out. I'll get to them later."

Jacob, who had heard the exchange, scurried out the door, head down, phone in hand, fingers still moving. I suspected he was in the middle of tweeting something along the lines of, *Kicked out of STEWie's lab, what in the world is going on.???*

Dr. Rojas, having finished off the granola bar, sent the wrapper flying into a trash can in a gentle arc. "Time travel. You wanted to know how it works. Hurtling yourself into a time period not your own and then finding a path once you're there—well, it's like trying to navigate a tricky maze with high walls." He seemed to be choosing his words with care, like he was explaining time travel theory to a journalist or a potential donor. "First you need to find a maze entrance—that is, a place to step out of STEWie's basket." I couldn't stop myself from looking in the direction of the basket, but one of the larger mirrors blocked our view of it from this angle. "Popular places to aim for are just inside a forest line at dusk, the outskirts of a city at daybreak, a beach after sunset. Once you arrive, invisible maze walls present themselves, limiting your ability to move with freedom, the reason for which is self-evident."

I winced. I had, more than once, strongly suggested to our academics that they refrain from using phrases such as *self-evident*, *obvious*, and *of course* when talking to visitors, donors, and journalists.

"Because, of course," the professor went on, making me wince again, "we can only tiptoe around in the past. We are mere visitors. Physical paths open up in a loop, permitting a walk there, a quick photo here, a minute's worth of video footage or five minutes' worth of eavesdropping. Perhaps even a conversation with a local, who might snicker at our outlandish accent but will soon forget about us. Our presence in the past never leaves a trace, our footprints on the path of history remain invisible." (As I said, we all took pains to underline this fact at the drop of a hat.) "From a practical point of view, this means that it's easy enough to move within, say, the confines of a forest, but once you leave its borders, the probability of encountering a person or situation that could be affected by your presence grows rapidly and your options diminish accordingly. Simply put, you can only go where you can."

I saw Officer Van Underberg jot that down. The pair of whiteboards behind the officer held maps and lists of coordinates and destinations—one of them being Norway's island of Selja. (Dr. Edberg of the History Department was hoping to run into Sunniva herself, but her goal had thus far gone unrealized.) The whiteboards were also loaded with snapshots. Lots of snapshots. So many, in fact, that they had overflowed onto the walls (except for where the built-in wire shelves held rows of reference books), even the floor. Faces of ordinary people, caught on camera in villages and fields and battlegrounds. The subjects were usually poorly dressed, in some cases ill or underfed, and always unaware of the photographer as they went about the task of shaping their particular brick in the edifice that was History. Inequality in life had followed them here. A few of the photos might make it into the *History Alive* exhibition or into a journal article, but most of them wouldn't.

As for the photos that were destined directly for the exhibition, the ones of notable historical figures, we had an undergrad doing touch-ups and making enlargements.

The professor got to his feet and wound his way through several of the mirrors to STEWie's basket, with Chief Kirkland and me following and Officer Van Underberg bringing up the rear. The officer barely managed to avoid slipping on the icy patch under the platform that had been formed by the water dripping from the tank. I saw Chief Kirkland catch sight of the fish. He raised two dark eyebrows. "A zebra tilapia?"

"An experimental one. This one has been bred to withstand environments much cooler than its usual temperate habitat. I've sent it on a few trips." Dr. Rojas might have been talking about a leisurely weekend drive to the North Shore or an unhurried afternoon cross-country skiing in the woods on the east side of campus.

"Where did the fish get to go?" the chief asked.

"We started out with near time, the students and I. We sent the tank bobbing into the middle of Sunniva Lake of last August, then brought it back. Then into Sunniva Lake of 1890, the year the school first opened. Since those two runs went off without a hitch, we then jumped—so to speak—into the fifth century. Far time."

"Far time? Near time?" Chief Kirkland asked as Officer Van Underberg furiously took notes, his neat block letters degenerating into hasty scribbles as he cupped his notepad in his right hand and wrote with his left, his boots firmly planted on the chilly lab floor.

"*Near time* is what we call the past two, three hundred years, a time period for which we have reasonably accurate historical accounts and maps, making it relatively simple to find landing sites—entrances to the maze. Calculations are fast, ghost zones are easily avoided, and location errors, both temporal and physical, are small. For example, Chief Kirkland, if you told me that you wanted to snap a photo of the Declaration of Independence being signed, I wouldn't send you to July fourth of 1776." He chuckled and cracked the first smile I'd seen on his face since Dr. Mooney's accident.

I shook my head. I was having trouble getting used to the thought that it wasn't an accident.

Dr. Rojas went on. "Though that was the day the Continental Congress approved the wording of the declaration, the formal signing didn't take place until early August. So we'd want to send you there almost a full month later. Now getting you *into* the chambers of the State House in Philadelphia, well, that would require some real thought and planning..." He drifted off into contemplation of the problem.

"And far time?" Chief Kirkland inquired in the manner of one who was becoming accustomed to dealing with academic types.

"If you go a few hundred years into the past—sooner for some places, Minnesota being of them, much further back for others—well, things start to get complicated. *Far time.* Maps are vague, or simply wrong, or don't exist. Dates are, at best, educated guesses. Historical accounts are inaccurate, exaggerated, or wedded to myth and folklore. Ghost zones become more of a danger. Depending on what part of the world and era you want to go to, we usually end up making a best guess for where STEWie's basket can land safely." I saw Officer Van Underberg scribble down, *Far time: maps vague, ghost zones a danger.*

"So how did the zebra tilapia do in far time?" I asked.

"The fifth-century trip to Sunniva Lake—it was bigger then, by the way—didn't take. There must have been someone in a canoe or on the banks of the lake, watching. Instead we did a somewhat wild and quick run into 10,000 BC, when this area consisted of mostly ice fields."

"What did the tilapia think of all that?" asked Officer Van Underberg. He sent a sympathetic look in the direction of the fish. He hadn't seen it eat, of course.

"It seemed to get crabbier. Not because it didn't like the tour of Sunniva Lake through history, I think, but because we kept jerking it back. It seemed to enjoy being deposited, tank and all, just below the lake surface and then slowly popping to the top each time. At least it always came back with its stripes looking a bit brighter."

Chief Kirkland reminded us of the event that had caused us to gather in the TTE lab. "And you're saying someone purposely sent Dr. Mooney into a ghost zone. A nuclear test site, something like that?"

"Also known as death zones, cracks in time, and temporal quicksand. The landing zones that are easiest to get to—places where your presence won't leave much of a trace. Of course, it won't leave much of you, either. When a destination is decided on, the computer sifts through maps, photos, historical records, geological data, data from past runs, archeological archives, and so on until it finds a safe landing site like a forest—making sure to avoid forest fires and blizzards and such. Obviously this is easier to accomplish in near time than it is in far time. If someone disengaged the safety protocols we have in place—that is, bypassed the calibration which ensures that the next day's run has a safe landing site…well." He added after a moment, "On occasion we've sent our wheeled mobile robot to check for hazards or undertake the journey instead of human travelers. There is an inherent problem with sending WMRs, though."

"And that is?" the chief asked.

"They don't exactly blend in. It's not like the WMR can throw on a cloak and a pair of sandals. Plus, they're not great at deciding what makes a good photo and what doesn't."

"Even so, why didn't you use the robot for your Sunniva Lake tests instead of the fish? Because it's not waterproof?" the chief asked.

"Well, yes, the WMR isn't waterproof, as it happens. But that's not it. Our WMR had an—it had an accident last month. We're building a new one." Somewhat reluctantly, Dr. Rojas continued the story for Chief Kirkland and Officer Van Underberg's benefit (I already knew it). "We sent the WMR to pre-*Beagle* Galapagos Islands for a Biology Department project, but the robot, uh—it sank on arrival. It zoomed right into the water and kept on going until it became wedged between two large boulders on the ocean floor. We sent someone after it, but it was no use. Come to think of it, the WMR is probably still there at the bottom of the Pacific three hundred years later, rusting."

Chief Kirkland threw a glance in the direction of the fish. "And the night he was scattered across time, Dr. Mooney, having volunteered to take Kamal Ahmad's place, came to the lab to oversee the calibration for Dr. Baumgartner's eighteenth-century France trip."

"Not much to it, really. Just making sure the program doesn't get hung up. It can be indecisive sometimes when it needs to make a choice."

"And instead Dr. Mooney stepped into STEWie's basket… willingly or unwillingly. And then someone—"

"Sent him on a trip to nowhere."

∞

Dr. Rojas leaned against the frame of STEWie's basket, causing the zebra tilapia to charge angrily in his direction. He backed up and spoke with pride of the complex arrangement of steel and reflective glass that dominated the cavernous lab. "The laser-mirror array is STEWie's heart and soul. Would you like a short lecture on the theory behind STEWie's being, Chief Kirkland, starting with the basic physics of spacetime warping by light—?"

"Perhaps later," the chief said smoothly. "You found evidence of sabotage, you say?"

"Hmm? Oh, yes."

"Which ghost zone was it?" I asked.

The professor shook his head. "No way to tell. Does it matter, Julia?"

"I'd like to know, that's all."

Dr. Rojas went on. "I wasted a week checking STEWie mirror by mirror and laser by laser…then with the fish. My underlying assumption was erroneous."

"You assumed that it was an equipment malfunction?" the chief prodded him.

"Exactly. It wasn't. Someone moved the mirrors into a random position after Xavier's run, overwriting the original coordinates." In a rare display of emotion, sounding almost angry with himself, he went on. "Xavier was responsible for the practical side of things—perhaps I should have let Dr. Little or Dr. Baumgartner assist me, like they offered. Too many cooks, I thought. Maybe they would have found the answer sooner. You might want to get Dr. Little in here, Chief Kirkland, to see if he can glean something further from the computer."

"Let's hold off on that. I don't want to call in Dr. Little just yet." The security chief circled STEWie's basket, causing the zebra tilapia to mimic his movements and thinking out loud in short, choppy sentences as he paced. "Clothes folded onto a chair. Personal effects placed in the locker. Office undisturbed… Why do all of that? To mislead us into thinking Dr. Mooney went willingly?"

"His didgeridoo is missing," I said.

"I beg your pardon?" the security chief stopped and turned his square jaw in my direction.

"Aboriginal Australian musical instrument, traditionally made from a eucalyptus tree hollowed out by termites," I explained. "About four feet long. Makes a deep, rhythmic drone when blown into. Traditionally played by men. Xavier was given one as a present on one of his journeys to far-time Australia—he had a talent for finding nooks and crannies in History where he could interact with locals. He'd been practicing in his free time, and he got quite good. He played for us at the Thanksgiving party, remember that, Dr. Rojas?"

Officer Van Underberg was penciling down *didgeridoo* but had some trouble with the spelling.

"And it's missing?" Chief Kirkland prodded me.

The implication hit me suddenly. "You think someone struck Xavier on the head with the didgeridoo and tossed both it and him into STEWie's basket? And left his wallet and other things behind to make it look like the professor went willingly?" An unwelcome image entered my mind. Had someone made the professor disrobe before making him climb into STEWie's basket? I found the thought very disturbing.

"I'm afraid that's exactly what I think may have happened," the chief said grimly.

It was my turn to think out loud. "We've had problems with people outside the school who believe STEWie is dangerous, that it can change history in unexpected ways—which, as Dr. Rojas has pointed out, it can't. Rarely does a day go by when the dean's office doesn't receive a letter or phone call or fax or e-mail or text message insisting that the program be shut down. Sometimes they come by in person to tell us these things, though not often—one benefit of being rather out of the way." I added, "We also get the opposite—people who want to go into the past to stalk their favorite historical figure. We try to discourage them as gently as we can. Popular historical figures are often the most difficult to get near, anyway—remember, Dr. Rojas, the time Kamal tried to get close enough to talk to Gandhi for a class project? He couldn't get within a mile of him. It was almost like Gandhi was more aware of the people in his surroundings than the average person—the good guys tend to be that way." I went on. "We also get the occasional enthusiast with a pet theory, like that aliens built the pyramids or that the *Titanic* was sunk by an errant torpedo or that the Moon landing never took place, that kind of thing." (For the Moon landing hoax, I liked to turn them away by quoting Dr. Tyson, astrophysicist and director of New York's Hayden Planetarium: "Atop three thousand pounds of rocket fuel, where *else* do you think they were going?") I added, "But it's not likely a stranger would have managed to get past Oscar. Plus they would have needed the security code to get into the TTE lab."

"So it's impossible to change the past," said Chief Kirkland, emphasizing the last three words, "even if someone hijacked STEWie for their own ends? You're sure about that?"

"Not that it hasn't been tried, mind you. We tried it ourselves, in fact." Dr Rojas sighed. "We made an attempt to rescue the scrolls from the Library of Alexandria and the Mayan books burned by the conquistadors, but for the most part failed miserably. We were only able to make a few photographic copies. For good or bad, the burning of those books had deeply impacted history and could not be reversed."

"I'd like to get a feel for how it works," Chief Kirkland said.

"History?" Dr. Rojas asked.

"STEWie."

"You mean you want to see a test run with the zebra tilapia? I suppose we could do that, it's just that all the test runs are getting expensive, what with the power drain by the cooling equipment—and I've used up so much thorium already—not to mention that the floor is getting wet and slippery—"

"Is it safe?"

"Oh, yes."

"For people, too, not just fish?"

"Oh, it's safe." Dr. Rojas waved any concerns aside. "No reason not to return the tilapia to the Genetics Department and bring STEWie back online. We can restart runs tomorrow."

"Dr. Baumgartner has the first slot on the roster," I said. "I can ask her if she'd be willing to let you observe her run, Chief Kirkland, though there'll be a blogger coming to do just that, so it might get a bit awkward if you still want to keep the story from getting out."

In its tank on the platform, the zebra tilapia was suddenly looking rather dark bluish and swimming around in an angry burst of activity. I realized why. The squeak of the doors had announced Abigail and Kamal's presence; they'd ambled over to the tank without offering to share any of their not-very-nutritious lunch of popcorn with the fish. They were pretending not to notice us, though I suspected Jacob Jacobson had passed on the news that something unusual was going on in the lab.

I cleared my throat. Abigail and Kamal turned in unison, pretending to be surprised to see Chief Kirkland, Officer Van Underberg, and me in the lab talking to Dr. Rojas. Abigail offered us her popcorn.

"No, thank you, miss," Officer Van Underberg said in a serious tone, though his caramel mustache crinkled a bit. "I'm on duty."

I accepted some popcorn (the ham sandwich hadn't been very filling, not with all the exercise I'd gotten trekking around the science buildings with the budget forms) then sent Abigail and Kamal back to the grad student office. They had a right to know what was going on, but not yet. Chief Kirkland's gaze followed the students as they filed out. I hoped he didn't suspect them of any wrongdoing.

After the lab doors creaked shut behind Abigail and Kamal, the security chief spoke into the room over the sound of a science dean's assistant trying to discreetly crunch popcorn.

"You misunderstood me before," the chief said to Dr. Rojas. "I wasn't suggesting that I observe a run. I'd like to go on one."

I quickly swallowed a mouthful of popcorn, almost choking on it.

"You want to go on a test run, Chief Kirkland?" Dr. Rojas asked, raising two thick, graying eyebrows.

"I want to go, too," I heard myself say.

7

I felt my cheeks grow hot. I don't know what had gotten into me, where that had come from. I disposed of the last of the popcorn in the trash can, wiped my palms against each other, then turned back. "Sorry. What I meant to say was this. Dean Sunder has requested that I accompany Chief Kirkland on his investigations. I interpret that"—I coughed, perhaps because of a popcorn kernel stuck in my throat—"as including STEWie's basket and anywhere it happens to go while Chief Kirkland is in it."

Chief Kirkland raised a hand. "There has already been one incident. It might not be safe, Ms. Olsen—"

"Nonsense," I said briskly. "You heard what Dr. Rojas said. It's perfectly safe. Besides, you'll need a team to go with you. We can hardly send students along on an official investigation."

"I volunteer," Kamal said from behind me.

"Me, too," said Abigail.

"And I do, too," said Jacob, "though I haven't been on a run yet, so I don't know what use I'll be."

"Didn't I send you all back to your office?" I asked, a bit exasperated. Apparently the sound of the creaking door had signaled Jacob's reentry, not Abigail and Kamal's departure. We'd been too preoccupied with the chief's unexpected request to notice.

"Julia, we want to help find out what happened—"

"Dr. Mooney was my advisor—"

"Not mine, but he welcomed me to the lab—"

It was Dr. Rojas's turn to raise a hand. "Hold on, everybody. Even if we get Dean Sunder's approval for this—I leave that to you, Julia—there are still protocols to be followed. No one, not even campus security, can climb into STEWie's basket without adequate training."

"When do we start?" Chief Kirkland asked.

∞

Dean Sunder did not like the idea at all.

"Why does he want to go?"

"Chief Kirkland said," I explained, handing the dean a guest list for the wine-and-shrimp afternoon fundraiser he was about to attend, "that the only way to solve a crime is to feel it, to get under its skin, so to speak."

(More precisely, Chief Kirkland had said, "If a wallet is stolen, I like to know its color, thickness, whether it was leather or man-made, carried in the left back pocket or the right or in a bag... It gives valuable insight into both the victim and the perpetrator. I try to imagine how it feels to rifle through another person's belongings, to take what you wish. Since Xavier Mooney was lost to time, then I must find out all I can about STEWie: who had access to the machine, the knowledge to program it, the impulse and the need to use it as a weapon. In other words, I need to know everything, which includes getting into STEWie's basket and trying it out myself.")

Dean Sunder ran a practiced eye over the guest list I'd handed him for the fundraiser. It was being held at the observatory. "Anything I should be aware of?"

"Don't mention STEWie to Mrs. Butterworth. I don't think she's ever forgiven us for proving that Shakespeare did write his plays by snapping a photo of the bard penning—or would it be *quilling?*—*Romeo and Juliet,* given her firm conviction that it was actually Sir Francis Bacon." I added, "Since she also has an interest in astronomy, perhaps a private viewing session this evening with one of our researchers?" That sounded vaguely inappropriate, so I amended the statement. "A viewing session of the night sky at the observatory for Mrs. Butterworth and the other members of the Butterworth Supporting Science Foundation. That's always popular. By the way, Ewan Coffey's assistant called to say the donation check for the new STEWie generator is in the mail."

"Excellent, especially since my meeting in St. Paul yesterday didn't bear any fruit. The donor had heard about the accident in the TTE lab." The dean added, "I have to say, I'm not convinced that someone did this on purpose and I plan to tell the board that." The dean's conference call with the Board of Trustees and Chancellor Jane Evans was set for 6:00 p.m. "I think Chief Kirkland put the idea into Gabriel's head by hanging around the lab, asking all those questions. I hope he's not spreading the story around."

"Chief Kirkland asked that we keep things under wraps for now. He's still calling this an accident inquiry." The trustees would have to be told, of course. There were legal and other ramifications to consider.

"Still, these things have a way of getting out." He folded the guest list into his pocket, adjusted his cuff links, and reached for his coat. "There hasn't been a murder on campus in twenty years, certainly not in the short time he's been security chief here. Where did Chief Kirkland get so much experience with serious crime that he sees it everywhere? In the parks?"

I had wondered about that myself. The chief hadn't been very forthcoming with the details of his years at the Boundary Waters Canoe Area Wilderness (BWCAW), with its thousand small lakes near the Canadian border, or why he had left the Forest Service, where he had been a member of law enforcement. (I'd once asked my soon-to-be-ex, Quinn, what he and the chief talked about when fishing. "Fish," he had said.)

"Should I tell Chief Kirkland that he can't go on a run, then?"

Dean Sunder cocked his head. "No. I still don't like the idea, but I suppose we'll have to let him have his test run."

I took that to mean that it was okay for me to tag along, too.

The dean added as I followed him out, "If it was murder, let's hope the chief finds whoever is responsible quickly and that it leads away from the school. See if you can help him in any way. And Julia?"

"Yes?"

"I suppose it's too much to hope that the story will stay under wraps for long, but let's do what we can."

∞

One question about this whole incident had been nagging at me. I returned to my office, spoke with Ingrid, the caterer, who reassured me that all was well for the observatory fundraiser, and had just reached for the phone again when it started ringing. A penetrating, insistent voice came over the line. I knew the type at once.

"The final grades for fall semester freshman Human Biology," I said, keeping my tone firm but polite, "are already in the system, but I can't disclose your son's grade to you and your husband... Why not? Well, your son is eighteen, is he not?"

"Nineteen," came the high-pitched answer through the phone.

"And therefore an adult. Legally, we cannot release students' grades to anyone without their permission...no, not for any of your son's classes... I'm sure he did well in the class and will go on to be a fine doctor...it's school policy, sir—" A gruff voice had replaced the shrill one on the line. "Yes, I understand that you're paying for his education...you could ask your son directly...well, I'm sorry you feel that way—"

The father hung up the phone after a few choice words. I shrugged off the conversation (calls like this were becoming more frequent as stronger-than-ever parent-child bonds were stretched to the limit when the newly minted adults arrived to face freshmen issues; a term had even been coined for the overprotective behavior—"helicopter parenting") and rang Oscar's post in the TTE building. He answered at once. I got straight to the point. "Oscar, I want to go over what happened the Monday night we lost Dr. Mooney."

"Like I told Chief Kirkland, it was a quiet evening," Oscar began, his raspy voice crackling down the line. "Not too much student partying going on, what with the kids studying for the week's exams. The campus was deserted except for the occasional kid out for a late-night snack or biking back from a study group— you could tell which it was by whether they were balancing a pizza box or textbooks on their handlebars. Just before eleven, I saw Dr. Mooney nearing the building, his headlamp visible from afar. The snow had just begun to fall. Chief Kirkland asked me if Dr. Mooney seemed upset or distracted and if that was why he forgot to lock up his bike. I told him that the professor seemed like his usual self. He dropped off an unwrapped gyroscope for Toys for Tots, but didn't linger to tell me about his latest time travel trips, like he sometimes did. But that wasn't unusual. He was a busy man. He seemed like he was in a hurry to get out of the snow and into the lab, that was all. Kamal Ahmad came out not long after the professor went in, maybe fifteen minutes later, carrying a stack of textbooks. He saw that it was snowing, said he wished he'd brought a knapsack for the books, waved good night, and left, stuffing the textbooks inside his jacket."

I knew Oscar hadn't fallen asleep at his post, but everyone had bodily needs. I took a moment to compose the question delicately. "Did you, uh—did you have to leave your post at any time during the night, Oscar?" Had someone stood in the shadows as the snow fell, hidden, waiting?

"Once, briefly," he admitted.

So someone could have sneaked in, I thought, though that late in the day the building would have been locked and an electronic pass would have been needed to get in, not to mention the door code to the lab. I wondered if Oscar, after the bathroom break, had noticed a trail of fresh footprints in the snow leading to the front door of the building, perhaps from one of the neighboring ones or from the direction of the visitor parking lot.

He hadn't.

∞

"Ms. Olsen, do you have a minute?"

I almost dropped the stack of paper I had been about to feed into the printer. The incident with Dr. Mooney had made me jumpy and I'd had to resist the urge to lock my office door. During winter break, the campus was quiet and the hallways emptier than usual. It was slightly spooky. I beckoned in Chief Kirkland and slid the pastel-green paper (for flyers about the upcoming science guest speaker series) into the printer tray. I hadn't seen the chief since early afternoon, when I had committed to going on a trip into the past with him. I picked my glasses up off the desk and put them back on as the printer started spewing out copies with a repetitive *whoosh-whoosh*.

Chief Kirkland took the chair across from me. He leaned forward and directed an intense stare at me. "I wanted to get something into the open."

I pushed the cookie jar—oatmeal chocolate chip this time—toward him, but he only shook his head. "No thanks, I'm not one much for junk food."

I took a cookie for myself and asked, "What is it that you wanted to get out into the open, Chief Kirkland?"

"The word."

"Which?"

"Murder."

The word had been said before, but hearing him say it made it seem more official somehow. There was no going back.

"The *who*, *how*, and *why* are the three questions that need answering," he added.

I almost jotted those three words down.

He went on, "The *how* we'll put aside for the moment. The *who* possibilities include everyone with a TTE building pass and the code to the lab—really, just the lab code. Someone could have hidden in one of the bathrooms or classrooms as the building emptied for the day. As to the *why*—I need you to think, Ms. Olsen. Who had a reason to kill Dr. Mooney?"

"No one."

"Nonsense." He ticked off potential answers on his long fingers. "One, a student unhappy with a grade. Two, an envious or slighted colleague. Three, a jilted lover. Four, the inheritors of his estate. Five—"

I briefly closed my eyes, tired from double-checking budgetary forms, and stopped him. "Let me answer those in order.

One—students. We get a disgruntled student or two every semester, that's true, mostly undergrads. Occasionally one of them threatens St. Sunniva with a lawsuit or parents withholding donations if we don't pass the student in all of the semester's classes. But I can't imagine that would lead to... Well, we don't take too much notice of them, to be honest. Besides," I added, "the door code to the TTE lab is changed monthly and never given to undergrad students, only to those grad students whose research requires it.

"Two—Xavier's colleagues. He got along reasonably well with all of them."

"You mean that they all worked well as a team, he and Dr. Rojas, Dr. Baumgartner, and Dr. Little?"

I paused to eat a second cookie. "Academia is not like that. Think of it as..." At a momentary loss about how to describe the peculiarities of the academic world, I caught sight of the walleye pin that Quinn had once given me, now sitting in a little box of office odds and ends. It was from the fishing club that both he and the chief had belonged to. (I was pretty sure that Quinn, who was not particularly outdoorsy, had joined the Walleyes to have something to do on the weekends that wouldn't interest me. Spending hours in waders in a fishing boat—or bundled in a parka in a fishing shack above a hole drilled in the ice—was just not my thing.) I'd used the pin to puncture holes in the wedding photo that used to sit on my desk. I had kept it because it was handy for opening envelopes.

"Think of academia as a fleet of fishing boats bobbing on Sunniva Lake, each boat captained by a professor, manned by graduate students, and producing a steady catch of scientific finds and journal papers. Most of the catch is little fish but the fishermen bump into each other's boats as they compete for the big fish—funds, grants, lab space, publicity, Nobel Prizes. It's a rare person who can keep a level head and not get pulled into the fray. Xavier Mooney was that rare person. Not because of any conscious decision on his part—on the contrary, in fact. He was always so brimming with ideas that he was simply oblivious to the politics of it all." I shrugged. "He didn't notice that sometimes others would get heavily invested in a single idea, or were desperate for funding, or were holding on for dear life until tenure."

"Any recent or unusual conflicts that you know of?"

I shook my head. "Xavier Mooney was an experimentalist and Gabriel Rojas is a theoreticist. On occasion they liked to engage in a friendly bet about whether a detail in history would turn out to be true, with Dr. Rojas trying to reason it out and Dr. Mooney insisting that History's particulars were rarely predictable, even if you knew their outcome. Then one of them—usually Dr. Mooney—would go back and obtain photographic or video evidence. The results were about fifty-fifty either way." I paused. "Xavier Mooney would have had a part in deciding whether the department should offer tenure to our two junior professors, Dr. Baumgartner and Dr. Little."

"Was he going to come down on their side?"

"Too early to say. Junior professors are initially appointed to two-year contracts and an evaluation is done every two years until the tenure review in the eighth year. Dr. Little has been here just over nine months. Dr. Baumgartner's first evaluation is coming up in the spring." To obtain tenure, a young professor had to have it all—an excellent research and publication track, positive teaching and peer evaluations, successful supervision of grad students, and a glowing recommendation from Dean Sunder. Chancellor Evans had the final say. I added, "I suppose we could check Dr. Mooney's notebooks and computer for any notes he may have jotted down on the matter. The movers have packed up his office, so we'll have to pull his things out of storage. Or you could talk to Dr. Rojas about it."

"Speaking of Gabriel Rojas, can he be trusted? I have to take what he's saying about STEWie's software being tampered with at face value."

"I can't think of a reason why he would have felt the need to get rid of Dr. Mooney—and then tell us about it."

"I can't either. But that means nothing."

"I suppose not."

"At this stage everyone who had the door code is a suspect."

"Including me?"

"Do you have the code to the TTE lab?"

"Copies of all the security codes are made available to the dean's office in case of emergencies."

"Would you have had the time-engineering knowledge to reprogram STEWie and make it seem like the focuser had malfunctioned?"

"Would I have—no."

"Then you're not a suspect."

I almost asked him if that meant he could call me Julia now that I had been cleared of any involvement in Dr. Mooney's death, but, brow furrowed darkly, he steered the conversation back to his original question. "What about jilted lovers or inheritors of his estate?"

"Xavier did go through a rather acrimonious divorce with one of our linguistics professors, Dr. Helen Presnik. But that was years ago, before my time here in the dean's office. And," I finished, "Xavier left all his worldly goods to the school. What's number five?"

"I beg your pardon?"

"Earlier you were about to tell me about murder motive number five—"

"Ah, yes. The incidental murder. The professor may have gotten in someone's way at the TTE lab, someone who was bent on going on an unauthorized run. Speaking of which, Ms. Olsen—" He cleared his throat and looked straight at me. "Remember what we now know—in one of the science departments, probably the Time Travel Engineering lab itself, there is a person who presents a danger to others."

Was that a not-so-subtle warning for me to stay out of his investigation? It was all very well for him to say so, but he didn't have researchers deluging him with messages asking—demanding—that STEWie be brought back online as soon as possible. Not to mention the fact that the dean had asked me to accompany the chief throughout his investigation.

"You say Dr. Mooney was married to a professor?" the chief added. "Is she still here at St. Sunniva?"

"Yes, Dr. Presnik works in the English Department."

"I'll speak to her first thing tomorrow morning."

∞

Chief Kirkland didn't get the chance to speak with Helen Presnik first thing the following morning because we were both summoned to Dr. Rojas's office. The professor had talked Erika Baumgartner into letting us squeeze in a run before hers. It wasn't much of a concession on her part—a short near-time run for Chief Kirkland's benefit wouldn't delay her own run to eighteenth-century France by much. She was planning on being there just about a full day, which was fifty minutes in the lab; we only needed an hour or so, which would pass in a jiffy in the lab—133 seconds. (No one quite knew why precisely 133 seconds passed in the present for each hour you spent in the past. Dr. Rojas had spent the last five years trying to figure it out.)

"There are three more rules you should know." Dr. Rojas was giving the security chief and yours truly a crash course on time travel basics from in front of the old-fashioned chalky blackboard that took up one corner of his office. (It might have been the last one left on campus. Whiteboards, with their colored markers, had proliferated on campus like mosquitoes on Sunniva Lake in the summer, in offices, labs, cafeterias, meeting rooms, hallways. Someone had argued that we needed them in all the bathrooms as well, for impromptu discussions and exchanges of ideas, but that had been ruled out as being too exclusionary of one gender or the other.)

Dr. Rojas picked up a piece of chalk and, just below *One hour there = 133 seconds here*, wrote in large, slanted letters:

History protects itself.

I jotted the two rules down in my notes as (1) and (2), even though I already knew them.

He turned back to face his audience of two. (Kamal, Abigail, and Jacob had not been invited on the run with us despite all their pleading; and Helen, who would accompany us as the senior faculty member, didn't need the crash course.) "Remember this well, Julia and Chief Kirkland. History protects only itself, never you. It's not going to stop you from doing something stupid like falling off a cliff or being hunted down and eaten by a grizzly bear—unless it's likely that someone would find whatever is left of your body and notice your modern tooth fillings or strange underclothes."

"Grizzlies don't hunt people," the chief interrupted him. "They only attack if they're surprised or if they're protecting their food or offspring. But point taken."

"Rule number three. *Blend in.*"

He wrote that on the blackboard under *History protects itself* and I added it to my notepad under (3).

"To take even a step or two away from the landing site, it's necessary to minimize how peculiar you appear to the locals. When Dr. Presnik's team went back to Shakespeare's time to prove that he wrote the plays, they made sure to don seventeenth-century clothing, dull the whiteness of their twenty-first-century teeth, and avoid indulging in period-inappropriate behavior like washing hands before eating. We're only sending you back for a short hop," he continued, "so hand washing and white teeth shouldn't be a problem. Even so, on occasion you might find yourself unable to take a step farther or to speak—say, if you were about to interfere with someone's walking route or inadvertently divulge knowledge from the future, such as telling them that it's a good idea to invest in instant noodles but not in slide rules."

"Is it possible to meet yourself in the past?" asked Chief Kirkland as if the thought, which had nothing to do with the investigation, had just occurred to him.

I opened my mouth to answer—I knew this one—but Dr. Rojas was already shaking his head. "History only allows a person to travel to a time period *before* they were born. Observing and documenting your own life, that's for the memoir-writing folks over at the English Department." He gestured toward the squat building by the bend in the lake, which was just visible through the wide windows of his office. "Since you'll want to stick close to the present, we'll go by the birth date of the oldest person on the team."

Yikes, I thought. I hadn't been keen on telling people my age since I'd passed the three-decade mark four and a half years ago. As for Chief Kirkland, who was sitting on my left, intently following Dr. Rojas's remarks, my best guess was that he was in his late thirties or early forties. Clothes were usually helpful for this sort of thing, but the campus security uniform ruled that out.

Plus something about him discouraged speculation, as if he was who he was and a data point as irrelevant as age would never be of consequence in his professional or personal life. It added to the air of mystery the man carried around with him. What *had* made him leave his job at the BWCAW? I supposed I could check the security office hiring records if I really wanted to find out (that would tell me his age, too) but doing it that way seemed a bit underhanded.

Dr. Rojas continued, "The birth date of the oldest person on the team will determine the threshold year—"

"Yes, that would be me." Dr. Helen Presnik stuck her head into Dr. Rojas's office and saved me from having to answer. "Before anyone asks, I turned forty-seven in June."

This surprised me. Helen wasn't one of the professors under my care, but I had chatted with her many a time at school-wide events over the years, and had always assumed her to be at least a decade older. But some people acquired gray hair early in life.

"Dr. Presnik, good to see you," Dr. Rojas said from the blackboard, perhaps a touch more formal than he usually was.

"Hello, Gabriel. How's Lane? And the triplets?" Lane was Dr. Rojas's wife and the triplets were all grown up and out of the house.

"Fine, fine," he said.

"Dr. Presnik, thank you for agreeing to come with us on this STEWie run," said our security chief.

"Helen, this is Campus Security Chief Kirkland," I introduced him.

"You're most welcome, Chief Kirkland," said Helen. "Are you almost done here, Gabriel? Erika is impatient for us to get going so that she can proceed with her run. She says that a blogger's coming to observe her."

"Penny Lind of the *Les Styles* blog," I explained. "Ear muffs. Pencil-thin eyebrows. Not a walker."

Without changing his facial expression, the chief said, "I'm sorry I'll miss seeing her."

"She'll probably be here when we get back."

"Her blog has hundreds of thousands of followers. It's a real coup for Erika," Helen said. "Shall I tell her you'll be a few more minutes?"

"I just need to explain rule number four and then we'll be right over."

"Rule four…that's the most important one, isn't it?"

Helen's head disappeared from the doorway and Dr. Rojas turned back to face the blackboard. "Which is—*There's always a way back*." He wrote that under the other three rules (I did the same on my list), then turned back to face us. "If it seems like you're stuck with no way out, unable to take a step in any direction, that's just History protecting itself by keeping you in place. That is, you won't be able to leave the area until the maze paths have had the opportunity to rearrange themselves and it's safe to proceed. If that happens, wait it out. Circumstances can change quickly. Sometimes," he added, "they change painfully slow. My team was once stuck for seven hours behind a rocky outcrop in the New Mexico desert, with only one bottle of water and half a granola bar among us. Finally, at long last, as the sun was sinking below the horizon, a small band of Anasazi passed us on their way westward and we were able to move. Only later did I realize that had we crossed the plain earlier, the Anasazi would have noticed our footprints in the dust of the desert floor."

I had a sudden vision of being unable to move and speak, like a temporary paralysis of limb and tongue, and for the first time experienced a doubt whether volunteering for the run was a good idea.

Noticing my expression, Dr. Rojas added gently, "It's not as weird as it sounds, Julia. Well, not once you get used to it." He himself had never gotten used to it, I thought. Gabriel rarely went out on runs, preferring to do his research with pencil and paper, while others stepped into STEWie's basket. The professor added, "Remember, we can't go wherever we want in our own time period either. We don't try to walk through trees or buildings, we automatically go around them." He wiped chalk dust off his fingers and onto his slacks. "Any questions?"

"Only one," I said. "Where are we going?"

"Let's keep it simple. Given Helen's birthday and age, we'll be able to send you to, let's see...May 1964 or earlier."

It occurred to me that going back in time by a week and staking out the TTE lab would be a good way of figuring out who had killed Dr. Mooney, only we'd need to send a newborn or a mounted camera. The arrival of either would have probably startled anyone who happened to be working in the lab.

"I was going to leave the choice up to you," Dr. Rojas continued, "but it's a good idea to keep it simple and not go back too far. Let's stick with the sixties."

The sixties. I was a child of the eighties and nineties; the sixties, so different from anything that came later, had always held a certain fascination for me.

"Perhaps you'd like to snap a photo of Penzias and Wilson ruling out that pigeon droppings were causing the strange signal in their antenna, thereby discovering cosmic microwave background radiation?" Dr. Rojas suggested. "Or shoot footage of Rosalind Franklin taking the first X-ray photos of DNA? Or—"

"The best destination for our purposes," Chief Kirkland, who really *was* getting accustomed to dealing with academic types, said firmly, "might be a crowded site like a sporting event or a racetrack. Someplace where we won't stand out much."

I pushed my glasses farther up my nose and raised my hand. "Can we go see the Beatles?"

8

I was pretty sure that my question had been driven by my desire to contribute to the investigation by suggesting a practical destination, and had nothing to do with the fact that the Beatles had always been my favorite band.

Even though the British Invasion of the United States was pretty well documented already, Dr. Rojas agreed that traveling to catch a glimpse of a young John, Paul, George, and Ringo, while not exactly the epitome of academic seriousness, would be acceptable. Having STEWie slip us directly into New York's Carnegie Hall without tickets was overruled as being too delicate a maneuver for a test mission, so we settled on plan B—watching the Beatles' first press conference on US soil. A busy airport and thousands of fans would nicely fit Chief Kirkland's criteria of a crowded urban site.

Helen, the chief, and I relocated to the TTE conference room, where we spent fifteen minutes watching black-and-white footage of the Fab Four stepping off their Pan Am flight 101 from London to the roar of thousands of airport-roof fans. Then we headed off in separate directions to procure sixties-style clothes, leaving Dr. Rojas in the lab to oversee the necessary calculations. He assured us that a short hop into a well-mapped area such as New York's still-existing airport would require only a quick calibration.

I hurried to my car, drove the five minutes home, left my boots in the mudroom, and went into the bedroom, leaving a trail of jacket, scarf, hat, and gloves on the furniture. I opened my bedroom closet. The sixties. Miniskirts, go-go boots, Twiggy, psychedelic colors. Fortunately, all of those postdated the arrival of the Beatles on US soil. Something a bit more prim and proper would be just the ticket. Wishing that Penny Lind of the *Les Styles* blog had arrived in time to provide some sixties fashions advice, I rummaged around the closet and finally chose a red button-down blouse, then dug up a basic black pencil skirt that had been a wardrobe staple in my twenties and which I had optimistic expectations might still fit. I wiggled my way into it, just managing to close the zipper on the side. Next, I pulled out my nicest pair of boots, black suede ones with a small but definite heel. The boots only came out on special occasions, like when I accompanied Dean Sunder to a fundraiser or a couple of weeks ago when I had gone to a lawyer's office to initiate divorce proceedings. Seeing the Beatles in person definitely counted as a special occasion, and the boots would help keep me warm in the chilly February temperatures in New York City.

I rummaged around the boxes at the bottom of the closet. I came across a box of Quinn's fishing magazines (I wondered briefly if Chief Kirkland might want them), then a box of Quinn's winter-wear, which would be going to charity, before finally finding what I was looking for in a box of miscellaneous items. Cat-eye glasses, black-rimmed ones with sparkly faux diamonds in the outer corners. I had bought them for a feline-themed Halloween costume the year Quinn went as a dog. I donned those as well.

I had been hearing shrieks and other sounds of merriment as I readied, and finally took a look out the window. Students wearing ski masks were racing dorm-made sleds down the hill at the park end of the street. It looked like one of them had ended up lodged in a mailbox. I made a mental note to organize a winter safety seminar for the students later in the week and thought how odd it was that soon I'd be one of the crowd at New York's airport. When the Beatles landed there, it had just been renamed John F. Kennedy airport, having previously been called Idlewild.

I threw on a short chocolate-brown wool coat on the way out, decided against a hat—I wasn't about to go see the Beatles with droopy and flattened hat hair—and hurried into the garage, leaving the front door unlocked. It was Tuesday, and Terry from Housekeeper's Express always came around on Tuesdays. Terry had done wonders for the state of my little blue-and-white bungalow—he wielded a dust cloth with a fanatic's touch, and had a secret formula for rendering bathroom surfaces sparklingly clean. Quinn's departure had not affected things one way or another, as his contribution to the housework had essentially been nil. To be fair, my own contribution had been essentially nil, too, I conceded, folding myself into my aged Honda in the tight skirt. In retrospect, hiring a housekeeping service seemed like a no-brainer; but the issue of household maintenance had become a tug-of-war for Quinn and me. Whose turn was it to throw out the trash? To vacuum the living room? To make a grocery store run in the snow for milk? To cross the road to the mailbox to pick up the mail?

Now Terry took care of the cleaning, I ran errands during my lunch hour, did the bulk of my grocery shopping on the weekends, and ate out often. Martha, my next-door neighbor, tended both her yard and mine—which was a good thing as I tended to kill plants—and in exchange, I did her taxes and helped organize her files and balance her checkbook.

The Honda started up after a moment of cold-induced indecision and I inched back out of the driveway, which had been narrowed down to car width by my latest attempts at shoveling.

Clearing the driveway was a job that Quinn and I had always shared. I made a mental note to stop by the hardware store first thing Saturday morning to pick up a gas-powered snow blower.

I turned the street corner, sighing as I watched the bungalow disappear from my rearview mirror. The snow was a practical problem that could be tackled. As to the rest—I had gone from living with my parents to living with college roommates to being married. Quinn and I had moved into my parents' old bungalow after they went to Florida to open a retirement community. Now that Quinn was gone, the discovery had crept up on me that living alone was a skill, one I was still working on developing. I was not a pet kind of person, so there was no one to greet me in the evening when I returned from work. Maybe renting out the tiny back bedroom with its separate entrance would be the way to go. Not to students, of course, but perhaps to visiting research and teaching fellows, who, despite the title, were women as often as men.

I drove back to campus humming "Strawberry Fields Forever."

Oscar complimented my cat-eye glasses as I hurried up the front steps of the TTE building. Once inside, I stopped to consider whether I should have dropped off my shoulder bag in my office. Dr Rojas hadn't given us instructions one way or the other. I decided not to waste time making a side trip to the History of Science building. Besides, the black, square bag with a snap mechanism would fit seamlessly into 1964 (or many another modern time period) and would be handy in case I needed a tissue or something.

"Julia," a voice stopped me as I started down the hallway.

Dr. Little, dressed in a blue-green plaid vest, had poked his head out of his office. I had a feeling that he'd been hovering just inside the door trying to figure out what was going on. Asking directly would have put him in the position of admitting to ignorance, something I suspected he disliked immensely.

"I hear Kirkland is going on a run," he commented, inviting more information.

"He is."

"Where?"

"It's just a test run."

"Who's accompanying him? I should have been contacted. Is it Erika?"

"Dr. Helen Presnik."

"Dr. Presnik? From the English Department? That's ridiculous."

"She's been on many runs. Besides, it wasn't up to me." As far as everybody but Dr. Rojas, the dean's office, the security office, and the board of trustees was concerned, a laser focuser had malfunctioned. Chief Kirkland had been the one to ask for somebody outside the department. Helen, while she had some personal involvement with the case, was the most experienced traveler who wasn't a member of the TTE Department. Plus it would give Chief Kirkland a chance to ask the professor whatever questions he had for her.

Dr. Little seemed to notice my outfit for the first time. "Are those new glasses?"

"Sixties style," I said noncommittally. "I really should go."

His eyes went from the cat-eye glasses to my boots, and back up. "I have great respect for Chief Kirkland," he said slowly, "but in this case I think he's overstepping his bounds."

"He is investigating a—an accidental death. There are no bounds."

"I'm concerned that he is merely using Mooney's unfortunate demise to indulge in living out his fantasies." He eyed my boots and glasses again, his eyes narrowing.

"You think Chief Kirkland has a time travel fantasy?"

"Everyone has a time travel fantasy."

He probably had a point there, but I wasn't about to admit it.

"Well, fantasies aside," I said, "the chief needs to familiarize himself with STEWie so that he can write up his final report. Dean Sunder has asked that we give him our full cooperation."

Dr. Little looked like he was far from convinced that the security chief had anything to offer on what he (as far as I knew) assumed was a technical matter. I hoped I hadn't said too much. "Unless you'd like me to convey to Dean Sunder that you disagree. I could do so later today, when he and I make a preliminary pass at next year's budget—"

"Of course, of course, I only meant…" He turned and stalked back into his office, mumbling something about STEWie roster priority, research deadlines, and—I was almost sure—uppity secretaries. I felt a sudden and totally underserved stab of satisfaction that I was a good half a foot taller than he was.

Outside the TTE lab I ran into Dr. Baumgartner, who had her hand on the door handle to the travel apparel closet. "Julia, are you back? Has the chief found out what caused the focuser to malfunction?"

"Back?" It took me a moment to parse what she meant. "No, we're just on our way out. We're moving as fast as we can," I added somewhat snappishly. My exchange with Dr. Little had left me a bit testy.

She seemed taken aback. "Julia, I didn't mean—it's just that Gabriel said that he exchanged the faulty focuser, so everything is fine now and I don't see why the chief—well, let me know when you get back. I'll change and then wait in my office."

"Thank you, Dr. Baumgartner. I'll see you in a few minutes."

I heard the tap-tapping of heels and turned to see Penny Lind, paper coffee cup in hand, approaching in a whirlwind of activity. She greeted us, complimented me on my glasses—"The fifties are making a comeback, might get a pair myself"—and followed Erika into the travel apparel closet before I could explain that I had been aiming for a different decade.

Inside the lab, I found Gabriel Rojas and Helen Presnik standing side by side. A grim task had brought us together, but I couldn't help but crack a smile at Helen's outfit. It was like a winter version of tropical. The boxy, lemon-colored jacket had large gold buttons and a fur trim. There was a matching skirt of the same yellow. She saw me staring. "I know, Julia, I look rather—matronly. I found the suit in the travel apparel closet," she added, as if wanting to make sure everyone knew that she would never own such an outfit. "It's woolen. It should be warm enough. Are the shoes acceptable? I don't usually wear modern apparel on runs."

It was a strange use of the word *modern*. "Helen, where did you find those?" The orange pumps had large gold buckles. Penny Lind of *Les Styles* would have choked on her fat-free latte.

"I stopped by the retirement home and borrowed them from my mother." Helen had a purse slung over one shoulder, which meant I could definitely bring mine, too.

Chief Kirkland walked in, wearing a navy suit that was one of his own and not a TTE travel apparel one, judging by the way the material fit over his tall frame. He still managed to look very uncomfortable in it. A dark-gray overcoat lay draped over his shoulders, and he'd chosen a dark-gray tie to complement it. The shiny black of his hair completed the look. He was alone. Officer Van Underberg, I knew, had been dispatched to fetch Xavier Mooney's things out of storage to start going through the boxes, looking for anything that might shed light on the murderer's motive. Oscar had gone to help him.

Dr. Rojas chuckled. "Chief Kirkland, your hair is longer than the Beatles'. I believe you need a hat." I watched him leave the lab and cross the hallway to the travel apparel closet. I was glad to see that the professor seemed more relaxed. Perhaps passing the baton to Chief Kirkland had done the trick. It would be up to the chief to solve the crime; all Dr. Rojas had to do was compute the coordinates for our JFK landing site, and he could do that sort of thing in his sleep.

Abigail bounced into the lab. Before I could open my mouth to say anything, she announced, "Dr. Rojas said I could go." Her short hair was back to its natural blonde state. She was wearing a lime-green cotton sweater, pink three-quarter-length pants, and little white sneakers. She looked like she was ready to go flower picking in a spring meadow, which is to say, she looked very unlike her usual self. I could just picture it. She had asked Dr. Rojas if she could go, and he'd given a vague wave of agreement after barely registering the question. I tried to catch Chief Kirkland's eye. All of Dr. Rojas's test runs had gone off without a hitch and I was pretty sure that STEWie was safe from an engineering perspective. Still, was it right to let students—plural, because I had no doubt that Kamal was somewhere changing into a sixties outfit—climb into STEWie's basket without letting them know we had a killer loose on campus? As I tried to figure out whether I should say something, Chief Kirkland sent a barely perceptible shake of his head in my direction. That settled it. "Where did you get the outfit?" I asked Abigail. "From the travel apparel closet?"

"It's my own stuff. I don't usually wear the pink and the green together, though." She had a tiny backpack slung across one shoulder and a large, folding-type Polaroid camera in her hands. "It's authentic, from the early sixties," she said of the camera. "Found it on a shelf in the travel apparel closet. We got a whole bunch of stuff off eBay a while back."

"Aren't you going to be cold, dear?" Helen asked as Abigail set the camera on a table, opened a film pack, snapped it in, and carefully pulled out the protective black strip.

"I plan on insinuating myself right into the middle of the crowd and taking a photo or two—if anything, I'll be too warm, Dr. Presnik."

The doors opened again and Kamal strolled into the lab like he had every right to be there. He still had jeans on but had exchanged his sneakers for brown leather shoes and the *So you want to be a PhD, not a* REAL *doctor?* T-shirt he'd had on earlier with a tie-dyed one. It looked like he had slicked down his thick, dark-brown hair with either water or a hair cream of some sort.

"I didn't know what to wear," he said somewhat sheepishly. "I usually don't have to worry about fitting in, except for having to blend into foliage and stuff."

Kamal's thesis had to do with cataloging safe landing zones in Neanderthal Eurasia.

"Tie-dyes are more of a late-sixties fashion item, aren't they? Plus you'll be cold," I said, "unless, like Abigail here, you plan on insinuating yourself right into the middle of the crowd."

"I probably do, but I'll go get a coat," he said, and hurried out of the room.

"I'm not sure those boots of yours are quite 1964 either, Julia," Helen said with a smile, "but I think we'll do."

"If you don't want the students to come along, I can tell them so," I said to the chief in a low voice as Abigail and Helen headed toward STEWie's basket.

He shook his head. "Let them stay. Students are part of STEWie runs. I want to observe a run that's as typical as possible."

"How long will we be gone? I left a research program running," asked Kamal, who had hurried back in with an overcoat.

Behind him was Jacob Jacobson, who looked like he would dash off to the travel closet to change at the first invitation. Dr. Rojas brought up the rear, carrying a gray felt fedora. He handed it to the security chief. "You'll have an hour there. STEWie will drop you off behind the arrivals building. Find your way to the upper arcade—that should be the best viewing spot. Enjoy yourselves. Don't go looking for public phones to call your relatives."

Helen tapped an impatient orange pump. Being an expert in Shakespeare's English and other bygone languages, she seemed bored with our destination and hadn't bothered to say much during our viewing of the airport footage in the conference room. I got the sense, without her ever saying a word on the subject, that she had an inkling of what was going on and had volunteered to accompany us because she was rather peeved that someone had done away with Xavier Mooney, as if the job should have been reserved for her and her alone.

"A big crowd, everyone focused on the arriving band, we should be able to move around with relative ease," she said as the five of us gathered around STEWie's basket. The fish tank was no longer there, the moody tilapia having presumably been returned to the Genetics lab.

Kamal and Abigail, who had been on a dozen of these runs, scrambled up onto the platform and took standing positions inside the wall-less basket. Dr. Presnik fetched a small stool and used it to step onto the platform. I followed her and, after making sure that we were all secure, Chief Kirkland hoisted himself up, too.

"It will take a few minutes to upload the coordinates," we heard Dr. Rojas say. One of the larger mirrors blocked our view of what he was doing at the workstation. "I'm sending you to the JFK airport of 1964, more precisely, to the seventh of February—a Friday…early afternoon, a few minutes before the

Beatles' plane lands…but one can never be too careful. We don't want you arriving at the wrong building or in the middle of the runway."

He was starting to make me nervous. The thick glass of the platform under our feet distorted and dimmed the floor lights. The steel frame of the basket gaped open like an unfinished house waiting for its builders to return. I repeated Dr. Rojas's rules in my head—*One hour there = 133 seconds here. History protects itself. Blend in. There's always a way back.* Seemed simple enough. I put my coat back on and felt more comfortable in the chilly lab.

Helen spritzed something into her nose. "For our own protection. Probably not necessary for 1964, but protocol is protocol. Here." She passed out the disposable sprays to the rest of us. "We'll sanitize again—hands, too—when we get back."

Jacob, clearly disappointed that he hadn't been invited along, dropped onto a lab stool, phone in hand.

"No tweets, Jacob," I said from the basket, spritzing my own nose.

"But Julia—oh, wait, is this trip supposed to be a secret? Oops. I didn't know that. No one told me."

"It's not a secret," I said. "That doesn't mean we want everyone on campus receiving a play-by-play of what we're doing. Put the phone away."

"I'm kind of excited we'll get to see the Beatles," Abigail said as Jacob complied with my order. "Should we scream and swoon with the other fans to blend in? Per Dr. Rojas's rule number three?"

"Rather than joining you and Julia and the other adoring Beatles fans on the upper arcade," said Dr. Presnik, "I think I'll walk around the airport listening to people's conversations. Maybe take some notes," the linguist added. "I know it's policy for the team to stay together, but in this case it doesn't seem necessary—"

"Let's stick to the usual protocols," Chief Kirkland said. "Though I think I'm going to feel out of place on the arcade, too."

Helen backed off the idea. "Fine. You've got a touch of the exotic about you, Chief Kirkland," she added. "People will probably assume that you're an international traveler who's just arrived from abroad. What's your background?"

"I'm from Duluth."

We could hear Dr. Rojas muttering to himself as he worked. "The seventh of February, 1964...let's make it 13:15...final coordinate check..."

The lab phone rang jarringly. Dr. Rojas picked up and absentmindedly said, "TTE lab, yes?"

There was about thirty seconds of silence on our end, then we heard the professor's voice again. "Does it have to be now? I'm in the middle of something... I suppose it can wait a few minutes... I'll be right there."

He called out, "Give me five minutes, I'll be right back," and the lab door creaked open and shut as he hurried out.

Kamal and Abigail sat down cross-legged on the platform. Abigail took a test photo with the large Polaroid camera. After some investigation, she discovered that tugging a white strip out of the camera released the photo. After giving it a good minute, she peeled the photo away from the negative and showed it to us. There was the chief, who had wedged his dark strands under the fedora Dr. Rojas had dug up, and one pretty fab (I'd like to think) science dean's assistant.

"Well, I have to say I'm kind of excited about this," I said, having decided that I was too old to squat beside Abigail and Kamal, not to mention the tight skirt. "Traveling back in time may be old hat to some of you, but it's not for me. I just wish it was happening under different circumstances."

"While we're waiting, Dr. Presnik," Chief Kirkland said to Helen, "do you mind if I ask you a few questions about Dr. Mooney? For my, uh—report."

"Ask away, my dear man. What is it that you want to know?"

"Your marriage to Xavier Mooney, how long did it last?" was the question Chief Kirkland chose first, tilting his fedora back as he spoke. Like me, he seemed to think that Helen had figured out what was going on. I hoped he didn't assume that I'd told her. Kamal and Abigail, for their part, looked surprised at the nature of the question.

Helen raised an eyebrow at the chief. "Our marriage? Just over sixteen years. Xavier and I met and got married when I was a graduate student and he was a junior professor. There is a fourteen-year age difference between us. We were in different departments, of course."

"Was it a happy marriage?"

Helen was silent for a moment, then said, "It wasn't an *un*happy one."

Jacob was still sitting on the lab stool, eagerly watching us with his mouth open. "Why don't you go see what's keeping Dr. Rojas?" I said. His face drooped but he headed out of the lab, his shoulders bent as if to say *How unfair*. He would probably tweet that, too.

"And the divorce? What was the reason for that?" the chief asked Helen.

She sighed. "Some people, my dear Chief Kirkland, cannot figure out how to live together even after sixteen years of trying. I walked out one evening in a huff. But really, it was mutual."

"Any interest on his part in your love life since the divorce?"

"Really, Chief Kirkland. What an idea."

"And vice versa?"

"Even more absurd."

"I think I hear Dr. Rojas," Abigail said thankfully as the lab doors opened and closed with their usual creak, and got to her feet.

"Dr. Rojas, are we good to go?" Helen called out, her strong voice reverberating around the cavernous lab.

There was no answer, but we heard the clicking of keys and, after a moment, the whole lab suddenly seemed to come to life, the quiet hum of the computer equipment vanishing under the rumble and *brr-brr* of motors powering to life. They were just needed to move the mirrors; the specifics of the generator that powered STEWie itself were above my pay grade. (About all I knew was that it involved thorium, the element discovered by a fellow Norwegian, the Reverend Hans Morten Thrane Esmark, and named after the Norse god of thunder.) The mirrors pivoted and inched into position around us like they were executing a slow, complex dance routine.

"Shade your eyes," Kamal reminded the chief and me.

I positioned myself next to the grad students and felt another pang of doubt about the wisdom of taking them with us. I had a responsibility for their well-being. But would they really be safer if we left them behind? After all, there was probably a murderer loose on campus. I ran out of time to consider the question as the brightness in the room increased to a painful level and I shielded my eyes with my hands—then wished I had an extra pair to cover my ears as the hum of STEWie's generator grew. There was a high-pitched whine and the platform beneath our feet started to vibrate—gently at first—then harder—it got brighter—louder—I heard a *thump, thump*—I was having trouble keeping my feet steady—the world shook harder than ever—*thump, thump*—I lost my footing—warm air hit my face—

"Ouch." I let out a sound as my body hit a surface much rougher than the polished glass of STEWie's platform. I stayed still for a moment, my eyes clenched shut, my ears abuzz, my body aching, then slowly felt around me. My hand touched a patch of grass, dirt, then something squishy. I sensed somebody else moving nearby, then cried out in pain as my fingers met something sharp—my cat-eye glasses, shattered into pieces where I had landed on them—and opened my eyes in the direction of the one sound, the thumping, that was refusing to go away.

PART TWO: IN THE SHADOW

9

I was in a vineyard, on all fours behind a boulder. Down a row of vines heavy with small unripe grapes lay a cobblestone road. An oxcart bounced along it, a figure in a tunic spattered with road dust wearily leading the animals. Odder still was what was *on* the cart—a bloated leather pouch, almost as big as the cart itself. Leather straps secured it in place. An extra strap had been tied to the throat of the pouch to prevent whatever was inside from spilling out.

"So...not New York City, then," I heard Chief Kirkland whisper behind another boulder, to my right.

Thump, thump. The repetitive clatter of spoked, iron-rimmed wooden wheels striking rut and stone. Instinctively, the chief and I waited until the cart and its unusual cargo had passed before we pulled ourselves to our feet. I steadied myself on the boulder, which felt slightly cool in the shade of the tall tree we were under. My head throbbed from the lights and sounds we had been subjected to in the TTE lab. The brightness was still there, but now it was from sunlight, not STEWie's artificial rays.

"Julia," a voice said from behind the tree. Abigail's. She was crouching on the tree's braided aboveground roots. She rose and brushed off her hands. "*That* was odder than usual."

Kamal was also behind the tree. He stepped out and looked around at the grapevines in their neat rows, then up at the tree, then down at the ground as if he expected it to open up and swallow us whole. Meanwhile, Abigail was pressing keys on her cell phone. "I don't understand—this is definitely not the airport—" The alarm that was evident in Kamal's face was there on hers as well.

The air was warm. *Quite* warm, in fact. I proceeded to take off my coat and folded it over the boulder. Next I removed the clip from my hair and let it fall down around my shoulders. Wherever we were, one thing was for sure—there was no need to project an aura of efficiency and competence.

"Here, Ms. Olsen." Chief Kirkland bent down and picked up my cat-eye glasses from where they had been crushed by my landing. A few of the faux diamonds had been dislodged from the rims and one of the lenses had fallen out and broken. The other had weblike cracks spreading from the center.

"Will you be able to see?" the chief asked. He picked up his gray fedora from where it had tumbled off his head and slid it back on. "You did bring your everyday pair along for backup, didn't you? In that bag of yours?"

"What? Oh, the cat eyes. They are plain glass. As it happens, my everyday pair are—uh, plain glass as well. As a matter of fact," I said and took a deep breath of the unexpectedly warm air, "I have twenty-twenty vision." Why was he harping on eyewear? We had more pressing matters to attend to, like figuring out where we were. Maybe even *when* we were. I stepped over one of the tree roots and reached out to touch the trunk.

"A fig tree," said Kamal. "An old one."

The gray bark felt smooth under my fingers. I hoped it wasn't some side effect from moving around in time, a dulling of sensation perhaps. No, that was silly. My broken glasses hadn't felt smooth. The new cut inflicted by the shattered lens had reopened yesterday's wound from the Geology Department rock, which had started to heal nicely. The fig I'd landed on had left a sticky spot on my other palm—it itched slightly—and I rubbed it off on my skirt. Now there was a sticky spot on my skirt.

"Julia, are you all right?" Abigail asked, moving the cell phone left and right as if searching for better reception. I wondered why she was trying to dial it, since there weren't any cell towers in 1964—if that was even the year we were in. And where was Helen? I pulled myself together and attempted to explain about the glasses. "Before I started wearing the glasses and the hair clip, I'd often get mistaken for a student. An undergraduate student. I'm told I'm a bit baby faced."

"Yeah, without the glasses you kind of are, Julia," Kamal said, temporarily distracted. "You do look younger, not at all like you have a real job. Your face is round and your nose is so small—"

Chief Kirkland grunted in agreement (I couldn't tell which way he meant it—whether he preferred the baby-faced look or my usual look of efficiency and can-do) and took a few steps forward to examine the grapevines, his back to me.

In every movie I'd ever seen with a female assistant or librarian as a character, the assistant would at some point remove the glasses and hair clip that had up until then inexplicably hidden her glamour, beauty, and luxurious locks. Then she would proceed to sweep the hero off his feet. If only. Besides, I had no intention of trying to sweep anyone off his feet—Kamal was a student, and the security chief... Well, his jaw was too square and he called me Ms. Olsen. Not to mention that I wanted a roommate, not a romantic entanglement.

Helen emerged from the overgrown grass by the edge of the stone road. She was holding one arm awkwardly, her eyes following the diminishing outline of the oxcart as the road took it down the gently sloping terrain. All around us lay a veritable tapestry of orchards, farmhouses, and sun-drenched vineyards. In the direction the cart had come from, the road steepened. We had landed on the lower flank of a small mountain.

"There you are, my dears," Helen said, turning. "We have clearly arrived somewhere *rustic*. Has anyone spotted a landmark of any use? An electrical post? A plane—or the contrail of a plane? Heard the sound of a car?"

It took me a moment to figure out that by "landmark" she meant an anchor not in space but in *time*.

"Well, we're definitely not at JFK airport," Chief Kirkland pointed out the obvious. "Nor does this look like any part of New York state that I'm familiar with. Could we have arrived on the wrong coast? This place reminds me of California wine country. Napa Valley, I'd say, except for that mountain."

He had a point. It did remind me of California (Quinn and I had eloped in a quickie beach ceremony in San Diego). The sun had jumped higher in the sky and shone brightly and warmly, too warmly. It was a summer sun. I took another deep breath. Winter was a quiet season for the senses on the St. Sunniva campus; here the air hung heavy with heat and there was a sweet aroma to it, like a flower and herb garden in full bloom, and also something else. The unmistakable scent of marine life, of air heavy with salt, of a breezeless summertime seaside.

"I'll give you the sunshine and grapevines, Chief Kirkland, but the cart that just passed—it was carrying a wineskin, not exactly a modern contrivance." Helen adjusted her right arm and winced. "I fell. It almost felt like the ground shifted a little just as we landed. Odd."

"Not so odd for California, perhaps," Chief Kirkland said, watching a seagull pass high above us in a smooth, wide-winged glide. "And don't you smell the ocean?"

"Leather wineskins, dear Chief. Oxen. Stone roads…"

"It could still be California," he countered stubbornly. "They have cattle there. As for the cart—maybe we're in the middle of a movie set."

I opened my mouth to point out the ridiculousness of the suggestion, when an almost imperceptible rumble shook the ground beneath us. A purple-green fig fell down by my boots, a large, five-pronged leaf still attached to it.

"There it is again, see?" said Chief Kirkland. "A small earthquake. California. They have fig trees there, don't they?"

Helen carefully pulled her injured arm out of the sleeve of the fur-lined wool jacket, which would clearly not be needed in the mild climate of wherever we were, California or otherwise, and said briskly, "Mr. Ahmad and Miss Tanner, which one of you has the Callback?"

"I do," Abigail said, holding up what I'd assumed was a cell phone. On second glance, it didn't look much like one. The device was more like an old, clunky handheld calculator, with a screen and a number pad.

Chief Kirkland, who had been scanning the road with a frown that belied his insistence that we were on the West Coast in the middle of a movie set, turned back and asked, "What is that?"

"STEWie's Callback. It reconnects the basket sections and launches us on a reverse trajectory," Kamal explained, not helpfully at all, I thought. He was glancing up occasionally, as if he expected an asteroid to come crashing down on our heads any minute. I didn't think he was merely watching out for seagull droppings.

"Imagine that there's a twisted elastic band that winds through time and connects us to the TTE lab," Helen said. "A band stretched so thin it needs the merest touch, the smallest release, to unwind and send us home. That's what the Callback does."

"Apparently not," I said.

"Here, let me try." Kamal thrust out his arm.

"It doesn't matter who pushes the keys. It's not going to work for you either," said Abigail, but she handed it to Kamal anyway.

"Maybe we're too far away? Let's all stand exactly where we were when we arrived," Kamal directed us.

Abigail shook her head, but she went back behind the tree. Helen took the lane between the vines back to the road where she had landed in the overgrown grass, and the chief and I went to crouch behind our respective boulders. Kamal returned to the fig tree, turning knobs and pressing buttons.

Nothing happened.

"I told you so," we heard Abigail say.

"Here, let me see it."

Kamal tossed Chief Kirkland the Callback. "The second knob on the left. Turn it counterclockwise, then press the Escape key."

The chief went into his crouch behind the boulder again, turned the knob counterclockwise, pressed the key. Nothing happened. He shook the Callback. "It's broken, then?"

"It's not broken," Abigail said in a small voice from behind the fig tree. "The basket is gone. We've been disconnected from the TTE lab."

The chief got to his feet and loosened his tie. "So. Dr. Mooney's murderer has played another card."

10

"Murderer?" Abigail asked for the fifth time.

Kamal was perched on what I'd come to think of as my boulder, scratching his head.

Helen, for her part, looked calm, like Chief Kirkland had merely confirmed her suspicions. "The sky doesn't seem to be falling," she said. She had taken off the yellow jacket to reveal a frilly white shirt and was resting with her back against the fig tree, legs stretched out, cradling her injured arm. I had joined her in the shade as our wait for rescue stretched on. I could see what she meant, I thought, swatting away a fly. If we were in a ghost zone, it sure seemed like a tame one. Butterflies fluttered all around, the unripe green grapes basked in the sun, fluffy clouds moved unhurriedly across a blue sky, cicadas chirped, the stone road stretched silent in the afternoon heat. It was, at a guess, a good sixty degrees warmer than the St. Sunniva campus.

As if we were all thinking the same thing, Kamal spoke up from his perch on the boulder. "Yeah, this doesn't seem like a ghost zone. Only—I can't figure out why the basket left without us."

"Are we sure STEWie's basket is gone?" I asked. "I mean, it's invisible, right? How odd that is."

"It's not that odd," Kamal said. "All sorts of things in nature aren't visible to our eyes—X-rays, oxygen, gravity waves, viruses… I've always imagined that if we *could* see STEWie's basket, it would look like a blob of water suspended in midair."

"I've always pictured it as sparkling silver Jell-O floating freely in large clumps," Abigail said.

"There is no such thing as silver Jell-O," Kamal said. "Trust me, I know. I've tried all the flavors in the grocery store."

"There is in my version of what STEWie's basket looks like."

"So, the basket?" I prompted them.

"It arrives in fragments, one for each traveler. In our case, there was one by this boulder for you, Julia, and another by that boulder for Chief Kirkland"—Kamal pointed—"and two behind the tree for Abigail and me. And in the ditch by the road for Dr. Presnik. That's what the Callback does, it closes the loop between the basket fragments, and we're sent back."

"I thought the basket only returned empty if the travelers were—"

"Dead," Kamal said.

"And we're not dead."

"No."

"So—?"

No one had an explanation.

Chief Kirkland had been circling the fig tree in what could only be called an angry stomp, stepping over its roots. "I didn't think—I mean, there are five of us—safe, I thought, a middle-of-the-day run—a brazen move—" He stopped, took off his hat, and faced Abigail and Kamal, looking stricken. "I owe you two an apology. For letting you come along without giving you all the facts. Dr. Presnik, you as well."

I had to give him credit. I felt guilty, too, but I hadn't spoken up about it.

"I understand what you said about Professor Mooney, Chief Kirkland, but what happened to us could still be an accident, right?" Abigail said.

"It could be, but I think not. I think whoever attacked the professor has struck again. They never do the smart thing—lay low and let events take their course."

He didn't say who *they* were, but he didn't have to. I pushed out of my mind the image of Gabriel Rojas's gaunt face, crisscrossed with worry lines since Dr. Mooney's murder, in sharp contrast to his relaxed demeanor as he readied our coordinates.

"Chief, what was your goal with this run?" Helen asked bluntly.

The chief defended his method. "It didn't seem like a risky thing to do. Dr. Rojas's test runs with the fish went off without a hitch. Like I said, five of us, in the middle of the day... As to my goal, well, it was simple. I wanted to observe a run as they usually are, uh—run. To gauge how easy it would be for somebody to slip away unnoticed by the rest of the team, for whatever reason. I suspected it would be very difficult to do so. Meaning that someone who wanted a run to themselves might have chosen that Monday night to do it, perhaps with Dr. Mooney's approval."

"No," four voices said at once.

"Well, without his approval then, which might explain why Dr. Mooney was sent on a ghost run and all the evidence was erased from the computer log."

"By Gabriel?" Helen said, considering the chief's words. "Is that what you're suggesting? That Gabriel wanted a run and Xavier got in his way, so Gabriel sent him into a ghost zone after he was done. And now he's gotten rid of us, too. Forgive me, but that doesn't make much sense. Why would Gabriel need an unauthorized run? TTE professors have priority where roster spots are concerned."

This was a bit of a sore point in the other departments.

"Maybe he didn't want people to know," Kamal suggested.

"He has no need for secrecy," I said. "We don't publish destinations until after the results are in. That's just standard protocol."

"Maybe he didn't want *us* to know," Kamal elaborated.

"Oh," I said.

"Maybe he needed a STEWie run for off-the-books research, maybe he needed it for personal reasons," the chief said. "Or maybe we're on the wrong track completely and it *was* an accident."

Abigail tapped a white-sneakered foot, her tiny, triangular backpack on the ground next to her. "I for one think Dr. Rojas did send us here by mistake. I know you all think it's unlikely—"

"Very unlikely," Helen said drily. I felt a little surprised that she was so quick to condemn Gabriel, whom she'd known for years. She turned the conversation to practical matters. "We're not in New York City of 1964 and the basket is gone. Does anyone have any idea where we could be?"

"Somewhere where they have figs and grapes," Kamal said.

"This farmland looks irrigated. Wherever we are, we can't have gone that far back in time," the chief said.

"Dr. Rojas will look for us," Abigail tried again. "He'll figure out we didn't make it to JFK airport. We've been here just about an hour. That's only 133 seconds in the lab."

"At best it will take them a few hours to figure out what went wrong and recalibrate, which means that *days* will pass for us here," Kamal said glumly. "Assuming this isn't a ghost zone and we aren't about to be caught in a sudden brushfire or something."

"And if Dr. Rojas just tells everyone that the basket returned empty?" asked the security chief.

"Then there is no hope of rescue," Helen said matter-of-factly. "Everyone will think we're dead. I don't know why STEWie's basket returned without us. We can sit under this tree and discuss it further or we can go and find out where we are. I vote for the latter. We can always return here to see if anyone has been by looking for us. Besides, I don't expect we'll get far dressed like this." She pushed herself to her feet with her uninjured arm and rolled her jacket into a ball and shoved it into a shrub. The rest of us did the same with our coats. Leaving the shade of the fig tree behind us, we took the lane between two rows of grapevines to the road, and turned in the uphill direction. The mountain—it struck me as being like a giant anthill, cone shaped, with a narrow flat area at the top—would offer a bird's-eye view of wherever we were.

I regretted my choice of footwear almost at once. Beneath our feet, blocks of gray stone lay fitted together like roundish jigsaw puzzle pieces, large ones, each the size of a chair seat or a side table. The road was not much wider than the cart that had passed in the opposite direction, and parts of it were overgrown with grass. Between the unevenness of the stones and the wagon ruts worn into them, the heels of my special-occasion boots kept getting caught and I had to concentrate to avoid falling.

Something else was bothering me. Dr. Rojas had said to expect insurmountable maze walls as we moved around in a time period not our own, but so far I hadn't noticed a single limitation on my steps, other than the awkwardness of my boot heels on the cobblestones. The decision of whether to hike up the mountain or walk farther into the plain had been our own, made with no interference from the overseeing entity called History. In fact, everything seemed perfectly normal, other than the fact that we had no idea where we were, which was very disconcerting. Could the chief's first theory really be correct? Were we somewhere in California?

Clusters of shady pines, palm trees, and what I guessed were olive trees lined the sides of the road. The upper slopes of the mountain, above the vineyards, were heavily wooded. The plateau at the top, where the ants would go in and out if the mountain were a large anthill, was bare.

"What are you doing, Dr. Presnik?" Abigail asked the professor.

Helen was peering into the roadside ditch. "Looking for trash. Not a soda can in sight. No gum wrappers, no cigarette butts. Just some animal refuse…a few pottery shards…"

For a moment I debated whether to ask her if our freedom of movement was a point in favor of present-day California, but decided to hold off and see if I could run into any maze walls.

I waved my arms in the air, twirled on my heels, and shuffled over to the side of the road.

"Ms. Olsen?" Chief Kirkland asked.

"Just testing one of Dr. Rojas's rules."

Two graceful pines stood on my side of the road. Beyond them was a small vineyard with a farmhouse nestled at its center. With their broad, umbrella-shaped canopies, the trees blocked much of the sunlight, and the soil underneath was covered with a soft layer of pine needles and sparse grass. I proceeded to weave between the pines, touch the gray-orange cracked bark, and kick a pinecone, barely managing to avoid twisting an ankle in the process. I was sure I looked like an idiot.

The boy staring at me from his perch on the crumbling log of a fallen pine must have thought so, too.

∞

I brought the arms I had been waving in the air like an overenthusiastic hockey fan down by my sides and said, "Well, hello there."

The small boy, his face tanned to a deep brown, was straddling the tree trunk and whacking something on the other side with a leafless stick, raising a small cloud of gray dust. The thumb of his other hand was in his mouth. He had on a loose, rather grubby tunic and his sandaled feet were dirty and scratched up.

"Hello, there," I repeated. "I wonder if you could tell me where we are. Do you know the name of your town?"

The boy glanced at the others behind me, stopped whacking whatever was on the far side of the log, and pointed the stick in my direction.

"*Suhl-way.*"

"What was that?" I said. I often have trouble understanding small children, especially if they happen to have something in their mouth.

The boy took his thumb out of his mouth. "*Suhl-way.*"

A call came from the farmhouse, a worried parental voice.

The boy hopped off the tree trunk and over to where I stood and poked one of my boots with the stick.

"Hey, kid, don't scuff up my boots." I caught a whiff of something in the air. The smell—rancid, like food gone bad—suddenly permeated the umbrella pines. For a moment I thought it was the boy, but then noticed all the flies on the far side of the tree trunk where he'd been perched.

The boy poked my boot with the stick again and spoke a long sentence in a tongue that was completely unfamiliar to me. It wasn't Norwegian or Spanish, which was about as far as my expertise went.

The call came again, louder, and the boy took off in the direction of the farmhouse. I could hear a dog barking as it ran out to meet him. I hesitated a moment, then took a step over to the fallen pine to see what had so interested the boy.

A swarm of flies buzzed above the blackened remnants of a bonfire. The odd thing was, the half-burned fish guts and bones scattered around the pale gray ash didn't seem like the leftovers of someone's dinner. They looked more like they had been thrown into the fire as part of some kind of ancient fish-burning ritual.

"Ugh," I said, covering my nose and backing off.

"What is it, Julia?" Helen asked as I clambered back to the road.

"Fish. Overcooked in a bonfire."

"Wineskins, locals in tunics, fish remains by the wayside." Chief Kirkland took his gray fedora off, adjusted its brim, adjusted it again, then put the hat back on. "All right, so it looks likely that we're not in California."

"No, my dear Chief Kirkland," said Helen, "we're not. That child was speaking Latin. I'm afraid we're in far time."

11

Given that we'd all pretty much suspected this already, Helen's announcement that we were in far time landed without much of a splash.

"Dr. Rojas made it seem like there would be many barriers for us to navigate," Chief Kirkland said as we picked up our pace, a sense of urgency suddenly enveloping us, as if knowing where we were would somehow solve the problem of us being here. "Akin to a maze, he said. But the experience itself isn't proving to be anything of the sort. Ms. Olsen seemed to have no problem engaging the boy in conversation."

"I don't know about engaging him in conversation," I said, wishing he would stop calling me Ms. Olsen already. "The boy poked my boots with a stick and said something I didn't understand. You're sure it was Latin, Helen?"

"He said hi," said Abigail, who had a working knowledge of that language.

"That's right. *Salve.* Hello, greetings, that kind of thing," Helen explained as we hurried along. "Also that you looked strange. I had a bit of trouble understanding him. It wasn't the scholarly kind of Latin. What's been rather haughtily termed *vulgar* Latin."

"That term has always bothered me," Abigail said.

"What about the fact that Ms. Olsen interacted with the boy easily, even though he found her to be, uh, strange?" the chief asked.

"It's not good," said Kamal.

"If we had been dropped into a ghost zone, we'd be dead by now, Mr. Ahmad," Helen said. "Chief Kirkland, interaction with youngsters is often easier than with adults when one is in a time period not one's own. Children accept new and unusual things without thinking twice about them. Even if they do mention seeing something strange, not much notice is taken of it. Children, as everyone knows, have a very vivid imagination. Still..."

We hurried on uphill, passing orchards, small fields, and row upon row of grapevines. Goats and sheep grazed about, dogs lounged in the shade, here and there a few figures could be seen hunched over, working in the midday heat against the song of the cicadas in the background. As the road took us higher up the slope of the mountain we had unexpectedly landed on, my boot heel got caught in a crack between two of the smooth-surfaced stones. Just barely managing to stay upright, I reminded myself of Dr. Rojas's final rule—*There's always a way back*. Perhaps Abigail was right and he had simply miscalculated—somewhat wildly, that was true—and needed some time to find us. Rescue would come. I wouldn't mind a side trip to an exotic location as long as I got back to my office in time to ready the spring class catalog.

Ahead of me, the chief was taking long strides along the road, Helen on his heels; behind me, Abigail and Kamal bickered as they tried to guess the latitude from the position of the sun.

"I'm thinking forty degrees," Abigail was saying.

"I don't know, that seems a little high for palm trees—"

I picked up my pace to catch up with the chief and Helen. "So, Latin. *Mens sana in corpore sano*. A healthy mind in a healthy body. *O tempora, o mores!* Oh what times, oh what customs. Uh—well, I can't think of any other ones." That was the extent of the Latin I'd picked up from my education and from seeing copies of ancient texts in the Coffey Library. As several snow-white sheep turned their heads to look in our direction, then went back to grazing unconcernedly, I added, "Latin—Rome—just think, we might get to see it during a famous emperor's reign—maybe one of the more unpleasant ones—Caligula, Nero—"

An odd feeling had taken hold of me. I wasn't a historian. But I suddenly understood the passion with which the TTE professors and students had committed themselves to the *History Alive* program. Even though I only worked a building or two away and had seen photos from successful runs, up until now it had all seemed quite—well, academic.

"I don't know how close we are to Rome itself," Helen poured cold water on my enthusiasm as we left the road and entered a field. "Remember, Julia, that the Roman Empire lasted for centuries and at its height stretched from modern-day Scotland to Sudan and from Spain to Syria. We're not in the north, obviously, but beyond that—"

The grass under our feet was yellow and dry from the summer heat, unlike the clearly well-watered orchards and vineyards; but what really caught my attention was the color of the soil beneath—it was black, like we were walking on a bed of coal. But grass does not grow in coal.

"It's a hot day for scaling mountains," Kamal called out from behind us. "I'm getting thirsty."

He had a point. Drops of sweat had broken out all across my forehead; Helen was fanning herself with a notebook she'd taken out of her orange purse; the chief had slung his jacket over one shoulder, unbuttoned the top two buttons of his shirt, and rolled up his sleeves; and everyone had complained about his or her shoes at least once, except for Abigail, whose sneakers and pink capris seemed ideal for the climate.

The uphill hike took a lot out of us and we all came to a stop in the vicinity of a two-story, terra-cotta-roofed villa far grander than the farmhouse with the boy and the bonfire. Despite its obvious luxury, it was a working country house—an orchard and a garden lay to one side, and pigs snorted and jostled in an enclosure just outside the courtyard wall.

I thought I'd take a look at the pigs, for no particular reason, really, but after a step or two I ground to a halt without much choice in the matter. My legs had lost all will to move, a reaction way too strong to be accounted for by all the uphill walking we had done in the heat of the day. It reminded me of the numbness you get after finishing the first snowshoe run of the season, when each step is a giant effort because of sore muscles, but without the pain. Before I could investigate this curious phenomenon further, Helen called out from by the courtyard wall. "We should take a peek over."

Wondering what, if anything, was so special about the pigs oinking and jostling in their pen (Was one of them destined to be tonight's dinner? Would my presence have affected which one was chosen? Or was it some other, unfathomable quirk of History?), I turned away from the pigsty, somewhat reassured by this proof of at least one of Dr. Rojas's rules. I joined the others at the courtyard wall, which stood well above our heads. Muffled voices could be heard from inside the house as the work of the day carried on.

"Right. Give me a boost," I said to the security chief.

"What if they see us?" he asked.

Helen waved the objection aside with the confidence of a seasoned time traveler. "If the courtyard is empty, we'll be able to look over the wall. If it's not, we'll still be able to look over if it's all right for us to be seen history-wise. And if it isn't, then we won't be able to do it."

The chief hesitated the merest moment, then leaned against the wall, cupping his hands. Abigail gave Kamal a pointed look. He said, "Oh," made a show of wiping sweat off his brow with the sleeve of his T-shirt, then joined the chief by the wall.

The chief lifted me up and I steadied myself on his shoulders, then took hold of the top of the wall and peered over. Next to me Abigail did the same.

A storage area of some sort stood to one side of the courtyard—a dozen sunken earthenware jars, evenly spaced, their tops and lids just peeking above ground. To the other side, in the shade of the house, stood a donkey cart. Two-wheeled and smaller than the one we had seen on the road, it was still big enough to carry a couple of people and a light cargo. The chestnut-colored donkey placidly chewed on grass, while its partner, its coat a patchwork of white and brown, fidgeted and hee-hawed occasionally, as if it preferred to be moving rather than hanging about in the shade.

Their mistress, an older woman, was tilting a small glass bottle back and forth as if to mix its contents. Her long-sleeved dress and the shawl draped around her head and shoulders seemed too warm for the season. As Abigail and I watched, she threw a quick glance at the villa door, which was tightly shut. Satisfied, she set the bottle on the cart next to a pair of wicker baskets that were filled with dried herbs and such, then took down the ladle hanging by the house's front door. She squatted near one of the terracotta jars in the storage area, a wince of old-age discomfort passing her face. The handle of the jar seemed to be giving her some trouble, so she pried the lid off with the non-scoop part of the ladle and, with another quick glance at the villa door, lowered the ladle inside. My knowledge of farming and grape growing was exceedingly limited—if you needed someone to organize a champagne-and-shrimp fundraiser or to order a grape-and-cheese basket as a thank-you for a donation to the school, I was the woman to call—but I rather thought I knew what was in the sunken pots and what she was doing, sampling the wine. She drained the ladle, wiped her mouth, then lowered the lid back in place. After returning the ladle to its spot on the wall, she went back to the cart.

As she chose an herb, perhaps mint, and crumbled it into the glass vessel, I heard Kamal grunt softly and Abigail's head disappeared back under the wall. I took a last glance around, searching for clues as to the time period and location, and was startled to see a pair of eyes watching me. Right below me, in the short shade of the courtyard wall, was a girl of maybe thirteen years of age. She had something in her hands and her hair fell in long, dark locks over strong shoulders under a plain, wheat-colored dress. I could have reached down and touched the top of her head. Curiosity, not alarm, registered on her features, as if I was a strange and novel thing to be investigated. I took a closer look at what she was holding—her steady hands gripped a wooden tablet whose long grooves were filled with beads.

Without turning around, the old woman barked something out, and the girl grinned at me and hurried over to the cart. She carefully wedged the abacus between two of the wicker baskets and followed the old woman, who was vigorously swirling whatever was inside the glass jar, into the house.

I heard the security chief grunt and hastened to get down.

"What did you see?" he asked, blowing on his reddened hands.

"Wine jars. Donkeys, a pair of them. An old woman and a young girl with an abacus, I think. I'm not sure any of it will help us figure out where we are, will it, Helen—Helen?"

Helen was not there. Or rather she was, but she had silently walked into the garden. This was an elaborate affair, with a footpath leading between rose beds and under decorative arches to a marble sculpture in the garden's center. Helen's back was to us as she examined the sculpture, which, upon a closer look, turned out to be a large sundial. Kamal and Abigail immediately set about trying to interpret the clock face. "It's past noon… two p.m., maybe…two thirty?" For a moment I thought that's what Helen had been trying to do as well, but then I noticed that her eyes were focused not on the face of the sundial but on the inscription on its base.

The letters were strange, backward E's, N's, S's, and R's. One looked like the number 8. Dots separated each clump of letters.

Helen had fallen to her knees in front of the inscription and was almost—*drinking it in* was probably the right way to say it. She moved her fingers from right to left, as if the letters were meant to be read that way, gently touching the marks and grooves.

"Helen?" I said.

"Oscan," she called out in wonder, "as I live and breathe, Oscan!"

For a moment I thought the heat had gotten to her and she was imagining she had seen Oscar, the doorman to the TTE building back home.

"Dr. Presnik, what's on the sundial?" Chief Kirkland asked.

"I haven't the slightest idea, my dear chief. It seems to be some kind of dedication. But I recognize the alphabet—it's Oscan. The language used to be spoken in the central and southern Italian Peninsula before the Romans moved in."

"So we're somewhere in the south of Italy?" Abigail said.

The sundial already looked old and chipped in places, I noticed, like it had been at the center of the well-tended rose garden for a long time.

Helen had risen to her feet and was staring over my shoulder. Following suit, we all turned to look, for the first time, at the vista enjoyed daily by the villa's inhabitants.

Even though I had expected it, for a moment my mind tried to fight what I was seeing. Make it fit into a Lake Superior or Pacific view, perhaps. But it didn't work.

Nestled between a harbor and the foot of the mountain lay a small town encircled by a defensive wall. Wisps of smoke rose from the hearths of its terra-cotta-roofed houses. Marble temples gleamed white in the afternoon sun. A broad, mellow river beyond the town flowed into a half-moon bay where a bevy of colorful wooden ships and fishing boats bobbed in the azure, shimmering water. A mountain ridge just beyond the town jutted out into the sea.

We all spoke at once.

"I've—I've always wanted to go abroad," I said.

"What a lovely little town," Abigail said.

"This won't fit into my research at all," Kamal said.

"The shape of that bay looks familiar," said Helen. "Now where—?"

"Who's going to feed Wanda?" Chief Kirkland said, fedora in hand.

12

Bowing down to some kind of twenty-first-century reflex that an urban area was the place to go, we headed down the mountain in the direction of the town. Helen muttered to herself as we trudged along in the oppressive afternoon heat, her orange pumps clicking on the large cobblestones. "Oscan. Well, I can't be sure about the date... That sundial looked like it has been here for ages and the child spoke Latin. The river beyond the town, could it be the Sarno? The fish on the bonfire by the roadside, that's probably from the Vulcanalia festival—but that would mean—no, it can't be..."

We covered probably a good four miles before nearing the town. On the way, we passed the remnants of a second bonfire. Occasionally Helen would pull us out of the way of a passing cart (one of them carrying the old woman and the girl back into town)—"I'd rather not try to interact with locals just yet," Helen said—but the sounds of activity had mostly ceased in the vineyards, orchards, and farmhouses adjoining the road. Probably everyone was taking an afternoon siesta. I could have used one myself. The parts of the road that were lined with trees provided some relief, but it was *really* starting to get scorchy. "Let's not add dehydration to our problems," the security chief said, and we discreetly helped ourselves to a smattering of figs and grapes from the greenery by the road. It didn't help much—the unripe grapes, especially, were tart and very seedy.

"We need to find another inscription to confirm—or, hopefully, disprove," Helen whispered through parched lips as we passed from a shady part of the road into full sunlight.

"We could go into one of those little buildings," I suggested, pointing, "and see if someone will give us water and information."

We had left the cultivated farmland behind us. Here the road was lined with small stone buildings of varying heights and shapes, all the way down to the town gate. A couple of circular stone benches, which looked like they had been placed there for weary travelers such as us, were interspersed with the small buildings. At the end of the street, the gate gaped like an elongated mouth in the defensive wall, an unmanned observation tower rising to the right of it.

"And ask what? *Ubi sumus? Quid annus est?* Where are we? What year is it?" Helen said. "It's unlikely that the locals would know the year. Besides, those are tombs, dear Julia, not houses. But you are right, they are exactly what we need," she added. "Tombs always have inscriptions."

We waited behind a square, squat tomb with a decorative column rising from its top as Helen translated the inscription. It had been built for one Septumia, daughter of Lucius, she said. No date was given. Two women who had been conversing in the shade of the town wall disappeared through the gate, and when they were out of sight we moved from Septumia's tomb to where a stone tablet, rather like a modern tombstone, stood set into the ground. The letters looked familiar, but the text was illegible to me. Helen peered down at the inscription, then squatted and swept at the grass so that she could read the bottom line.

"Oh, dear," she said.

"You've figured out where we are in far time, Dr. Presnik?" Chief Kirkland asked in the tone of one who was prepared for anything.

Abigail had also read the inscription. "Yikes," she said.

Pallor had driven the pink tinge of exertion from Helen's face. She moved aside as the rest of us huddled around the upright stone. "Abigail, why don't you translate for us."

"Sure, Professor. It's a proclamation, right? The tribune Titus Suedius Clemens…on the authority of emperor Augustus…has restored to the town some lands illegally taken by private individuals… The bottom lines are the interesting ones. The land was restored to the citizens of—Pompeii."

I stared at the stone. It read:

> EX AUCTORITATE
> IMP CAESARIS
> VESPASIANI AUG
> LOCA PUBLICA A PRIVATIS
> POSSESSA T SUEDIUS CLEMENS
> TRIBUNUS CAUSIS COGNITIS ET
> MENSURIS FACTIS REI
> PUBLICAE POMPEIANORUM
> RESTITUIT.

"Pompeii?" the chief asked.

Helen gave a small twitch. "That's right, dears. The town just over that wall, I'm afraid"—she pointed at the pockmarked stone blocks of the wall that towered over us—"is Pompeii. And the cone-shaped mountain with the lovely vineyards and orchards on its slopes must be the Vesuvius volcano. I'm afraid, dears, that we *are* in a ghost zone."

13

Pompeii.

The word conjured up images of hot ash and scorched rock, of a mountain erupting and changing the outlines of land and sea forever, of a town and its residents entombed by a fiery flow. Vesuvius, which had seemed like a peaceful mountain gracing an idyllic seaside town, now positively loomed over it—and us.

A cold wave of panic had coursed through my body at Helen's words. My feet moved of their own accord, away from the town wall and back to the open road. Stretching into the sky above us, the volcano was silent. A misleading, pregnant silence. Because ghost zone meant only one thing. An eruption—surely any second—followed by oblivion.

"The mountain reminded me of Mount St. Helens before the 1980 eruption," the chief said quietly. "Didn't want to say so." He had walked up beside me, and Kamal and Abigail were silently trailing him.

"Helen!" I called out.

"Yes, Julia?" she said, joining the rest of us after a short delay, as if reluctant to leave the tablet with its telling inscription.

"Should we seek shelter in the town? Find a road that will take us away from the mountain? Check to see if anyone has come to look for us yet?"

"Is there any point in trying to flee? The eruption must be imminent." She started listing the salient points as if she were holding an impromptu workshop on the matter. "One, the basket returned to the lab without us. Two, the twenty-fourth of August in the year 79 is believed to be the day of the eruption—and the Vulcanalia festival, with its sacrifice of small fish meant to appease the god of fire, took place on the evening of the twenty-third of August, just like it did every year." She went on, still pale, in the same calm tone. "Three, the ease with which we've been able to move around. Four, the tremors we've been feeling... You can't outrun an eruption, can you?"

"I don't think you can outrun them on foot, no," Chief Kirkland said. "Ships?" he added as if he were suggesting that we hail a taxi. He pointed in the direction of the sea and the town's harbor. "Can we get on a ship and escape that way?"

Helen started. "Yes, I suppose we could try. The letters by Pliny the Younger to the historian Tacitus—the only surviving eyewitness account of the eruption we have; I assign it to my Intermediate Latin students on occasion—the two letters tell of the death of his uncle, Pliny the Elder." She pronounced the name to rhyme with *skinny*. "The elder Pliny was a scientist and a scholar, and also the commander of the Roman fleet, which was stationed at the port of Misenum, across the bay—*is* stationed at Misenum—as I said, the younger Pliny wrote about the death of his uncle and also gave a very touching account of what he himself, in his late teens, went through during the eruption—"

"Helen!" I said.

"So this Pliny junior—obviously—survived," Chief Kirkland prodded her.

"He and his mother were staying at his uncle's house in Misenum, just out of reach of the worst of the eruption. It's been a while since I've reread Pliny's account myself, but I recall him saying that the disaster began with a cloud appearing over Vesuvius, then there were extended earthquakes...the sea retreated...and the cloud descended down the mountain—"

"A pyroclastic flow," Chief Kirkland said in an emotionless voice.

Helen nodded and went on. "The older Pliny left the safety of Misenum and sailed into Pompeii's harbor in an attempt to get a closer look at the strange phenomenon and to help save friends and others. He never made it out. He died on the beach from toxic fumes." Facing the volcano and shading her eyes with one hand from the sunlight, she gave it a piercing look and added, as if we needed more grisly details, "The town of Herculaneum, some ten miles up the coast, will be buried completely in ash and volcanic debris. Pompeii, though not buried quite as deeply as Herculaneum, won't fare much better."

Somewhere far off, a sheep bleated, then another. Cicadas chirped. The street of tombs lay deserted in the heat of the afternoon and the silence of what was essentially a cemetery was punctuated only by the sheep and cicadas and the sounds of activity on the other side of the town wall. For a moment, I was aware of my own heartbeat, which sounded as loud as a jackhammer, but then realized that the steady beat was actually a blacksmith's tool hammering metal in a workman's shop somewhere close by.

A terra-cotta urn perched in a niche on a nearby altar suddenly fell, probably displaced by the last tremor we'd felt. It broke in two, spewing forth a small pile of gray ash and blackened teeth.

We all lost our heads at that point. In unison we fled in the direction of the sea, away from the tombs, toward the azure water with its sprinkling of fluffy clouds above it. Always, the shadow of the mountain hung above us. We ran without regard for roads and paths, roughly following the line of the town wall, past villas and small orchards, across a second street of tombs, away from the danger of the mountain, the hot ash and fiery rocks that would surely come. I could hear Helen and Kamal panting as we followed a turn in the town wall, cut across a dirt road, and ran past a villa into an apple orchard. The heel of one of my boots came clean off and the chief caught my arm as I stumbled. "This way." He pointed to where the land met the cliff's edge, beyond which lay the sea, and pulled me along through the orchard—the dark-red fruit hung heavily, much more heavily than apples did—the cliff edge was within reach—pomegranate trees, the thought flew through my mind, not apple trees—and then that thought was replaced with nothing as I came to a jolting stop.

The force of the impact knocked the breath out of me. I realized I was on the ground again, as I had been when we'd arrived, but this time it wasn't an earthquake that had caused me to lose my footing. I put my hand up and felt the air in front of me.

There was nothing there but I couldn't push through.

14

The chief and Abigail had been able to stop themselves in time, but Helen was also on the ground, to my left. The chief picked up his fedora, which had flown off his head, pulled me up, then went to help Helen. Kamal was bent over as if his stomach was cramping from the run, his breathing uneven, reminding me of the morning he'd burst into my office with the news that Dr. Mooney had been scattered across time. Though barely a week had passed, it seemed like a lifetime ago.

"Let's back up a bit and try another way," the chief said grimly, offering Helen a steadying arm. "C'mon, Kamal, get to your feet." On the other side of the invisible wall lay some patchy grass and a glimpse of a steep path leading down the cliff to the harbor.

"This is good news in a way, really," Helen said, wincing as she got to her feet. "For the residents of the town, I mean. The more our freedom of movement is limited, the larger the percentage of the local population who will survive the eruption."

"That is good news," I said, thinking of the boy by the pine trees with the dirty feet, and the older girl with the abacus.

"Not this way either," Abigail said from in front of Chief Kirkland. She had been forced to come to a stop.

"There must be an exit," Chief Kirkland said. He proceeded to move around the edges of the orchard, feeling his way around like a mime and trying to occasionally push a foot through. Abigail took the opportunity to scale one of the pomegranate trees, on which red fruit hung on long stalks like elegant Christmas tree decorations. "We're a bit up from the harbor...I can see the statues on the piers...trading ships and fishing boats...warehouses... lots of activity... I suppose we'd have caused quite a commotion if we'd scrambled down the cliff face dressed like this and tried to board a ship or dive into the sea, right?" She jumped off as the branch swayed dangerously under her not-very-considerable weight.

"What if we retrace our steps *exactly*—that is, we back out of the orchard as if we were never here?" I asked, since no one else seemed to have any suggestions.

But History would not let us do that either.

Abigail and Kamal exchanged a look and a shrug and joined Helen, who, looking grateful for the respite, had lowered herself into the shade of one of the pomegranate trees after conceding, "We seem to be wedged in on all sides by historical paths that cannot be disturbed." Abigail picked up a plump pomegranate from the ground and started attacking it with her nails. I joined her.

The chief, having made another full circle, came back and sat down in defeat.

∞

"Does it matter who sent us here?" Helen asked, briefly looking up from her notebook. The linguistics professor was sketching what we could see of the town and its harbor to complement several photos Abigail had taken with the sixties Polaroid camera. ("We're here, might as well make ourselves useful," Helen had said.) I had helped her immobilize her injured arm by making a sort of a pillow of her purse by stuffing Abigail's green sweater into it. The notebook was propped up on her knee as she worked.

"Certainly it matters," said the security chief.

I was with him on that. If I was about to be flattened into nothing when the mountain blew up, I wanted to know who was to blame. Now that I'd had some time to think about it, I didn't believe that Dr. Rojas had done this to us. I said as much. It was a bit hard to explain why I didn't think it was his hand that had sent us here, but it came down to this—I'd always thought I was a good judge of character, especially when it came to the people in my administrative care.

Chief Kirkland looked unconvinced. "Mystery novels and crime shows aside, the person who's most likely to be guilty usually does turn out to be guilty," he said in what I'm sure he thought was a sensible statement. "The spouse. The company partner. The beneficiary of the will—"

"But Dr. Rojas is a theoreticist!" I objected.

"Meaning?"

"It's the experimentalists in our departments who tend to take matters into their own hands and hammer diplomas onto their office walls or put together office furniture, causing Maintenance to complain that their territory is being encroached upon. I can see Dr. Rojas mulling over murder as a theoretical problem, perhaps even deciding on it as an optimal solution, but to actually do it, to get his hands dirty—once for Dr. Mooney, and then again for us—very messy, to send five people into a ghost zone…"

"It's not a particularly elegant solution, is it?" said Abigail.

"Poor Erika Baumgartner," I said. "She won't get to go on her run. After what happened to us, Dean Sunder will probably cancel all runs for a while, maybe permanently. She might never get to snap color photos of eighteenth-century French fashions and publish them on the *Les Styles* blog."

The security chief did not seem to think it was the right time to worry about Dr. B. "She'll find something else to do."

I decided to add the main point in Dr. Rojas's favor. "We didn't actually see Gabriel operate STEWie, did we? The phone call. The one that got him to step out of the lab. Maybe someone sent him on a fool's errand while they snuck in and changed our destination."

"Or," the chief said, "Dr. Rojas set it all up and pretended to step out for Jacob Jacobson's benefit."

There was no way to counter that. I remembered Jacob's fingers moving speedily as he tweeted a play-by-play of the proceedings just before I sent him out of the room. It was certainly some kind of alibi.

For a while we sat in silence. Sounds of activity drifted up from the harbor, the shouts and banter of fisherman, sailors, and merchants, the *thwack* of cargo being loaded and unloaded. Closer by, the rhythm and pulse of building work in a nearby villa rung out in the still air; occasionally, we caught sight of a young, muscular local in a loincloth (he reminded me of the movers in Xavier's office) pushing a loaded wheelbarrow down the road, a pair of mangy dogs running around his feet. Helen jotted down some of the louder banter of the workmen, who were oblivious to our presence. It felt like an unseen hourglass hovered above us and the town, one only we knew about. And the sands were about to run out.

"Look, only a handful of motives cause people to turn to crime," the chief finally said. "We are all, every one of us, at the mercy of our emotions. The usual suspects, I find, are few: Greed. Jealousy. Desire. Fear. Desperation."

He listed them evenly, as if he'd never experienced any of them himself, which was ridiculous, of course. Everyone has. I had experienced at least four of them myself since we'd arrived—fear that I was going to die, a desperate desire to get home, jealousy of all the people at St. Sunniva who were safely snug in their offices and labs. Well, if he could keep it under control, so could I. "Five possible motives," I said as matter-of-factly as I could muster, "and five intended victims? Or was only one of us the target and the rest of us happened to be in the wrong place at the wrong time?"

"That's the question, isn't it? On the surface of things, it would seem that the most likely target was myself," the security chief said without a trace of vanity. "I am in charge of solving Dr. Mooney's murder." His voice deepened in thought. "Except that I don't know why anyone would feel the need to get rid of me. Everything I learned during my investigation of Dr. Mooney's murder was duly recorded by Officer Van Underberg and will be available to whoever replaces me on the job.

"If I wasn't the target, then our next possibility is you, Dr. Presnik," he added. "You have a particular connection to Dr. Mooney."

"My dear Chief Kirkland—perhaps we better dispense with the formalities if we are to be soon engulfed in a rain of rock and ash. I don't think I know your first name?"

"Nate."

"Nate, you mentioned a Wanda earlier. Is she a pet you have at home?"

The chief nodded. "A spaniel. Cavalier King Charles."

I hadn't expected him to have such a pedigreed dog. "I'm sure Officer Van Underberg will see to her," I reassured him. "The basket returned without us, so Dr. Rojas will sound the alarm immediately." He would do so whether or not he was the source of our current predicament.

"About your connection to Dr. Mooney—"

"What, that I used to be married to him? Other than work matters, I haven't said more than a passing hello to the man in years," Helen said.

I could not recollect Helen ever saying a passing hello to Xavier Mooney in the seven years I had been the dean's assistant.

The chief clarified. "I meant someone might have assumed Dr. Mooney had told you something in confidence."

"Like I said, we did not speak much."

The chief turned to Kamal and Abigail. "Moving on, then. I don't suppose you two saw anything around the lab that would have connected Dr. Rojas or anyone else to Dr. Mooney's murder? No? Did one of you come up with a brilliant scientific idea in tandem with the professor that someone might have wanted to steal?"

"I wish," said Kamal, watching a lizard dart across a boulder.

"Which brings me to you." The chief turned his square jaw toward me.

"What about me?"

"You've been nosing around, asking questions, isn't that true?" He sounded annoyed, like I had overstepped some boundary between civilian and soldier.

I wasn't going to deny it. "Dean Sunder asked me to see what I could find out. I talked to Oscar and also the cleaning staff in the TTE building, though I didn't learn anything of interest from them. I didn't mean to step on your toes, uh—Nate." Why shouldn't I call him by his first name? Besides, it wasn't my idea, it was Helen's.

"Did you—hold on a minute."

The offshore breeze had picked up and stirred the orchard foliage, briefly parting two of the fruited branches to reveal a small, circular stone wall overgrown with ivy. It supported a wooden shaft on which a rope and a bucket hung.

The chief sprung nimbly to his feet. (*He* hadn't had to do all that running in high-heeled boots and a tight skirt.) He picked up a pebble and tossed it through the invisible wall of History and into the well. I thought I heard a small splash.

"All right, then," he said. "I'm just going to get some water. I have no intention of leaving this sunny orchard…" He continued his commentary as he slowly and purposely headed for the well. "Quite happy to stay here, just need some water…"

Kamal pursed his parched lips and looked away. We were all desperately thirsty by now.

"I'm not sure History can hear you, Chief," Helen began. But the security chief had already been brought to a full stop by the invisible wall.

He came back, sat down without a word, and picked up where he had left off. "Dean Sunder asked you to see what you could find out."

"He relies on me to solve problems, small or large, that make their way into the dean's office."

"Well, did you find out anything that you haven't told us?"

I shook my head, uneasily recalling how I had stood looking over Dr. Rojas's shoulder at his workstation's screen, the window into STEWie's innards, which had revealed the fact that Dr. Mooney had been scattered across time on purpose. I hadn't understood any of the information on the screen, but if Dr. Rojas had something to hide, he might have forgotten that not everyone who spent time around the TTE lab had savvy computer skills. I shook the thought off. No, I was sure he wasn't responsible. Besides, why would he tell us that Dr. Mooney's run had been sabotaged if he had been the one to do it? "If I had found something out, I would have said so."

The chief studied me for a moment, but instead of pushing me further, he moved the conversation along. "Well, one of us must have seen *something*. Kamal, you were probably the last person to talk to Dr. Mooney, other than the murderer."

Kamal looked pained, like he should have noticed whatever it was that he was supposed to have seen. "We exchanged a few words about the scheduled calibration, then I said good night and headed home in the snow. I miss snow." He licked his dry lips. "I ended up pulling an all-nighter for Dr. Little's exam."

"And you, Abigail?" the security chief asked.

"I had exams all day Monday and spent the evening in the library, finishing a project. I didn't come into the lab until Tuesday morning."

"But you did go into Dr. Mooney's office this week," I said.

"What's this?" the chief asked, sitting up under the pomegranate tree and bumping his head on one of the lower branches.

Abigail, sounding embarrassed, explained how she had gone into Dr. Mooney's office after his memorial and spent some time looking at the books, photos, and musical instruments the professor had collected on his time travels. She pulled apart another pomegranate to expose its honeycomb interior of bright red seeds and white pith and offered Kamal a segment. He looked a little green at the prospect of sucking on more of the tart pomegranate seeds. "The didgeridoo was missing. That was odd, I suppose," Abigail went on. "But I did tell you about it, Julia."

"And I told Chief Kirkland."

"What's this about the didgeridoo being missing?" Helen asked, puzzled.

"It wasn't in his office," I explained.

"The instrument's absence was duly noted in Officer Van Underberg's notes. That can't be why we were targeted. But I wonder if someone watched you go into Dr. Mooney's office, Abigail, and perhaps thought you were on to something—but what?" Chief Kirkland swore under his breath. "None of this makes sense."

Helen shook her head. "Not in the least, my dear Chief."

∞

A warm, breezy evening approached. Occasionally we'd hear the rattle of a cart returning from town and the drivers' banter; then the cart would pass and there would be another period of silence. Activity in the harbor had mostly ceased. The repetitive *swoosh* of the sea as it gently washed against the rocky shore drifted up to the ridge. Stars had started to come into view, a whole lot of them, like coarse salt crystals shaken onto a dark tablecloth.

Kamal tossed a picked-over pomegranate shell through the invisible barrier History had placed around us and said, "Pretty."

The entire Astronomy Department would have given an arm and a leg for this view. The moon had not risen yet. Faint pinpoints of light on Vesuvius's slopes revealed the locations of villas and farmhouses. The mountain carved a tipless triangle into a sky alive with stars, unspoiled by light pollution from headlights, streetlamps, and overilluminated car dealerships. I thought about home. Quinn wouldn't have to bother with the divorce paperwork, a temp would take over my work duties until a permanent replacement could be found, Wanda the spaniel would need a new home.

I was about to say something befitting the moment when Helen turned on the light on her wristwatch and said, "I'd like to set it to local time—nine o'clock, perhaps? I've been trying to remember what time the eruption started, as described in Gaius Pliny's account."

"Too bad I didn't choose Mount Vesuvius as my project for Dr. Mooney's Ghost Zones in Time: How to Find Them and

Avoid Them," Abigail said. "We might have a better idea what time of day the eruption occurred, right? No, I had to go and choose Tunguska."

Helen sounded as if Abigail had just leveled an accusation of incompetence at her. "When you read as much history as I do, Abigail, the details sometimes get put aside, but I assure you—"

"Oh, I didn't mean that, Dr. Presnik—"

We were all tired, snippy, and in need of food, water, and a safe haven far from the danger of the volcano.

"Perhaps you better put the watch away, Dr. Presnik. For blending-in purposes," Kamal said, coming to Abigail's rescue. He had been periodically getting to his feet to check if the invisible wall was still there and he got up to do so again.

"I usually do not permit students to address me by my given name, but given our situation you can call me Helen, Kamal. You, too, Abigail."

"Okay, Helen," Abigail obliged.

"Everyone—most everyone—calls me Julia already," I said.

The security chief cleared his throat and said, "How's it looking, Kamal?"

Kamal was at the edge of the orchard, on the side where the builders were working, trying to poke his foot through. We heard him give a small cheer.

"They're gone," he called out. "The guys working on the addition to the villa."

Chief Kirkland scrambled to his feet. "Is that why we've been stuck here? Until the workers finished up for the day?"

"Who knows what kept us from leaving this place?" Helen said, joining him. "Quite often it happens that one simply does not know."

The first thing we did was to lower the bucket into the blackness of the well and, after some effort, as there only seemed to be a shallow pool of water at the bottom, gratefully drink. The water was lukewarm, not cool like I had expected, and tasted vaguely of earth.

The second thing we did was walk over to the edge of the cliff. Below us, the steep path ended on a flat coastal plain and disappeared into the darkness of a rocky shore. We could see the outline of the harbor docks, the statues adorning them like still ghosts in the night. Figures holding pinpricks of light moved among the statues and on the decks of the ships.

"On reflection, I'm not sure the harbor is a good idea," Helen said. "Even at night, there will be crews attending to ships and their cargo. How would we manage to sneak on board?"

The chief nodded. "All right then. We head out on foot and find a road that leads away from Pompeii and Vesuvius. Which way is Rome? All roads can't lead there, regardless of the saying."

"Rome, yes. Northwest from here, probably a good week's worth of travel up the coast. But even if we manage to obtain a horse and cart, we won't necessarily be able to take any road we want—I don't know if we can get far enough from the mountain in time—"

15

"Why aren't we dead?"

The security chief lifted the fedora, which he'd angled over his eyes during the night, and addressed our small party. Stubble covered the lower half of his face, under eyes puffy with little sleep.

It was an apt question, given that we were in a tomb and it was morning.

Kamal ran a hand across his hair—it continued to stand straight up—and said, "I noticed that, too. We're not dead."

"I've been thinking," Helen said. "By the way, my arm feels better. I think it was just a sprain. My neck, however—" She stretched her neck from side to side and added in a thoughtful tone, "We seem to be early."

Yesterday, as we left the pomegranate orchard behind, I'd pictured us rousing the nearest sleeping household, explaining the danger (Helen would need to be our spokesperson), and accepting the thanks of the grateful family and a horse and cart we could use to zigzag our way to Rome through History's maze.

But darkness—and History—had defeated us.

With only my cell phone and Helen's watch to serve as faint flashlights, we proceeded unsteadily through the unfamiliar terrain in the moonless night. The first villa we attempted to enter by knocking on the gate in its property wall may or may not have accommodated a horse and cart within. We never found out. The same for the second. Each time, History would permit us to reach the gate, but we were unable to raise a hand to knock. We could only pass by like ghosts, unseen by the inhabitants inside as they slept peacefully in the warm Pompeii night.

We found ourselves back on the street of tombs, the one with the telling tablet bearing the town's name. Silently admitting defeat and agreeing that the sturdy stone walls of a tomb would offer us more protection from the volcano's wrath than an open road, we chose a house-shaped one whose shadowy, eerie niches held stone busts of those interned inside.

In the utter, disconcerting blackness of the tomb, the silence punctuated only by an occasional cough or exhalation by one of us, we settled in to wait out the night. The volcano would do what it would. We couldn't do a thing about it. I leaned back against the cool stones of the tomb wall and let my mind drift back over the events of the past week. I almost felt like something *had* been nagging at me—something about that unfortunate Tuesday when Kamal had brought the news about Dr. Mooney. Was it something he had said? Or something that I had heard or seen later in the day but hadn't internalized, distracted as I was by the day's events? Not a new piece of information, more like a reminder of something I had already known… No, there was nothing. I gave up trying to figure it out and let my mind drift off into tired nothingness.

Every disturbance outside, whether it was the shouts of drunken tavern patrons just inside the town gate or the clatter of cart wheels as dawn neared, jolted us out of an uneasy sleep and had us peering out of the tomb.

Now it was morning and we were still alive. Very much so. My stomach growled with pressing hunger. The locals seem to be early risers and the increasingly familiar rattle of carts drifted into the tomb. We'd chosen it because of its size—it was bigger than the altar-shaped ones around it and had four sturdy walls and a roof. A family tomb, I decided; the six stone busts outside, in the niches above the archway, shared a name: *Nigidius*. A shaft of light streaming through the archway illuminated the prints of our twenty-first-century shoes in the dirt. Garland-decorated urns sat in the equidistantly spaced niches above our heads. In one corner was an object that I'd assumed in the dark to be a small bench, but the morning sunlight had revealed it to be an intricately carved wooden chest with a vase or urn on top. Kamal was sitting with his back against it.

My stomach growled again and I suddenly remembered the snack I usually carried in my shoulder bag. What was the matter with me? I wasn't thinking straight. I unsnapped the bag and started to rummage. "Wallet, keys, notepad, tissues—those might come in handy—cell phone… Here we go."

The package had gotten sandwiched between my cell phone, which was *way* out of range and whose signal bars were simply flat, and the bottom of the bag. I turned off the phone to conserve whatever was left of the battery and popped the plastic package open. Five thin crackers and cheddar cheese in a separate compartment, highly processed and an unnatural yellow. I gave everyone a cracker and we took turns dipping them into the cheese. It was not much of a meal, but it was something. The cheese, softened by the summer heat into a gooey mess, was particularly delicious. Then again, at that point anything would have been.

"I don't know if this is worthy of the name *cheddar*," the chief said, "but I'm glad you had it in your bag."

"Do you have any more, Julia?" Kamal asked, licking cheese off his finger.

I shook my head.

"I think," Helen repeated, "that we're too early. For the eruption."

Nate lost interest in the cheese. "Hold on. You said the date seemed right, judging by the bonfires and all."

"I think yesterday *was* the twenty-fourth of August."

"Then—?"

"But I believe we may have gotten here weeks, if not months, before the eruption. Whoever sent us here hasn't spent much time reading recent journal articles about Pompeii."

"Let's assume it was Dr. Rojas for argument's sake," the chief said.

"I don't like to assume, but if you insist. Gabriel—or whoever did this to us—may have thought he was sending us into a ghost zone. August 24 has long been assumed to be the date given by Pliny the Younger in his two letters to the historian Tacitus. But the letters, written a quarter of a century after the eruption, have been lost. We only have medieval copies—ones made by hand, of course, which is a far from perfect process, especially where Roman dates are concerned. Pompeii residents fleeing the town who didn't make it"—she winced—"left behind impressions in hardened ash that suggest they were wearing heavy, warm clothes. And even if we assume that they overdressed to protect themselves from the ash, there is also the question of winds. High-level winds blow inland in the summer and toward the sea in the fall—and the ash cloud dispersal pattern carved into the landscape suggests fall winds, according to an article I read recently. I feared the worst when we found out that we were in Pompeii. It seemed inevitable that the twenty-fourth of August was the correct date after all. Ironically, I had planned on proposing a run to definitely determine Vesuvius's eruption date."

She added, "If it *was* Gabriel, he clearly forgot his own unspoken fifth rule—*Always check your dates.*"

The chief asked with some disbelief, "He meant to drop us into the middle of the eruption, but miscalculated? What about the tremors we've been feeling?"

"They must be just early precursors."

"Are we sure about this?" I asked. I noticed that my voice sounded rather high. "All this yo-yoing is starting to get to me. First we thought we were in a ghost zone, then we decided we weren't, then we decided we were after all, and now it turns out we aren't?"

"Seems like it," Kamal said.

"But why did the basket return without us, then?" Abigail was sitting with her knees drawn up to her chest, her back against the wall.

Helen shook her head. "That I do not know. But I do know this—if History had dropped us into a ghost zone because of a STEWie equipment malfunction or software glitch, it wouldn't have gotten the date wrong and we'd be dead by now. Which proves, once and for all, that there is a human hand behind this. Perhaps Gabriel's, perhaps not. Either way, I'm afraid we're on our own. We might be stuck in the past," she continued, her voice strengthening, "but whoever did this hasn't succeeded in killing us."

"Hear, hear!" Kamal said. "Not yet, anyway."

"I've thought of something." I hesitated, then went on reluctantly. "There have been rumors, well-substantiated ones, that Dr. Rojas and Dr. Mooney were up for a Nobel Prize next year. This sounds stupid—but perhaps Dr. Rojas didn't want to share."

"How would Dr. Mooney's dying change that?" the chief asked.

"You can't get a Nobel Prize posthumously. And there is money involved. Quite a bit of it." My firm conviction that Dr. Rojas couldn't possibly be the murderer temporarily forgotten, I scrambled to my feet. "If that's the case, let's make sure he doesn't get the Nobel Prize. Let's make sure that justice, at least, is served. There must be a way to send a message back and let everyone at St. Sunniva know what happened. After that—well, we can make our way to Rome and fashion some kind of lives for ourselves."

"Hear, hear!" Kamal repeated. "I've always wanted to try my hand at being a gladiator. Just kidding. What did scholarly types do in ancient Rome? Scroll copying? Library tending? Teaching little Romans?"

Even the chief seemed carried away by the moment. I could tell that the state of inaction we had been subjected to since yesterday afternoon had started to get to him. He pushed himself up to his full six feet something. "Sounds like a plan. A note letting them know what happened, perhaps with the guilty party's name. You say we're safe for the moment, Helen?"

"More than a moment. Until the fall, it seems, which will give us plenty of time to get to Rome."

By now we were all on our feet. Though we were doomed to stay in far time, it felt good to have a goal, even one as strange as trying to fashion a message that would outlast us by two thousand years.

∞

Kamal disposed of the cheese-and-cracker container in the plastic bag that Helen had brought along in her purse ("I don't like to leave trash items, however small, behind me on time runs," she'd told us) and said, "The crackers made me even thirstier. I'm glad the volcano won't kill us any minute now, because it means we can concentrate on important matters of survival, like finding food and water."

He had a point. A weight had been lifted off our shoulders—being stuck in the past with no way of getting back home seemed like small potatoes in comparison to being caught in a mammoth eruption—but it had also brought into sharp relief our immediate bodily needs.

We'd all taken turns using impromptu bathroom facilities in the overgrown area behind the tomb as the sun rising above the mountain ridge to the east did away with the cool crispness of the dawn. We had no choice but it still felt wrong—we had essentially spent the night in a cemetery and were now defiling it. It didn't make me feel any better that the area was already filled with plenty of trash and donkey and dog refuse.

"Maybe there's something useful in here." Kamal was on his knees by the wooden chest. He lifted the vase off, looked inside, and tipped it over. Dried rose petals, their original white yellowed with time and desiccation, fluttered to the floor. Setting the vase aside, he swept a thin layer of dust off the chest lid with the hem of his T-shirt, and opened it. We all leaned forward to look. Two matching bronze pots and a stoppered bottle made of thick glass sat upright on a length of folded brown wool. "Lamps and"—he uncorked the bottle and took a sniff—"oil for the lamps. Olive oil." He clicked his tongue in disappointment.

"This is Roman Pompeii. It will have fountains," Helen reassured him.

"I'll be glad to get away from this street of tombs," I said. "It's a little creepy."

"Romans always built their tombs outside town walls—the town itself is only for the living. We do something similar, if you think about it," Helen said. "We place our dead in carefully tended cemeteries, strictly separate from the rest of our lives, only to be visited on anniversaries and special occasions. No one wants to be reminded of death."

Kamal had lifted out the two bronze lamps. They were shaped like a left foot and a right foot, with a loop handle in the heel and a hole in each big toe for the wick and flame. Next he pulled out the brown woolen cloth on which the lamps had sat. Underneath was a second one. He shook each of them in turn, raising a cloud of dust, and coughed. "Cloaks."

"Those things will come in handy," the chief said. "The dead don't need them. Survival is our highest priority."

"Not mine," Helen said. "We have a responsibility toward future archaeologists to disturb ancient sites as little as possible."

"If we take them, are we sure we're not depriving some poor soul of light and protection during the eruption when it comes?" I somewhat agreed with Nate, but still felt compelled to ask.

"I can't guarantee that," Helen said after a moment. "All I can tell you is that History would not have let us enter the Nigidii tomb if our being here would significantly impact someone's life. This tomb might be destroyed in the eruption, or buried under layers of ash only to be looted by vandals, or left untouched until excavated in our own time—or possibly as yet undisturbed. Still, I suppose we need the cloaks to get into town. We can put them back when we are done. They might be needed for a family ceremony. We'll have to go in pairs so that we can all get water," she added.

We decided that Helen, with her academic-if-not-vulgar knowledge of Latin, should go through the town gate first. Kamal, who seemed to be the thirstiest of us, would accompany her, then Abigail and I would go, and finally Helen or Abigail would pay the town a second visit with the chief.

"I'll see if I can confirm the date. I wonder if people will find it odd if I asked if Titus has just succeeded his father as emperor." Helen pulled the cloak over her head, adjusted the hood, then ran her fingers through her long silver hair in an effort to untangle the knotted strands. I could have used a comb myself.

Kamal pulled the other cloak over himself, and he and Helen headed out and seamlessly became part of the street-of-tombs activity, a slice of which we could observe through the low arched door of the Nigidii tomb. A few locals milled about, presumably paying their respects at family tombs; merchants readied wares to supply the tomb visitors; weary animals pulling carts loaded with jars and wicker baskets holding farm produce passed us on their way into town, trying to beat the heat of the day. The cloaks were not quite long enough to cover Helen and Kamal's shoes as the street took them in the direction of the town gate. Helen's orange pumps looked particularly noticeable as they peeked out from under her cloak.

As the three of us sat down to wait, I asked Abigail, "I don't suppose we could chisel a message into stone and bury it for someone to find and pass on to Dr. Mooney—letting him know to bring an armed guard that fateful Monday night? Or a message telling ourselves not to step into STEWie's basket?"

It wasn't easy to come to terms with the fact that we were permanently stuck in the past. The basket was gone. No one was coming. I threw out the questions even though I already knew the answers.

She shook her head. "It wouldn't work. If we did write a message telling Dr. Mooney to bring an armed guard with him, events would conspire so that the message wouldn't be found until *after* Dr. Mooney's murder and our getting stuck here. We can't change stuff that's already happened, right? So it doesn't matter whether we chisel our message into stone in Latin or write it in pen on notebook paper in English. The note won't be found before it *can* be found."

The security chief got to his feet and started to pace the small tomb, muttering to himself. "We need to tell them to question Gabriel Rojas and everyone else who had the door code in connection with the murder of Dr. Mooney. Maybe the guilty party could also be charged with attempted assault with a deadly weapon—a volcano?"

Abigail unzipped her tiny backpack and tore a blank page of graph paper out of a lab notebook. She looked around for a handy surface to write on and settled on the wooden chest, sitting down cross-legged by it. She thought for a moment, then slowly wrote down a short paragraph in neat block letters with the Sharpie she had brought along in anticipation of a Beatles autograph. I was reminded that hers was a generation that didn't have much use for cursive, or handwriting itself really. "I still think he's too nice to do anything of the sort, but…" She passed the note to me. I read it, then passed it on to the chief, who read it aloud:

FORWARD THIS MESSAGE TO ST. SUNNIVA CAMPUS SECURITY. DR. ROJAS SCATTERED DR. MOONEY ACROSS TIME, THEN SENT TO POMPEII GHOST ZONE THE FOLLOWING PEOPLE: DR. HELEN PRESNIK, SECURITY CHIEF NATE KIRKLAND, JULIA OLSEN, KAMAL AHMAD, AND ABIGAIL TANNER.

The chief shook his head. "I don't know about Dr. Rojas being too nice to commit murder, but there is such a thing as presumption of innocence, Abigail."

We left it at that.

Helen's eyes shone with wonder when she and Kamal returned a half hour later. It took her a moment to get the words out.

"Marvelous, my dears, *marvelous*. The people, the buildings, the smells, the *colors*…a historian's dream. We went a little way into town and peeked into shops and doorways. I wish I had my audio recorder. I want to take notes on the local dialect. And photos with Abigail's Polaroid camera."

"Of us?" I asked as Helen pulled the cloak off over her head and passed it to me. "To include with the message Abigail wrote?"

Helen caught sight of Abigail's message where it lay on the wooden chest, read it, and raised an eyebrow. "I'll see if I can reword it. The photos wouldn't be of us but of the town—for future archaeologists, should STEWie be put out of commission because of what has happened. I'd like to visit the Forum, the Amphitheater, the public baths…Kamal and I didn't make it that far in before History stopped us, just a block or two. I think it was the shoes."

"Money," Kamal spoke for the first time since he and Helen had bent their heads to reenter the tomb. "We need local money. We passed a bakery. It smelled so good—" He rolled his eyes upward.

Abigail cocked her head. "I've got an idea. Julia, do you mind if Kamal goes again with me?"

"Well—all right." I handed her the cloak.

"Of the two future Nobel Prize winners, whose name would have come first?" the security chief asked as Abigail readied herself. I noticed that his eyes were still fixed on the note.

"Dr. Mooney," Kamal said without hesitation.

I sat down on the wooden chest and thought for a moment. "It's the eternal question, isn't it—which came first, theory or experiment? The two of them attacked the question of time travel from complementary directions—Xavier Mooney was a tinkerer and Gabriel Rojas is more interested in the theory of it all, so they made a good pair, wouldn't you say, Helen? It took them years to get STEWie up and running, theory propping experiment, experiment propping theory. Along the way Dean Sunder lent them as much support as he could in the form of grants." I added, "The dean brought on two junior professors to expand the program and inject some fresh ideas into it now that we're about to have competition from the bigger schools. Dr. Erika Baumgartner—Abigail's advisor—has a joint appointment with the History of Science Department. Dr. Steven Little—you remember him from the TTE meeting, Chief Kirkland, on the short side, sweater-vest—"

"I know him."

"Despite the name of the lab—Time Travel Engineering—he's the first professor with an engineering background to actually work on the project. Both he and Dr. Baumgartner are impatient to prove themselves. It made for somewhat of an awkward quartet, I suppose. Dr. Little, in particular—"

Kamal interjected, "Dr. Little seems to channel Ernest Rutherford," as he helped Abigail wiggle into the cloak, which was a couple of sizes too large for her.

"Who?" Chief Kirkland asked.

"The father of nuclear physics," Kamal answered, the unsaid *of course* hanging in the air.

"Ah, *that* Ernest Rutherford," the chief said. (One of the first tasks I had set for myself after being hired as the science dean's assistant was to read up on my science history. I began with the names that graced the science buildings, all of them of women: Mary Anning, Marie Curie, Emmy Noether, Hypatia of Alexandria, Rosalind Franklin, Ada Lovelace, Maria Mitchell. I was by now quite well versed in the subject.)

"Lord Rutherford was of the opinion that physics is the only real science and that the rest is just stamp collecting." Kamal snorted. "Ironically, the Nobel Prize he went on to receive was in chemistry, for his work in radioactivity."

"And he ended up *being* on a stamp, in his native New Zealand. Serves him right for being so mean to everyone else," Abigail said, pulling her cloak tight around her. It dragged on the ground behind her by a good inch.

"Steven Little has been doing simulations to try to figure out if time travel runs can be implemented in parallel," I said. "So far the answer seems to be no."

"Apparently you can't have two STEWie baskets side by side in the same time period," Kamal explained further.

"And Erika Baumgartner?" the chief asked.

"She has a lot of Dr. Mooney in her. For her, STEWie isn't about the physics of time travel, but about what you can *do* with it. She's been researching the lives of eighteenth-century scientists as she works on optimizing landing zones in that century. She has each of her graduate students pick a historical figure from that era."

"She gave me a choice of several scientists," said Abigail, "including Gauss, Euler, and Fahrenheit. I suggested Marie-Anne Lavoisier. Dr. B pointed out that Marie-Anne wasn't considered a true scientist. I countered that that made her an interesting research subject—if Antoine was the father of modern chemistry, was she the mother? She made sketches and kept records of her husband's experiments and translated chemistry texts into French for him to read. I know *I* wouldn't be able to translate a scientific text unless I knew a lot about the subject. It took a while to convince Dr. B to give me the chance."

"Could she have wanted to steal your idea for herself?" the chief asked.

"It's not that big of an idea as far as time travel research goes. Plus she gets her name on all journal articles I publish in any case, right?"

"But your name would be listed first," I pointed out. Every journal article published by a graduate student had the advising professor's name on it, too. And Erika Baumgartner had a large contingent of graduate students. Which wouldn't hurt come Dr. B's final tenure review a few years down the line. Still, the journal articles where your name was the first one listed were the ones that really mattered.

The chief looked over at me. "Hardly seems like enough to justify trying to murder five people."

I shrugged. "The tenure process is, well, what it is."

"Plus it wouldn't explain what happened to Dr. Mooney."

Helen offered a frank evaluation of the four TTE professors, starting with her ex-husband. "Xavier tackled research problems on his feet and with his sleeves rolled up. Gabriel is more the sit-down-and-think-about-it type. As to Erika—she attacks problems head-on and sometimes too fast, in my opinion. It's like she feels she doesn't have the luxury of taking her time. The pressure of a tenure-track position, I suppose. And Steven Little solves problems virtually by running simulations and doesn't seem to want to have much to do with people, students or otherwise. That last bit is, like with Erika, probably due to the pressures of a tenure-track position," she allowed charitably.

"Junior professors tend to mellow up a bit once they achieve tenure," I said. Noticing that I had dirt streaks on my skirt, I attempted to swat them off.

"I don't think I have, Julia, have I? You should see some of the things my students have written on their class evaluations.

Really, all I want is for them to perform their best, but much of the time they'd rather be surfing the Internet or partying. All in all, though, I'd rather set the bar too high than too low."

"So Xavier Mooney and Gabriel Rojas are the old guard," the chief summarized, "and Erika Baumgartner and Steven Little the new. It can't be easy trying to make your mark in the shadow of two potential Nobel Prize winners. Or to have young colleagues trying to muscle in with new ideas."

"I don't know if I'd put it quite that way," I objected. "And that doesn't mean one of them did away with Xavier—"

"A fish is most likely to be eaten by another fish," the security chief said somewhat cryptically as Abigail and Kamal headed out.

∞

The grad students returned carrying something my nose registered before my eyes did. Bread. Round, about the size of a dinner plate, and marked into wedges by a design on the top. The sweet, yeasty aroma made my stomach growl with hunger. "Where did you get that?" I asked the pair as Kamal wiped his hands on his shirt (a useless gesture in terms of getting them clean, since his shirt was equally grungy). He proceeded to break the bread into sections and pass them all around.

It was Abigail who answered, mouth full. "I—yum—distracted the bakery shopkeeper while Kamal borrowed the loaf."

"Borrowed the—Abigail! Kamal!" Helen chastised them, shocked.

"You should have seen her," said Kamal, who didn't seem chagrined at all. "She all but fluttered her eyelashes at the baker." He offered the professor a wedge. "Dr. Presnik, if any of our actions threatened to significantly impact someone's life or change History, we wouldn't be able to undertake them. You know that."

"Still—one does not alter one's morals according to the difficulty of the circumstances, Miss Tanner and Mr. Ahmad."

It seemed to me that the opposite was true and that sometimes circumstances did need to dictate our actions. The bread must have been fresh out of the oven, and its oatmeal-white interior was warm and dotted with nuts and raisins. Suddenly realizing how ravenous I was, I attacked the piece. Kamal and the security chief proceeded to dig in as well.

After a moment, Helen relented and took a bite. "I've always felt that our researchers should carry along a bag of gold nuggets for emergencies. When we get our hands on a denarius or two—no, I don't have any ideas yet about how we can do that—we'll go back and reimburse the baker."

"Fair enough," the chief said through a full mouth. For a police officer, he sure didn't seem too bothered by the idea of consuming stolen goods.

∞

While the chief and I got ready for our expedition into town, Abigail tore up the note she'd written blaming Dr. Rojas. Using a pen from her purse, Helen reworded the note in neat cursive:

> *Finder, please convey this message to Campus Security, St. Sunniva University, Minnesota. Marooned in Pompeii ghost zone. August 25, year 79. Presnik, Kirkland, Olsen, Ahmad, Tanner.*

"There," she said. "Let them sort out the details at their end."

Next we needed something to encapsulate the note so that it would be protected from the destructive elements it would face.

Helen's purse turned out to be pristinely clean. All it held was more paper, pencils for sketching, pens for notes, and the plastic bag into which we'd placed Abigail's crumpled-up note and the rest of our trash, mostly strips and backing from the Polaroid films.

The camera took up most of Abigail's backpack. There was also an extra pack of film, the useless Callback, and her research notebook.

Nate and Kamal had nothing in their pockets.

From my shoulder bag I pulled out my wallet and matching change purse, the cell phone, a couple of black-ink pens, a dozen paperclips, and a list of names, the first pass at the guest list for Dean Sunder's annual π-day cocktail party (π being 3.14, the party was held on March 14, which also, in a cosmic coincidence, happened to be Albert Einstein's birthday). I shook the shoulder bag but nothing else came out except for a palm-full of cracker crumbs and a piece of gum that had come loose from its packaging and was covered with lint.

"I really should clean my bag more often," I said, slightly embarrassed.

But the others weren't even looking in my direction. Their eyes were fixed on something in Kamal's hand.

"Perfect!" Abigail said. Kamal had retrieved the empty cheese-and-cracker package from the bag in Helen's purse.

"We're going to bring someone to justice using trash?" I asked.

Nate snapped the package open and shut a few times. "Why not? This should last a good while."

"Long enough for our purposes, I imagine." Helen sighed at the thought of contaminating an archeological site. "Assuming the plastic doesn't melt in one of Vesuvius's eruptions, that is."

"Eruptions?" I said. "There'll be more than one?"

"Besides the upcoming one? Yes, there will be other, smaller ones through the centuries. One as late as 1944. We'll have to choose a hiding place well."

"Why don't we slip it into one of those urns?" Abigail suggested, pointing to one of them.

"Abigail!" I exclaimed, shocked. "Somebody's ashes are in that."

Helen took my spot on the wooden chest as I donned one of the cloaks. "Let me think about this. We need a hiding place that will be safe from the force and heat of the eruption, once it comes, and all of the subsequent ones, too. The note must stay undisturbed for two thousand years. From what I remember about Pompeii's history, there was looting immediately after the eruption by rightful owners, thieves, and treasure seekers, who dug tunnels into the ash and looked either for their own valuables or those of others. In time both Pompeii and Herculaneum were forgotten… In the early eighteenth century, a villager digging a well came across marble—Herculaneum's theater, as it turned out—and excavations began. Pompeii's Forum and Amphitheater have long been excavated and well explored, so we can't hide a message there." She wrinkled her nose in thought. "I can try to remember which houses are currently undergoing excavation…the House of the Painters at Work…the House of the Chaste Lovers…but, to be honest, I have no idea how we'd figure out where they are in AD 79 without a modern map of the site."

Chief Kirkland and I left while she was still puzzling out the problem. Even though my cheeks were sunburned from yesterday's wanderings around the foot of Mount Vesuvius, the sun felt pleasant on my face as we walked toward the town gate.

"There is a fountain just inside," Helen had instructed us. "Go straight in, you can't miss it."

I adjusted my cloak. The itchy brown wool was musty and smelled like olive oil; I hoped fumes were the only thing it was harboring. On the plus side, keeping my balance on the large cobblestones was easier now that my boot heels were gone. After one of them had broken off, I had gotten rid of the other by whacking it against a stone. The chief had tried rubbing dust onto his black leather shoes in an effort to conceal their modernity, but his cloak reached well above his shins. In the end he'd removed his shoes and socks. "I hope I don't step on anything sharp," he'd said, rolling up his pant legs so they disappeared under the cloak. His calves, I noticed as we walked, were hairy and had round marks on them from the elastic in the socks.

As the chief and I passed under the town gate, I noticed that it seemed a little askew, perhaps due to displacement from recent earthquakes. The square building next to it was the town's water reservoir—the *castellum aquae,* Helen had called it. I could hear the gurgle of water as the aqueduct, which started in the mountains beyond the town and ran somewhere underneath our feet, emptied into the brick building. I reached out to touch one of the thin orange-red bricks of the castellum aquae, but was unable to do so, as if the mere gesture would have immediately pegged me as an intruder. We turned away and I asked the chief, "Which of our TTE professors do you suspect?"

With the caution of a law enforcement officer, he said, "Anyone can pull the trigger under the right circumstances. If one of them felt their survival or long-desired goals were at stake—well. It might not even have been personal. Do you understand what I mean?"

I didn't answer. I was too caught off guard. It was clear that I'd have to throw all my preconceived notions about life in a Roman town out the window. I'd been picturing toga-clad citizens standing around in fancy gardens dotted with gleaming white statues, debating the finer points of law and aqueduct building. What I saw was much different. The town teemed with life—shops, eateries, and workshops lined the narrow cobblestone street on both sides, shaded by the awnings and wooden overhangs of the cream-colored buildings whose terra-cotta roofs we'd seen from Mount Vesuvius. The men wore tunics and the women had on long dresses and wraps of ochre, red, blue—the colors fresh, the cloth, though not fancy, nothing like the long-faded, drab, depressing historical costumes one sees in museums. There was not a white toga in sight. Probably they were reserved for the upper crust, people who didn't do their own errand running. I expected that togas would be more plentiful around the Forum, which, according to Helen, stood on the opposite side of the town, facing the harbor.

"Here," said the chief. We waited for our turn at the fountain. A faucet protruded from the carving of a flask and emptied into a square tub. The water was cool and it tasted of the mountains, or so I imagined, as I cupped my hands under its flow and drank deeply, then splashed my face. As the chief took his turn, I noticed a peculiar wall painting above one of the shops. The subject matter made me raise an eyebrow but I decided not to point it out. "Let's keep walking," I suggested after Nate had splashed his face and taken his fill of the water. "The others will be waiting, but going in just a bit farther won't hurt."

"Yeah."

It was easy to see why the others had taken their time, too.

Brightly painted gods and goddesses stared at us from above shop entrances—a blue-gowned Venus on a chariot pulled by elephants, a plump Hercules wrestling a snake, Bacchus draped in a cloak of grapes, and a host of others I didn't recognize. Some had clearly been composed by experts, and others were just crude sketches. The colors were bold and brilliant—rich ochre, cornflower blue, warm red with a hint of orange... There were also the *other* decorations, a lot of them. I decided I'd have to ask Helen about that later. The street seemed to be a main one, with deep ruts worn into the paving stones by long years of cart traffic. It gradually sloped downhill and was narrow by modern standards. It was lined with a raised sidewalk, and a half a dozen steps, or three hops on the large stepping-stones that served as pedestrian crossings, would get you across it. The building facades were painted reddish orange up to head height and were covered with notices and signs for businesses. I spotted long cracks in the plaster here and there—more damage from the recent or past earthquakes.

Near a bakery (probably the one we owed money to) we stepped off the sidewalk onto a stepping-stone crossing, which allowed us to avoid the animal refuse, kitchen trash, broken pottery, fish bones, and other elements lodged among the cobblestones. The mixture had baked in the sun, releasing a foul smell. I imagined rain torrents rushing down the sloped street in the winter, washing the caked refuse in the direction of the sea.

A narrow side lane caught our eye and we turned into it, dodging a bucketful of slops that had been thrown from above. The side lane was quieter, with no shops fronting it, only back doors. A mousy-looking man with a line of warts down his nose worked in the shade of one of the walls, squinting at a half-finished line of text, a brush in one hand, a small pot of paint in the other. Graffiti? Or perhaps an ad or an election poster? I was curious, but my legs suddenly felt heavy again, stiff, like I had been transported to a planet with a stronger pull of gravity. I came to a stop with no choice in the matter.

"I'll never get used to this," the chief said next to me.

"Maybe we stand out because the street is mostly deserted?" I suggested in a low voice as we made a U-turn. "Or the sign painter might be a crux person—someone nameless, an ordinary local who is key to history in some fashion that they themselves will never know. It's almost like there's an impenetrable bubble around such a person, I remember Dr. Mooney saying."

"Or maybe it's simpler than that. We might have startled him and caused his hand to slip."

"Dr. Mooney would have probably pointed out that possibility, too."

As we merged again with the shoppers, merchants, and well-tanned children running about on the water-reservoir street, he asked, "You miss Mooney, don't you, Julia?"

It was the first time he had called me Julia. It was an odd moment for him to have chosen to do so, but life is full of odd, seemingly unimportant moments.

"A dean's assistant isn't supposed to have favorites," I said.

"If Gabriel Rojas wasn't the one who got rid of the professor, it must have been one of the others."

Earlier, he had asked me again about the door code to the TTE lab. "It's like I told you before," I'd replied. "The TTE professors and their grad students have the code, as well as our postdoc researchers. The cleaning staff. Professors and researchers from other departments with spots on the STEWie roster, like Helen here—"

"My code didn't work this time. Gabriel had to let me into the lab," Helen had said.

"New policy," I'd explained, smacking my head with the heel of my hand. "I'd completely forgotten to mention it, but the code had been changed after Dr. Rojas had found evidence of sabotage. The dean's office had been giving out the new code on a strict need-to-know basis. "I'd just started giving out the new code to teams with runs scheduled this week, starting with yesterday's for Dr. Baumgartner. Today's run would have been Dr. Little's. Tomorrow—Thursday back home—would have been Dr. May's from the History Department, but I hadn't gotten around to giving her the code." I added, "None of the students had the new code yet."

"I did," Kamal said. "Dr. Rojas gave it to me when I volunteered for this trip."

"Me, too," Abigail said. "And I gave it to Jacob. But only because he needed to go in and out and he was on the authorized list."

"No one suspects Jacob Jacobson," I said and continued talking as Nate opened his mouth to say something. "Did you give the code to any other students, Abigail? Sergei went home to St. Petersburg for the winter break, didn't he?"

"Dr. B wasn't too happy with him. And Tammy is still working at home because of the broken leg. Skiing accident."

Sergei and Tammy were Abigail's other office mates. Sergei was one of Erika's graduate students, and Tammy was Dr. Little's.

The chief had summarized. "So besides us, three professors had the new code—Rojas, Baumgartner, Little—and one student, Jacob Jacobson. I'm confident of one thing," the chief said, ending that conversation. "Between the five of us, we can figure out which of them did this and why. One of us must know something without realizing it."

It wasn't until we were strolling down a sunny Pompeii street, trying to do our best to fit in, that I noticed the worry lines etched onto his face. It dawned on me that he felt responsible for the five of us being here. I understood how he felt. I felt guilty for having let Abigail and Kamal climb into STEWie's basket.

The chief ticked off the names on his fingers. "Drs. Rojas, Baumgartner, Little; and one student, Jacob Jacobson. How I would love to sit each of them down and have a little conversation.

As it is—let's take them in turn. We've already talked about their backgrounds, but what are their flaws?"

"Flaws?"

"Yes. Everybody has at least one character flaw. Nothing wrong with that. It's what makes us human. One of these days I'll tell you all about my character flaws. Let's start with Gabriel Rojas. From what I've been told, he's a gentle man, happily married, devoted to his work and his wife and three grown sons. No one has said a bad word about him. So what's his personal flaw?"

I considered the mild-mannered, gray-haired Gabriel Rojas, who spent much of his time lost in thought. "Well, he tends to forget to show up for meetings and turn in department forms. That's about as far as his failings go, I'd say... Except for one thing. He's been reluctant to forgo the chalk and blackboard and embrace modern teaching methods like smartboards and online homework problems. He prefers to have his students take notes in class. By hand. He says it helps them think more deeply about knotty physics problems. We've tried suggesting that some changes might be in order, with no luck. I've heard that the students call him the Dinosaur. To be honest," I added, "the dean hasn't pushed very hard. The promise of a Nobel Prize doesn't come to St. Sunniva often—we're a small school. We take a lot of pride in Dr. Rojas's and Dr. Mooney's work. And with Dr. Mooney now gone—" I caught myself. My good opinion of him aside, Gabriel Rojas was still the most likely suspect. He had a motive, after all.

We passed a street shrine for a goddess holding a shield and a spear. I didn't recognize her, but her broad shoulders and height reminded me of the taller of our two junior TTE professors. "As far as Erika Baumgartner goes," I said, "she's eager to prove herself, helpful on committees, and stretched thin between her research load and her teaching load to the point where, rumor has it, her marriage is beginning to suffer." I could sympathize with that, I thought but didn't say. "She's taken to going for long jogs each morning—cross-country ski runs lately. As to a flaw—that's easy. An inability to ask for help, to admit that she has taken on too much."

"There's no weakness in asking for help, but sometimes it's hard to see that. Will it be easier for her to get tenure with Dr. Mooney gone?"

"You mean because of the empty spot? Possibly. I know Dr. Mooney did suggest to her in passing that she might want to cut down on her teaching load, and I suppose she could have interpreted that the wrong way. She might have thought he was implying she couldn't handle all the hats her position required—teaching, research, mentoring—and that he'd turn in a negative vote come tenure review."

"And Steven Little?"

"Rude to the point of being insufferable, avoids committees assiduously, and, like Erika Baumgartner, stretched thin between his research load and his teaching load. I haven't heard any rumors about *his* marriage, other than that he and his wife are expecting their first child in the spring. He came over from a postdoc position at Berkeley, where he was a small fish, but prolific in publishing journal articles." The image of the clean-shaven professor hunched over his keyboard in his trademark button-down vest, fingers moving swiftly, came to my mind. "I know that Dr. Mooney and Dr. Rojas have tried to get him to see the importance of more involvement with students and the rest of the faculty, with mixed results. I would say that's his flaw—Dr. Little always puts himself first. He often pounces on perceived inequalities in the assignment of STEWie roster spots."

"So he views the academic world as being an unfair place?"

"Which it is, in many ways. Things can get very political."

"Like the assignment of roster spots?"

"The assignments go through the dean's office and I sometimes have to juggle them and soothe frayed nerves, yes."

"And finally, Jacob Jacobson," he said as we shook our heads at a toothless jewelry hawker who had approached us hopefully, a multitude of medallions and amulets—gods, goddesses, and gladiators—hanging around his neck and both arms. He moved on down the street, continuing to call out the dubious merits of his wares.

"Jacob's navigating the pitfalls of graduate school as best as he can, I think. It's too early to say if he'll find a place for himself in academia. Not everyone is cut out for a PhD, and sometimes it's not even a matter of academic ability. Dr. Rojas aside, the stereotype of the mild-mannered professor working serenely in his lab for years on end doesn't apply anymore—if it ever did. Once Jacob chooses a research topic, he'll have to become skilled at actively seeking funds, guarding his results, publishing as much as possible…and somewhere in there he'll also need to learn how to run a lab and teach."

"And Jacob's flaw?"

"Too much twe—tweeting—"

I had come to a halt so abruptly the security chief ran into me.

"Julia, what—"

A familiar-looking donkey cart, loaded with sacks and pottery jars, was weaving its way up the street. The driver was walking beside the cart, his hand on the harness of one of the animals. The donkeys' hooves moved in rhythmic unison, but while the chestnut-colored one gave the impression of weary acquiescence, the spotted one occasionally strained against its harness as if it wanted to move faster. The bearded figure accompanying them seemed to be singing into the spotted donkey's ear, perhaps to calm him down.

I elbowed the security chief in the side and shaded my eyes against the sun in an effort to see better.

"What's gotten into you?" Nate whispered.

Then he, too, saw—or rather heard—what had stopped me in my tracks. The donkey guide's merry song was accompanied by the jingle of cart bells and the clang of iron-wood wheel on stone pavement.

I didn't recognize the tune that came to my ears. The words, however—

There's no such thing as empty space
    it jitters
    it foams
Wherever you roam
There's no such thing...

16

I opened my mouth to speak but no words came out. It wasn't that I was struck silent by the sight or at a loss for words. I knew exactly what I wanted to say—the words simply would not come out. My tongue was frozen, immobile. In a flash I realized what the problem was. History. I had been about to shout at the top of my lungs, in the middle of a crowded Pompeii street, in English.

I took a step forward and raised my hands.

The cart ground to a halt. The spotted donkey, its nostrils flaring, brayed a hee-haw at me.

I saw Nate open his mouth, then close it again. He looked at the bearded figure with its hand on the spotted donkey's mane, and back at me. I realized he had never met the professor in person and made an attempt to introduce them. The words would still not come out.

Standing still in the middle of the street like statues frozen in time, we were starting to attract attention. A raggedy child of indeterminate gender tugged on my sleeve and the donkey guide took a coin from the leather bag on his belt and passed it to the child, who gleefully took it and moved on.

The donkey guide, for his part, seemed positively annoyed to see us. He gestured with his head for us to follow him.

"Dammit," the bearded figure said with feeling after we turned the corner into the lane where the sign painter had been, which was now empty, a single line of text left behind drying in the sun. "I thought I made it quite clear that I didn't want to be found."

17

"Nate," I said, "this is Dr. Xavier Mooney, our missing TTE professor. Xavier, this is Campus Security Chief Nate Kirkland. I don't believe you've met."

The men shook hands.

Xavier Mooney, professor of physics and time travel engineering, saw me staring at his beard and said, "How long has it been since I left, Julia?"

"Eight days," the chief answered for me.

That didn't seem quite right. Xavier's gray hair, usually trimmed to a close crop, hung below his ears. He sported a salt-and-pepper beard and a deep tan. The tan carried from his face and arms past his thigh-length tunic to his bare legs, all the way down to his feet, which were enclosed in strappy leather sandals. He smelled vaguely like fish stew.

"Dr. Mooney, did I understand you correctly? You came here of your own accord?" Nate looked over the two donkeys and the cart's cargo—the cloth sacks and tall earthenware vessels—as if the answer might lie there.

"Let's drop the titles, doctor and such, shall we? We're a long way from the exalted halls of academia, unless you count the Greeks, of course, but Greece is far from here. Yes, I'm here of my own free will. I don't need rescuing. Now go away."

"We'd like to," I said. "It's a bit more complicated than that."

∞

Kamal was the first to notice the cart and its driver. He and Abigail were sitting cross-legged just inside the doorway of the Nigidii tomb. Abigail had her Polaroid camera out, as if they'd been furtively taking snapshots of passersby. Kamal got to his feet and nudged Abigail with one foot. I saw her mouth the word *What?* and then turn in our direction, the camera in hand. She slowly rose to her feet.

Helen poked her head out of the tomb at the commotion. I heard her emit a gasp as Abigail let the camera fall to the ground and tore out of the tomb, jolting to a stop in front of the cart. Both donkeys brayed in protest, bells jingling furiously. Abigail dodged the donkeys and ran into the professor's arms for a bear hug.

Helen stared at her ex-husband, framed in the tomb archway like an angry goddess.

"Xavier," she said with a touch more timbre to her voice than usual. "Not dead, then?"

"As you see, Helen." He added, looking down, "Let me breathe, child."

Abigail released the professor, but did not move away, as if she were afraid he might disappear again. "I was hoping for something like this when the same thing happened to us."

"Not quite the same thing. The professor came here of his own free will," Nate said, making it sound as if we were having a normal conversation.

"We thought you had been scattered across time, Xavier." This from Helen. "Couldn't you have left a note? It would have saved everyone a great deal of trouble. We had a memorial for you."

"You did? Did you go, Helen?"

"Xavier, you made a fool of all of us." Helen turned on her heels and stalked back into the tomb. If there had been a door to slam, she would have slammed it.

Xavier rubbed the spotted donkey's mane without seeming the least bit apologetic. "Really, I thought I was being perfectly clear. I left Scarlett unlocked in the bike bay for whoever wished to take her. I put all my affairs in order. My will has long been on file—I left everything to St. Sunniva. And I graded the final projects for my classes and left them on my desk. Julia, did you find them?"

I was sweating, in desperate need of a shower, and my boots were hurting my feet. I tugged at the shirt that was sticking to my back under the itchy cloak. "We found the graded projects, Xavier. A note clipped to them saying that you had decided to relocate into the past would certainly have been helpful."

He led the donkeys into the shade of the Nigidii tomb, tied the reins to a tree, and accompanied us inside. "I didn't want anyone stopping me or coming after me, pestering and badgering me to come back. I programmed the computer to erase my destination from memory by having it randomly move the mirrors after I left so that no one could trace me. How did you manage to find me?" He caught Helen's eye and went on. "The night I left, I folded my biking clothes on a lab chair—again, I thought I was being perfectly clear—changed into a tunic I had made, and left my watch, cell phone, and other small items in the locker."

"But Xavier," I had to ask, "Why on earth did you come here just as Vesuvius was about to erupt?"

He hesitated for the first time since we'd run into him.

"It's a bit of a long story. We can talk about it later."

"And why are you so tan?" I added.

"I've been here for six months."

"I thought you looked even older, Xavier," said Helen in a ringing voice from deep within the tomb.

"Time is relative," the lean, tanned professor said to a confused-looking security chief and me, his gray hair loose around his shoulders. Apparently, even though only eight days had passed back home, six months had passed for the professor. If I had been the type to clutch my brow, I would have. I was still trying to wrap my head around the fact that Dr. Mooney was alive.

"What is the date, Xavier?" Helen asked in a tone that reverberated around the tomb and could only be described as *glacial*.

"August twenty-fifth. The eruption would be in full force by now if the Pliny camp was correct. I had a hunch that they weren't, but still," he chuckled, "I spent a nervous afternoon and night peeking out of my room at any unusual sounds. A party of some kind was taking place in the tavern across the street and between the noise of the musicians and the intoxicated sailors, I think I must have opened the door of my rental room a dozen times during the night to look outside—"

"Your rental room?" the chief interrupted. I glanced down at the faint impressions our bodies had left on the dirt floor of the Nigidii tomb.

"I've been living the life of a trader. I made my way down from Britannia via Singidunum by foot and boat—or, at least, that's the story I've been telling. What I really did was step out of STEWie's basket just outside one of the town gates, with silks and spices to trade and a handful of coins. You have no idea how much planning it took to sneak everything past Oscar. I had to bring in the supplies bit by bit for several weeks and store them under my desk and behind the larger of the musical instruments."

"That explains the cinnamony smell in your office. Wait, is that why you took that sewing course? To make a tunic for yourself and sacks for the spices?" I asked. "I thought it was because you were trying to expand your social horizon."

Somewhere in the dark part of the tomb, Helen snorted.

"I knew that spices—saffron threads, cinnamon sticks, peppercorns—would fetch a good price on the market here. Silk, too. I ordered traditionally made silks and had them shipped to my house. There was quite a pile of stuff. If I could have figured out a way to pull it off, I'd have snuck a horse and cart into the TTE lab. I wrapped up my affairs, got everything ready, and stepped into STEWie's basket. Once I got here, I hid everything behind a tomb until I sold off a bit of the saffron and some silks and obtained rental quarters and the use of a cart."

"But why come *here*?"

Xavier sent a concerned look in the direction of Abigail, who was sitting on the wooden chest, arms wrapped around her knees. Then he caught Helen's eye as she came back into the sunlit part of the tomb.

"Well, Xavier?" she said sharply. "What is it?"

"I've been diagnosed with an immune system disorder. Crohn's. The details don't matter. I knew what it meant."

"No more time traveling? If so, that would have been the right decision," Helen said. "Because if there was a heightened risk that you could bring something back, even with the nasal and hand sanitizer and other precautions—"

"—like the plague, you mean? Modern antibiotics deal with the plague very effectively. Still, I didn't want to take the chance. I decided to find another way to be useful. The pursuit of knowledge would be better served not by sitting at my desk, I reasoned, but by relocating to the past and making a cache of photos and detailed notes for historians and archaeologists to find. I had so many destinations to choose from—I had been planning to look for al-Khwarizmi's *The Book of Sundials* before I was diagnosed, but in the end I chose Pompeii. I reasoned that I'd have significant physical and social freedom here—that the coming eruption would mean that I'd be able to move around freely and talk to people."

"That makes sense," said Kamal. "The freedom of movement part, I mean. Has it worked, professor?"

"Mostly, though perhaps not quite as well as I expected. How's your research going?"

Kamal's thesis topic was Safe Landing Zones in Neanderthal Eurasia.

"It's only been a week, professor, plus we've been doing test runs with a cranky tilapia because we thought something was wrong with the equipment."

"Right, right. Sorry about that. I had hoped that Dr. Little would take over as your advisor." Kamal looked aghast at the prospect. It seemed like Xavier was just beginning to realize how much his departure had affected everyone at St. Sunniva.

"Were you planning on leaving for Rome as the eruption day neared, then? To document their contribution to science or something of the sort?" I asked.

"The Romans?" He snorted. "Don't get me started. They wouldn't recognize a mathematical proof if it tapped them on the shoulder. No, my intent was to, uh, make my way from here to Alexandria, then perhaps the Levant, Greece, China…"

Kamal started at the mention of Alexandria, as Egypt (albeit an Egypt that was two thousand years in the future) was home to him. "You'll get to see the lighthouse," he said with wonder.

"We might get to see it, too, right?" Abigail said.

Xavier turned to Nate.

"Chief—Kirkland, is it? I'm glad to see you here."

"Well, thank you, but—"

Xavier raised a hand. "I don't know how you found me. It doesn't matter. We're in sore need of an investigator. A crime has just been committed."

18

He meant a local crime, not the one that had landed us in the past. A burglary.

"My friend Secundus runs a *garum* shop. That's his cart outside."

"A what?" Nate asked.

"A specialty shop of sorts. Secundus is a freedman—he and his family used to be slaves. When their master, the owner of a laundry in Nola, died, the family was granted freedom. Secundus's older brother went to Rome to look for a trade and a wife and Secundus came here to Pompeii to open a shop with his mother and daughter."

"We've seen the cart before," I said. "Parked in front of a villa outside town."

"Faustilla—Secundus's mother—uses it when she needs to deliver an ointment to a wealthy client, for curing gout and warts and such. Secundus and I met when I sold him spices for an herbed sauce he manufactures on-site. He offered me a room for rental above the shop. The shop also sells pickled vegetables."

"So, specifically—"

"Beets and such."

"No, I mean what got stolen?" Nate clarified.

"Money from his cash box. They destroyed what they couldn't take. Jars of pickled vegetables upended onto the floor into a soggy mess. Garum containers smashed. You wouldn't believe the smell garum generates when it's mixed with pickled beets—"

"Garum?"

"A local delicacy. It's the sauce Secundus manufactures in the garden behind the shop. You don't want to know what's in it."

"I do," said the chief, reminding me of his statement that an investigator needed to know everything about a crime, no matter how trivial.

"It's a fish sauce used for flavoring dishes, made from discarded mackerel bits steeped in salt and left to ferment in the ground for up to three months."

"Ugh," I said, remembering the pile of fish guts and bones in the bonfire by the roadside. Nate, for his part, looked a bit regretful that he had asked.

"Romans love the stuff. A pint of it will set you back twenty denarii. You can buy a tunic for about four, a cup of quality wine for a quarter of a denarius." He added, "I need you to give Secundus a professional opinion as to who might have done this, Chief Kirkland." The chief opened his mouth to say something, but before he could (I assume) protest that he knew nothing about the criminal underworld of ancient Pompeii, Xavier added with a frown, "Hold on. If everyone thought I was dead and you weren't looking for me, then why are you here? And why, for heaven's sake, are you dressed like that? Helen, why didn't you have the team dress in Roman-wear?"

"We were aiming for JFK airport of February 1964," Helen snapped across the tomb.

His frown deepened. "That's quite a slipup."

"Someone sabotaged us, Dr. Mooney," Abigail explained quietly.

"We were trying to figure out who murdered you, Professor, by scattering you across time—but since you're alive and well—" I stopped awkwardly. Sick or not, his cheeks had a healthy glow under his tan and his frame was lean and muscular, like he had been getting a lot of exercise. Scarlett had always kept him in good shape, acting as a counterbalance to his sweet tooth, but this was a step beyond. I went on. "Anyway, once we realized we'd arrived in Pompeii, well—we thought Dr. Rojas did it at first."

"You thought *Rojas* murdered me? By scattering me across time?"

"There was a rumor going around that the two of you had garnered a significant number of nominations for next year's Nobel Prize," I mumbled.

"You thought Rojas murdered me so he wouldn't have to share the Nobel?"

Hearing him say it like that did make the idea sound ridiculous.

"So no one attempted to murder you, Professor," Nate said slowly.

"No."

"And no one knew your destination."

"No."

"And yet someone sent us here, to the same spot at very nearly the same time."

"That is odd, yes."

Xavier glanced in the direction of the mountain as if its conical shape was visible through the thick walls of the tomb. "August twenty-fourth has passed. Preparing for the trip, I remember being surprised that Gaius Pliny hadn't mentioned that the eruption happened the day after the festival of Vulcanalia. It seemed likely that he would have made some comment about the festival's failure to appease the god of fire." He added, "Still, I didn't want to be foolhardy about it, so a few days ago I trekked up the mountain to see if there were signs of an imminent eruption."

"And there weren't?" I asked.

"Well, there were actually. Once you get to the summit, above the tree line, you come to a flat, barren place devoid of vegetation. It looks like a giant campfire burned itself out eons ago and left behind blackened rock and scorched earth. I saw a couple of vents and cracks with sulfurous steam seeping out. There was also a recent landslide. I wasn't familiar enough with the terrain to be able to tell if any bulging of the mountain was going on. Just in case, I got all of my belongings ready yesterday morning. The eruption, according to Pliny, started in the afternoon—"

"Ah, that's right," said Helen.

"—but when the day and night passed without anything happening, I decided it was safe to make a round of the town to sell more of my wares and some of Secundus's remaining garum. Which is where you ran into me."

"What are the other dates in the medieval copies of Pliny's account?" Nate asked.

"Frankly, they are a bit of a mess. I looked into it before I left. The most famous of the manuscripts, where the traditional date for the eruption comes from, is the ninth-century *Codex Laurentianus Mediceus*—"

"In the Florence library," Helen added.

"The codex tells us the date is nine days before the Kalends of September—August twenty-fourth—but we know that's wrong. To answer your question, Chief Kirkland, other sources give the month as October or November, or don't give the date at all. I was planning on being the one to settle the debate once and for all." Xavier glanced at Helen's orange pumps and said, "You'll need to get out of those clothes and into something more appropriate for this time period," just as Helen said, "Clothing is our first priority."

Helen put her hands on her hips. "Xavier, I'm the team leader here. Finding you changes nothing."

"I'm the more senior research member."

"Only by age. Your specialty is time travel engineering, not history."

"Yours isn't history either."

"No, but historical linguistics is closer. And I teach Latin—"

"And during the past six months I've drastically improved upon my working knowledge of Latin. And I'm the one with the money bag—"

Nate raised a hand to stop them. "Hold on. I'm head of campus security and this is still an investigation."

"Given our predicament, maybe a democracy is in order?" Kamal suggested.

"Yeah," Abigail said, in what was for her a rather sharp tone. Watching her turn away, back held stiff, my suspicions were confirmed. It had just sunk in that Xavier Mooney had purposely cut himself off from everyone at home. I had seen it before. Students sometimes had trouble coping with the fact that their advisors had lives of their own, which occasionally took precedence over the students' needs. (And sometimes it went the other way around, too—St. Sunniva's student union had recently won a legal battle against a chemistry professor who'd felt that a seven-day maternity leave and a zero-day paternity leave were more than adequate for his graduate students who were facing impending parenthood. The postdocs and senior grad students in his lab had staged a quiet rebellion and the policy had been amended to something more reasonable.)

I almost pointed out that Dean Sunder had put me in charge and that everyone's paychecks—except for Chief Kirkland's and Helen's—made their way across my desk before being sent out, but decided it would be best not to prolong the who's-the-boss conversation.

"I think the suggestion of getting us some clothes is excellent," I said, settling the matter.

∞

"We all solve puzzles of one kind or another," Nate said. He and I were accompanying Xavier back into town, having left the others behind in the Nigidii tomb. Helen was still livid, Abigail was sulking, and Kamal was more than willing to let us do the walking in the midmorning heat while he took snapshots. We had left the donkeys in the shade of the tomb, the chestnut-colored one chewing on thin grass and the spotted one staring at us with sad eyes.

"Puzzles," the chief went on as we walked through the town gate. "Small ones, large ones. Julia, you solve office and personnel problems on a daily basis. In police work, it can take anywhere from a few months to a year or more. And in scientific research—"

"In science, solving a problem in a single year would be considered extraordinary," Xavier said. "You might get lucky, of course, but more often than not you have to count in decades, if not lifetimes. Even if a solution strikes suddenly—*Eureka!*, like with Archimedes—it's preceded by years of study and rumination. Take Fermat's Last Theorem. In 1637, Pierre de Fermat wrote in the margin of a copy of *Arithmetica* that he had a proof of the theorem but it was too long to fit in the margin. It wasn't until almost four hundred years later that the theorem finally found a proof at the hands of mathematician Andrew Wiles of Princeton and Oxford. He was knighted for his accomplishment."

"How long was it then?" Nate asked as we turned a corner into an alleyway.

"Hmm, Chief Kirkland?"

"Wiles's proof, would it have fit in the margin?"

"No. It's over a hundred pages long. There is a sense of unease in Pompeii," Xavier added as we navigated a segment of the road where a trench had been dug up to fix water pipes probably damaged by the recent earthquakes. "There are repairs going on all over town, practically on every block. The older folks remember the big earthquake of seventeen years ago and the damage it did. They're worried about another big one, what with all the tremors." We passed the entryway to an elaborate villa. Unlike some of the others that had the word *HAVE*—"Welcome"—spelled out on the floor mosaic just inside the threshold, this one featured *CAVE CANEM*—"Beware of the dog"—and a mosaic of a chained guard dog with bared teeth. Beyond, I caught a glimpse of a fancy atrium and a colonnaded garden, where the real dog could perhaps be found; what other riches and decorations waited inside were blocked from the view of mere passersby like us. Shops and tiny living quarters faced the street all around the block, serving as a buffer between the villa at its center and the rest of the world. This seemed to be the standard arrangement throughout the town.

We had stopped by a second entrance, which was not at all like the fancy one we'd just passed—a plain wooden gate, it was just wide enough for a cart to fit through. "Wait here. Let's make you presentable first and then you can meet Secundus." As Xavier pulled the gate open and walked through it, I caught a glimpse of a small stable and a garden.

"You know what's really odd?" I said to Nate as we waited for the professor to return.

"Being stuck in the past with no way to get home?"

"That, and not knowing why someone did this to us. We're back to square one now that we know that Dr. Mooney's disappearance is unrelated." Next door was a small shop selling foodstuffs from an open counter. The brightness of the midmorning sun made it difficult to see much deeper into the shop, but I thought I caught a glance of someone sweeping the floor. Directly across the street, a proprietor readied his tavern for the day, and farther down there was a street fountain. Only a thin trickle ran out of the open mouth of a theatrical mask, a tragic one. It was unsettling. I pulled my mind back to what I was saying. "I keep thinking I'm the one who was targeted. Abigail said she feels the same way. Kamal, too. And Helen. But if it *is* me, I don't know what I might have done. It keeps eating at me, though. I wish I could keep a professional detachment like you do."

He had been leaning against the wall next to the gate, his bare ankles crossed under the cloak. He straightened up at my words. "No, trust me, Julia, it's personal, *very* personal. I'm barely—with some effort—managing to keep myself professionally detached. There is a reason why officers aren't supposed to work on crimes committed against themselves. Just like a lawyer shouldn't defend himself in court, or a doctor should not try to diagnose—herself," he added quickly, as if he was worried I would judge him on his choice of pronouns.

"I'm not sure that's true in every case," I said, digressing from the subject at hand. "I, for one, do all my own paperwork and taxes. And though I have never seen his house, I'm sure Terry keeps it as immaculate as he makes mine every Tuesday. And my neighbor, Martha, is a retired horticulturalist who does her own gardening... I wonder why it's suitable to apply your work skills at home for some professions, but not for others."

"Speaking of skills, Julia, I've been wondering about something."

"Yes?"

"What about dinners?"

"I beg your pardon?"

"What do you do when you invite someone over for dinner at your house?"

Was this a roundabout way of asking me out on a date? If so, it was a very odd way of doing it. The timing wasn't so great either. "Uh—I'm still not following," I said.

"You said you don't cook. Do you never have people over for a dinner party?"

"Oh, that. I get events like that minicatered."

"Minicatered?"

"I get delivery from the Panda Palace over on Main or pick up something from Ingrid's on Lakeshore. And I throw in some wine and ice cream, too," I said, conscious of sounding a touch defensive. "And I *can* make coffee." From instant packets, I didn't add.

"I never picked up any of the languages my grandparents spoke—if I had been more enterprising I could have learned four—but my father's mother, Mary Kirkland, taught me to cook. If we can get our hands on the right spices, I can make shrimp curry, my favorite dish, for us."

"Thanks. Uh—it sounds spicy."

"I'll make it mild."

"Are there any basic skills that you lack, Chief Kirkland, or are you good at everything?"

I half expected him to say yes, but he thought for a moment and said, "I'm terrible at gift wrapping. Birthday presents,

Christmas presents, doesn't matter. Even square ones like jigsaw puzzles come out looking like shapeless blobs."

"I can teach you. You measure out the paper, fold the edges, tape, then add a ribbon and curl it using a scissor blade—"

"The nearest Hallmark store is two millennia away," said Xavier, who had returned. He had a lit lamp in one hand, and with the other he was hugging against his chest a wicker basket filled with clothes. He passed the basket to Nate, then motioned for us to follow him. We walked through a one-room stable, and into a small courtyard planted with several fruit trees and a tiny herb garden. To one side, a sunny spot held three jars sunken into the ground, like at the villa on Vesuvius's slopes, for the fermenting layers of fish, salt, and herbs that Xavier had mentioned. I'd expected there to be a smell, but there wasn't. A crudely executed painting on one wall—flowers, birds perched on tree, a bubbling fountain—made the garden seem larger than it really was.

"In here."

It was cooler inside, with the heat of the day kept out by the thick stone walls. My eyes took a moment to adjust to the darkness. Herbs and drying flowers hung from racks. Tables held stoppered jars and earthenware vessels filled with mysterious liquids and pastes. Something simmered in a pot sitting on a tripod brazier, releasing a sharp, acrid smell into the room. To one side, a curtain cordoned off what I guessed was a sleeping area.

"We're behind the shop. Secundus's mother concocts ointments and salves in here with herbs from the garden. This way."

I caught a glimpse of a bald man of medium height sweeping with a twig broom before Xavier led us up a narrow staircase to the upper story of the house. A balcony overhanging the street fronted two doors. Xavier opened the second and motioned us in, closing the door behind us. The sliver of light coming in through the slit that served as a window didn't do much to illuminate the dark, dingy space, explaining the need for the lamp in Xavier's hand. Its small halo of light caught the didgeridoo, propped up in one corner against the wall. (I supposed you had to bring a little bit of home wherever you traveled. I decided to ask Xavier later, at a more private moment, what else he had brought with him. I was sorely missing soap, a toothbrush, and toothpaste, not to mention toilet paper.) Xavier set the lamp on a small table, the only piece of furniture in the room other than the bed. The bed was a simple affair, a wooden frame supporting a straw-filled mattress. In one corner were a couple of large, unwieldy sacks—Xavier's silks and spices. The room, like his office, smelled of a Thanksgiving feast.

    I looked over the clothes in the basket we had brought up. Xavier explained, "I purchased a few things from the household downstairs. We can pick up stuff for the others on our way back. That's Sabina's mother's dress," he said of the somewhat faded, but carefully folded blue linen dress I had pulled out of the basket. Before I could ask who Sabina was, he and Nate left the room so that I could change. I made a little pile of the cloak, my boots, skirt, and blouse, then donned the dress and a pair of sandals I found in the basket. After lacing up the sandals, which fit reasonably well, I tried to figure out what to do with the two cord-like, woven belts that had come with the dress. I tied one around my waist and had just dropped the extra one back into the basket when the door opened and a dark head poked through. "Salve."

    It was the girl I had seen in the villa courtyard, the one with the abacus. I waved her in. She said one more word, "Sabina," and looked at me expectantly. I assumed that was her name and replied in kind. "Julia." She closed the door behind her and repeated that, but with a soft *j*: *Yoolia*.

    There was a double-sided ivory comb in her hand, and she held it up, then motioned me over to Xavier's bed. Looking around, I realized that the room contained neither a mirror nor a chair. I sat down at the foot of the bed. The girl commenced brushing my hair by the flickering of the lamp. A simple ritual, the brushing of hair, one that had remained unchanged through the centuries. The delicate tines of what looked like a family heirloom kept getting caught in my thick strands, but it was still a very touching gesture.

As she moved around me, I noticed an amulet hanging on a thin leather strap around her neck. (I'd been brushing up on my knowledge of deities since we'd arrived—Greek, Roman, Egyptian, they were all over Pompeii in large numbers. Xavier had been very informative. The early Roman spirits of fields, streams, and the home and hearth had merged with the Greek deities from Mount Olympus into one large family, which absorbed new gods and goddesses as state borders grew, explaining why there was a temple of Isis in the middle of the town. To add to the mix, kosher garum was available for purchase and Xavier mentioned that he might have spotted a wall graffito referencing a small, new monotheistic cult, but he wasn't sure.) The amber crescent moon that hung over Sabina's wheat-colored dress I recognized as Diana's—*Dee-ahna*, goddess of the hunt, the moon, and childbirth. The girl's dress was a simple one, two rectangles sewn together, leaving space for the head and arms, with a belt at the waist. The soft light of the lamp revealed the strong arms underneath. Like her kin downstairs, this was a working-class girl.

After ten minutes or so, Sabina stepped back to take a look at her handiwork. She frowned, as if displeased with something, looked around, and spotted the extra belt where I had dropped it back into the basket. I pointed to the one I had already tied around my waist. She nodded as if to say, "Yes, but that's not all," and wrapped the other one just under my bust line.

"Oh," I said. "Never would have thought to put it there."

Lastly she loosely draped a thin, rectangular piece of material, like a cross between a scarf and a shawl, over my shoulders.

"Thanks," I said. I bundled up my twenty-first-century clothing under her curious gaze. She didn't seem too surprised that a traveler from far Britannia might not know the local customs regarding proper dress, but I suspected that she had to be curious about the strange material of my skirt (rayon), not to mention the plastic shirt buttons and the zipper on my boots.

We stepped back out onto the terrace, my hair looking much better than it had since our arrival. Nate said, "What took you so long?" and went in to change. He emerged a minute later wearing a light-brown tunic, pretty much like a long sleeveless T-shirt with a belt tied around the waist. His strappy leather sandals were a good two sizes too small and his toes stuck out uncomfortably. I repressed the urge to giggle, not at the outfit but at his obvious discomfort at how revealing it was. The tunic reached about midthigh.

"Pants—why don't they have them?" he mumbled.

"The climate is mild. Pants may be worn in Britannia, where we're from, but not here." Xavier went back into the room to stuff our clothing bundles under the bed.

Once that was done, we headed back downstairs. Nate paused at the top of the narrow staircase and said quietly, "I'd like to take a look around the shop, examine the scene of the crime."

"Yes, I'd like your opinion," Xavier said, his voice not at all low, from the bottom of the stairs. "By the way, I told Sabina's father that Julia here—nice Roman name, by the way—that Julia is my niece, and that you're her husband."

"What?" Nate and I said simultaneously. Xavier added as we came down the stairs, "I explained that you're in town from

Britannia with your two young adult children and an older relative. It seemed like the easiest solution. Why, is there a problem?"

I was glad Helen wasn't there to hear herself described as an "older relative."

Xavier remembered to add, "I've explained that you don't speak a word of Latin."

That was true enough.

We got our first proper look at the shop.

It was a mess.

Pottery jars lay strewn all around, smashed into pieces and dripping some sort of dark sauce. The smell defied description and I realized that whatever was simmering on the brazier in the other room had been meant to counter it, unsuccessfully. The bald man I'd spotted earlier was working on sweeping the mess into the street, past the shop counter. The counter faced the street; the three round openings set into it held dry goods, undisturbed. Above, bronze ladles and funnels were suspended from a wooden rail—also undisturbed. A scruffy brownish dog lay to the side, lazily asleep in a shaft of sunlight. Deeper inside the shop, an old woman was wiping a wall where a jar had been flung against it, leaving a dark stain. I recognized her at once. I had last seen her in the courtyard of a Vesuvian villa, as she enjoyed an illicit scoopful of wine. Her dark shawl was gone and today her dress was sleeveless; I couldn't help but stare at her arms—the skin was dried and cracked with age and use, but the strength was clearly still there. I looked away, not wanting to be rude.

Sabina's father came over and greeted us, broom in hand. He was somewhat scruffy, with dark stubble under prominent cheekbones. When he turned to me after greeting Nate, our eyes locked for a moment. His gaze was bright, keen, alive. And suddenly it all felt so real. Secundus, Sabina, the woman wiping the wall, they weren't figures on History's stage anymore, but living, breathing human beings at the mercy of the forces of the disaster that was about to descend on their heads. I had to tear my eyes away from Secundus's gaze. I felt like he could see deep inside me. I felt like the harbinger of death. I didn't want him to read all that I knew in my face.

The woman cleaning the wall, a much older and more sour-looking version of Sabina, shot us a disinterested look. When she noticed Sabina behind us, she barked something at the girl through a mouth missing several of its yellow teeth. Sabina hurried over, the Diana medallion around her neck bouncing against her chest. The old woman pointed at a spot on the wall where what looked like wine stains or dark-colored juice marred the plaster. Sabina dipped a cloth in a vessel, squeezed the excess water out, and started scrubbing at the stain, but I doubted it would give and felt a pang of pity for the girl. Her attempts at cleaning the wall seemed to have the effect of removing bits of plaster more than anything else.

Secundus said something to Nate.

"You have a beautiful wife," Xavier translated, and it took me a moment to parse who he meant. "Your daughter must be a picture of beauty as well... He wants to know what business you engage in, Chief Kirkland."

"Uh—tell him I'm the caretaker of a school."

Xavier proceeded to do so.

"A strange occupation for a Briton," Xavier translated Secundus's reply. "He's heard you're all warriors who paint yourselves blue."

"Tell him we're sorry about what happened to his shop," I said, deciding that I wasn't going to be relegated into the background while the men conversed. I watched as Xavier relayed my words and a cloud descended onto the man's proud, strong-boned face. He said something back, with a quick glance in my direction. "All of his profits gone, months of work ruined," Xavier translated. "He doesn't know how he'll cover the rent or get his shop back on its feet. It's hard enough competing against Scaurus as is."

Xavier didn't bother to explain who Scaurus was, but added, looking around, "I'm a bit chagrined that I didn't hear the intruder even though I was lying in bed awake, worrying about the volcano. Secundus had gone over to join in the festivities at the tavern, as he usually does in the evening. I decided not to because I wanted to keep an eye on Vesuvius. Sabina and Faustilla were asleep in the room next to mine. They didn't hear anything either. Someone came in through the side gate, even though Secundus swears by all the gods that he had locked it after shuttering the shop for the night. Whoever it was went into the shop through the garden, emptied the small box Secundus used as a till, and proceeded to smash whatever they couldn't take. The gate was swinging open when Secundus got back."

During the professor's explanation, Sabina's father had been leaning on his broom, occasionally nodding when he recognized a name. I studied his features, not because of any sudden physical attraction, but because I felt a strange kinship with him. He was a man with a shop, a garum shop—about as far as you could get from the paperwork and organizing skills needed for my own job—but I understood. The shop was Secundus's way of making his mark on the world, not just a means of supporting himself and his mother and daughter (not to mention his dog). I nodded my head toward the animal, still asleep in a corner. "Didn't the dog hear the intruder?"

Xavier shook his head. "Celer is not much of a guard dog. He only barks at birds. He was asleep in the garden under the pear tree."

The security chief nudged one of the broken garum jars with his foot. It broke into two additional pieces along the length of a crack. "It looks like an amateur job."

"Why do you say that?" I asked.

"A professional would have taken the money and beat a fast retreat. Wanton destruction like this speaks of a personal animosity, of anger. I'd say someone has a personal beef with Secundus."

"A local who had a bit too much to drink at the tavern? Did Secundus insult someone without realizing it?" I was throwing out ideas as they came to me, surveying a sad glob of smooshed olives on the sole of my sandal. Faustilla gave her son a sharp look and he went back to sweeping the shop, with, I swear, a wink at me. "It's horrible to see anyone lose their livelihood like this."

"You're forgetting, Julia," the security chief said quietly.

I didn't know why he was speaking in a low voice since neither Secundus nor his mother or daughter spoke a word of English, but I lowered my voice, too. "What am I forgetting?"

"The volcano."

I hadn't forgotten.

∞

As we headed back toward the town gate, Nate carrying the clothes we had purchased for Helen and our two grad students, I asked Xavier, "Doesn't it bother you that Secundus and Sabina and her grandmother will most likely perish in the eruption? We were able to interact with them so easily…and you have as well, for what—six months?"

"Julia, you can't let yourself get attached," he said evenly.

I didn't believe him for a second. I struggled to find the right words. "Secundus—he looked straight into my eyes. I felt like he could see deep into my soul and read the secret about his town that we all carry."

"Because he said you were beautiful? You did seem to be fascinated by him, Julia." This from Nate, on my left.

"What? No, I'm sure he was only being polite."

"Deep into your soul, huh?" Nate certainly seemed to have forgotten that only yesterday he used to call me Ms. Olsen. His gait was off as he struggled to walk with his knees together and in the too-small sandals. "I didn't feel like he could look deep into *my* soul."

"Stop it," I said, irritated at his effort to make light of what I was saying. Was this his way of trying to make me feel better? I didn't want to feel better. "I'm serious. It must bother you, Xavier. I know it does."

Xavier was staring straight ahead as he walked, his face expressionless above his salt-and-pepper beard. "Everyone I've ever met on my time-traveling runs was already dead, in a sense," he finally said. "Just not at the time."

"True, but you could say that about anyone, even back home. *Not dead yet.*"

He sighed and looked over at me. "I find it's a little easier when you're facing your own illness and mortality, but only just. If you must know, my plan had *not* been to go to Alexandria and escape the eruption. Forget what I said. I was going to secure my cache of notes and sketches, then share the town's fate. I know it's a bit dramatic, but I wasn't thinking clearly. However—" He paused to formulate his words as we passed the flask fountain, which, unlike the theater-mask one, still seemed to be going strong. "I've come to believe that much of the town will evacuate in time. I haven't had as much freedom of movement as I thought I would. Hardly a day goes by that I don't encounter a crux person or a path that closes itself off to me. So when I'm able to interact with people easily, like Secundus and his family, I assume that they'll die when the eruption comes. It's a problem," Xavier admitted. "I know very well that nothing I say or do in Secundus's presence can alter his fate. He is either going to perish or he won't."

As we walked through the town gate and onto the street of tombs, he quoted the poet and mathematician Omar Khayyam, in what might have been written as a motto for the Time Travel Engineering lab: "The Moving Finger writes; and, having writ, Moves on: nor all your Piety nor Wit Shall lure it back to cancel half a Line, Nor all your Tears wash out a Word of it." He went on, "Still, many a time I've wanted to tell Secundus to drop everything and leave town before it's too late. That the fate of the store and the garum jars matters not in the least."

"And?" I asked.

"I could never get the words out. Not because of History. It just—it seemed like I would be trying to play the role of one of their gods."

"Is there a chance that"—I paused to frame my words carefully, but they still didn't come out as I intended—"the impact of Secundus's life on history is so insignificant that we might be able to get him and his family out in time? Maybe he's the opposite of a crux person," I attempted to explain, thinking of that proud man with the deep eyes. I meant what I was saying with no disrespect. Not all of us were meant to move mountains and lead armies. Including me.

"I don't believe in that possibility for a second," Xavier said sharply. "Either scientifically or philosophically. All people's lives, no matter how ordinary, impact their loved ones, their neighbors, strangers passing through town... Think of all the people Secundus's shop has fed, the garum varieties he's flavored, the dinners he's elevated with his sauces, the wisdom he's imparted to his daughter, the dogs he's taken on as pets. We can't just pluck him out of the fabric of History as if nothing he'll do between now and the eruption, and perhaps afterward, matters."

"Xavier," I asked without thinking, "do you feel bad that you left St. Sunniva and your lab and all your friends?"

Nate gave me a pointed look over the wicker basket, as if I had asked something inappropriate, but I thought bringing the issue out into the open might help Xavier. We had come to a stop just outside the Nigidii tomb.

The professor had gone a deep red from the neck upward, either out of anger or embarrassment. I rather thought it was a combination of the two. "Yes, I feel bad that I left. I feel bad that I'm ill. I feel bad that Vesuvius will erupt. I feel bad that many people in this town will die. I feel bad that there's nothing I can do to save them. By the way, Julia," he added, shaking off his mood, "the dress is supposed to go down to your feet."

The dress was too long for unencumbered walking, so I'd hitched it up a bit by folding the material into the lower of the two belts, the one circling my waist. After the boots, the sandals were a delight for my blistered feet. "You mean because I'm wearing nail polish? Dusty rose is not a very bright color. I was hoping no one would notice."

"No, it's just proper dress code for this era."

I decided to bring up something else. It had been impossible to miss as one walked along Pompeii's streets. "Speaking of propriety, what's with all the, uh—explicit imagery above doorways and on walls and fountains? The male genitalia with wings and bells and stuff?"

"Those are for luck. Different times, different hang-ups," he said as we entered the tomb.

∞

"We're here. The Stabian Baths."

The six of us were standing at the crossroads of two of the town's main arteries, next to the somewhat gaudy statue of a man in a short red cloak and white tunic holding a spear. "Marcus Holconius Rufus. Local bigwig. Never mind him. The women's entrance is down that alley," Xavier added. The baths took up the entire block, with various shops and eateries at their front. We had decided that cleanliness took precedence over a sit-down meal, though it was somewhat early in the day to be heading to the baths, Xavier said. I wasn't quite sure what to expect from communal facilities, but clearly anything would be better than our current situation.

"The men's side is closed for renovation," Xavier explained, "so Chief Kirkland, Kamal, and I will go down to the Forum Baths. Here, you'll need to give a tip as you go in. Do what others do and try to blend in."

"I've been on a few of these runs before," Helen said. "As has Abigail."

"I was addressing Julia."

Back at the tomb I had asked him if he thought our group would draw undue attention to itself.

"You mean because we have a spectrum of faces and skin tones among us—the ladies on the light side and Kamal and our campus security chief on the dark side?" Xavier had said, misinterpreting my meaning. I had merely thought that splitting up into smaller groups might make it easier for us to move about town.

"Don't like that term," Nate had muttered.

"Did you say something, Chief Kirkland?" Xavier asked.

"Don't like that term."

"Skin tone?"

"The dark side. It makes it seem like I'm on the wrong side of the law and that rankles the law enforcement officer in me."

"I agree," said Helen, possibly to spite Xavier. "After all, the word *light* denotes brightness, radiance, buoyancy. *Dark*, on the other hand, is often used as a synonym for gloomy, sinister, evil, which really is not—"

Xavier raised both hands in defeat. "All right, all right. What I was going to say is that skin color doesn't determine social status here. Yes, there are numerous slaves in villas, on farms, in shops, some even owned by the town itself. But they come from all over the empire, and are in their position because of family circumstance, war, trade, piracy—Gauls are said to be good herdsmen, Britons excellent for physical labor, Greeks for teaching and secretarial positions, Egyptians for amorous purposes."

"Really?" said Kamal, straightening his posture and slicking his hair back.

"Probably not in the way you think. If freed, like Faustilla and her sons were when their master died," Xavier went on, "a former slave can run a business and own slaves himself. Not to mention that the town is full of merchants and sailors and traders from all over the Mediterranean. By the way," he added, "I've put about the story that Julia is my niece, the security chief her husband, and that you two, Abigail and Kamal, are their children."

"I had them quite young apparently," I commented. "In elementary school, in fact. I'm only—what?—seven or eight years older than Kamal."

"I'm maybe thirteen years older, so that's a bit better," said Nate.

"And did you think to include me, Xavier?" Helen asked.

"You're the maiden aunt on Julia's side of the family."

That ended *that* conversation.

Helen wordlessly accepted a handful of coins from Xavier. The men continued downhill in the direction of the Forum Baths and we turned into a somewhat seedy-looking side street. The outer wall of the baths, which was painted reddish orange up to head height, had no windows for us to peek into. "This must be the entrance," Helen said of a door that stood open. Moist air wafted out from within.

We stepped inside and let our eyes adjust to the darkness. A long, narrow passageway led around a corner. We followed it to a room at whose door sat a remarkably old woman. Helen poured coins into the woman's leathery hand and she handed us three towels from a table and muttered something listlessly. "Bathrooms through the changing room and out into the palaestra and to the right," Helen translated. "We must stand out as being from out of town."

In the changing room, niches in the wall held folded piles of clothes below a vaulted, richly decorated ceiling. Two women stood by a bench, chatting as they disrobed. A squarish pool with stone sides took up the fourth wall, by the entrance. Lamps twinkled all around. We left our towels on a bench, then went through a door that looked like it had been put in as an afterthought, and through a colonnaded walkway into what Helen explained was the palaestra, a grassy area where men would be getting their exercise if their side of the baths was open.

"In there, I think." Helen pointed.

The bathroom. Communal, but luckily empty. There was a large U-shaped bench of wood on stone, with regularly spaced, keyhole-shaped seats in it. In front, beyond where the feet would go when sitting down, water ran through the room in a shallow channel. There were sponges on sticks next to each of the holes. "Roman toilet paper," Helen explained.

Once we were back in the changing room, we wrapped ourselves in the towels, having left our clothes in a niche, and donned clogs with thick wooden soles, which stood stacked in one corner.

The towels, to someone spoiled by twenty-first-century luxuries, were not what you might describe as soft or plush.

Abigail glanced at the two women, who had moved over to the square pool, and whispered, "Helen, Julia."

"What is it, Abigail?" I whispered back. The other guests looked over as if they were surprised by our whispering. Apparently it wasn't the thing to do.

"I have a tattoo."

Einstein's famous equation, $E = mc^2$, decorated her right shoulder blade.

The women were still staring and I gave them a frank stare back, and said to Abigail, in a normal tone, "Well, cover it with a towel."

We hung about a bit to let the two women go ahead of us, then, following their example, took a quick dip in the changing room pool—cold water—before stepping into the next, notably warmer room, where a masseuse and a hair plucker worked by lamplight, and finally into the hottest of the three rooms. This one had columned walls under a vaulted ceiling, a washbasin at one end, and a marble pool with steam rising from it at the other. Heat radiated from under hundreds of miniature floor tiles, explaining the need for the thick-soled clogs. The walls felt warm to the touch, too, as if a furnace in a nearby room was sending hot air circulating behind the walls and under the floor (the opposite of STEWie's lab, it occurred to me). Above the birdbath-like washbasin, which was round and the size of a dining room table, was an opening in the ceiling. Sunlight streamed in and sparkled and danced on the water in the basin. Birds and garlands and other beautiful imagery decorated the walls.

"I've been wondering if Jacob did it," Abigail said as we lowered ourselves into the pool, having left our clogs and towels on the double steps that ran alongside it. The water was *very* warm—the ancient equivalent of a hot tub—and smelled vaguely of massage oil and perfume. The two women we had followed in were deeply engaged in conversation but they occasionally sent a stare in our direction. Abigail moved a bit, her back to the tub wall, so they would not be able to see her tattoo.

"Are we doing something wrong?" I asked Helen after a few minutes of this.

She shook her head, her silver hair wet from the shoulders down. "Not necessarily. Staring—people watching, if you will—is the norm in most cultures. To our modern sensibilities it might seem rude, but really it's nothing of the sort. Just ignore them. Now, what were you saying about Jacob Jacobson, Abigail?"

"Don't get me wrong, Professor, I like Jacob a lot. His tweets can be quite funny, especially when he's talking about his classmates. There was this story about a missing umbrella—never mind." She went on, "But this is his first semester as a grad student. Kamal says Jacob is struggling in his classes, that he didn't do too well in Ghost Zones in Time. Not only is he supposed to be studying hard in all his classes, he needs to find a research topic, right? Maybe he snapped after Kamal told him he had to redo the final project for Ghost Zones."

Helen considered this as a hair-plucker-induced shriek echoed in from next door. "Most students who decide they don't like graduate studies simply leave after the first semester or two. The ones I worry about are those who stick around for years, flailing in their research, never managing to get any concrete results or publish anything."

I considered her words, leaning back against the side of the pool and feeling my sore leg muscles relax. Kamal, who was the teaching assistant for Ghost Zones, would, I thought, make a fine professor one day. Jacob and Abigail were at St. Sunniva on research assistantships. Would Abigail make a good professor one day? It was an odd question to consider while I was sharing a hot tub with her. But I rather thought so, even if she was still working on finding a place for herself in the world. And Dr. Rojas's new ginger-haired student? "Jacob might be struggling," I said, "but he seems committed to sticking around. I'm optimistic that he—"

Splash. A wave of warm water hit me in the face. A portly woman with several chins and a mole above one nostril had plonked down into the pool, sending water onto the floor and effectively ending our conversation. I guessed she was well-off by (a) the size of her person, (b) the size of her earrings, and (c) the way the bath attendant (or slave) hovered nearby after helping her into the pool. She dismissed the attendant, ran her eyes over the two women we'd followed in, who did not look as well-off and hadn't been offered help by the attendants, then turned to us as if she considered us to be the more interesting choice. Haughty eyes contemplated us above sagging breasts for a moment, then she said something in Latin. Helen answered in the hesitant speech of someone who was used to reading, but not speaking, a language. I heard the word *Britannia*. As they chatted, Helen haltingly, the portly woman with gossipy interest, I noticed that she took pains to keep her head above the level of the water so as not to dampen her elaborately styled beehive or wash away the chalky powder that whitened her cheeks and whatever had been used to darken and extend her eyebrows. She reeked of rose-scented perfume; whether she and the other bathers wore copious amounts of perfume as a mark of vanity or to conceal body odor, I didn't know, and it was probably better not to speculate.

I closed my eyes and tilted my head back, enjoying the luxury and pushing away the suspicion that the water in the pool didn't get changed much. The truth of the matter was that grad students were at the bottom rung of the hierarchy at St. Sunniva.

This was true of most schools. The uninitiated often assumed that *under*graduate students were at the bottom rung, but undergrads were the paying customers, or at least their parents were. And paying customers needed to be kept happy. Grad students worked for the school as teaching and research assistants—TAs and RAs—but weren't really proper employees, and as such they weren't entitled to the benefits that, say, a cataloger in the Coffey Library received. Then there was the fact that they had to learn to leave behind passive studying and test taking, which was what most of them had been taught in their school careers up to that point, and learn how to actively attack research problems and come up with new ideas, all while being poorly paid. Like Helen had said, a not insignificant number of grad students left after a year instead of sticking around to work on obtaining their PhDs. Who could blame them? Industry paid more and had better benefits.

Still, all that was a far cry from sending people into a ghost zone. Besides, I rather suspected that Jacob Jacobson had found an outlet for graduate-school stress—his steady stream of tweets.

Someone had bypassed the safety calibrations and sent us into a ghost zone, that much was certain. But this wasn't just *any* ghost zone. Which brought up the question, I thought, sitting back up and feeling the water stream down my neck and shoulders, of how that person had known that Xavier Mooney had purposefully relocated to Pompeii.

And what had pushed one of the four people on our list of suspects—Gabriel Rojas, Erika Baumgartner, Steven Little, Jacob Jacobson—to the point where they felt that the only way out was to send us on a one-way trip?

19

Feeling refreshed, if not completely clean, we headed back into the changing room wrapped in the towels. The baths were getting busier now and, among the dozen or so bathers and bath attendants, I saw a couple of familiar faces. Faustilla had just walked in, Sabina trailing behind her. The girl gave us an inviting smile—"Yoolia! Helena! Avi-gail!" Grandmother and girl, sweaty and dusty from putting the shop to rights, claimed an empty niche in the wall. As they took off their sandals, I noticed that Faustilla's heels were cracked, her toenails stained and misshapen. It wasn't only from old age. Sabina's were like that as well.

As if sensing my gaze on her, Faustilla turned to look at us. Her glance rested lightly on me, then Helen—disinterestedly, for we were, after all, foreigners and not very rich ones at that—then finally on Abigail. Her eyes lingered on Abigail, who was lacing a sandal, for a long moment, a calculating look on the old woman's face.

With a shrug I bent down to lace up my own sandals. I was in danger of becoming something of a people watcher myself. First I couldn't tear my eyes away from Secundus's proud face, and now I was having trouble ignoring Faustilla. "I get the feeling Faustilla doesn't like us very much," I commented, straightening back up.

Abigail was studying the intricate designs on the vaulted ceiling. "Sabina is nice, though, isn't she?"

"It's not that simple," Helen replied. "We know very little about the complexities and nuances of Pompeii society. After years of being at somebody's beck and call, Faustilla is now a freedwoman—can you imagine what that must be like? It's customary for slaves to tack on the *praenomen* and *nomen* of their former master to their own name after being freed. This family didn't."

I probably wouldn't have, either, I thought.

"I just wish she were a little nicer to Sabina," said Abigail.

"I'm sure she has the girl's best interests at heart. Practical skills, like Faustilla's herb growing and ointment making, are essential if the girl is to marry and find a place in society. We can't impose our twenty-first-century sensibilities on them without any regard for this time and place and their station in life."

At Helen's words, I resolved to be more understanding of Faustilla. As we headed out, I saw her dip one corner of the sleeve of her dress into the cold basin to scrub a stain off. Though it didn't seem any less hygienic than rinsing soiled body parts, the deed struck me as particularly off-putting.

The men were waiting for us on the busy street outside the baths, looking impatient. They'd all had a shave, Xavier's missing beard leaving a pale pink crescent on the bottom half of his face. "Lunch next," he said.

∞

"What are these meatbally things?" Kamal asked, eying one of them. The leather satchel by his side hid some of our twenty-first-century indispensables, namely pencils and paper and Abigail's Polaroid camera with its last pack of film. We were in the tavern across the street from Secundus's shop. The chief had asked to go there, saying he wanted to familiarize himself with the neighborhood.

"It's a fish-and-egg mixture," Xavier said of the meatballs.

"Ugh, fish," Abigail said.

Kamal tried one. "They aren't bad." There was also salad, bread, seasoned olives, dried figs, and cheese that looked very much like ricotta. The proprietor had followed us over to our table. He tipped a rooster-shaped flask to pour grape juice into bronze cups for us. He seemed to know Xavier very well and gave the professor a hearty pat on the back as he left to attend to other patrons, leaving the flask on the table.

"By the way, Julia, what happened to your glasses?" Xavier asked and downed much of the juice in one long sip.

"They were fake," Abigail answered for me.

A motley collection of locals had given us the usual people-watching stare as we made our way to the last empty table, with Abigail garnering most of the attention due to her short blonde hair and her youth. I picked up one of the bronze cups—had it been more elaborately designed, I would have called it a goblet—and took a sip as conversation resumed at the other tables. It wasn't grape juice. Wine, watered down and lukewarm. I took a second sip. It was refreshing in its own way. "I wore them to project an aura of efficiency and competence," I explained to Xavier about the glasses.

"She thinks she's baby faced," Nate said.

Before Xavier could say anything, Helen pitched in, "I know what you mean, Julia. When I first started out as a graduate student, I only wore pants, never skirts. I still got treated differently."

"Never by me, Helen," Xavier said, popping an olive into his mouth.

"No, never by you, Xavier." They were the first kind words I'd heard them say to each other since we'd arrived.

"And I wore ties to impress you, remember that?" Xavier said, then ruined the whole thing by adding, "I was quite foolish at that age."

Helen's facial expression didn't change, though I thought I saw a muscle above her right eye give a slight twitch.

Kamal lifted up his cup and sniffed the reddish liquid inside. "Is this wine?"

"I figure it's safer to drink than plain water," Xavier said.

"I think I'll get something else. Uh—Professor, can I have a denarius or two...?"

"The denarius is a silver coin. You don't need that much." Xavier put his cup down and opened the coin purse hanging on his belt. "Here, have an *as*."

The as was a copper coin a bit larger than a quarter.

Kamal got to his feet, said, "Abigail, come and translate," and they wove their way around tables to the front of the shop, leaving Xavier to explain, "I have to confess I brought I few coins with me. I didn't want to arrive with completely empty pockets. I obtained authentic coins from, shall we say, rather unsavory sources—don't lecture me about the antiquities black market, Helen, this was a special case. Anyway, I noticed that one of the coins I brought was minted in September of this year. I meant to hold off on using it until then, but accidentally paid with it for a snack at a gladiator match."

Helen clicked her tongue in disapproval.

"How were the women's baths, Julia?" Xavier asked with the clear intention of changing the subject.

"Social," I said. "We ran into Sabina and her grandmother. Faustilla doesn't seem to like us very much—except maybe for Abigail."

Xavier chuckled. "She might be thinking that Abigail would make a good second wife for Secundus."

I almost choked on a fish ball. "What? But he's a good twenty years older than she is."

"More like ten or fifteen, Julia," said Nate. "Besides, what do you care? Don't forget that you're married to me and therefore off limits to Secundus."

"Very funny," I said. "That's not what I meant."

"If it makes you feel better, Faustilla's never liked me either," Xavier said. "Secundus lets me borrow the cart to peddle my wares around town when he's not using it to pick up fish or deliver garum jars—you've seen them, the thin, long-necked ones. Faustilla thinks it's unnecessary wear and tear on the cart and the donkeys. Abigail would fulfill one of her goals for her son, a second marriage. Her other goal is to convince him to move to Rome, where Primus, her firstborn, lives. She's been arguing that the sacking of the shop is a sign, like the increasing earthquakes, that it's time to leave."

"I don't know about the first part, but she's right about the second," Helen said. "Secundus would be wise to listen to his mother in this instance."

"Everyone would be wise to listen to their mothers," said Kamal, who was back with Abigail and a different drink, something thick and sweet smelling. I hoped Abigail hadn't heard the bit about being good marriage material. "Mine told me to go into medicine, not grad school to study physics. She thought time travel would lead to trouble—and here we are, stuck in the past."

"Then there's the matter of Sabina," Xavier went on as Abigail and Kamal sat back down. "Faustilla thinks I'm encouraging the girl to behave outside her station in life because I've bought her an abacus and a couple of reading scrolls. Which is nonsense. Behavior outside her station in life must already be part of Sabina's temperament, or History wouldn't have allowed me to give her the scrolls and the abacus in the first place, not that I can offer that explanation, of course. Secundus approves. Sabina learned how to read and write from the children of the household they served. A waste of time in Faustilla's opinion. Sabina is of marriageable age. She should be learning useful skills."

Abigail snorted at this.

I decided not to ask what *useful* skills were. Sewing and such, no doubt. Probably cooking, too. I scratched the spot on my finger where I had cut it on the cat-eye glasses yesterday. It had started to itch.

"Well, now that we're clean and fed," said Nate, who had downed the food and wine with impressive speed, "and have discussed all the reasons Faustilla doesn't like us, we need to get on with the business of finding a suitable place to bury our cheese-and-cracker-package note."

"Cheese-and-cracker-package note? What is this?" Xavier asked.

Nate explained.

"Contamination of an archeological site, Helen?" Xavier asked in a clear attempt to needle her.

Nate hurriedly answered before Helen could say anything. "We need to get the message to someone at St. Sunniva—someone who can be trusted—so that they'll know what happened to us."

"I have the utmost confidence in Rojas," Xavier said. "Address the note to him."

Nate shook his head. "I'd like to hide it where archaeologists can find it and forward it to the police or St. Sunniva campus security. You can help us there, Professor, with your knowledge of the town," he added.

∞

We left the tavern somewhat tipsy (except for Xavier, who had acquired a tolerance for the wine, and Kamal, who hadn't drunk anything alcoholic), and headed in the direction of the Forum to seek a good hiding place for the message.

"Okay, *that's* kind of odd," Abigail said, stopping almost at once. She signaled across the street with a nod of her head.

"Is that one of those, what are they called, Porta Potties? The Roman version?" Kamal asked.

Across the street, a man stood with his back to us, relieving himself into a large vat sitting on the sidewalk. None of the locals paid him the least bit of attention. A moist stench emanated from the neighboring workshop, spreading across the street.

"It's a fullery," Xavier explained. "A laundry and cloth-dyeing workshop. The urine is used for washing clothes. Passersby contribute it and the urine is thrown in a tub with some other stuff, then slaves work the clothes with their bare feet, like grapes at a winery." I caught sight of a large tub inside where three slaves were doing exactly what Xavier had described. He added, "Secundus's old master ran a fullery in Nola, and Secundus and his extended family worked in it, including Sabina from a young age. There was a matter of a debt that had gone unpaid by Secundus's late father. They were technically indentured servants, not slaves, but practically speaking there's little difference. When the master died, his will released the family from the debt, and Secundus returned to his father's trade, garum making. He likes to say that, in comparison with the fullery, he doesn't mind the smell of fish or garum one bit."

"We better move along, we're starting to attract attention," Helen said, looking like she was itching to pull her notebook out of the leather satchel slung across Kamal's shoulder and take copious notes and sketches of the fullery. Her long hair had dried tangled below her shoulders, her face was sunburned, and her arm was probably still sore from yesterday's fall, but Helen Presnik didn't seem to mind any of it.

"Abigail, do you have the camera?" she asked as we left the fullery behind us.

"It's in Kamal's bag. I almost left it back at the tomb, thinking it might get wet in the baths."

"I took good care of it." Kamal tapped the leather satchel. "Stuffed it under my clothes in the changing room. We figured no one could steal the bag with its modern contents anyway."

"—but that wasn't the real reason," Abigail went on. "I'm feeling weird about it, right? Usually I have no problem snapping pics or shooting footage of locals, even though I know they're long since dead. It's bothering me this time, I can't explain why. It's almost like we're intruding."

"It's certainly been bothering me," I said, thinking of those deep eyes of Secundus's.

"I know why," Helen said. "It's because the people we usually see or meet on our time travels may have years yet to live—ten, twenty, thirty. Aside from famous historical figures, we have no idea what their fates will entail. Here—it's like there's a sword waiting to fall."

The description was apt. A sword waiting to fall and nothing we could do about it. The moving finger writes.

"I'm hoping Sabina and her family will leave town at the first rumble from Vesuvius," Abigail said optimistically.

"There's a chance that Secundus might have to leave sooner than that. Primus has been by again asking about the rent," Xavier said.

"Primus?" Nate asked.

"Not the brother in Rome. The slave of one Gnaeus Alleius Nigidius Maius." Xavier threw out the long name with the ease of one who's had months of practice.

My ears perked up as I parsed the long name. "Nigidius? Is he related to our tomb family?"

"I believe the Nigidii are his birth family, yes. But that tomb isn't of interest to him anymore. He was adopted by the powerful Alleii family, which must have been in need of a male heir, and now he prefers to go by Alleius Maius. He's a local bigwig, a politician—the kind that puts on gladiatorial games. He owns rental property around town. I've seen him in the neighborhood—a portly fellow of about my age. Since Secundus was late with his rent, Alleius Maius sent his slave Primus by—"

"Wait. Can we call him Nigidius even though he wouldn't like it? I'm having trouble keeping track of all the names," I said.

"Nigidius, then. An Oscan name, by the way, one which predates the Roman takeover of the town a century and a half ago." Xavier went on, "If he forces Secundus to vacate the property, Secundus will have no choice but to sell off his wares and make his way to Rome to join his older brother."

"That would certainly make Faustilla happy. Why don't we invite them to come with us?" I suggested as we let a cart pass and then crossed the street via the stepping-stones.

Helen shook her head. "We shouldn't try to meddle."

"Shouldn't we at least attempt to save them? Even if—no, *especially* if they aren't destined to survive?"

"Destined is the wrong word," said Xavier, sounding a touch fed up with my perseverance.

"To change their fate, then."

"Fate isn't the right word either." This from Helen.

"Fine, what is the right word?"

"Their future, the world's past," Helen said.

"It's all twisted together, isn't it?" Kamal said as we passed under a wide arch and into the Forum. "Like some temporal Möbius strip. From our twenty-first-century perspective all of this already happened a long time ago, that man who was using the urine vat, that group of children playing by the temple, that woman hurrying somewhere." He pointed. "History, as chiseled into stone and in the documented record that society keeps. And yet we're here watching it happen. I told my parents I couldn't study medicine because I don't like the sight of blood—who does, really?—but my mother, like I said, was sure time travel would be worse. Disturbing, confusing, strange."

"Yeah," said Abigail.

∞

The hot afternoon stretched on, made somewhat bearable by an offshore breeze; the six of us were temporarily time-stuck at one end of the Forum, near the stately marble temple of Jupiter, Juno, and Minerva, the triad at the top of the god food chain. Xavier had been playing the part of tour guide, pointing out the Basilica, or town hall, and a temple that housed bronze statues of the twins Apollo and Diana; to the other side was a large marketplace and a long hall built by Eumachia, town priestess. All around us were brightly painted equestrian statues, toga-clad citizens, beggars crouched in dark corners, children playing hide-and-seek, and shoppers haggling with merchants who were hawking shoes, cloth, jewelry, gladiator figurines, and, most disconcertingly, in one large area, slaves.

"I know what you're going to say, Julia, and there's nothing we can do about the slaves for sale or trade here," Xavier informed me, forestalling the comment I was about to make. Helen was taking the opportunity to grab a quick sketch of the gabled roof and garland-decorated columns of the temple of Jupiter. "This area will be damaged by the Allied bombing of

1943," she explained. "We can include the sketch with the note. Abigail, see if you can get a photo."

"I know that there's nothing to be done," I said to Xavier. "I was merely going to lament about it." What I really wanted to do was to holler at the top of my lungs, "Can't you see what's coming? Flee, all of you, *now*, before it's too late. Heed the signs of the earthquakes, of the failing fountains, *go*. There is still time." Not only had there been another small earthquake, but *something* was making its way into the water pipes, lowering the pressure to a trickle in many neighborhoods. The well-off woman with the multiple chins had told Helen about it at the baths. It was another sign. The clock hands were moving closer to midnight. A bull sacrifice had been made as an attempt to regain the good will of the gods, the woman had said.

I commented on the futility of this.

Xavier shrugged. "All the blood sacrifices of animals, the ritual reciting of prayers, the vows and offerings at the temples… They've worked so far, haven't they? Rome is great."

He left it at that. I felt Nate's eyes linger on me as Helen finished her sketch. Another few minutes passed by, and we were finally able to leave the Forum. We took a drink of water at a fountain decorated with a somewhat spooky face of a Gorgon, where children splashed in the water, leaving the pavement wet, and continued out of the Forum to the double-arched Marine Gate, which faced the sea. The larger of its two archways served cart traffic coming up the steep road from the harbor and its warehouses, and the smaller was reserved for pedestrian traffic. Helen stopped to sketch the houses that sprouted above the town walls on either side of the gate. "The people living up there must have nice views of the harbor," I commented in an effort to prove to everyone that I could be as calm and dispassionate about the fate of the town as they seemed to be. I had, after all, asked to go on a time trip.

Xavier pointed to a terraced, three-story villa to the left of the gate. "That one, over there, belongs to Secundus's main competition. One Aulus Umbricius Scaurus, the number one garum producer and exporter in town. Scaurus owns extensive facilities and warehouses down in the harbor. His ex-slaves sell the stuff in shops all around town and he exports it, too."

I imagined the garum maker on the terrace of his villa, keeping an eye on his warehouses and watching merchant ships carrying his fish sauce sail to faraway lands.

The security chief's ears had perked up, but, "That's quite a place," was all he said.

"What, you suspect him of trashing Secundus's shop because Secundus is elbowing in on his turf? But Secundus's shop is such a small place," I protested.

"Small businesses are the ones most easily intimidated and driven out of town. We should go in and talk to the man."

"Is that a good idea?" I asked.

"I'm a police officer. If I suspect someone of wrongdoing, the first thing I do is talk to them. I don't speak Latin, but one of you can translate for me."

I would have probably tried to spy over Scaurus's garden walls but Nate's method made sense, too.

"It will only take a few minutes," Nate said.

Xavier hesitated, then said, "Just the chief and I."

Helen, our two grad students, and I were left to cool our heels (literally) by the Gorgon fountain with its wet pavement. We didn't have to wait long for Nate and Xavier.

"What happened? What did Scaurus say?" I asked.

"We didn't get to talk to him. One of his slaves, a burly overseer—the kind you don't argue with—informed us that his master wasn't accepting visitors, at least not rabble such as ourselves. He said we should come back tomorrow at dawn," Xavier said.

"At dawn? Why at dawn?" asked Abigail. The invitation did have the suggestion of a duel about it.

"Of course. For the patron visits," Helen said.

"Patron visits? Who is the patron?" I asked.

"Scaurus himself. Those of lower socioeconomic status come by to ask him for favors. It's a measure of his power and influence," she explained.

"It put us in our place," Xavier said.

"We could spy over his walls," I suggested.

Nate sent a look in my direction. "If Scaurus did have something to do with the damage to Secundus's shop, he wouldn't have gotten his own hands dirty. I don't like the look of that overseer—Thraex, you said his name was, Xavier? Latin sounds like gibberish to me, but even I picked up on his tone. I'd like nothing better than to get my hands on his fingerprints and dust off Secundus's shop."

"What about Secundus's landlord?" I asked.

"Nigidius? What about him?" Xavier said.

"Maybe he was irked that Secundus was late with the rent, or he doesn't like the fact that Secundus is subletting one of the rooms above the shop to you to make extra income. He could have sent his slave to trash the shop as a warning."

"I doubt it," said Xavier. "I've seen Primus around the neighborhood. Mousy-looking fellow. Warts on his nose. Goes around painting *Rental Quarters Available* signs. Wouldn't hurt a fly. He was most apologetic when he told Secundus he would have to leave if he didn't come up with the rent."

"We've met his wife," Helen remarked. "Nigidius's, I mean."

"We have?" I asked.

"At the baths. Claudia."

"You mean the portly woman with the hovering attendant, the large earrings, and the sagging—Did she say anything of note?"

"She wanted to know all about us when she heard we were staying in her block. She thinks her cook uses some of Secundus's fish sauce. I told you about the rest—we mostly talked about the strange goings-on with the water pipes, and how she was forced to come to the public baths after the pipes to her house ran dry. A kink appeared where the pipes meet up with the street...*meet up*—" She stopped and sucked in her breath. "Yes, of course. I don't know why I didn't think of it before."

"Helen?" Xavier asked.

"You may be content to live in the past, Xavier, but I am not."

"Oh?" Xavier said.

"I've thought of a way to get us home."

20

"Am I correct, Julia?" Helen said. "I thought I remembered that Dr. May wanted to propose a run to Rome in the spring."

I was burrowing in the wooden chest of the Nigidii tomb, where we had stashed most of our twenty-first-century things, stuffing the cloaks and lamps back on top to hide them. I wondered if the fact that we had been able to leave them there meant that the members of the Nigidii family weren't likely to visit their ancestors anytime soon—or if they did, perhaps wouldn't open the chest? My cell phone had STEWie's roster in its memory. I hoped there was enough battery life left to turn it back on. I had almost drained it the night before, when we'd used the phone as a flashlight to guide us to the tomb.

The phone was dead, very much so. I shook it, which didn't help in the least, and said, "As I mentioned the other day, Dr. May was up next after Dr. B and Dr. Little. She was planning to go to 41 BC Egypt to try to snap photos of Cleopatra. But I'm pretty sure she was on the roster for another run during the spring semester... The dedication of the Roman Colosseum, yes, I think you're right, Helen."

"Do you remember what month and year she's jumping to, Julia? Have we missed it?"

"Don't you know what year the Roman Colosseum was built, Helen?" Xavier asked.

"No, I don't. Not offhand." Her cheeks were crimson. "Do you?"

I was beginning to see why Xavier and Helen had gotten a divorce—it wasn't just the fourteen-year age difference. Their strong personalities grated against each other. On the other hand, a sharp cheddar was best paired with a strong wine (or so I had once read on a cheddar cheese wrapper).

Still kneeling by the chest, I closed my eyes and tried to visualize STEWie's roster. I remembered the note I'd included in the information field for the Colosseum run: *Lavish and over-the-top affair, lasted a hard-to-believe hundred days. An easy target for a run.* A hundred days of celebration and carnage, with gladiator battle after gladiator battle. And the year...was AD 80, I was pretty sure. I opened my eyes. We hadn't missed it.

"It's going to be tricky to meet up with Dr. May's team given that we don't know the exact day they'll arrive, but we can worry about that later," Helen said, restacking our items back into the chest.

"We can let her know to be on the lookout for us in the cheese-and-craker-package note," I said "I'm glad we don't have to decide whose name to put on it. Still—"

"Yes, I'd like to have a good idea of who to confront when we return home," Nate finished my thought. Was there a slight emphasis on the "I" in that sentence, as if to remind me this was *his* investigation?

"For now, the main thing is to get ourselves to Rome," Helen said. "We have a comfortable buffer of a few months to find our way there. Then we can try to cross paths with Dr. May to hitch a ride back home in her basket. Assuming they haven't shut the program down, that is," she added.

"Why would they shut the program down?" Abigail asked with all the optimism of youth. "STEWie is so important."

"They think they've lost six people. It's going to be hard to justify continuing the program in its current format to the board of trustees," I explained.

Helen agreed. "It could very well set the program back a decade or more."

Xavier took the opposite view. "It will make the news and Lewis can use that to bring in new funding. And no, I'm not suggesting that as a motive for whoever sent you here. Lewis will have his work cut out for him. Meeting up with Dr. May isn't a bad plan, Helen," he added.

"You can stay here if you prefer."

"I can't. You'll need funds to go to Rome. I'll have to sell off my wares. Rome, huh? I've heard a few things about Rome while I've been here. Some of them good. By the way, if we really wanted to move along freely in the Eternal City, we could use the Cloaca Maxima."

"What's that?" I asked.

"Rome's great sewer. I don't think so, Xavier," Helen said, speaking for all of us.

∞

Xavier lifted a coarsely sewn woolen sack filed with peppercorns—it left behind a small pile of black granules—into my arms. We had all squeezed into his rental room to help him carry what was left of his wares downstairs so that he could make a circuit around town in the morning to sell everything off. "There's a notebook under my bed with the notes and sketches I took when I first arrived in town," he mentioned. "Since then I've mostly tried to keep my activities limited to the quarter of town between the Vesuvius Gate—the one you've been coming in and out of—and the Nola Gate to the north, where the road leads inland to the town of Nola."

"Why only that part of Pompeii?" I asked.

"It hasn't been excavated yet. In 2011, I mean. I theorized that I'd have more freedom of movement than in areas that had already been thoroughly explored and documented."

"Makes sense," said Kamal, who was sitting cross-legged on the professor's bed.

"Xavier, you've been contaminating a future archeological site for six months," Helen said, aghast.

"My presence has left only traces. I'm living as a local, doing what they do. I'm a single bee in a beehive, a worker ant in an anthill. The didgeridoo is the only nonessential item I brought along, and I chose it because it's wooden and therefore will not survive the eruption. I've played it a few times for Secundus and Sabina, by the way. Other than the didgeridoo, everything I brought with me is made from perishable or time-accurate materials…except for—well never mind that."

"Except for what?" Helen wanted to know.

"I said never mind."

"Xavier, you're not keeping anything from us, are you?"

"Why would I do that?"

"Maybe you could play the didgeridoo for us one evening, Professor, before we leave," Abigail suggested in a clear effort to diffuse the tension. The instrument stood propped up against one wall.

If we didn't manage to connect with Dr. May in Rome, the professor would have time to play it for us on many an evening, I thought but did not say.

"You said you had a tough time getting this stuff past Oscar—how did you do it?" I asked as we carried the woolen sacks and the silks down to the ground floor, leaving a trail of peppercorns on the steps.

"You wouldn't believe what you can hide in a down jacket, Julia."

∞

The tavern across the street from Secundus's shop was bustling with locals who were out for dinner, a dice game, a celebration, their faces illuminated by table lamps. Shouting a bit to be heard above the din and cacophony of voices, Xavier explained to us that except for the owners of luxury villas, Pompeians lived in small apartments with no kitchens, like his own rental quarters, and ate out—in taverns, snack stands, marketplaces. It was in the villas of the wealthy, like Nigidius and Scaurus, that slaves prepared food in small kitchens and served it in elaborate dining spaces with couches instead of chairs. It all sounded very—Roman.

"Is there pork in this?" Kamal asked of the stew the tavern proprietor had doled out for us. At the table behind us, four locals, fisherman perhaps, played some sort of gambling game, one of them rubbing a phallus-shaped good-luck charm that hung around his neck before each throw of the dice. To my admittedly untrained ears, it sounded like they were speaking something other than Latin, and Helen hissed, "Oscan," under her breath and looked like she would have given an arm and a leg for an audio recorder.

"It's goat. I can't complain about the local cuisine," said Xavier, then proceeded to do so. "It's just that I've been missing some foods." He ticked off items on the fingers of one hand. "Coffee. Potatoes. Tomatoes. Pumpkin pie. Chocolate. I ate as many pumpkin pies and chocolate bars as I could before I left."

"No tomatoes? But we're in Italy," I protested.

"Tomatoes are a sixteenth-century import to Europe from North America," Helen explained. "Same with chocolate."

"Interesting," I said, marveling at History's quirks. I dipped some bread in the stew, then had to drop it in. "Ow."

"What is it, Julia? Stew too hot?" Xavier asked.

I shook my head, staring at my right hand.

"My finger hurts where I cut it on my glasses when we arrived on Vesuvius."

"Let me see," Helen said. "Looks a bit red. It might not have been a good idea to go to the public baths with an open cut. Why don't you pour some wine on it as an antiseptic?"

"Rinse it in saltwater tomorrow morning before we leave," Abigail suggested. "In the sea."

Kamal looked away. "Ugh, let's not talk about this at the dinner table."

I took Helen's suggestion and poured a tiny bit of wine on my hand, earning a puzzled look from one of the game players at the next table. Kamal's squeamishness aside, since we were already talking about a medical issue, I took the opportunity to say to Xavier, "You don't seem ill. Except for being a bit thinner."

"It's all the walking I've been doing. And the change in diet. I have to say, I think something in the food itself—perhaps the lack of sugar—is helping to control my symptoms. All those pumpkin pies and chocolate bars I ate before I left probably didn't do my body any favors."

"*Ad multos annos!*" came the cheerful call from a nearby table. A quartet of locals raised their cups in celebration. "It's someone's birthday," Helen explained.

"I'd like to try garum," Nate said out of nowhere.

"It's flavoring the olives, I believe," Xavier said, nodding toward the side dish. "But if you want the undiluted thing—"

"I expect it's similar to Thai fish sauce, which I've cooked with, but I'd like to be sure. It might have motivated Scaurus's act of intimidation and I always like to experience everything related to a possible crime. It's why I wanted to come on a STEWie run when I thought we were investigating your murder, Dr. Mooney."

"Even if we figure out who did the damage to Secundus's shop, we might not be able to tell him," I pointed out.

"Maybe we have more leeway because the whole damn place is going to go up in flames anyway, in October or November."

Xavier got up, went to the counter, and came back with a small dish filled with a reddish-brown liquid. The chief took a whiff, then downed a good bit of it, all without a change of expression.

The rest of us stared at him.

A sweaty redness broke out where his brow met his hairline and spread to his nose and cheeks and down to his square jaw. He coughed violently and grabbed his cup and downed the wine. "More," he croaked.

Xavier hurried to pour more wine for him.

After the red tinge in Nate's cheeks had subsided, I asked, "Well?"

"Piquant. And salty. Very salty."

∞

Merriment and melody emanated from the neighborhood bars and taverns in the warm Pompeii evening as shopkeepers closed up for the night. Secundus's shop had been shuttered, but the side gate had been left unlocked for us. "I obtained a second room for the night from Secundus in exchange for some of my wares," Xavier explained, sounding pleased with himself. "Ah, there's the man himself."

Secundus had been attending to something on the upper floor. The clay lamp in his hand illuminated his way down the steps, his sandals tap-tapping on the wood. On his heels was Celer, moving his squat body down in a sort of swinging motion. The scruffy brown dog's name, pronounced with a hard *k*, translated to "Speedy" in what was clearly meant to be a joke. The bags under Secundus's eyes seemed deep in the flickering lamplight, but he greeted us warmly. The shop had been mostly set to rights, except for the stains on the floor and the walls. Celer gave us a lazy look, then toddled off into the darkness of the garden. Under the pear tree was where, after further discussion, we had decided to bury the message for Dr. May at the next opportune moment.

As Xavier and Secundus chitchatted, I found myself unable to meet the garum maker's eyes. Guilt on my part. How had Xavier managed to spend six months here knowing what he knew?

"Tell him I'd like to examine the side gate more closely in the morning," Nate said. "After our visit to Scaurus—and Nigidius, too. Why not."

I threw a glance in the direction of our two grad students. "Wait, I thought we're leaving in the morning? I'd like to help him out, too, but we have a responsibility to the students. We don't know how long it will take us to reach Rome. We'll undoubtedly keep getting time-stuck, like in the pomegranate orchard."

Kamal looked like he was about to say something, but Abigail beat him to it.

"We're not kids, Julia," she said angrily. "We can be told—things—even if they are bad, right?" She was pointedly not looking at Xavier Mooney. "And we can certainly decide for ourselves if we're willing to stay a day or two longer to help Sabina and her father. We have plenty of time to get to Rome and meet up with Dr. May."

I was reminded once again that Abigail had no family other than the large scholarly one she was part of at St. Sunniva, where she had found a place after leaving her foster family at age seventeen. It wasn't that there was anything *wrong* with them, she had once told me. They were nice and all, but she had felt like a visitor the whole time she lived there. Sometimes those things worked out well, and sometimes they didn't. That was true of any social contract, I remembered thinking at the time.

Abigail was still eying me defiantly.

"Does everyone feel this way?" I asked the group. My hand had started to throb, I noticed. Hopefully the wine had helped disinfect the cut.

It was unanimously agreed that we would stay as long as it took to figure out who had ordered the sacking of Secundus's shop—Scaurus, the town's top garum maker, or Nigidius, the landlord.

During our conversation, Secundus had been standing by silently. I imagined that for him it was like watching a soap opera in another language, with the characters arguing over intangible things. He nodded as Helen explained our decision and said something back, a cascade of swift sounds rolling off his tongue. I wondered if that was how we sounded to him. With a small bow, he went into the shop. We heard the sound of the jars being rearranged on a shelf. At least something had survived the intruder's wrath.

"What did he say?" I asked Helen.

"He would like to know who did it, if only to spit at the man's feet—or, better yet, to have a curse tablet made."

"Wow, how does that work?" I asked.

Xavier replied before Helen could. "You write down the name of the person you want to curse, the details of whatever nasty thing you'd like to have happen to them, and what you promise to your god of choice or underworld spirit in exchange. Then you drive a nail into the tablet, right into the name of the person you've cursed, and take it to a tomb or temple."

"Yikes," I said.

"And if your wish comes true, you bring your offering as promised. It's all very quid pro quo. Oh, here's Faustilla. I've asked her if she has a poultice or salve that might help your hand, Julia."

Faustilla tut-tutted over the swelling index finger of my right hand. She pulled me into the back room and sat me down on a stool, Helen trailing along to translate and Abigail to hold the lamp. As Faustilla rummaged among the small jars and vessels, finally choosing one that held a pea soup yellow powder, Sabina came in from the curtained area to see what the commotion was about. Under her grandmother's supervision, she was given the task of sprinkling water into the powder to moisten it.

When the mixture had turned into a goopy yellow paste that met with Faustilla's approval, the old woman sloshed some vinegar on my hand, then dabbed on a liberal amount of the mixture. That being done, she turned and gave Abigail a frank stare. After a moment she asked Helen a question.

Abigail's mouth popped open. Helen's eyes crinkled a bit, but she translated for me. "Faustilla wants to know if Abigail's recently been sick and if that's why her hair is so short."

"You better explain we're leaving for Rome soon," I said, forestalling Abigail's answer.

"Roma," said the old woman, recognizing the word, and then began a long monologue.

Helen translated while Faustilla continued to work on my hand. "She'd like to see Rome one day. Her son—her firstborn, her pride and joy—went there to seek his fortune and a wife... She's not sure exactly what he's doing, but no doubt something important. He is busy and does not have much time to arrange for a letter to be written and sent to his mother. She is blessed that the gods gave her a younger son to take care of her."

It struck me that Faustilla didn't exactly treat her younger son like she appreciated him.

As Celer waddled in from the garden and made himself comfortable by my feet, Faustilla added something, her voice rising and falling. Abigail's cheeks were getting pinker by the minute.

"She is lamenting the fact that Secundus doesn't have a son of his own. She has been urging him to take a new wife, but he won't listen. Your daughter—she means Abigail—she wants to know if she's unattached. If so, she and her son might make a good match."

"Well, now. Let me mull that over for a bit," I said, then, at Abigail's outraged stare, relented. "Tell her…tell her that Abigail has a betrothed back home."

"I do," Abigail said, loudly. "His name is Dave and he is a graduate student in the Athletics Department. Well, he's not my betrothed exactly—we've only been seeing each other for three months—why are we even talking about this?"

Faustilla seemed disappointed as Helen relayed my words. She wrapped a strip of cloth around my hand and tied a knot, perhaps more firmly than necessary. She made a remark. Abigail snorted and Helen smiled.

"What did she say?" I asked.

"That your children—Abigail and Kamal—don't look very much alike."

"Don't look very much—what's she insinuating? Tell her that Abigail takes after me—my hair was a bit lighter when I was younger—and Kamal takes after Nate." I added, "What happened to Sabina's mother?" It was something I'd been wondering about.

"Sabina told me that she died a few years back," Abigail explained.

"How did it happen?"

The only answer was a noncommittal shrug. It was quite possible that the family didn't even know what had caused her illness.

Poor Sabina, I thought, rubbing Celer's furry head with my good hand as Faustilla went on what can only be described as a tirade, Helen translating. "It would be wise of her son to heed the gods' warnings, with the break-in to the shop and the increasing tremors… She remembers the earthquake of a generation ago—the buildings danced like embers in a bonfire and the angry gods made tiles rain down from rooftops. She thinks another big one is coming. The fountain down the block has gone almost dry, like something underneath the very stones of Pompeii has been angered."

"She's right of course," said Xavier, who had wandered in. He reached into the cloth purse hanging on his belt to pay Faustilla for her efforts, but the offer was waved away. An unexpected bit of graciousness on Faustilla's part. The second one. We had learned that the additional room Xavier had rented for the night belonged to her and Sabina. They would make do with the back room; I had spotted blankets and pillows on the floor in the curtained-off area, next to where Secundus had been sleeping. Xavier was compensating them, but I still appreciated the gesture.

Once upstairs, we left the men in Xavier's room—the chief and Kamal would sleep on the floor (a rather tight fit)—and went into the adjoining one, carrying a lamp.

"I don't mind sleeping on the floor," Abigail said.

Envying her younger bones, I lowered myself onto one of the two beds. The mattress was stuffed with straw and it smelled of it, too. It was a step up from sleeping on the floor, both literally and figuratively, but just.

Tired as I was, my impressions of the town (not to mention my throbbing hand, though Faustilla's yellow paste seemed to be helping) kept me from dozing off immediately. What a thriving, alive place Pompeii was—an intricate social web of family, hospitality, entrepreneurship, hard work. And yet a leisurely pace of life was on display everywhere, people engaged in conversation, gossip, and discussion on corners, in cafés and taverns, in the baths, by their front doors.

Helen worked with words, Xavier with numbers and symbols, and I—I was a people person, which is why my job suited me. Students, postdocs, and professors came knocking on my office door every day (or, more likely, e-mailed or called me), and if I could, I solved their problems and sent them away happy. If I couldn't, I offered a sympathetic ear, a shoulder to cry on, or served as a venting board or a focus for their anger. It was all part of the job. I'd always felt that there were as many personalities in St. Sunniva as there were people. I rather felt that way about Pompeii, too.

"Helen?" I whispered. Abigail was already asleep, judging by the sound of her breathing. "Are you awake?"

"I am, Julia, what is it?"

"If we don't manage to meet up with Dr. May, I've decided what I'd like to be."

"What?"

"A barmaid."

"Why a barmaid?"

"I'm a people person. People could come into my tavern and tell me their problems and I'd serve them wine and try to make them feel better."

"Hmm. I'm not sure it would turn out to be all that you imagine. And History might not let you do it, anyway." She paused. "You and Chief Kirkland have a lot in common, you know."

"We do not," I protested. "I can't make him out at all. Sometimes he's very pleasant to me, other times he's reserved, and sometimes he's downright obnoxious."

"I meant his job has to do with working with people and their problems, too."

We both snickered at the thought of the tall and outdoorsy chief spending his days doling out stew and wine from behind a tavern bar. Helen added in a more thoughtful tone, "It's complicated for him, you know. He blames himself for what happened to us. I think his interest in the crime at Secundus's shop stems from a need to keep his mind busy. His real concern is getting us home safely and finding out who sent us here."

"Well, he doesn't have to blame himself for me being here—I wanted to come along. I've spent a lot of time thinking about who might have done this," I added.

"Have you?" Helen said, and then paused as a yawn overtook her. I heard her turn on her side, toward the wall. She mumbled, "See? You two do have a lot in common."

∞

A sunny day dawned, sending a strip of brightness and the din of neighborhood activity into the room. I woke up groggy, already hoping that the others would be willing to adopt the local custom of a midday siesta. All this early rising was getting to me.

Judging from their steady breathing, Helen and Abigail were sounder sleepers than I was. I quietly opened the door and stepped outside onto the terrace. Unwinding the strip of cloth Faustilla had wrapped around my hand, I checked the cut. It was hard to tell if it looked any better because I couldn't see past the yellow. It throbbed a little less, I decided, wrapping my hand back up.

Secundus had reopened his shop, I saw as I headed down the stairs, though most of the shelves gaped empty. Sabina was manning the counter. Faustilla, who was much kinder now that we were paying lodgers, nodded a grudging good morning and handed me my share of the breakfast, which I assumed Xavier had paid for on his way out. He'd slipped a note under the door to let us know that he and Nate had left before dawn to pay the twin patron visits with Secundus: one to Nigidius, whose villa was the grand one with the floor mosaic of the chained dog in the entryway, and the second to Scaurus.

I ate the porridge in the garden, then spent some time looking at Faustilla's herbs, trying to identify them all, until Abigail, Kamal, and Helen joined me. I greeted them with an idea that I had been brooding over. "I suppose it's unrealistic to suggest that we obtain all necessary materials and build a STEWie from scratch here, but wouldn't History be on our side for that?"

Kamal shook his head. "Materials are only half the problem. We need a computer. Figuring out how to jump from one place to another, that's a calculation that's—what's the expression?—hair-raisingly complex. Say that we wanted to jump from this spot here"—he pointed to a row of mint plants—"to the same spot in modern Pompeii, the tourist town. It seems like we could just keep standing still as we traveled forward in time. But this spot on the Earth *constantly moves*. The Earth rotates once a day. The continents are drifting, with Europe and North America moving apart at the rate of, what, four centimeters per year? The Earth itself is moving in its orbit around the sun... Not to mention that the sun is traveling around the galactic center, carrying the whole solar system with it."

Helen took up the explanation. "Also, the ground level typically rises as one moves forward in time due to the layers of trash and other detritus added by people and by nature. That would especially be true near a volcano like Mount Vesuvius. Layers upon layers of ash and rock will be deposited by the imminent and subsequent eruptions. Which means that Secundus's Pompeii lies below the modern ground level. You have to go down to get to the excavated parts."

"Not to mention all the funky things going on with the Julian and the Gregorian calendars, skipped days, leap years, lack of year zero, and so on, making calculations even trickier," Abigail said.

"In short," Kamal concluded, "let's just say there is a reason we needed whiz professors like Dr. Mooney and Dr. Rojas to get STEWie operational in the first place."

"Just thought I'd ask," I said.

Kamal wandered over to the crudely drawn painting on the garden wall, with its eternally blooming flowers, birds chirping on a tree, and bubbling fountain, and studied it for a moment.

"Kamal, isn't there something you and Abigail need to do?" Helen called out to him. "The money that we owe the bakery?"

"We tried yesterday, Professor, we really did." Abigail said. "History wouldn't let us pay them back."

"Well, try again today."

"I hope we're not doomed to spend the rest of our lives here. It might be okay if we could move around freely, but as it is—" Abigail didn't finish her sentence. She opened her palm, revealing the two-sided ivory comb that Sabina had used on my hair. "When Sabina heard we were leaving, she gave me this."

Abigail's Latin was sketchy and halting, but I could easily picture the conversation. Sabina would be eager and excited for her new friend who was going to Rome, wonder shining in her eyes, dark and hauntingly deep, so like her father's. The girl had heard many implausible-sounding things about Rome, Abigail told us, including that there were armies of giants there and more people than there were fish in the sea.

"Faustilla has invited some guy she's decided is the perfect match for Sabina to stop by tomorrow," Abigail said abruptly. "Apparently it's all pretty much settled. Sabina doesn't know anything about him, other than that he's an apprentice in a pottery shop. Weird, isn't it? I mean, she's only, what, thirteen?"

I sighed and tried to put a positive spin on things. "Many arranged marriages work out very well. It's an old tradition."

Kamal had lost interest in the wall painting. "My parents have an arranged marriage," he informed us.

"How did that turn out?" I asked.

He gave a shrug, the usual reaction people had to personal questions about their parents. "Fine, I guess."

"Sabina is just about the age Anne-Marie was when she got married. I suppose that turned out all right," Abigail allowed. "At least until Antoine was guillotined," she added.

Anne-Marie was Madame Lavoisier, Abigail's thesis topic.

"Speaking of Faustilla and arranged marriages, Abigail, have you noticed her interest in you?" Kamal asked.

"I have." She whipped around to face me. "Julia, promise me you won't marry me off if we have to stay here. Not to Secundus or anyone else."

"Faustilla didn't seem too discouraged when you mentioned Dave. But don't worry." I patted her shoulder. "I won't marry you off. Nor you, Kamal."

Kamal snorted and Helen said, "Let's just do our best to meet up with Dr. May in Rome," ending the conversation.

∞

Nate and Xavier returned from Nigidius's villa looking glum. They hadn't been able to get past the front door. It wasn't that they weren't *allowed* in, History's hand had stopped them. It had taken some explaining to Secundus, who was a bit baffled by how quickly they had changed their minds. They would try again later in the day.

I asked about Scaurus as we all filed into the room where Helen and Abigail and I had slept.

After waiting on a bench outside the gaudy villa with the other callers, they had been led into a large atrium open to the sky, its floor a mosaic with garum jars proclaiming "Best fish sauce." (Advertising or bragging? It wasn't that different from what many modern companies might do.) Beyond the atrium was a colonnaded garden with a fishpond, and that was about all they saw of the house. Scaurus himself had turned out to be a toga-clad, large-nosed, heavyset man with a booming voice that carried across the villa. He had sat in a high-backed chair, playing the part of a royal. The overseer, Thraex, had stood by his right hand the whole time, and, on his left, a lavishly decorated strongbox had held unseen valuables.

"Did he seem like the type of person who would order his overseer to trash Secundus's shop?" I asked.

"He didn't seem like he *wasn't* the type," Nate answered.

Xavier said thoughtfully, "Secundus told me a bit about Thraex, Scaurus's overseer. He has plans for the future. He aims to run a shop that sells his master's garum, just like Abascantus and Agathopus—two freedmen who were previously slaves of Scaurus. Scaurus likes to free his slaves after a certain period of service, to encourage loyalty in the current crop and to impress others with his wealth and generosity."

I tried another avenue, remembering a conversation I'd had with the chief about the crime that had stranded us here. "What's Scaurus's character flaw?"

Nate didn't even take a moment to think about it. "Pride. He seems to want to display to the world everything he owns, all his accomplishments. Really, who keeps a slave on one side and a strongbox on the other when receiving clients?"

Xavier mentioned a piece of gossip he'd overheard on the bench outside the villa—the garum maker hadn't been the same since the death of his son. It was rumored that he was channeling all his energy into his business. The son, Aulus, had done his father proud—he had been an elected official of Pompeii and, upon his death, the town had built an equestrian statue of him in the Forum. I didn't remember seeing it, but I put it on my Pompeii to-do list.

As he spoke, Xavier was looking over the Polaroids we'd taken since arriving in Pompeii, the ones of the harbor and Secundus's street, faces, wares, graffiti, the theater-mask fountain with its trickle of water. It seemed like he was about to suggest something, but all he said was, "These are all right. They'll make a fine addition to the *History Alive* exhibition, Helen."

"What?" Helen said.

"I didn't say anything. I was paying you a compliment."

"But?"

"Well, since you ask, it seems to me that it might be a good idea to take a snapshot of Vesuvius itself for the Geology Department. After all, the mountain will look much different after the eruption."

Helen looked chagrined that she had not thought of it herself.

"There are two Polaroid films left," was all she said. "We can go take care of it right now."

"Let's head over to the Amphitheater," Xavier suggested. "It will be deserted. August is a dead month for gladiator games. Too hot. We should be able to get a good view of the mountain from there."

Nate stopped on the way out to take a look at the lock mechanism on the side gate. "Looks undisturbed. It would have been easy enough for someone to slip in and hide in a dark corner of the garden before Secundus went out for the night."

As we wound our way through the town in the direction of the large stadium with its oval shape and graceful arches, Xavier said, "I read up on Pliny the Younger's account in order to have an idea of what to expect when the eruption came. It was something he wrote that led me to believe that coming here was the right thing to do. I'll tell you more about that in a moment. I met him, you know."

"Who? Pliny?" Helen said.

"Well, I saw him in the street. I visited Misenum one morning and someone pointed out the admiral to me. With him was a pimply, bookish-looking youth with curly hair combed forward. I attempted to make a sketch from memory later, but it didn't turn out terribly well." Xavier explained that he had not only studied Gaius Pliny's account before traveling here, but had also perused modern volcanology textbooks. "A quiet period in Vesuvius's life is about to come to an end," he said. "It's been seven hundred years since the volcano last erupted. When it comes, the eruption will make itself known with a sudden, mammoth explosion. Hot gas and ash will shoot high into the sky. Pumice and other debris will rain down on Pompeii and its countryside."

I wasn't sure what exactly pumice was, but it sounded unpleasant.

"Streets will become impassable, and roofs will collapse from the extra weight of pumice and ash by nightfall. Phase two," he added, "will be worse. The gas and ash column will collapse under its own weight. Deadly surges, six of them, will travel down the mountain at devastating speeds, burying everything in their path. Pyroclastic flows. The first will bury Herculaneum completely. The last three will reach Pompeii. The sixth will be the biggest, bringing with it unsurvivable heat and debris.

I expected to die in that one. It will sweep across the bay and reach Misenum and the island of Capri, both thirty kilometers away. Eighteen miles," he added for my benefit, but I had long ago familiarized myself with the metric system so that I could follow cafeteria conversations and understand funding requests. "When it's all over, Herculaneum will be under twenty-some meters of debris—seventy-five feet. Pompeii will fare a little better. Rooftops and temple gables might peek out above the ash when the sun reappears three days later. Land will push back sea perhaps by almost a kilometer."

Xavier shaded his eyes—the sunlight was strong in the clear blue sky—and faced the mountain. "How about we take the pictures from here?" he said, his tone matter-of-fact.

Here was the grassy area by one of the outside staircases of the Amphitheater. The stadium was quiet in the summer heat, but at other times of year it would be humming with morning animal fights, lunchtime executions, and afternoon gladiatorial combat. Nearby a vineyard lay within the town walls, and there, framed between umbrella pines, was the mountain itself. Xavier continued to speak as Abigail turned the Polaroid on the mountain. "Gaius Pliny wrote this of the disaster he was caught in: 'I believed the whole world was perishing as wretchedly as me and this was a great consolation to me in my mortality.' He was only eighteen at the time." Xavier paused. "And completely wrong, I've discovered. There is no consolation in everyone around you dying while you are. In fact, I had come to take a certain comfort in the fact that everyone I left back at St. Sunniva was alive and well."

Including whoever had sent us into this mess, I thought, taking a look around at our little group. Which one of us had someone wanted to do away with? And why not run that person down on a slippery winter night instead of subjecting others to the same fate? Perhaps it was merely a matter of opportunity—or a need for speed.

Nate stood with his large, sandaled feet planted firmly on the ground, doing a visual sweep of the area, as he always tended to do, as if danger lurked behind every statue, pine tree, and lavender bush. Back home, he had just started his inquiry into what we thought was a murder, having sent Officer Van Underberg to go through Dr. Mooney's effects. As he himself had pointed out, his officer knew just about everything he did, so getting rid of him didn't make much sense. Unless something had been said just before we stepped into STEWie's basket, when Officer Van Underberg wasn't present—something that had doomed us all from that moment on. Which would narrow down the pool of suspects to two—Gabriel Rojas and Jacob Jacobson, mentor and student, the only ones from our list of suspects who'd been present at the time. I tried to remember everything that had been said as we prepared ourselves for the Beatles' arrival at JFK airport. Abigail had wafted in after asking Dr. Rojas if she and Kamal could come along, Kamal had left a program running on his computer, Dr. Rojas had found a hat for Chief Kirkland, I had told Jacob not to tweet a play-by-play of the proceedings. Not much to go on, really.

I turned to look at Helen, who was making a quick sketch of the Amphitheater. She was as much at home here in far time as she was at St. Sunniva. Now that her connection with Dr. Mooney no longer mattered, I couldn't think of a single reason why anyone would have wanted to get rid of her. She didn't demand a ton of spots on the STEWie roster; when she did ask for a trip, it was usually a for a good reason, like with Shakespeare's plays, or more recently, when she had gone back to copy the letters destroyed by Jane Austen's sister after the novelist's death. (The letters had turned out to contain as much scheming, misunderstanding, and jealousy as one of Austen's own novels, all of it regarding one clergyman and potential suitor to the sisters, Dr. Samuel Blackall.) Given Helen's penchant for picking successful projects, perhaps professional jealousy had played a part.

Then there were our two grad students, who were currently bickering over what spot and angle would yield the best photograph of the mountain. They settled on taking a photo each. It was preposterous to think that someone would have wanted either of them out of the way—Kamal wouldn't hurt a fly, and Abigail's successes were so hard-won. The chief had suggested that perhaps someone wanted to steal one of their ideas, but it wasn't like anyone did their research in a vacuum—roster spots had to be justified months in advance, funding proposals put together, papers published, seminars given. It wasn't easy to steal other people's research.

That left yours truly.

I couldn't think of anyone who'd want to do away with me. Really.

Not that I thought everyone on campus necessarily liked me—I had ruffled a few feathers rearranging class schedules and STEWie roster spots, and delegating shared lab expenses. Erika Baumgartner had lost a STEWie spot early in the school year when, with Dean Sunder's encouragement, I had made room for several last-minute runs for Dr. May to gather snapshots of British royal coronations for the opening of the *History Alive* exhibition. The truth of the matter was that bringing in funds sometimes took precedence over research goals. Erika had said she didn't mind, but it was just about then that she had started her early morning jogs.

Steven Little had wanted early-morning time slots for his fall semester classes, but 8:00 a.m. wasn't a popular time with students for obvious reasons, so I had overruled him and scheduled his classes for various times throughout the day. Dr. Little didn't hide the fact that he disliked me and thought I was an interfering busybody who sent way too many committee requests his way. I had no doubt that he was happy to be rid of me, but probably considered me too unimportant to bother doing away with. Still, I couldn't rule him out.

As for Gabriel Rojas, I'd doubted him at one point, but I was sure he would not have used STEWie, his pride and joy, for something as boorish as this.

And I couldn't think of a single reason why Jacob Jacobson would have wanted me dead, other than the fact that I kept telling him to put away his cell phone.

It struck me that sending a group of people into a ghost zone was certainly a clean way of getting rid of them. No bodies to be found by the police, no blood on the guilty party's hands. Clean and quick.

Abigail surrendered the Polaroid camera to Kamal like they were siblings who had been told they had to share. She joined me in the shade of an umbrella pine. "A penny—no, an *as* for your thoughts, Julia," she said, carefully peeling the backing off the print in her hand.

"Just mulling over who might have sent us here and why," I said as we watched the photo come to life.

Kamal nonchalantly went down on one knee by the Amphitheater staircase, as if he needed to relace his sandal. He framed the mountain in his hands, trying to find the perfect shot before taking his photo.

Abigail said to me, "Twenty possibilities."

For a moment I thought she was counting everybody in the TTE building, whether they had the lab door code or not, but she went on, "Dr. Little is my top suspect. Maybe he wanted to get rid of Chief Kirkland, or you, or Dr. Presnik, or me, or Kamal... What's he doing? That's not a great angle, he'll get a lot of glare. Anyway, that's five possibilities right there. Or Dr. B wanted to kill Chief Kirkland, or you, or me, or Dr. Presnik, or Kamal for some reason. That's five more possibilities right there. Or it could have been Jacob, or Dr. Rojas—"

"That's the problem," I said. "Too many possibilities."

"It's actually more than twenty. It could have been a combination of culprits and victims, like maybe Dr. Little and Dr. B conspired to get rid of the security chief and you for some reason, or maybe all four of them conspired to get rid of all five of us for some reason. I could total up all the possibilities—"

"Let's see if we can rule out some people," I said. "I don't think Dr. Rojas did it, for one."

"I don't either. And I don't think Jacob did it. Dr. B has been looking a little stressed out lately," she said quietly. "She's forgotten about our weekly meeting a couple of times. Sergei said that she was late grading midterms this semester. She is really hard to please, generally speaking," Abigail added, as if easygoing people were never criminals. I knew that some of Dr. Baumgartner's colleagues and students thought the professor could be best described as pushy and ambitious. Both were qualities that could be helpful in academia, in my opinion.

"If Erika wanted something, she would go for it openly, not like this," I said.

"Which brings us back to Dr. Little," Abigail said.

"Who you both happen to dislike the most," Nate said from behind us. I hadn't noticed him standing there.

"Doesn't mean he didn't do it," I said. "Though I can't think of a good reason why he would have sent us all here."

"I can. To get rid of me."

∞

"Do you and Dr. Little know each other personally?" I asked. I couldn't think of any reason why Dr. Little would want to kill Nate that was related to the case.

"We're next-door neighbors. There was an incident during the summer, just after I moved in. I had requested that Dr. Little and his wife cut down a red oak that was swaying during thunderstorms and was in danger of falling on my new house. Dr. Little wanted me to pay for it. But the law is the law. The tree was on his side of the property. He seemed to think I was abusing my police powers somehow."

"You think he sent us here, Chief Kirkland?" said Abigail. "Because of a personal grudge against you?"

"You'd be surprised what behavior people will to stoop to with their neighbors. But there's something more to this, something that's eluding me," Nate said. "Someone wasn't just using STEWie as a weapon. There's a significance to how our disappearance was staged. It's bound to affect the program itself, isn't it? Make it harder to get funding?"

"Probably," I agreed. "You think someone doesn't approve of us knowing more about the past than we used to? Like Mrs. Butterworth?"

"Who's she?" Abigail asked.

"A frequent and generous donor to the school. I wasn't really suggesting her as a suspect, only giving an example. She wasn't too happy that we ruled out Sir Francis Bacon as the penner of Shakespeare's plays. I suppose there have been other things our researchers have confirmed or disproved that may have rubbed someone the wrong way. If it's someone within the department, especially an untenured professor, he or she may not wish to rock the boat by saying something openly against the program. This way—well, like Xavier said, Dean Sunder will have his work cut out for him. He'll need all the help he can get from donors like Mrs. Butterworth and Ewan Coffey to keep the lab going."

"Ewan Coffey? You mean our library donor?" Helen asked as she and Xavier came over to where the four of us were gathered in the shade of the pine. "I've never seen any of his movies, but he has done a lot for the school."

"He was the lead in *Robin and Marion*," Abigail explained in a dreamy voice, "and in *Antony and Cleopatra* and *Juliet's Romeo*—though the movies themselves," she added more briskly, a touch of pink rising in her sunburned cheeks, "were silly history-wise, of course."

"They should consult us on these things," Kamal, who had ambled over after taking his photo, concurred.

"Whatever happened with the new STEWie generator, Julia?" Xavier asked as we watched Kamal's photo appear on the print. "Was Lewis able to arrange for one?"

"He was, through Ewan Coffey. Though everything was put on hold after you, uh—left."

"Sorry."

"I've heard that Ewan Coffey is coming to campus for this year's graduation, Julia, is that true?" Abigail demanded.

"He might," I admitted. "Don't spread this around if we make it back, but there's been talk of giving him an honorary degree from the Drama Department." Technically, Ewan Coffey wasn't an alum because he had never finished his studies, but that was a minor point when it came to generating good publicity for the school.

"Do you think there's a chance he might stop by the TTE lab?" Abigail breathed.

I opted not to remind her that two-thousand-some years separated us from Mr. Ewan Coffey and his smoldering good looks. "Is anyone else keeping any secrets?" I asked, with a look at Nate. I felt a little irritated that he hadn't told us about his trouble with Dr. Little. He seemed to think this was his investigation only. It was part of my job to help figure out what had happened and why. Dean Sunder had instructed me to do so.

"Well..." Helen said.

She glanced at Xavier.

"What?" he said.

"Well—Gabriel and I went out on a few dates. Before you and I met."

"I know. Rojas was the one who introduced me to you. He said it didn't work out."

"I was the one who broke it off. He was a little—too polite, I suppose. I could never tell what he was thinking. He didn't seem to mind when I broke things off. Then he met Lane and it didn't seem to matter that you and I were getting married. But all these years, even after he married Lane, I've rather thought that he might still have feelings for me. At your memorial service, as Lane was putting a basket of flowers by the enlarged photo of you that Julia had ordered, Gabriel quietly asked me out for coffee."

"Dr. Rojas?" Abigail asked, incredulous.

"Professors are human, too," I said, impatient to hear more of the story.

"Coffee, huh? And what did you say, Helen?" Xavier asked.

"I said no, of course. I would have said no even if he had asked at a more appropriate time and place. Again, he didn't seem to mind, and his behavior as we prepared for the New York City trip was as usual, but—"

"—here we are," Nate finished the sentence for her. "Well, crimes have certainly been committed for lesser reasons."

"Let's hope Dean Sunder manages to keep the program going so Dr. May's team comes to the Colosseum dedication as planned. And that it happens without delay at their end," Helen said. "If things are put on hold for a year or two or ten, everyone we know will be older when we make it home—even your Ewan Coffey, Miss Tanner. That would certainly be strange."

"It would be very strange," I said, thinking of a new dean's assistant taking my place in the small office on the ground floor of the Hypatia of Alexandria House, of Dean Sunder retired, of Jacob Jacobson with a *Dr.* in front of his name, of Officer Van Underberg in charge of campus security. I felt melancholy, like all signs pointed to us having to stay in the past, never to set foot again on the sprawling St. Sunniva campus. I stared at the volcano, mesmerized by its hidden power. "Vesuvius is beautiful, isn't it? The vineyards, the rich farmland, the orchards, the power and beauty of the mountain itself..."

"As powerful and beautiful as a coiled snake," Kamal said. He had obtained sweets earlier and he pulled out a handful from the satchel. Abigail accepted a piece. "You want some, Julia? Chief? Professors?"

To my surprise, Nate took one of the sticky sweets.

I shook my head at Kamal's offering. "Got a bit of a headache. I think I just need some water."

"We should be getting back anyway," Nate said. "I want to see if we can accidentally run into Nigidius by his front door so that we can ask him some questions." He popped the sweet into his mouth.

Abigail was looking at me with concern. "I thought you said you felt better, Julia."

"Let's see your hand," Nate said through a full mouth.

"Well—all right." I unwrapped Faustilla's cloth. The yellow paste, dried and cracking, enveloped my index finger and hid whatever was underneath. But the underlying redness and swelling had spread to the neighboring fingers in thin reddish streaks, even up my hand a bit. "I guess Faustilla's ointment didn't work,"

I said. Kamal had moved away and stopped eating the sweets, his face a little green. I noticed that Xavier was staring at my hand as if debating something, but he only bit his lip in thought.

I rewrapped the hand and changed the subject. "What's pumice anyway?"

"Hmm? Pumice? Superhot, frothy lava that cools fast and solidifies into sponge-like chunks upon being ejected from a volcano," Xavier explained.

"Sponge," I said slowly.

"Exactly. A light rock with many air pockets."

"No," I said. "Sponge. Not as a noun but as a verb. Faustilla—when we saw her with Sabina at the baths, she was scrubbing a darkish stain off the sleeve of her garment. I think it was garum. From the broken jars."

"You didn't mention that before," Nate said. It was his turn to sound irritated. "But most likely the stain got there as she was cleaning up the mess in the shop," he suggested, as if to rule out that possibility before jumping to any conclusions.

I visualized the scene again—Secundus sweeping, Faustilla wiping down the wall, Sabina being chastised for wasting time talking to the foreigners from Britannia. I shook my head. "She had on a sleeveless dress when we saw her in the shop. Any splatter would have gone on her arm. The dress at the baths—I'm pretty sure it was the one she had on yesterday morning, in the villa courtyard. She must have changed back into it—"

"The stain could have been from making beet juice," Xavier said. "She sells it to clients. It's supposed to be an aphrodisiac."

Nate took charge. "If there's a chance that Faustilla's responsible, we had better hurry back. Professor, you saw how Secundus was looking at the town's top garum maker. He may head over to spit at his feet. If Scaurus is blameless, that can only end badly."

21

"Do you realize what it means if Faustilla did trash her son's shop?" Nate asked as we hurried along. The others had been immediately behind us, but History had blocked them from taking the same street and they were forced to take a longer route back to Secundus's shop.

"What?"

"I tasted garum for nothing."

"Ow," I said as my right hand brushed against a building wall.

"Your hand?"

"I didn't want to say it before, but it's *really* starting to hurt."

We found Secundus outside his shop. His mother was behind the counter, and they seemed to be arguing about something. As we approached, we saw him give a dismissive wave to end their conversation, as if to say, *Enough, I'll do what I must.* Then he turned and left.

"Secundus, wait!" Nate and I called out at the same time and ground to a stop.

The urgency of our tone halted the shopkeeper. He looked almost comical as he stood midstride on the pedestrian stepping-stones outside his shop, staring at us in puzzlement.

I pointed to Faustilla and then the pile of refuse by the stepping-stones—the broken jars and dried-up pickled vegetables that he had swept into the street yesterday morning, now covered with flies. I didn't say a word, but I didn't need to. My meaning could not have been plainer.

Secundus looked down at the fruits of his labor, mingled with grime that had been lodged against the stepping-stones by long-passed rain torrents and refuse newly discarded by the proprietor of the tavern across the street. I felt for him. It was through no fault of his own that he was not his mother's favorite, but the mere accident of birth order. Those deep eyes of his rose to meet Faustilla's and she didn't look abashed, just angry that she had been found out. Proud and defiant, she met her son's gaze for a long moment, then turned to Nate and me. For a second I thought she might follow Secundus's plan and spit at our feet, but she merely turned and went into the back room. She had destroyed her son's carefully nurtured garum and her own pickled vegetables, but had not been able to bring herself to do the same to the ointments and mixtures that she kept in the back.

She returned a moment later with a cloth purse in her hands. She released it and it landed with a loud clink on the stone counter. The take from Secundus's till. One of the coins, a chipped brass one, rolled out and I watched as it came to a stop and settled on the counter. I didn't understand what Faustilla said to Nate and me, but I imagined it was something along the lines of everything being fair in love, war, and the battle for personal happiness. She had been willing to let her son confront Scaurus, something that was bound to end disastrously, rather than admit the truth.

She went into the back room for a second time, came back with a shawl, and, draping it over her head and neck, hurried past Nate and me without looking at her son. I knew where she was headed.

"She's gone off to have a curse tablet made," I murmured to Nate. "We are about to be one cursed married couple."

Secundus had wordlessly taken his mother's place at the shop counter. His shoulders seemed squarer, his back straighter. He sent us a look of thanks—intermingled with something in the vicinity of *Family, what can you do?*—and picked up the change bag and threw it behind the counter, then began hawking his wares to passersby.

"Well," Nate said uneasily, "that went better than I expected."

∞

"Now that Secundus has all the facts, he can make an informed decision whether to stay here or sell out and join his brother in Rome. I rather hope it's the second, of course, what with the volcano and all," I said as Nate and I headed to the theater-mask fountain. Xavier had asked us to fill a couple of jugs with water for our journey. Abigail and Kamal had gone down to the harbor with Sabina, and Helen had stayed behind to help Xavier ready everything. It was time to leave. The sun was just about at its highest point in the sky, meaning that we would face the full heat of the day, but none of us wanted to stay a minute longer under Faustilla's hostile stare. We had buried the note addressed to Dr. May under the pear tree in the garden behind the shop. If it got to her in time, she would know to keep an eye out for us in the vicinity of the Roman Colosseum.

"Whatever he decides, it will be the same decision he would have made anyway, whether we came here or not. Right, Julia? Otherwise we wouldn't have been able to say anything. I have to believe Secundus would have changed his mind about confronting Scaurus even if we hadn't stopped him."

That nicely deflated the pride I had felt about solving the case and helping out a fellow human being.

"Justice is a complicated thing," the chief said, noticing my crestfallen expression. "Sometimes all you get is knowledge, understanding—the who, the why, the how—and that has to be enough."

"And you? Would you be satisfied if we knew for sure it was Dr. Little"—for we all suspected him, though we kept bickering about his possible motives—"who marooned us here, even if we fail to hook up with Dr. May's team in Rome? If all we were able to do is write down his name and bury another note and hope it's found centuries from now?"

He grunted an affirmative.

I wasn't sure I believed him. Knowing who did it was all well and good; getting a message to St. Sunniva to bring our attacker to justice—the prison kind—even better; but the best scenario of all was to get home, look our would-be killer in the eye, and *then* send him or her to prison.

I wondered how many people Nate had sent to prison in his time. Watching as the thin trickle of water slowly filled the first of the two jugs, I asked, "What did you do at your previous job?" The future Boundary Waters Canoe Area Wilderness, which was near the border with Canada, probably didn't look hugely different in this century than it did when I had visited during my college days. Lakes and forests, except with Sioux and Ojibwe settlements here and there instead of park visitor campsites.

He stuck the first of the filled jugs in my good hand and set the other jug under the fountain faucet. "What did I do at the BWCAW? There's an old saying that the park ranger's job is to protect the park from visitors, the visitors from the park, and the visitors from each other."

A burly man with a hoe over one shoulder and his head down bumped my shoulder as Nate bent down to shift the jug so it captured more of the trickling water. A short line of Pompeians had formed behind us, the disappearing water clearly the main topic of conversation. As we left the fountain behind us, I felt myself getting a bit misty-eyed at the thought that these sturdy-stoned streets would be choked with debris in perhaps a soon as a month, the houses with their awnings and back gardens crushed under falling rocks. The life of this town was nearing its end, and its citizens would have to flee.

I didn't have much of a chance to stay misty-eyed as we turned the corner. The burly man with the hoe was blocking our path, standing with his sandals shoulder-distance apart in the middle of the narrow lane, which, I was suddenly aware, was otherwise deserted. High, windowless walls and a shuttered door or two stood to either side of us. The figure blocking our way swung the hoe over one bare, beefy shoulder. He said something in a low growl.

"This guy seems to know us," I said to Nate.

"That's Scaurus's overseer, Thraex. We must have given the wrong impression this morning."

Thraex growled again at the mention of his master's name.

"The wrong impression? That we were suspicious that his master might have ordered the trashing of Secundus's shop? That's exactly what we were thinking. He's bigger than I expected," I added.

"Julia, turn around and walk away. Find a different route to Secundus's shop."

"I don't think so. Besides, two is better than one when facing muscular Romans armed with large garden implements."

"I can handle him."

"I'm sure you can, but I'm not leaving. Should I scream for help?"

"Julia—"

"Or we can both make a run for it. Or—"

"Or what?"

"Or we can explain to Thraex here that our interest in his master was purely an investigative one and that his innocence has been proven beyond doubt."

"And you know how to translate that into Latin?"

Thraex had been following our exchange like a tennis fan at a close match. He swung the hoe off his shoulder and wielded it up menacingly.

"I think we could outrun him," I said and winced. A sharp pain shot through my head as I tensed my muscles. My body was sore and aching, like I was coming down with the flu. "You try and pass him on the left, I'll take the right—"

The burly overseer took a step forward and thrust his face near mine. He had bad teeth and bad breath.

I edged back.

Nate tapped him on the shoulder, and Thraex turned and swung the hoe. The chief jumped out of the way, the water splashing from the jug he was holding onto the sun-warmed cobblestones.

The overseer now stood between us, his muscular legs planted firmly on the ground.

A loud pop, like a car backfiring, distracted Thraex for a moment. He looked around for its source.

"That's strange," I said. "It sounded like a car backfiring, which is of course impossible, but I don't know what else would—"

Thraex glanced at me, making the rest of the sentence die in my throat. He smirked, then turned back toward the chief, who was holding the earthenware jug in front of him like a shield.

I opened my mouth to scream and summon help.

Not a sound came out.

I tried again.

Nothing.

I threw my jug at the overseer's back. It bounced off him and shattered into pieces on the cobblestones—not loudly enough to summon help—and made him growl but not turn.

The overseer raised his hoe and took a step toward Nate, who was trapped with his back against the wall—

"Julia! Chief Kirkland!"

Xavier was hurrying toward us, his hair streaming behind him. He ground to a halt, trying to catch his breath. "It has begun."

"No," I said, "quite the opposite. As you know, we've wrapped up the investigation quite nicely—we just need to explain that to Thraex here—" I tapped the big man on the shoulder and he turned toward me, looming over my head. "Your master has been cleared of the crime," I said loudly, as if raising my voice would help him understand me, then went into some version of pidgin English. "*Cleared.* Yes, you understand?"

Thraex simply stared at me, like I was as much of a threat as a buzzing mosquito.

"The mountain, Julia—didn't you hear—"

"The popping noise?" Nate interrupted. "We heard it."

I looked over Thraex's shoulder at the mountain. Everything was quiet. The wind had changed direction, I noticed, and was now coming from Vesuvius rather than the sea. It gently blew my hair back from my forehead—a pleasant feeling in the heat of the day. Maybe I wasn't coming down with the flu. Maybe it was just the heat.

"*Cleared,*" I repeated for good measure for Thraex, then said, "Are you sure, Xavier? I'm as ready to panic as the next person, but that wasn't anything I'd call an explosion—"

"According to geologists," he said, punctuating the words with sharp intakes of breath, "a minor explosion of steam and ash on the eastern flank of the mountain preceded the eruption.

"It has begun," he repeated.

22

"How much time do we have?" I asked, giving in to the panic. Xavier had explained to Scaurus's overseer that we were more than happy to leave his master alone and Thraex had ambled off (apparently he had only been trying to scare us out of town, and was mollified by Xavier's pronouncement that we had every intention of leaving). At the end of their conversation, the professor had pointed to the mountain and said something insistently, but judging by the leisurely pace Thraex set for himself as he continued down to the harbor, it was clear that he had not understood.

"How much time do we have?" I repeated.

"Not much. Leave the jugs, let's go."

"Are the others back yet?" Nate asked as we willed ourselves to walk at a normal pace. Town life was still going on around us as usual. The harbor was where Abigail and Kamal had taken Sabina to say good-bye and to help her gather seashells for one of Faustilla's mixtures.

"They're not back yet. And Helen has gone to the Nigidii tomb to gather what's left of your twenty-first-century belongings—she didn't want to leave anything behind. I tried to reason with her, but you know Helen." Xavier tugged at his hair. "We need to split up. You two go find Abigail and Kamal, I'll see if I can catch up with Helen, then we'll meet up at the Secundus's shop."

Nate took charge. "No, that'll take too much time. Julia—can you make it to the harbor?"

"Certainly. My hand may hurt but I can still walk." It suddenly struck me how convenient cell phones were. I desperately wished that we all had them—and a cell tower, too. I felt the breeze on my face again, gentle and warm, from the direction of Vesuvius.

"You bring back Abigail and Kamal, and I'll see if I can find Dr. Presnik. Dr. Mooney, you get the cart and the donkeys ready and whatever else we need," Nate commanded. "We'll all meet up by the Nola Gate. Is everyone clear on the plan?"

Xavier went off without a word. Despite all he had read about the eruption and all of his preparations, it seemed like he couldn't believe it was actually happening.

"What should I do with Sabina?" I asked quickly, impatient to get moving.

"Drop her off at her father's house. It'll be on your way to the gate."

∞

Kamal, Abigail, and Sabina looked young and carefree as they bounded up the steep road from the harbor, their sandals in their hands, their feet still wet from sea dipping. Celer followed a few steps behind, an air of indignation hanging about him, as if he disapproved of all the physical activity he had been subjected to.

They had not heard the small pop.

We all heard what came next.

Thunder, the loudest I'd heard in my life, reverberated through the town, shaking house and garden walls and the very stones under our feet. All around us, the residents of houses and shops and temples, slaves and masters alike, spilled out into the street to see what was causing the blue-sky storm, probably expecting to see an angry Jupiter hovering above the town flinging thunderbolts. In the commotion, a merchant bumped into me—his large nose, toga, and heavy figure perfectly matched Xavier's description of Scaurus—and I watched apprehension replace bafflement on his face as fingers started pointing in the direction of Vesuvius. A gray, billowing column was rising from the top of the mountain—a terrible, deadly cloud.

The town doesn't matter one bit, the people do, I thought. But they stood frozen in place, not knowing how to react, and there was no warning we could give.

"Let's go," I croaked as Sabina and the grad students hurriedly put their sandals back on.

We ran then. Or tried to. The path would not open for us, only for Sabina and her dog. She looked back at the three of us as we stood frozen in place. She wasn't scared yet, only puzzled by our strange behavior and the even stranger behavior of the mountain that had lain dormant for her entire life. She skipped a few steps back to where we were and tugged on Abigail's hand. Abigail looked stricken.

Kamal shook his head. "We might have to let Sabina and Celer go back to the shop alone while we head for the Nola Gate."

"Kamal is right, unfortunately. We have to let them go," I said in what I hoped was a firm voice. "There is nothing we can do."

But my words didn't matter. Sabina had picked up on our anxiety and would not leave without her new friends.

More slowly than we wanted, one foot in front of the other, together we wound our way back to Secundus's shop, Sabina not quite sure what to make of our antics as we crossed streets for no apparent reason and made unexplained detours to go where History would allow. Kamal had picked up Celer, grasping the squat, brown animal firmly in his arms. All the while, the dirty gray cloud billowed up from the mountain—rising slowly, cruelly, like an accidental toxic release from a factory smokestack. Higher and higher.

We made it back to Secundus's shop as ash and the pumice Xavier had mentioned—white, hard, and dangerous—started descending from a suddenly overcast sky. The smokestack cloud had flattened into a wide disc that blocked out the sun—the umbrella pine described by the young Pliny, who was watching from across the bay, I thought in a detached way. Pumice began to rattle down onto roof tiles like an especially loud hailstorm. We ran inside through the garden gate and into the back room where Faustilla's mixtures and salves lay unattended—she was not there—and into the shop. At the counter, Secundus was wrestling the shutters closed as debris rained down on the cobblestones of the street fronting his shop. The graduate students and I turned to leave so that we could meet up with the others, but Secundus called out something and pointed upstairs.

Xavier looked up, lit lamp in hand, as the three of us stumbled into his room. He seemed calmer, like he had accepted what was happening. "Good, you're here," he said in a businesslike tone.

But I suddenly realized that something else wasn't. The cart and the donkeys had not been in their place in the hay-strewn stable downstairs.

23

Abigail and Kamal stared at the professor as if this entire experience was a project he had assigned and they needed a little help to finish it. The professor, for his part, looked like he needed some help himself, but I couldn't think of anything to say. I had hoped that Nate and Helen had already taken the cart to the Nola Gate, but Xavier just shook his head when I asked him. We would have to make our way out of town on foot. We were helping Xavier light the rest of the lamps in preparation for facing the dark volcanic night when Nate burst into the room, covered with a fine layer of ash and breathing heavily. "Helen—" He paused. "Why are you all still here? Why haven't you headed for the gate?"

I closed the door behind him and asked, "Where's Helen?"

He looked around the small room wildly. "She didn't make it back here? I ran all the way to the Nigidii tomb and back, didn't see her, but it was damned hard to spot anyone with all the people running about in the ash." He took off his felt fedora, which he must have picked up back at the tomb, and shook it, dislodging a shower of ash onto the wooden floor. "All of our stuff was gone except for the hat, which was on the ground outside the tomb—Helen must have dropped it. You don't think she's gone to the fig tree on the slopes of the mountain to fetch our overcoats, do you?"

Xavier stopped what he was doing to answer Nate. "Helen might just be foolish enough to do that."

"Could she have headed straight for the gate?" I asked.

"Does she have the cart?" Nate asked.

"Faustilla has it," Xavier said, passing a lit lamp to Nate. "She took it this morning. She should have been back by now."

The first time we had seen Faustilla, she had taken the cart to the villa that rested high on Vesuvius's slopes, higher than the fig tree, to personally deliver an ointment. Disliking her as I did, I still hoped that today's visit had taken Faustilla in the opposite direction, farther inland to Nola, perhaps, where we were planning to go ourselves, or Nuceria, in the hills. I didn't necessarily like her underhanded method of trying to get her way. But her position in life—being wholly dependent on her son—was such that it might have seemed like the only course of action available to her.

The missing cart was not a good development, but it had eased my conscience somewhat. I had been worried that we were depriving Secundus and his family of their only means of escape. (Xavier had negotiated a price for the cart—all of his silks—but the silks would do little to help the merchant if he didn't survive the explosion.) Now we were all in the same boat.

"None of the dates listed in the medieval manuscripts are right. Curious, isn't it?" Xavier said, crouching by the bed as he filled the last of the lamps. "I had assumed that *one* of them must be right. History never fails to surprise me."

Nate put a hand on Xavier's shoulder. The professor looked up at him, a numb look on his face. Our plan, so carefully crafted, had fallen to pieces.

"So, no cart," the chief said. "We head out on foot, then. You've prepared lamps, good. We'll need pillows and blankets, too."

"Xavier," I said, squeezing around Nate to crouch by the professor. "Did you have a plan B?"

24

I raised my voice as the clatter of the pumice hitting the roof above our heads intensified. "What were you going to do if you decided not to stick around for the eruption after all, Professor? It would have been hard to find a spot on a merchant ship in a hurry and impractical to rely on a donkey cart. You have some sort of portable version of STEWie, don't you," I said. It wasn't a question.

My head was pounding, loudly—the volcanic storm outside was making it difficult to think—but I rather suspected I was right.

"What is this?" Nate said, the first time I'd heard his voice vibrate with anger. "Professor, what is this?"

Xavier hesitated slightly before pulling out a chamber pot from under the bed. He retrieved a bundle from behind it, and unwrapped it to reveal a rectangular black box, bigger than the Callback, like a chunky briefcase with knobs and displays all over it. "It's meant for one—a personal, portable STEWie. I have been doing some local sightseeing with it—that's how I went to Misenum. Yes, it could get one of us safely to Rome."

"One of us?" I said.

"Yes. The battery—a little something the Engineering Department came up with for me—still has some life. Enough for one person to make a short hop up the coast. Rome is one of the destinations I had preprogrammed."

Kamal had cracked open the door and was looking out onto the balcony. Cupping his lamp with one hand, he watched the strange, thick, gray snowfall, one that brought darkness and heat, not cold. An early night had descended on the town. He closed the door and turned to face us, his face illuminated by the flickering flame of the lamp like he was telling a campfire story. "I'll be the one to say it first. Yes, we could use your portable STEWie to send one person to Rome, Professor, while the rest of us try to make our way out of Pompeii on foot. Here's the thing, though. If we send Julia because she isn't feeling well and is the least likely to make it out"—he stopped me from protesting by raising a hand—"it still may not help her. Julia's hand is getting worse. She needs antibiotics. And if the rest of us manage to make it out on foot—a big *if*—we're more likely to get time-stuck somewhere than meet up with Dr. May. I don't want to live some half life where I can only take roads History allows and where I may never find a wife. I don't want my parents to think I'm dead. I want to eat a hamburger and drink Diet Coke in an air-conditioned restaurant and see the next Ewan Coffey flick with Abigail and the other TTE grad students at the St. Sunniva theater—yes, I'm admitting that I like his movies, sappy though they are. I want to get a flu shot and have a dental checkup. I want to write my thesis and get a job somewhere continuing your work, Dr. Mooney, and Dr. Rojas's, too. And, Dr. Mooney—you know we won't need much battery power, not if we're heading in the direction of home. I don't know if your device can accommodate all of us. I say we find out."

It was a rather long speech for Kamal, and we had all stayed silent as he spoke.

Something crossed Xavier Mooney's face. "It's not that simple. Look, using the portable STEWie to try to get home would be tantamount to—to *surfing* ghost zones."

25

"Dr. Mooney," Nate said in his best security chief tone, the one that made everyone stop and listen. He had to practically shout because the pumice hail continued unabated, and a new element had been added to it: the sound of tiles breaking and slipping off the roof. "The roof will soon be in danger of collapse and the air is only going to get more toxic. We need to come to a decision."

"I second the motion that we go back to see the next Ewan Coffey flick. I'll even buy the popcorn and the drinks," Abigail said. "And Dave was going to teach me how to play golf."

"Even if we send Julia to Rome, it will be month's before Dr. May gets there. Julia doesn't have that kind of time," Nate said. "An infection in a world without antibiotics is no joke."

"Do you think I don't know that? I've been thinking of nothing else since I saw how bad her hand looked, weighing whether it's better for Julia to take her chances here or use my device to try to make it home—"

"I'm fine," I protested. "Besides, antibiotics are made from mold, aren't they? I'm sure they have mold in Rome. Once we get there, we just have to figure out what kind I need, where to get it, and how to make an antibiotic from it while we wait for Dr. May."

"Now it's a different equation, right?" said Abigail quietly. "Not whether we'll manage to meet up with Dr. May, but whether we can get out of Pompeii alive."

"Dr. Mooney, Abigail is right," Nate said. "Would using the portable STEWie to reach home really be more dangerous than trying to battle our way out of town on foot?"

"Possibly," said Xavier. He retrieved a cloak from under the bed, at the other end from where the chamber pot and the portable STEWie had been stored. He threw it on the bed and added a blanket, a pillow, and another cloak to the pile. "Look, I've had a lot of time to think while I've been here. When I embarked on this journey, I was very sure I didn't want to go back. However"—he threw another blanket on the pile—"I'll admit that it hasn't been as much of an adventure as I'd expected it to be. In the beginning, yes, but after a while you settle down to the minutiae of everyday life. It would appear that the university life suits me better than a trader's life. Don't tell Helen. Besides, I seem to be feeling healthier." Having run out of things to add to the pile on the bed, he turned to face us. "Fine. Let's go see if the basket will accept all of us and get us home."

Abigail piped up. "I've thought of a problem. *Our* basket left us under the fig tree, and returned back to the lab empty."

"Meaning we're dead no matter what we do?" Kamal said. The flickering lamp in his hand wouldn't be of much help outside, I thought, in the darkness of the ash and pumice rain. He added, "Otherwise our basket would have stayed. I've thought that all along."

"It returned because my basket was already here. Your basket wasn't needed anymore," Xavier said.

"But that makes no sense, Professor. Your basket arrived back at the lab empty. We saw it," Kamal said.

I wondered how they were so sure—the basket was, after all, invisible; then I remembered how Dr. Rojas had once explained to me that the basket gave off a faint high-frequency hum that could be detected by sensitive instruments. Kamal meant that they had "seen it" on the lab instruments.

"I figured out how to splinter off a small part—a Mooney-shaped piece, if you will, though not literally, of course—and send the rest back. That was all I needed for the portable STEWie. You didn't notice anything different about the basket?"

"Not a thing. I'm dying to see the theory behind your work, Professor," Kamal added. It was perhaps not the best choice of words under the circumstances.

"The basket must have stretched back out," the professor said. "It is an interesting phenomenon."

"Maybe we could suggest it to Jacob as a thesis topic," said Abigail.

Nate threw a look in my direction. Like me, he couldn't believe his ears. Why were they discussing the finer technical points of time travel? It was time to go. Only—I sat down on Xavier's bed, next to the pile of blankets and pillows, my knees suddenly weak.

Abigail put her palm to my forehead. Her skin felt cool. "Julia, you're burning up."

"It's nothing," I said.

"Here, Julia, let me help you," Nate said, pulling me to my feet. "Where is the basket fragment?" he asked Xavier.

"Where I left it. Just beyond the Nola Gate. In a tomb."

"These tombs sure are handy," I said.

Nate took one of the blankets and folded it roughly into a square before handing it to me. I realized he wanted me to balance it on my head, for protection once we left Xavier's quarters and their illusion of safety. "We better tie something around our faces so that we're not breathing in the fumes and ash," he said. "And wet it with water."

"Yes—downstairs, in the back room. The silks I gave Secundus in exchange for the cart." Xavier picked up the portable STEWie and clutched it in front of him like a shield. "I want to make sure everyone understands that I don't have the coordinates to the TTE lab and we have no way of computing a safe trajectory. We'll be jumping blind, so we'll gravitate toward ghost zones. To put it bluntly, we're going to fall into a few before we make it home."

A particularly loud thud overhead signaled the descent of a large rock. The professor's didgeridoo slipped and we watched it fall to the ground. The roof had started to sag in that corner.

"What about Helen?" I asked.

"Let's hope she's waiting for us at the gate."

"Lead the way," the chief said, sliding a pillow over his fedora.

∞

"A night blacker and darker than any other," quoted Xavier. "Gaius Pliny."

The ash came down hot and thick; the pumice—no longer white but gray—was bruising and dangerous. Tongues of thunder crackled on the mountain and fires were bursting forth all over the upper slopes, like flames seeping out from hell itself. The ground shook. I realized that the donkey cart would probably have been useless in any case—the street was already ankle deep in pumice and other debris. Scorched rock bounced off rooftops and landed by our feet. One hit the blanket I was balancing on my head, jolting me and making me pick up the pace. It took all my concentration to keep within an arm's distance of the others;

I couldn't see even a few paces ahead, my eyes gritty, teary. The ash felt hot on my sandaled feet and the rotten-egg stench of sulfur permeated the cloth around my face. Figures passed us like ghosts in the night, their flickering torches and lamps disembodied halos of light, calling out as they tried to meet up with relatives or friends. Others peered out at the strange phenomenon from within their rooms and shops as if they were trying to decide what to do. We passed a man who was calling something out over and over again, as if all traces of sanity had left him.

But many of Pompeii's citizens were hastily throwing their possessions onto horses, wheelbarrows, and carts. A steady stream of people headed with us in the direction of Nola and safety.

In the passageway of the Nola Gate, Xavier stopped, straining to see in the dark volcanic night. There was no sign of Helen. He hollered through the cloth wrapped around his nose and mouth. "Let's move a bit farther down. We'll have to go tomb by tomb until we reach the one we need. I'm having trouble orienting myself—"

A fiery rock whooshed past us, shattering a statuette on an altar.

"Hurry," the chief urged, as if we needed any human encouragement.

"There." Xavier pointed.

One by one, we stumbled into a tomb barely large enough to hold us all. Sabina hesitated by the door as if she wasn't sure she wanted to come in. Xavier made the decision for her, pushing her inside.

∞

We had not meant to bring her with us.

With a lamp in his hand and a blanket over his head, her father had left to look for Faustilla, but not before entrusting Sabina to us.

Xavier had attempted to explain that we ourselves were leaving, urging him to follow us out of town, but to no avail. Secundus, resolve firm in those deep, dark eyes of his, had been adamant that he needed to find his mother. He would not, in any case, want to leave his shop. If the gods decreed it to be so, he would die in peace as long as he knew that Sabina was safe. Besides, he had added in a sudden burst of practicality, who could guarantee that the gods' anger didn't extend to Nola as well?

We had no answer that we could give.

Still, he had seen the STEWie device slung over Xavier's shoulder by its leather strap—had even extended a calloused hand to touch it. Plastic was two millennia away and the device with its wires and buttons and display screens had held his attention for a long moment. Perhaps it was that more than anything that had made him place Sabina in our care. "Friends, take her with you to a safe place," he had said, looking straight at me for a long moment before turning to go. "Diana will keep an eye on her."

And so we had brought Sabina with us, and she had brought Celer.

As we helped each other swat ash off our clothes, Xavier turned back toward the tomb archway. "Wait here. I'll go back outside to see if I can find Helen."

Nate pulled him up by the shoulder. "You're the only one of us who knows how to operate that portable STEWie of yours, Professor. I'll go. If I'm not back in fifteen minutes…" He tied the cloth back around his face, grabbed a pillow for his head, and, bending his head, headed back out through the tomb archway.

"Hurry," Xavier yelled after him, but Nate probably didn't hear him above the clatter of pumice on the tomb roofs and street stones.

I was having doubts, serious ones. "I don't think we should do this on my account. This portable STEWie thing sounds very dangerous."

"You'd do the same for us," Abigail said.

"You don't know that. I might not."

She patted my shoulder. "I know you would, Julia. Besides, we all want to go home, right?"

"We gotta come up with a better name than portable STEWie," Kamal said in a show of bravado. "Mini-STEWie? STEWie Jr.? Slingshot?"

"Slingshot it is," Abigail concurred.

"Slingshot, then," said their professor, wiping soot off of his device and laying it on the floor. "If only I had a way of computing a safe trajectory. All I can do is point us in the right direction. I'll try to do it in as few jumps as possible—" He stopped speaking as a fit of coughing overtook him. It was getting harder to breathe.

"We have a problem," I said, thinking of Secundus, who was so trusting of his gods and goddesses even in the face of total disaster. I nodded toward Sabina, who was whispering something into the goddess Diana amulet as she crouched by the professor, her face pale with fear and ash. Next to her, Celer panted as he tried to get enough air.

"We're not leaving her here," said Abigail.

"Maybe she was meant to walk out of town," Kamal said like he didn't believe his own words.

"Are you suggesting we send her out there alone, into that shower of fire and rock?" Abigail protested. "Why don't we just bring her with us?"

"I have considered it," Xavier said without looking up. "Nothing like that has ever been tried. Besides, if she is meant to live, we won't be able to yank her from her own time period. And if she she's meant to die, it still might not work. What if her remains—or what's left of them—have been found already? The plaster cast of her body might reside in the museum at Naples for all we know." He sounded gruff, but I knew better.

An extended quake rumbled the ground under our feet, sending marble busts crashing onto the tomb floor. It seemed to go on and on, as if a subway train was passing beneath us. Debris and ash were piling fast in the archway; soon Nate and Helen's way back in would be blocked.

"We don't have much time," Dr. Mooney said. "If there's any hope of saving us, it has to be now." Hunched over the Slingshot, trying to shield it from debris, the professor entered commands into it in a rapid sequence.

I was at the tomb door, trying to clear some of the fallen pumice with my good hand, having wrapped it in a cloth so I wouldn't get burned. The gray projectiles piled up faster than I could work. "We can't go yet, Nate said to give him fifteen minutes."

Abigail and Kamal were on their knees, helping me clear away the debris.

"Look, all of you. This all started with my coming here," Xavier said and went into a fit of coughing. "If I had left a note—*cough*—none of you would be here except for Sabina and Celer. I don't want to be responsible for your deaths. We can't wait any longer, we'll be buried in here—*cough, cough*—there is no time—"

A voice broke in through the opening, which we were just managing to keep clear.

"I knew you were hiding something, Xavier. Didn't you think this portable STEWie of yours was important enough to share with the rest of the scientific community?"

Helen, balancing her orange purse on her head for protection. And behind her, Nate. They scrambled in over the pile of pumice, Helen first, then Nate.

Xavier's face lost some of its pallor. "I left the blueprints on my desk. I'm surprised that nobody found them."

"It's been only a week or so," I answered automatically, as if any of this mattered at the moment. "We haven't had a chance to go through your stuff yet."

"We're calling it the Slingshot," Abigail said, helping Helen shake ash off her clothes.

"I'm sorry to say I've lost almost all of our twenty-first-century items. I dropped the bundle with the clothes and shoes—everything got trampled. I was hurrying—I thought you might leave without me and then I ran into the chief here." Helen's eyes came to rest on Sabina's dark head. "Oh, Xavier."

"We can't leave her, Professor Presnik," Abigail said with a determined look on her young face.

Helen perceived the complexity of the problem at once. "It would severely violate time travel protocol in a way that, frankly, hasn't even been defined yet, not to mention that it might just be wrong. Who are we to decide what would be better for her? And she can't make the decision on her own—she doesn't know how different our world is from hers."

"It's better than—*cough*—dying," I said as another rumble sent us all to our knees on the dirt floor.

"I say we ignore protocol"—Nate grimaced, eying the roof—"and get the hell out of here. All of us."

"I second that," I said.

Abigail and Kamal were already standing by Sabina's side.

"Helen?" This from Xavier. He would leave the final decision to her. It had to be unanimous.

"But will it even work?"

"No way to know."

The corner above Nate's head had started to sag dangerously. "Now or never," he said.

After a pause that lasted so long I wanted to scream, Helen said, "The goddess Fortuna favors the bold. I think we have to try, Xavier."

Xavier swore. "All right then. We'll do this by experimentation. If it works, it works. Link hands, everyone!" he commanded.

I grabbed Sabina's hand to pull her to her feet and encountered something hard. She was clutching her Diana amulet so hard that her knuckles had gone white. Abigail grabbed Sabina's other hand. "Hold on," I reassured the girl as Abigail and I pulled her upright. "We'll be out of here in a jiffy." Sabina seemed to relax just a bit, perhaps trusting my tone even though she did not understand my words. I hoped I was right.

"How many?" Kamal yelled out above the volcanic hail as we all formed a circle. He had picked up Celer, whose brown coat was streaked with gray ash, his normally droopy eyes wide and round with alarm.

The professor was balancing the Slingshot on one arm. He hooked Helen's elbow with the other. "We'll need only one or two, I hope," he shouted back.

"One or two of what?" This from Nate.

"Jumps—*cough*—into time's ghost zones."

PART THREE:
ADRIFT

26

The air was clean. I tore the cloth off my mouth, took a deep breath that sent a shudder down my spine, and collapsed into a fit of coughing. I was coated with dust and ash—it was on my clothes, in my throat, on my hair, in my nose.

I willed myself to breathe normally. Small, regular breaths.

Someone was coughing next to me. Sabina. My uninjured hand was still wrapped around hers and I released it, tapping her on the back to help clear her passageways. On her other side Abigail was doing the same thing. I whipped around to check for others and breathed a sigh of relief. We were all there in one long, curved, limb-connected line with Sabina and me at one end. Pillows and blankets tumbled off heads and shoulders. Lamps were dropped onto the sand under our feet as we all fought for breath and our minds adjusted to the sudden change in our circumstances.

Wherever we were, it seemed to be just after daybreak; the sun warmed the marble temples and columns of a wide, sheltered harbor. Besides being wonderfully clean, the air smelled strongly of marine life. The sand felt soft under the leather of my sandals. For a moment I thought we had jumped forward in time to a calmer, posteruption beach on the Pompeian coast, but the mountain was nowhere to be seen and the sun arose to the right as we faced the sea, not to the left. And the sea—

The sea was gone.

The dry white sand under our feet met darker, wet sand five or six steps farther down the slope of the beach; beyond, gentle hills and valleys blanketed the exposed floor of the circular harbor. These were covered with writhing sea creatures, fish and starfish and octopuses. White-sailed wooden ships, beached, lay on their sides, towering over locals who milled around, gathering the defenseless sea life. A few nimble youths were trying to make their way onto the deck of a ship that rested on its side, climbing up its mast like gymnasts on a slanted balance beam. At the entrance to the drained harbor, on an offshore island linked to the mainland by a causeway, stood a lighthouse, multitiered and gleaming white.

History doesn't really want to kill us, Xavier had explained back at the tomb, coughing as he readied the Slingshot. It doesn't care that much. It just wants us out of the way. Getting us safely back to our own time period was the best way to accomplish that, even better than throwing us into an underground cave or in the middle of the desert.

"Wouldn't our bodies with their anachronistic trimmings cause a paradox if we ended up in a desert?" I'd asked as pumice pounded the tomb roof.

"Not if they were quickly covered up by sand," the professor had explained, fighting for breath with each word. "We're like a mosquito—History might give a general swat in our direction, but we still have a chance. With every ghost zone we drop into, I'd say the odds are even that we'll get through."

"So it's a coin toss whether we'll make it home or not." Under the circumstances, those were odds I was willing to take.

"No, weren't you listening, Julia?" Kamal had interrupted. "Our chances of surviving a *single* ghost zone are one in two. If we fall into *two* ghost zones, our chances of making it out are one in four. If we fall into *three*, they're one in eight—" And that was when Xavier had turned on his device with one last warning. "Surfing ghost zones is like a cog slipping in a mechanical clock—we'll move in some combination of distance and time as I sling us forward."

The first jump had landed us here, wherever *here* was. We weren't going to have much time to figure it out. In the forty seconds or so we had been on the beach trying to get our bearings, a roaring sound had been increasing in intensity. Beyond the waterless sea floor, a wall of *something* approached, something reflective that sparkled in the morning light. And it was moving fast and getting bigger by the second, about to engulf the harbor and its residents.

"Get us out of here, Xavier!" Helen commanded from next to Nate.

"I need a reference point in spacetime or we're jumping blind—"

"No time," I said, my mouth dry. I felt Sabina squeeze my hand, hard.

"Now, Xavier!"

"Professor, I know where we are—Alexandria's harbor—that's the lighthouse—the Pharos!" Kamal shouted. Celer peered out from between his arms, his body rolled into a protective ball.

"Alexandria, yes, the tsunami triggered by the undersea earthquake near Crete—but the year, Kamal, what *year* is it?"

"Three hundred sixty-five—but I don't know the day and month."

"Wait," I said, "we can't leave. If it's Alexandria and the year is 365, we need to check if Hypatia has been born yet. The History of Science building plaque is still missing her birth year—"

"Now, Xavier, the wave—"

27

We were on a narrow cobblestone street, the night sky a bright, smoky red, the air streaked with gently descending ash and glowing embers, a city ablaze all around us, carts upturned, streams of people heading every which way. My mind immediately went back to Pompeii, but then I caught sight of a cathedral, a large one with a missing spire and restoration work going on. The buildings all around it were burning and the wooden church scaffolding had just caught fire. Crackling orange flames shot up in the air, threatening to leap onto the timber beams of the cathedral roof at any moment.

"Old—St. Paul's," Helen coughed out with effort. "The Great Fire of London—1666—we've jumped forward more than a thousand years. The church caught fire on the third day of the fire, September fourth—"

Xavier was already entering commands into the Slingshot, shielding it with his body. Nate whacked at the professor's tunic where an ember had landed—

And then it was all like it had never been. Not if I did time jumps forever would I get used to this, I thought.

And it was cool, blissfully cool, and after almost being burned alive twice, the cold felt so lovely on my face, on my hands, on my feet, that it took me the better part of a minute to realize that I was standing ankle deep in snow.

We had arrived on train tracks. The snow was still coming down fast, the swirling, large flakes whipped into our faces by ferocious blasts of subzero-windchill air. We only had minutes before severe frostbite attacked our bare limbs and faces. A rotary or wedge plow engine had cleared off the majority of the snow, leaving behind a narrow tunnel—on either side of the tracks, snowbanks rose up to the height of a one-story house. I spun around in panic, certain that a train was about to strike us, but the snow had won: a brief respite in the wind revealed that the train was at a standstill farther down the valley on an offshoot of the main track. The black outline of the locomotive faced us, its smokestack smokeless and silent. The train and its railcars, which were stacked high with logs, had been abandoned until the blizzard passed. All there was around us was woodland and snow.

Sabina, who had certainly never seen that much snow before, covered her face with her hands, as if the cold would go away if she didn't look at the austere landscape. That we were back in Minnesota seemed likely, but where was the St. Sunniva campus and the safe haven it represented?

Nate bent down and used his fedora to clear off a section of the track, then looked up in the direction of the train. "A white pine logging train," he hazarded a guess. "Which would mean we're past 1886 or thereabouts."

"We seem to be bouncing between continents," Kamal shouted into the wind, shivering. "An interesting side effect. It would make a good thesis topic. Might suggest it to Jacob when we get back since he's looking for something to work on. Man, is it cold."

Through chattering teeth, I said, "My great-grandparents, the Olsens, moved to the state in 1894—wouldn't it be something if we followed the train tracks to the station and got our bearings and managed to find them—"

"And my grandmother's family might be nearby, on a Dakota reservation," Nate said. "But we're not dressed for the conditions. We could try to make it to the train and seek shelter inside the locomotive, make an attempt to restart the engine."

"A poor proposition in terms of our survival, I'm afraid." Snowflakes stuck to Helen's eyelashes and cheeks, leaving streaks in the ash and grime. Her lips were turning blue.

"The device wasn't designed for this," Xavier hastened to defend his invention. "I built it for jumping from a known location, Pompeii, around the Mediterranean for some sightseeing. Simple. This—"

"I am not criticizing your device, Xavier," Helen explained through chattering teeth. "In fact, I'm rather impressed by it. It will revolutionize time travel."

Xavier looked like she couldn't have given him a bigger compliment if she'd tried. He reached for the Slingshot.

∞

And we were at the edge of a lush, green forest, on the shore of a large lake—one of Minnesota's 11,842, I hoped.

"Oh—looks like we're still in Minnesota, but it's summer," Abigail said, surveying the area around us as we shook the snow off our clothes and bodies. "The trees seem right. And there's a lake. We must be home."

"It's so warm and sunny and bright that I don't care where we are," Kamal said. He let Celer down on the ground and blew on his fingers to warm them up.

I willed my limbs to move to get my circulation going. My fingers and toes were so icy they felt like they were on fire. We had jumped to a pleasant summer morning in the woods, one perfect for canoeing or hiking or fishing, if you liked that sort of thing. There were plenty of mosquitoes on the lake. That seemed about right for Minnesota, too.

Sabina had already shaken off the cold and was bending down to pick a wildflower. Even Celer seemed a touch energized. He started sniffing around and gave a short bark at a bird. He trudged after Sabina as she followed a trail of wildflowers deeper into the woods. Seconds later, we heard the girl cry out in surprise. I saw that she was trying to nudge a small, moss-covered stone with her foot. History was blocking her. She reached for a second wildflower instead, a thin-stalked purple iris, and I moved closer to get a look at the mossy rock. My hand wouldn't even wrap around it. For a moment I thought it was because my fingers were still icy and frozen stiff. Then it hit me. For whatever reason, the stone needed to stay in place. Now that Sabina was no longer in her own time period, she was subject to the constraints of History, just as we were. Celer, too. And that meant that we weren't home, not yet.

"What is *that*?" the chief asked suddenly, pointing to something above the treetops.

I followed the direction of his arm.

There were *two* suns in the sky.

The normal, yellow one, was already well up above the horizon. Higher still, unbelievably, was a second one—fiery, streaking across the blue sky, such a strange addition to the daytime celestial dome that I could not process what I was seeing. I couldn't look for long—it was impossible to stare at the fiery object for more than a moment. Whatever it was, it was *nearing*, getting closer by the minute.

"I know what it is," said Abigail calmly. She spun Sabina around by the shoulders so that the girl wouldn't hurt her eyes. "We're not in Minnesota nor are we in our own time period, so we'll have to jump again. I wish we had more of the Polaroid film," she added.

"Abigail?" Nate asked.

"We're in Siberia, in the Tunguska region. An asteroid—or comet—is about to explode above us and emit a shock wave that will level eighty million trees in an area of over two thousand square kilometers. The largest impact in recorded history." She sneaked a glance up. "I gotta say, to me that looks more like an asteroid than a comet—but it's hard to say if there's a tail with all that streaking."

Calmly I pondered where the moss-covered stone that wanted to stay in place would end up after the catastrophic event was over.

Xavier grabbed the Slingshot off the ground, where he'd dropped it as he stretched his fingers in the warmth of the summer morning, and barked, "Abigail, what date, remind me?"

"June seventeenth, 1908," she said promptly.

"You're sure?"

"No, wait, that's the Julian calendar. Gregorian—June thirtieth. And it's just after seven in the morning. Good to have previous experience with a subject, right?" she added.

"Previous experience—yes, of course," I said.

"Julia?" said Helen.

"Maybe she's becoming delirious," Abigail whispered loudly, as if I couldn't hear her. "Her hand looks really bad."

"I'm not delirious. Ask me later. Let's get out of here before the sky falls in."

"Unless we want to stick around to see if any large fragments will hit the ground?" Abigail suggested. "It's a matter of some debate, whether the whole thing exploded above and there was just a huge shock wave, or if a piece actually impacted—"

∞

"Julia, are you all right?" I heard someone say as wooziness overtook me and I staggered where I stood, which was in a columned square of some sort, in a pleasant night. Suddenly there were arms supporting me, steadying me as I sat down abruptly. I felt odd, both hot and cold at the same time, and my head swam and swayed. Helen felt my forehead under my hair. "Julia, you're burning up—"

"He did it," I said, struggling to break through the fog in my brain. "Dean Sunder did it."

28

"Where are we?" asked Abigail. "Back in Pompeii? This looks like the Forum."

Sabina certainly seemed to think so. She looked around the town square, its columns like blank, branchless trees in the night, with a mixture of relief and apprehension. The Siberian wildflowers fell out of her hands. I heard her inhale deeply, as if confirming that the scent of this place matched *home*. The moonless night didn't reveal any details beyond the columns, just vague outlines of stone walls and archways. Sabina's fingers clutched the amulet of Diana over her ash-stained dress, as if the place might disappear if she let go. Celer, by her feet, seemed spooked, like he didn't like being out at night. He inched as close as he could to Sabina's leg and started nervously chewing on the wildflowers.

"Did we go backward for some reason, Professor? Back to a pre-eruption Pompeii?" Kamal said slowly. "We do seem to be jumping all over the place."

"The device is turning out to be far less stable than I anticipated, but we should not have gone backward, no."

"We haven't gone backward." Helen carefully stepped over to examine one of the columns. She touched it gently. "It is the Forum. We're right by the temple of Jupiter, but the decorations are faded and mostly gone. There are weeds growing all around. This site has been excavated. We must be back in our own time."

Xavier heavily sat down on the ground by me, as if a large weight had just fallen off his shoulders. The Callback landed between us with a thump.

"You did it, Professor. You brought us back," Abigail said. She gave Sabina a hug as Kamal punched the air with a whoop.

I felt the stress leave my body. We had made it—defeated a volcano, a tsunami, a fire, a blizzard, an asteroid hurtling toward Earth…really, History itself. We were home. Now that my eyes had adjusted to the darkness, I could see the outlines of several modern-looking crates stacked by the temple of Jupiter, its columns bare and stunted, its glory long since faded. The marble pavement of the Forum was gone, too, dirt in its place. The equestrian statues that had stood regally in the front of the temple were missing, taken by the volcano or looters, or perhaps safe in some museum. Antibiotics were nearby and so was a good meal, a bath…and an airport. And the first thing I would do when we got back home would be to march, not into Dr. Little's office, but into Dean Sunder's, and look him straight in the eye.

Kamal and Abigail were giving each other high-fives and trying to teach Sabina, who looked utterly confused, how to do them. In her halting Latin interspersed with English, Abigail explained to Sabina that we were all voyagers in time and that she was one now, too. A traveler. *Viator.*

Sabina said something back, and Helen translated for me as she lowered herself to the ground by the neighboring column. "Sabina made a vow to Diana asking her to watch over us and keep us safe. Apparently Diana complied." She added, "It's too dark to make our way out of the ruins now. We'd be risking broken ankles. Julia, do you think you can wait another hour or two?

It's almost dawn. The site guides and tourists will start arriving soon."

"I'll be fine." I hoped that was true.

"Did you say you think Lewis Sunder is to blame for all of this? Do you have proof?"

"I remembered what's been nagging at me. It was such a small thing. The day it all started—the day you disappeared, Xavier—I went into Dean Sunder's office to bring him the press statement. The dean was at his office window with an old thesis in his hands. He wasn't perusing it—he was studying it. I assumed it was yours, Xavier, but it had a red cover."

"What did?"

"The thesis."

"I'm not following."

"You all worked together for a while, didn't you, Xavier—you and Gabriel and Lewis? He graduated with a physics PhD a couple of years before you and Gabriel, didn't he?"

"That was a long time ago. We weren't having much luck with our experiments and our funding had dried up. Lewis got fed up with having to scrounge for funds in a speculative scientific field—time travel was a technology that few people felt had any promise—and went with a safer topic. Good for him. Once he had tenure, he decided he could help out—he's good at getting people to see the big picture when it comes to research and donate big—so he ended up overseeing all of the science departments. I'd say he's been very good at it. What are you thinking he did, Julia?"

"I think he got the idea of a copycat accident while we were still trying to figure out what had happened to you. What year did you graduate?"

"Nineteen eighty-one."

"Exactly. That's what I'm saying. Your thesis would have had a blue cover. The school had switched to blue the year before."

"How do you know that?" Nate asked.

"I work in the dean's office. Believe me, things like this come up all the time." I added, "Was he rereading his thesis to give himself a refresher course on the physics, to help him compute the Pompeii coordinates? Does that even make sense, that he would forget the practical issues of something he himself had worked on as a graduate student?"

"You'd be surprised," Kamal said. He and Abigail had wandered over to listen in to our conversation while Sabina puzzled over the transformation of the Forum. "I myself have forgotten research ideas I jotted down only weeks before."

"So he wasn't reading my thesis," Xavier said. "My thesis wouldn't have helped him in figuring out how to send you to Pompeii. It was a first pass at a workable STEWie design. Quite wrong, as it turned out. His own thesis addressed spacetime coordinate systems without touching on the question of time travel. Like I said, it was a safer topic at the time. But that's hardly proof of anything."

I thought of something else. "And at first he wasn't enthusiastic about the idea of the chief going on a test run, but then suddenly changed his mind. I thought it was because he wanted the investigation over as quickly as possible, but now I wonder."

Nate was leaning against the nearest column, his face concealed by darkness. "Did you ever suspect him?" I asked.

"You said all door codes were made available to the dean's office in case of an emergency. Dean Sunder had access to the code to the TTE lab, just as you did, Julia, did he not?"

"Yes, why didn't you remind me of that?"

"I wanted to give your subconscious a chance to work on the problem."

"But why would Dean Sunder do such a thing?" Abigail said. After some circling, Celer made himself comfortable by her feet.

"Julia?" the chief asked.

"My subconscious may have spewed forth instances of Dean Sunder's odd behavior, but as far as motive goes..." I remembered his list of the usual suspects: *Greed. Jealousy. Desire. Fear. Desperation.* A list. Excellent. I could work with that. Sitting down—and being safe—was helping, but I still wasn't feeling all that great. "Not fear," I said, then added, thinking of the dean's suave demeanor, "and not desperation either." He was successful man, comfortable in his own skin, or at least seemed to be. "Jealousy and desire—perhaps. But I think, yes, greed might fit the bill." I was thinking of the one thing that Dean Sunder could be said to be passionate about.

"Money?" the chief said.

"More precisely, Ewan Coffey. He makes regular donations to the school and on occasion has given staggeringly large amounts. Hence the Coffey Library. Part of your research assistant funding, Abigail—and yours, Kamal—has come from his donations." I saw Abigail's eyes widen at the news of this personal connection she shared with Ewan Coffey. Xavier already knew this, having been on the receiving end of the funding. "However, he's not always careful with his checks. Some have reached my desk with the 'to' field blank. There's a large check on the way for STEWie's new generator." I added, "If Dean Sunder held on to it—we do send the actor a yearly summary for tax purposes, so a discrepancy might have been caught then—"

"Unless the dean planned to doctor the paperwork," Helen said, "so that Julia got the blame."

"If that's true, he wasn't trying to get rid of all of us—just you, Julia." Nate sounded angry. I was rather angry myself. So. The dean had gotten fed up with procuring funds for others and had decided to keep some for himself. Maybe he wanted to upgrade his BMW to a Porsche or something.

"It could be that he didn't mean to kill us," Abigail suggested, in what I thought was a far-too-kind interpretation of the events.

Apparently Helen agreed with me, because she said crisply, "He sent us straight into what he thought was a volcanic eruption. Is there any way he could have found out your destination, Xavier? Did you leave any notes or calculations lying around?"

"I did run into him one time at the Coffey Library—literally. I dropped an armful of books on Pompeii, and he helped me pick them up. He is also the only one who knew about my illness. I suppose he could have put two and two together when I disappeared and thought I committed suicide by sending myself into a ghost zone. You're going to have to work harder than that to convince me he's guilty, though."

"There's one easy way of settling the matter. We'll know when we see the look on his face after we walk through his office door," I said, conscious of a note of spite in my voice.

"Right." This from Nate.

Helen made herself more comfortable, her back propped against a column. "Be that as it may, there's nothing we can do about it right now. We might as well all snatch an hour of sleep."

"I'm too hyped up to sleep, what with all the ghost zones and Dean Sunder maybe having tried to kill us," Kamal said, opening his leather satchel, which had made it through with us in one piece. He crumpled a blank page out of Abigail's notebook into a ball and tried to play catch with Celer without too much success.

Sabina gave a small shrug at the strangeness of things and scrunched up against the base of a statue and closed her eyes.

Nate sank down with his back against my column, his long legs stretched out in front of him.

"Nate," I whispered after a moment, watching Sabina's gently rising and falling breast, "I've been thinking about death."

"You'll be fine, Julia. We're only a few short hours away from getting help." He reached over and gave my arm a squeeze.

Well, it was nice of him to be reassuring and all, but he'd misunderstood me. "I mean death in general," I explained. "I don't see how an afterlife would work."

"What are you talking about?"

"For one thing, what age would you be? And would you have all your memories, even of the moment of your death?" I was thinking of Secundus and Faustilla, but didn't want to say so; in the eerie dark of the silent and deserted town, it felt as if their spirits hung over us. "Or maybe it wouldn't matter how you had died because you'd arrive there at your best, at whatever time in your life you had peaked in happiness? But that would mean you'd lose all your later memories." The questions poured out fast and uncensored. "And would you have a form? Hands to touch things with, a mouth to talk with…and if you did, what would you talk about after that first day of greeting long-departed family members and friends?" Secundus's proud face came to my mind again, and Faustilla, with her dried, cracked heels and her scheming, unsuccessful manipulation of her son. "And would there *be* such a thing as a day? Or would you be stuck there indefinitely exchanging pleasantries? Are you allowed to be catty in heaven, to gossip, to be curious about how things work and ask questions?"

"Can't say I've ever thought about it, Julia."

"And if you found you didn't need to use those things—hands, eyes, curiosity, reasoning skills—would you be completely alien to yourself?"

I saw him give a small shrug in the dark. "Maybe that's the answer. Maybe after death we end up on some distant planet in a faraway galaxy. Formless aliens, interacting with others of our kind, feeding on ideas. And then in *their* afterlife, they turn into stiff creatures with arms and legs who require organic food and sunshine, and so on in an endless cycle."

The levity of his answer punctured my dark mood. With all my heart, I hoped mother and son had made it through the eruption, but either way they were long gone now. All that was left of Pompeii were its aged stones and dusty roads. "Well, look for me when we're both idea-gobbling aliens then," I said and closed my eyes for a moment. Soon, the sound of Celer and Kamal playing faded into the distance.

I woke up with a start. Dawn was still a while off, but the others seemed to be awake and on their feet.

"That plane is kind of loud, isn't it?" Abigail was saying.

A plane. I realized that I'd been missing twenty-first-century sounds, ordinary ones like the hum of car engines and the music blaring from students' iPods. Only this plane seemed to be droning above us steadily rather than roaring by.

"Sounds like an old plane," Nate said uneasily. "Is it possible we're not quite home yet?"

The faint drone of the plane had been steadily getting louder.

"You mean we've fallen into another ghost zone? Another Pompeii eruption?" Abigail sent a worried glance at Sabina, who had opened her eyes at the commotion.

"Could be. The last eruption was in 1944," Xavier said. "But I don't believe it affected the town. Helen, what do you think?"

She just shook her head, uncertain.

Nate was looking up into the moonless night sky. "That's too loud to be just one plane—"

Before he could finish, the sound of muffled thunder reached us.

The thunder went on and on, in a repeating fashion, not at all like the open boom that had spelled the end of Sabina's Pompeii.

"Dammit," said Xavier. "I know what this is and it isn't another eruption. Helen, the Allied bombing—"

"Of 1943? Yes, that's got to be it."

Xavier reached for the Slingshot. "Helen, do you happen to know the day, the month?"

BOOM.

"Only that it took place sometime in the fall and that a hundred-some bombs fell on Pompeii. The Allies thought the German army was encamped here or storing ammunition. There was even a rumor that the Allied Powers wanted to bomb Vesuvius to set off an eruption—"

"All right, so 1943, sometime in the fall," Nate interrupted. "Great. Let's get out of here, Dr. Mooney."

"Knowing the month would help—"

"How precise do we have to be?" I asked as the muffled thunder grew closer.

The strain was beginning to wear on Xavier and he was showing it. "How precise do you want to be in arriving home? There is no danger of arriving *early*—History won't let us travel into a time where we already exist—but I don't want to badly overshoot home time either. If that happens, we might arrive after everyone we know is dead—"

BOOM.

"But we've been gone only three days. Won't that be just a couple of hours in the lab?" I had been picturing us dealing with Dean Sunder before he even had a chance to leave his office for the day. "Or would it be more like a week, since it's your basket that we're hitchhiking in?"

Even in the dark, I could see Xavier shaking his head as he readied the Slingshot. "We're going to be coming in at such a high energy level that I'm afraid all bets are off. We can't make any more intermediate ghost zone steps—I'm going to be born in seven years. It's now or never. One last jump."

PART FOUR:
HOME

29

For a moment I thought that it was late fall and that we had missed both the spring and the summer semesters. Then I saw the green buds on the trees and the geese bobbing on the lake, its level swollen from the melting snow and the spring rains. Late April or early May, I judged. If we had gotten the year right, we had been gone several months. We were ankle deep in water among the reeds at the north end of Sunniva Lake, by the boat dock.

We must have been a sight to behold as we clambered out of the lake, our sandals dripping, our tunics and dresses stained with ash from Vesuvius and the Great Fire of London, our hair (and probably our expressions) wild. We drew a few strange looks as we took the path toward the science buildings, followed by a squat, slow-moving dog, but we did not get a *lot* of odd looks. St. Sunniva was a university campus, after all.

"Jacob," I said to Nate as we neared the Time Travel Engineering building, our feet leading us straight there as if we were being pulled by a homing beacon. I'd forgotten all about my throbbing hand and was focused on only one thing—finding proof of Dean Sunder's guilt.

"Jacob Jacobson? What about him?"

"His tweets."

"What about them?"

"I want to take a look at them."

We found the ginger-haired grad student at his desk in the graduate students' office, eating ramen noodles with a plastic spoon while he worked on a paper-and-pencil physics homework problem.

"You're—you're back," he managed to utter. The pencil had fallen out of his hand and lodged in the ramen noodles, right next to the spoon. "We thought you were all—"

"Dead?" Nate said. "Well, as you can see, we're not. What year is it?"

"The year? Uh, 2012."

"And month and day?"

"Friday, May eighteenth."

We had been gone almost five months.

Abigail slid behind her desk. Everything on it was covered in a thin layer of dust. "My stuff is still here, good."

"We've been in a sort of limbo, with the big accident and all—Dean Sunder said that come fall, we would regroup and make some changes in office space assignments and leadership—"

"How have you been, Jacob?" I asked.

"How have I—well, things are going a bit better with my classes. Oh, and I've started a blog, for when I want to say something that won't fit in a tweet. I'm calling it *The Eternal Student*."

"You've started a blog?" Abigail said, turning her computer on. "Good. Boy, have we got a story for you and it will *not* fit into a hundred and forty characters."

"Dr. Rojas has been arrested for the murder of Dr. Mooney and the rest of you. Who's that?" asked Jacob.

"That's Sabina, and next to her, Celer. Be nice to them, they just lost their family," Abigail said as she waited for her computer to boot up. "It's a long story. Never mind that for now. We need to take a look at your tweets from last week—I mean, from December."

"Really?"

"Are they archived somewhere?"

"Yup." Jacob pushed away his homework and the ramen noodles, and coasted over to Abigail's desk in his chair. Helen, Nate, and I came over to look at her computer screen from over their shoulders. Kamal went into the hallway and came back with two paper cups filled with water. He gave one to Sabina and put the other on the floor for Celer, who proceeded to drink it in slow, pink-tongued slurps. Sabina looked at the paper cup in her hand for a long moment, then drank. Kamal went back out into the hallway to fetch water for the rest of us.

Abigail tut-tutted. "Jacob, there are—you've gotta be kidding me—there are over seven hundred tweets since December. How long *have* we been gone?"

"My tweets tapered off a bit after I started the blog."

"We want the ones from the day we left." I was running on pure adrenaline. "December twentieth," I added, then with parched lips downed the water that Kamal had brought over to me.

A stocky body with a caramel-colored mustache burst into the room. "Oscar called me. *I knew it.*" It was Officer Van Underberg, looking a little more seasoned and comfortable in his campus security uniform. "No one wanted to believe me, but I knew you weren't dead."

"Thank you, Lars," the chief said.

It took us a minute or two to read through Jacob's stream of tweets from the day we'd prepared for a one-hour trip to see the Beatles and had instead ended up battling time itself. Sandwiched among Jacob's thoughts on other matters and his replies to his friends was a very telling sequence of tweets, ordered by time index, with the last ones first:

They are not coming back #imsad

Missed all the excitement. Something went wrong with Beatles run. Will try to find out more.

Stomach rumbly, off to cafeteria. Almost collided with Dean Sunder in hallway & he tut-tutted over my tweeting-while-walking #closecall

Dr Rojas just passed by grad office, some kind of delay in STEWie lab?

Kicked out of lab, back in office. Will try to wrap up some projects.

Campus policeman Kirkland questioning Dr Presnik. VERY curious!

I'm in STEWie's lab. Team going to watch Beatles land at JFK. Not invited :(

The updates from the rest of the day told of a department in uproar, of shocked reactions from students and staff, of Dean Sunder vowing to continue the program.
"Jacob, why didn't you tell anyone that Dean Sunder was in the building during our send-off?" I asked.
Jacob looked at me blankly. "I did. It's right there in my tweet."
"Never mind," I said.

"If you'd like, I can put it all up on my blog. I don't have that many followers yet. Classmates, mostly, but everyone will be thrilled that you're back."

"Not everyone. That reminds me, I should let Penny Lind of the *Les Styles* blog know we're back. I owe her a good story."

∞

Nate had said that we couldn't just march into Dean Sunder's office and arrest him on the spot. Helen and Xavier agreed with him, pointing out that a visit to the hospital was our first priority. They were right, of course, and Oscar called us an ambulance. We would all go to the university hospital, me to be pumped up full of antibiotics, the others to be checked out, and Sabina— well, that was a more complicated matter. Vaccines and other stuff to begin with, I supposed. And a visit to the vet for Celer would be needed, too.

Under the guise of needing to use the bathroom, I sneaked out of the TTE building and hurried over to History of Science, leaving Nate and the others to relate the details of our story to Jacob and Officer Van Underberg. I had a few minutes before the ambulance got here. The EMTs would find me easily enough.

The tidy brick building that housed History of Science looked the same as it always had, but Hypatia in her ankle-length dress in the photo by the front door seemed more real now that I had on a similar one. On the oak that shaded her image from the noonday sun, hummingbirds chirped on branches bursting with early spring leaves. The bags of road salt just inside the front door were gone. Five months had passed here; much less for me.

I went in.

The door to my office stood open. A young woman sat at my desk, her blonde hair tied back in a ponytail. She looked perky and young enough to still be in high school. There were potted plants all over my office—green, thriving ones. And she had replaced the window cabinet, where I kept my cookie jar, with a little fridge. I had been looking forward to a cookie.

She glanced up at the sound of dismay that must have left my lips.

"Can I help you with something, ma'am?"

"Maybe later."

I continued one door down, unsteadily.

Dean Sunder was at his desk, sipping iced tea and working on something. He did not hear me at first, the soft step of my soggy sandals silent on the office carpet. He seemed to be readying a presentation of some kind. My eyes went to the title at the top. *The Way Forward: Proposed Changes to the TTE Lab Operating Procedure and Research Staff.*

"Lewis."

He couldn't have been more surprised if I had appeared out of thin air in the form of a malevolent ghost with revenge on its mind. In fact that must have been the first thought to cross his mind as he pushed himself to his feet, his face ashen.

"Julia—how—"

"I'm back," I said. "You'll have to get rid of the new assistant. What's her name?"

"Brittany," he answered, still looking like a pale robotic version of himself. "But how—I don't understand—"

"You're wondering how I got out of the Pompeii ghost zone."

"Well—yes, I am. What an unexpected development—a pleasant one, of course."

"I can imagine."

"How—how *did* you come back, Julia?"

"With a lot of luck and some help from the goddess Diana."

The sheer exhilaration of being back had helped my headache a bit, but I still felt lightheaded, woozy. Against my express wishes—I wanted to face him standing—my body sank into the chair facing his desk. He sat back down and bent toward me, his face suddenly calculating and cold.

"Are you all right, Julia? You seem ill. Your hand—"

"A little infection I picked up in the past."

That made him pull back, I noted with satisfaction.

He was still studying me. "What happened to your glasses?"

"I don't need them anymore."

That probably didn't make much sense to him, but all he said was, "I see. Well, it certainly is pleasant to have you back, Julia. Brittany has been helping out, but you've always been so efficient and capable of arranging everything so nicely—"

It was entirely the wrong thing to say to me. I was done being nice.

I wanted to jump out of my chair, accuse him, shake his expensive, crisply starched collar, but I didn't have the energy to move. Instead my questions came out slowly, casually, like we were talking about the weather. "Why did you do it, Lewis? Was it the money? The check from Ewan Coffey for STEWie's new generator?"

He stared at me for a long moment, then got to his feet. I felt like speaking was enough of an effort and turning my head to watch him would be too much, so I didn't do it. I heard the door swing closed. He rounded the desk and sat back down, studying me as if seeing me for the first time in his life.

"Lewis—why?" I wanted to hear him say it *now*, before the lawyers and trustees and media came into the mix. "Was it the money?"

"You should know me better than that, Julia. I've had plenty of opportunities through the years to discreetly help

313

myself to funds, but I would have never robbed my researchers of the money. No, that wasn't it at all." He gave a sigh, not of sadness, but of newfound frustration. "I learned that Mooney and Rojas were at the top of the consideration list for this year's Nobel."

"But that's good news, isn't it?" What was he talking about? I didn't understand. A Nobel Prize would bring publicity, funds, and prestige to the school. Not to mention that Xavier Mooney and Gabriel Rojas deserved it. I said as much. "Against all odds, the two of them managed to crack a monumental research problem—how to slip into the past. A shared Nobel Prize would be great for the TTE Department, good for the school—"

"And what about me?" he spat out suddenly. "The two of *them* deserve it? I'm responsible for bringing in every penny that built the lab, not to mention the salaries of everyone in it. I was the one who fought for grants and donations and publicity and built the program into what it is today. If it wasn't for me, there would be no TTE lab, no STEWie in it, and no Nobel Prize on the horizon."

"So you staged the accident to...what, shut down the lab?"

He fought to get himself under control and said more calmly, "It was so—easy. I called Dr. Rojas from his own office pretending to be a delivery truck driver who was at the dock parking lot. It's happened often enough before. Rojas agreed to come pick up a generator part that had come in early. I went into STEWie's lab after I saw him leave. Erika was getting ready for her run in the travel apparel closet so she wasn't around. I had the Pompeii coordinates ready. It took only a minute to enter them in and send you on your way. Then—I waited. I've been waiting all this while. Come fall, I was planning on reopening the program after quitting my position as dean, and taking over for Rojas as director of the TTE lab. He has been arrested. It wasn't difficult for the police to figure out that the call summoning him from the lab came from his own office. They thought Rojas had rigged the phone to place an automatic call to the lab."

I finally understood. It had been different in the past—Galileo had worked under the patronage of the Medici family, King Ferdinand and Queen Isabella of Spain had sponsored Columbus in his voyages of exploration—but nowadays…well, no one knew the name of the person or persons who had provided Albert Einstein with a desk and a pencil or organized funding for the Moon landing. A dean of science might get a plaque with his name on it upon retirement; scientists under his care, if lucky and brilliant, would have their names chiseled into History.

My eyes went to the diplomas, accolades, and photos mounted on the wall behind Lewis's desk, one of them his own PhD diploma—a daily reminder of his early days at St. Sunniva, when he worked on the first unsuccessful attempts at time travel technology with Xavier and Gabriel, before STEWie. "One thing led to another," he had told me once, "and here I am today." Even then, I thought I had detected a hint of regret in his voice, like he wished he had stuck with the time travel engineering field now that it had shown itself to be a viable science.

In the end, for all of us, it came down to fighting for what was important. Faustilla's wish had been to live near her firstborn son in the urban wonders of Rome. For Dean Sunder, it meant fighting his way back into the TTE lab to partake in the glory. Maybe he had visions of new breakthroughs in TTE technology, of time-traveling runs that would address historical questions yet unanswered, maybe even his own Nobel Prize. But life just didn't work like that. Faustilla might have gotten her way if the volcano hadn't intervened, but it never would have worked for Lewis—because you couldn't go back, ever, no matter what you had been—a child or a single, thinner version of yourself or a young physicist with a promising future. That's why it had all gone wrong for him.

Lewis got to his feet and moved behind my chair.

I felt his fingers wrap around my throat, tighten.

So that was the way it was going to be.

I tried to grab his hands with my own, pull them away, but I don't think I really managed to, only in my own mind.

Then I heard the wail of an ambulance as it tore down the emergency route to the TTE building. That gave me the will to croak out, "Jacob is putting the story on his blog. Many, many readers—"

I felt his fingers stop, go limp. No doubt he assumed that the siren meant the police were on their way to arrest him. I gasped and fought for air as he stood hovering over me for a minute. Then I watched as he went back to his desk chair and sat down as if the air had been pumped out from his spine.

I heard running footsteps in the hallway.

It was over. Which was good, because I was about to faint. I felt myself slip out of the chair and slump onto the floor just as the door flew open with a crash.

30

I woke up in the hospital, with an IV line in one hand and the other wrapped in a bandage. Sunlight streamed in through the open curtains of the window. I felt my forehead. The fever seemed to be gone. Faustilla's curse tablet had not worked. We had made it back. We were safe.

Several get-well cards and a vase with flowers sat on the bedside table. I didn't feel like reading the cards just yet. I just lay there, enjoying the peacefulness of it all—and the modern amenities.

After a while, a nurse came in, asked how I was doing and if I needed anything—"Bathroom," I croaked—and after that and a sit-down shower had been taken care of, I learned that I had been out for forty-eight hours and that they wanted to keep me under observation for at least twenty-four more.

The day brought a steady stream of visitors—Helen and Xavier, who were back to their tightly buttoned-up academic selves, though I sensed a certain warming in their relationship; then a hospital physician with four residents in tow to check on my progress; then Kamal, looking clean-shaven and wearing a bright yellow St. Sunniva T-shirt; followed by the entire astronomy grad student section, who had made me a gigantic *You're a Star* get-well card. Dr. Rojas stopped by, freshly released from jail. He looked gaunt but he was smiling (I vowed to do all I could do restore his reputation in the academic community). Later Dr. Little came to see me, armed with a picture of his newborn daughter. He begrudgingly said, "You should write down an eyewitness account of all the places you saw. It will have academic merit." In an unexpected bit of kindness, he left his laptop so I could catch up on news and e-mail. Dr. Baumgartner, looking like the five-month STEWie halt had provided a well-needed rest, brought by a box of chocolates and Penny Lind, who took photos of a recovering science dean's assistant in a decidedly unstylish pale-green hospital gown for the *Les Styles* blog.

Abigail and Sabina stopped by midafternoon, which made me feel best of all.

I had been lying in the hospital bed, staring out the window at the birds bobbing on the lake, mulling over what would be best for Sabina. The child needed a safe, structured environment in which she could adjust to twenty-first-century life. Young people adapted easily, so it wasn't like I was expecting any problems on that score. It was just that I wasn't at all the motherly type. I couldn't even keep a potted plant alive, and I didn't know a word of Latin.

But Sabina needed a home.

Abigail, whose unconventional childhood had produced a practical and openhearted individual, set my worries to rest. She had always wanted a family, she said, and a sister would be more than she could have hoped for.

For her part, Sabina seemed to have taken everything in stride, including the news that Nate and I weren't married and Abigail and Kamal weren't our children. Abigail and Sabina were almost the same height, so the older girl's clothes hung only somewhat baggily on Sabina, no more so than they might on many a modern teenager. They looked like sisters who had inherited wildly different genes, Abigail's petite and Nordic, and Sabina's bigger-boned and Mediterranean. The crescent moon, which I'd learned was called a *lunula*, hung around her neck like a modern revival of an ancient religion.

"There's just one problem, Julia," Abigail added.

"What is it?"

"I'll have to move out of grad student housing. They don't really make accommodations for family members. I'll look for a place in town, but that might bring up some awkward questions."

That, at least, was easily solved.

"My house has a mother-in-law suite with a separate yard entrance. It was put in by the previous owners, before my parents bought the house," I said. "I was planning on renting out the extra space, so this will save me from having to look for a tenant. I don't cook, though."

"We'll manage, Julia."

"And we can build a doghouse for Celer in the yard," I said. "Speaking of Celer, where is he?"

"The vet wants to keep him for a few days, for shots and stuff."

There was only one bit of bad news—Dave, Abigail's boyfriend in the Athletic Department, had not waited for her. "I can't blame him." Abigail shrugged. "He thought I was dead. He offered to break up with his current girlfriend, but I said no. It would have been too weird."

As she and Sabina left, I heard Abigail explaining what a mall was in a mixture of English and Latin—like a long Pompeii street of shops, only indoors—and saying that a shopping spree might be in order. I heard Sabina exclaim at the idea that one's clothes should be changed and laundered daily.

∞

For dinner, the nurse brought me a tray with orange juice, fruit, toast, and a strangely colored Jell-O that reminded me of Abigail's vision of what STEWie's basket might look like. I was supposed to be replenishing my fluids and, as I nibbled on the fruit cup and sipped the juice—I couldn't say that I had much of an appetite yet—a thought kept rather unexpectedly popping into my head. Why hadn't Nate stopped by? Perhaps he was busy. There were reports to be given, Lewis Sunder to be processed, and he had to catch up on everything he'd missed during the time we were gone. I had just managed to convince myself that his absence meant that he was just swamped at work, when a gruff voice said, "That wasn't very smart, confronting Lewis Sunder like that."

His uniform was back on, as if we had never left. The small dog at his feet set about sniffing the room, its long chestnut ears vibrating with excitement above a chestnut-and-white coat.

"I suppose it wasn't," I admitted. I pulled the hospital blanket farther up. The visit from Penny Lind had left me keenly aware that the hospital gown was not the most flattering of outfits. At least I had showered and my hair was clean and combed. "I wasn't thinking clearly. I don't think I've ever felt sicker in my life—I thought I was going to die."

"You did look like crap."

Well, he was certainly being a lot less formal. Of course, the case *was* over.

"I went into Dean Sunder's office—he's not the dean anymore, is he?—into Lewis's office because I wanted to look him in the eye. I had to know for sure if he had done it...and why."

Wanda, having finished her examination of the small hospital room, came over and put her front paws on the bed to let me rub her silken ears and head. She seemed a cheerful sort. I wondered how she and Celer would get along. "Are dogs allowed in hospitals?"

"Probably not."

"She seems all right."

"Van Underberg's been taking care of her just like you said he would."

"Nate, why did you leave your previous job? At the Boundary Waters Canoe Area?" I asked, letting Wanda have some of what had turned out to be peach Jell-O.

He moved from the bed to the window and stared through it for a long moment.

"I resigned. There was an incident. It's a bit of a long story, but let's just say I got involved with a suspect. Someone had been setting fires throughout the BWCAW. I was positive the arsonist was one of the teenage kids camping in nearby Voyageurs Park, perhaps a group of them, not this one—uh, person who was up for the summer." He turned back to face me. "She was a photographer and I had been taking her out in my canoe in my free time. She had pretended to be a canoeing novice. Wanda was her dog."

"And it turned out that it was her all along?"

"She borrowed the canoe after hours to set fires at various points on the islands. Pretty soon we had our hands full fighting the spreading fire." His voice grew deeper. "The fire got out of hand and we lost someone."

"I'm sorry."

"I was blinded by her interest in me. No blame came my way, but I felt I had to resign. I applied for the job here and got it. Chancellor Evans, well, she seemed to think I would do fine here."

The door opened before I could say anything and the nurse shooed Nate and Wanda out, saying that dogs were not allowed, and in any case, visiting hours were over. I settled back down on my pillow as she checked my temperature, and thought about things.

It was the wrong time for both of us. I was working on living alone, not to mention that I had no idea if my divorce from Quinn had gone through after its weird legal limbo of five months. I'd have to give him a call and let him know I was alive. As for Nate—he had to come to terms with the fact that he was merely human, just like the rest of us. Mistakes were made, people got hurt, and sometimes it took time to move on. Still, I understood him a little better now. He had to learn to trust again.

I did notice one thing. He hadn't gone back to calling me Ms. Olsen, but he hadn't called me Julia either.

31

The enormity of what we had done took a while to sink in. We got chewed out by Chancellor Evans for breaking a long list of rules by (a) pulling Sabina and Celer out of their own time and (b) roaming around campus without first undergoing the necessary decontamination procedures. If plague-ridden fleas and lice appeared on campus, Chancellor Evans said, she would know who was to blame. But she did help us conceal some of the details of our story to protect Sabina's privacy. That part of the story did not make it onto the news. We also took pains to protect Dr. Mooney's reputation. Almost everyone on and off campus assumed that his disappearance to Pompeii had been an accident, one that had been exploited by Lewis Sunder; none of us corrected that mistaken impression.

As for Sabina herself, short of trying to organize exploratory time-travel runs, we had no way of knowing for sure what had happened to her father and grandmother. Going back to search for them would have been the time equivalent of looking for a needle in a haystack. I found peace by deciding that Secundus of the soulful eyes had found his mother and they had made it out of Pompeii. They had lived out their lives with the knowledge that Sabina and Celer were somewhere safe with us.

Abigail said that Sabina sometimes sat on the shore of Sunniva Lake in silence, watching the finger-size fish flit about. I suppose it was as close as she could get to the seashore she'd left behind. She had taped the photos we'd taken of her hometown above her bed; Abigail had promised her that the two of them would one day go to modern Pompeii and fulfill Sabina's vow to the goddess Diana. Not a blood sacrifice of a goat or a pig (which was what Sabina had wanted), but a less messy one in the form of a few drops of wine sprinkled onto the still-standing stones of the Forum temple where Diana's statue used to stand across from her brother's. Hopefully that much could be done without the tourist site guides noticing. For now Abigail and Sabina were taking it a day at a time and having fun with (and some odd discussions about) modern conveniences like pretzels, ice cream, computers, bras, toothbrushes, TV, hair conditioner, and chocolate.

For his part, Celer seemed to have decided that the whole house belonged to him, and he spent equal amounts of time sleeping in their part of it and in mine.

I had added a pushpin of a different color, red, to the smattering of blue ones on the STEWie map on my office wall.

There were only two problems. One, though Sabina's spoken English skills were improving drastically day by day, her writing skills were not keeping pace. In the end Abigail decided not to worry about it and to let Sabina use the computer, where the spell-checker was her friend. Sometimes I heard them laughing about a funny post on Jacob's blog.

Two, I hadn't heard back from Quinn yet and had no idea if I was divorced or not.

One particularly warm July afternoon, as I jotted down a note to call Maintenance to inquire when they would get around to spraying the rapidly multiplying mosquitoes on the lake, a knock came at my open office door. It was our security chief.

"Just stopping by to drop off some papers for Sabina and to ask for your advice about something—where are you going?"

Nate had a manila envelope in his hands, I noted as I rushed past him. "I left something in the microwave."

He followed me to the building kitchenette as I explained, "I'm preparing a cheese fondue for the new science dean—it's going to be Dr. Braga from the Department of Earth Sciences. She's moving into her office this afternoon and I wanted to welcome her properly." I opened the microwave door to reveal a congealed and unappetizing-looking yellow mess. "Well, that didn't work at all. Perhaps they'd let me use one of the Bunsen burners over in chemistry or a laser in one of the physics labs."

Nate threw an expert eye over the cheese bowl. "We'll have to start over. Do you have more of the cheese?"

I pointed to the hefty chunk of Gruyère sitting on the counter, of which I'd only used half.

"We'll need a touch of flour. Wine or brandy, too, if we can get our hands on some."

"There's cornstarch in the cupboard, left over from the non-Newtonian goo we made for Halloween, and I keep a bottle of wine in my office. For emergencies and such," I explained, leaving the room to get the wine.

My white cabinet had been in storage along with my other office things, and I had reinstated it next to Brittany's fridge, which I had decided to keep—it would come in handy for stockpiling snacks for department meetings. I had also kept Brittany, who was a graduate student in the Astronomy Department, first to help me out until I got back on my feet, and then as my part-time assistant. The school was happy to let me do it. The trustees were no doubt relieved that none of us had decided to sue, and I was almost tempted to ask if, once the excitement over our return and Lewis Sunder's arrest had died down, we could go see the Beatles after all.

I brought the wine back to find that Nate had scrubbed out the congealed cheese at the sink, dried the bowl, and cubed the rest of the Gruyère. He uncorked the bottle and added a good dollop of the white wine to the cubed cheese, which he'd already sprinkled with cornstarch and what looked like nutmeg. He seemed to be fitting in better on campus, I decided, though I don't know why the sight of him stirring wine into cheese would have led me to that conclusion. He placed the mixture in the microwave and turned it on. "By the way, I pulled some strings to get a birth certificate and a social security number issued for Sabina." He nodded at the manila envelope sitting on the counter. "That's what I came by to drop off."

"You did something illegal?" I was touched by this unexpected side of him.

"Not at all. Just pulled a few strings with Chancellor Evans's help. Turns out she has a lot of connections."

"Chancellors tend to."

"Really, it was no more than what would be done for someone who was headed into the Witness Protection Program. Everything she needs is in that envelope—a birth certificate that's a translation from an 'original' Italian one that's also in there, immigration papers, a newly issued social security card. We've made Abigail her legal guardian."

"Good. It will make enrolling her in school easier. What was the second thing?"

"Hmm?" The microwave beeped and he stirred the cheese mixture, adjusted the power level, and set it for another minute. "Oh, that. Sabina's birthday present. I don't know what to get her."

The party was tonight. We were sticking to the calendar date for Sabina's birthday, the Ides of Julius (that is, July 15) and had solved the math problems that had arisen from our jump in time by planning to double-celebrate her thirteenth birthday. Nate was making shrimp curry, Helen and Xavier were bringing walleye sandwiches, and I was contributing mint chocolate chip ice cream, Sabina's new favorite.

"I got her math books," I said. "Everything from elementary to junior high. She's been devouring them. There are no language barriers there, which I think helps a lot. That, and I think she'll be a scientist one day, though people say that children never grow up to be what you expect them to be." I thought of something. "You could get her a cell phone, she's been asking for one."

He stirred the cheese dip some more and put it back in for a bit. "Do you think she's ready for that?"

"It would help her keep in touch with Abigail throughout the day. And with Jacob. I think she might be developing a crush on him. She's fascinated by his tan eyebrows."

"Cell phones, crushes—I have to say, I'm not ready for that. I feel responsible for her, like I'm her uncle or something." The microwave gave a final beep and he reached for the cheese bowl. "Ouch, hot."

I handed him a kitchen towel. "I know what you mean. Any day now, I expect she'll start calling me Aunt Julia."

He watched me stack a box of crackers, a plate with apple slices, and the cheese bowl on a tray. I picked up the envelope, thick with documents, from the counter and slipped it under the tray. "See you at the party tonight. Come by early if you need help wrapping Sabina's new cell phone."

He held the kitchenette door open for me. "Good luck, Julia."

"With what?"

"The new dean."

"Well, she can't be worse than the old one, can she?" I said, sliding past him with the tray and hurrying over to Dr. Braga's office before the cheese dip crusted over.

Just outside her office door, my cell phone rang. I managed to answer it, balancing the tray and the documents one-handed. A familiar voice said, "Hey, Jules, it's Quinn. Not calling about the divorce paperwork. I know about Sabina. Don't worry, your secret's safe with me—but I need a favor in return. I want to go somewhere. The fourteenth century."

THE END

ACKNOWLEDGMENTS

St. Sunniva University is purely a figment of this author's imagination. There is no relation to St. Olaf College in Northfield, which is named after the better-known patron saint of Norway. I had more fun than I should have in painting the campus into Minnesota's landscape of lakes and trees and choosing the names of the buildings.

Like Julia, I am not a historian. It is an extraordinary thing to walk the ancient paving stones of Pompeii. I have taken the liberty of moving wall frescoes and a fountain found elsewhere in town into the as-yet-unexcavated parts visited by Julia and the others. The floor mosaic of Scaurus's villa did indeed proclaim "Best fish sauce." I have given Nigidius Maius a house and additional rental quarters beyond the ones he owned by the Herculaneum Gate.

A full translation of Pliny the Younger's eyewitness account can be found in Joanne Berry's *The Complete Pompeii*. In addition to Berry's book, I relied on Mary Beard's *The Fires of Vesuvius: Pompeii Lost and Found*, Peter Connolly's *Pompeii*, Jo-Ann Shelton's *As the Romans Did*, and Alison E. Cooley and M.G.L. Cooley's *Pompeii: A Sourcebook* as to what life might have been like in 79 AD. The 2007 article in the *Journal of Volcanology and Geothermal Research* by G. Rolandi, A. Paone, M. Di Lascio, and G. Stefani titled "The 79 AD Eruption of Somma" provided a helpful summary of wind direction studies and the debate surrounding the Vesuvius eruption date. Special thanks go to Tony O'Connor, tour leader extraordinaire, for patiently answering all the questions I pestered him with. (Where *did* the women go to the bathroom in the public baths?) It bears underlining that any errors, misinterpretations, or downright flights of fancy are my own.

Thanks go out to my agent, Jill Marsal, and to the book's awesome team at 47North: Alex Carr, Justin Golenbock, Katy Ball, and Patrick Magee. John Baron, Karen McQuestion, and Jill Marsal read an early draft (and, in the case of John, a late draft as well) and provided invaluable feedback. Angela Polidoro was the Jedi master of editing and wielded the editor's lightsaber with a firm hand and much wit. Jenny Williams went over the manuscript with a sharpened copy editor's pencil.

The Moon landing hoax quote on page 73 is from a tweet written by Neil deGrasse Tyson on May 25, 2011.

Thanks go out to both sides of the family, the Maslakovic side and the Baron side, for their unfailing encouragement and support. As always, my most grateful thanks go to my husband, John, and my son, Dennis, without whose support the journey in this book would not have been possible.

ABOUT THE AUTHOR

Neve Maslakovic is the author of the highly praised debut novel, *Regarding Ducks and Universes*, which was published in February 2011 by AmazonEncore. Before she became a fiction writer, Maslakovic was hard at work finishing her PhD in electrical engineering at Stanford University's STAR (Space, Telecommunications, and Radioscience) Laboratory. Born in communist Yugoslavia, she has called London, New York, and Silicon Valley her home and now lives near Minneapolis/St. Paul with her husband and son. *The Far Time Incident* is Neve Maslakovic's eagerly anticipated second novel and the first book in a new series of time travel adventures.

Printed in Great Britain
by Amazon.co.uk, Ltd.,
Marston Gate.